THE
SAGE

BY CHRISTOPHER STASHEFF
Published by Ballantine Books

A WIZARD IN RHYME
Her Majesty's Wizard
The Oathbound Wizard
The Witch Doctor
The Secular Wizard

STARSHIP TROOPERS
A Company of Stars
We Open on Venus
A Slight Detour

THE STAR STONE
The Shaman
The Sage

THE STAR STONE

BOOK TWO

THE
SAGE

Christopher
Stasheff

A DEL REY® BOOK

Ballantine Books • New York

A Del Rey® Book
Published by Ballantine Books

Copyright © 1996 by Christopher Stasheff

http://www.randomhouse.com

Library of Congress Cataloging-in-Publication Data
Stasheff, Christopher.
The sage / by Christopher Stasheff. — 1st ed.
p.   cm. — (The star stone ; bk. 2)
"A Del Rey book."
ISBN 0-345-39239-6
I. Title. II. Series: Stasheff, Christopher. Star stone ; bk. 2.
PS3569.T3363S24   1996
813'.54—dc20   96-2036
                                                      CIP

Manufactured in the United States of America
First Edition: June 1996
10 9 8 7 6 5 4 3 2 1

With thanks to
Peter D'Alessio

THE
SAGE

CHAPTER 1

The first stone struck Culaehra in the ribs; something cracked. He cried out as he doubled over in pain—and wrapped his arms around his head. The rest of the stones came thick and fast. He ran, his clan chasing, howling obscenities and throwing rocks. Culaehra cursed them back, even though the sound was muffled by his forearms as stones struck them, the hurt coming through to his head. He ran in among the trees, whose branches took the stones and even threw them back. But one tree caught a rock and dropped it onto his arm, half striking his skull.

Culaehra went sick for a moment, stomach pressing upward and feet staggering as the world swung about him. He blundered into a tree trunk, but he had taken many such blows before, ever since Ruckhose had slapped him for his interfering—but Culaehra had come back at him then, kicking him where a blow would disable any man; and he came back now. His head cleared; he gathered himself, pushing off from the tree to go lurching on through the forest.

Most of the voices dwindled behind him, but a few came on—Ruckhose's sons, ever eager to avenge their father. That by itself would have been only right, but they might have given a thought to their sister—many thoughts, since it had been eleven years before! One of their stones caught Culaehra squarely atop the head, between his upraised arms. It was small, so he only staggered, stomach-sick and dizzy again—but long enough this time for them to catch up and kick him in the rear. He shouted in anger and pain and turned on them, dizzy as a newly wakened bear, and as dangerous. He blundered into them, his fist cracking into Gornil's head, Nirgol's belly. But the third cousin fetched him a blow with a cudgel on the back of the head, and Culaehra went down, almost unconscious, darkness folding about him. He struggled against it, enough to hear old Dabalsh's voice coming closer. "Enough! You know you can't use any weapons but one-hand stones in an out-casting!"

"Bastard swung at us," Gornil groaned.

"The more fool you, to get so close! No, leave him—no killing!"

"He killed our father!" Nirgol grunted from his sore belly—for the hundredth time, as he ever had for eleven years, and Dabalsh's answer was the same as always.

"He killed him to save himself, killed him in the middle of an act even the gods abhor!"

"Whore indeed," Gornil snapped. "What's the crime in whoring? Culaehra has made a new whore, and you don't kill *him* for it!"

"A woman jilted isn't a whore, and Tambat has already betrothed her, pregnant or not!"

"The more fool he," Nirgol muttered, but without conviction—what was one wife more or less to Tambat?

"And the more fool you if you slay a man for a jilting!" Dabalsh's voice began to fade as he hauled the young men away. "Be off with you now, or you'll bring down the gods' anger on the whole village! It's for them to say if Culaehra lives or dies! Be off!"

The young men bleated protest, but their voices faded as Dabalsh drove them away. Culaehra lay panting—and hurting. He breathed carefully against the pain in his ribs—and his head, his arms, his legs, his chest, and his back. He assuaged his hurts by reflecting with vindictive satisfaction that he had, at least, stolen and hidden the village treasury, and they would be livid when they discovered it missing. Hard on that thought, though, came the realization of what the brothers would do if they came back and found him lying as he was, and unconscious. The thought shot enough strength into his arms and legs to pull him in under the low-lying bushes. There he burrowed into the forest mold, found one last bit of strength to lift a leaden arm and pull leaves down to hide his body, then lay, trying desperately to cling to consciousness . . .

And failing.

Ohaern moved a hand in a slow and languid caress, and Rahani shuddered, gasping, "Enough!"

"Never enough," Ohaern breathed, still caressing.

This time her answer was a moan. "I thought you had forgotten that game."

"I have never forgotten any game you have taught me, my goddess."

"But I teach you a new one every day, and it has been decades since we played that . . . Ohhhh! Ohaern . . . !"

"Decades? Can it really have been so long?" Ohaern kissed the rounded flesh so gently that his lips might have been butterfly's wings, so gently as to wring another groan from her.

"It has been five hundred years!"

"They have flown like swifts," Ohaern breathed, and his breath made her shiver. "Five hundred, and every day in Paradise! But how could they be else, when my beloved is my goddess?"

"Foolish boy." She caressed under his chin, lifting his face to kiss his forehead tenderly, gazing adoringly down at his face. "How many times must I tell you that we Ulin are no gods, but only an older and more powerful race than your own?"

"As many times as you wish," he murmured, "for then I hear your voice." And he made to move his hand again. But she caught his wrist and held it firmly.

"Enough, impetuous mortal! Is it not enough indeed? Have I only minutes ago given you satisfaction, a transport of ecstasy? And you must move me to crave more?"

"Yes, if I can—for how can any mere man be satisfied, with so infinitely desirable a woman beside him?"

He spoke only truth, for Rahani was the most voluptuous of the

Ulin, and had been even when there had been as many of her kind as there now were of humans—and the least of the Ulin women had been a queen of beauty, in human terms. But if she had felt the need to choose a human mate—which she had not needed, but had only desired—surely Ohaern was just such a one as a goddess would have chosen. Tall and broad-shouldered, with mighty muscles and a face with the strength of granite but so well-featured that he might even have been called beautiful, with jet-black hair and golden skin, large eyes and sensuous lips, he was all that a woman might desire, except that, on earth, he had been straitlaced—but with Rahani, he was quite otherwise, was unlaced indeed.

"Now, stop!" She tightened her hand again, but not in time— his caress drew a shiver from her breast and a writhing from her body. "Nay, my love! I must speak to you of serious things, and I cannot, if you stimulate desire in me again!"

"What can be more serious than love?"

"Life and death!" She would not let his hand go, but lifted her head to look straight into his eyes, a commanding glance, then a pleading one.

"Death?" Ohaern stilled. "Have I ceased to please you, then?"

"Never that." She softened, and the hand that held his wrist loosed it and lifted to sweep his hair back from his forehead. "Never could you bore me, Ohaern."

"You promised me that if you began to tire of me, you would tell me instantly!"

"Only because you demanded it of me—for I knew very well that I would never weary of your company, any more than you would weary of mine."

"But you are a goddess, and a woman of infinite variety! Whenever I might begin to grow accustomed to you, I discover something new about you, some aspect of your being that I had never suspected before, and fall in love with you anew!"

"And do you not see that the same is true of yourself?" She caught his chin, holding his head still so that he could not look away from her eyes—as if he might wish to!

"There was never as much to my soul as there is to yours," Ohaern protested.

"But daily there is more, for under my tutelage you constantly grow and change, though you remain forever the same dear, sweet boy I chose of all your kind to aid Lomallin in destroying Ulahane, thereby serving also me." She leaned down to kiss him again. "No, never will I tire of you, Ohaern, for there is ever new depth to you, even though it is I who must show it."

"It is you who make it!"

But she shook her head. "Learning makes the soul grow, and you have daily learned more and more of magic from me, yes, and more and more of the way the world and the universe turn and grow and churn about us."

"And daily learned a new facet of Rahani, and a new love-game!" Ohaern smiled and moved his hand again. She gasped and clasped his wrist. "I have learned how to please a goddess—but how can there be more of me for you to discover?"

"It is there within you, and ever was, for you alone of your generation were both shaman and warrior by nature—and it is both the shaman and the chieftain who must see what the future holds unless he changes it."

Ohaern groaned. "Must we think of the world, then?"

"It has been five centuries since I bade you do so," she reproved, and rose, gathering robes about her out of the very air itself. She stood, gesturing to clothe Ohaern's loins in a breechcloth. "Come," she said, "and look upon the world as it was, and as it may be."

He followed her to the edge of a precipice, knowing it was not real, telling himself desperately that what he gazed upon was only illusion. Where Rahani dwelled with him, he did not know, and had come to realize that it was not a place so much as a state of mind, a dream-realm like that of the shamans, a dwelling place for the soul—but the world that she chose to show him now was quite real, and he knew it.

"Gaze upon the clouds," she told him, and Ohaern did, watching the mist swirl and thicken. Its motion held him; his eyes lost focus and seemed to see only a gray, featureless wash of formlessness. It began to thin, to clear, first as a hole in the center, then as a widening area of clarity.

He stared at the face of a stranger, with black hair held back by a copper band, black moustaches, and a close-cropped black beard. The eyes glittered, and the mouth opened in a shout as the warrior raised a spear, shaking it. He grew smaller, and as he did, Ohaern saw that from the waist down he was—a horse! Instead of neck and head, this horse wore the torso, arms, and head of a human! And not just one—as the first grew smaller, he saw more and more about him, all half man and half horse, all shaking spears or bows and shouting! Smaller and smaller they grew, and as they shrank, Ohaern saw even more of them—and more, and more! Finally they were so small that they seemed like a field of pebbles, stretching as far as the eye could see in every direction.

"How many are they?" Ohaern whispered, awed.

"More than thirty thousand," Rahani answered, subdued, and Ohaern stared in shock.

He had never seen so many men gathered together, never even heard of it! "How?"

"How do they come to be so many?" Rahani's lips thinned. "Bolenkar came among them, when they were few and starving, and showed one tribe how to gain food by killing another tribe, taking all their stores and weapons, and killing the best of the victims as a sacrifice of thanks to Bolenkar. He gave their chieftains Ulin weapons, which they copied in bronze, and they took him for their god and worshiped him. He commanded them to go forth and conquer whomever they found, and to rape their captured women, both centaur and human, again and again, to bring forth babies to rear to do his fell work. He bade them also take as many wives as they wished, siring as many babes as they could upon them, and if they died in the bearing, or died because their poor bodies wore out, what matter? Women were nothing to Bolenkar."

Ohaern shuddered, remembering. There had been many, many Ulin at one time, but the cruelest and most vicious of them had been Ulahane.

When the Creator had brought forth new and younger races, Ulahane, in jealousy, had gathered a troop of Ulin about him to torment, enslave, and exterminate humankind, elfinkind, dwarfkind, gnomekind, and the others. Lomallin, incensed, had gathered those who were outraged by Ulahane's cruelty, and a war between

Ulin had resulted, with most of their number being killed—for, though the Ulin never died of old age or disease, they could be slain, and were: by one another. His army depleted, Ulahane swayed human beings to do his work against their fellows, posing as a god and demanding worship by battle. Few Ulin wished to fight the Scarlet One anymore, so Lomallin had gone among men while Rahani worked within their dreams and their hearts, and between them they chose Ohaern to gather a force from the younger races to fight Ulahane's corrupted human armies—the cruel soldiers of cities whom Ulahane had seduced, and the Vanyar, chariot-riding barbarians who came driving in from the steppe to conquer the free hunters of the land, then to pounce upon those cities that Ulahane had not yet corrupted. Ulahane had slain Lomallin, but the Green One's spirit had strengthened Ohaern and his nomad armies. Then Lomallin's ghost had slain Ulahane, and ghost had fought ghost among the stars. Below, Ohaern led the armies of Life against those dedicated to Death, and as Lomallin extinguished Ulahane's spirit, Ohaern had won. He had claimed his reward— five centuries in the arms of Rahani. But now he felt his spirit stir within him, and knew that he could no longer remain in bliss with her, for he read danger in the horde below him.

The centaurs began to move. As they ran, they shrank even smaller in his vision, until the whole army was only a roughening of a map showing mountains and rivers that bordered a vast land to the south. Into that land flowed the roughening that was the army of centaurs, like ripples in a pond driven before a storm, moving at the speed of running horses, not the slower pace of walking men. Southward those ripples sped until they struck a darker region, like deeper water. The turbulence swelled, growing larger and larger, until it resolved into clashing armies, then grew farther still, until Ohaern could see the two sides for himself. The centaurs fought tanned men with eyes of flint, men who fought from horse-drawn chariots with double-bitted axes and swords.

"The Vanyar!" Ohaern recognized his old enemies. "They who took Ulahane for their god!"

"And now take his son Bolenkar," Rahani said, her voice hard.

Ulahane had bred up his own war-leaders by the expedient of

raping human women, making them swell almost to bursting, then die in the bearing of huge babies—half-human, half-Ulin children: the Ulharl, eldest and most vicious of whom was Bolenkar. First and most lonely of his kind, he both hated and revered his father— revered him as any son will a strong and providing father; hated him for his cruelty and for the malice of the other Ulin folk who despised Bolenkar for being a hybrid. That anger and bitterness found its outlet now, in turning human against human, army against army—and the revering of his father, the constant craving for praise never given, found its outlet in continuing Ulahane's work of trying to eliminate the younger races by inducing them to kill one another. But Bolenkar had bade the Vanyar, too, to get as many babies as they could, and the two forces that clashed were almost equal in size.

The centaurs outfought the Vanyar, though, for chariots were no match for the quickness and agility of their tough pony bodies. The charioteers fled, leaving thousands dead and dying on the battlefield. Those survivors who managed to find their ways home packed up their families and fled—those who found their families still alive. They sent word, and families farther also packed and fled, leaving behind a rearguard of Vanyar who fought, retreating and dying, until their folk were all escaped or enslaved or dead. Then the survivors of the rearguard turned and fled, too, while the centaurs took their tents and their slaves and settled down to the task of learning to follow the great herds that had been the source of Vanyar life, and the survivors of which were now the core of the herds the Vanyar would tend, not follow.

For the Vanyar were boiling out of the vast grasslands toward the west and south—but not toward the east, for other tribes of centaurs were invading those lands. They set upon people weaker than themselves, looting and slaying and burning and enslaving; they attacked shouting the name of the god who led their conquest: Bolenkar. Aghast, Ohaern watched the fall and sacking of the glorious cities of the southern subcontinent and the slaughter of their people. Then the Vanyar drove on, leaving the glorious cities deserted, to crumble back into dust or be engulfed by the jungle.

They grew smaller in Rahani's magic cloud-circle, became again only ripples in a pond, ripples that stretched out toward . . .

"The Land Between the Rivers!" Ohaern cried.

The ripples engulfed that land in their flowing tide—a land in which Ohaern had walked and fought, in which he had saved cities and made friends. Loss chilled his soul as he realized they were dead now, those friends—long dead, and probably their descendants, too.

Rahani sensed his sudden desolation and wrapped him in her arms. "Peace, beloved. This is not what has happened or even what must happen, but only what may."

She knew that was not the true cause of the chill that had touched Ohaern's soul, and he knew she knew—but was grateful all the same. For the first time, he began to understand how Rahani herself felt, dwelling apart from the other Ulin—as she must, with so many of her race dead, and the few that remained sunken into hermitage. He felt some shred of her desolation, her loneliness . . .

Enough to make her console herself with a man of a lesser race?

He embraced her fiercely, determined to console her indeed—but his gaze dwelled still on the devastation before him. The rippling tide of Vanyar had engulfed all of the Land Between the Rivers and onward, all around the shores of the Middle Sea and even upward into the lands of the north and west, where Ohaern's home had been. Dizziness claimed him for a moment, as he wondered if there was still anything left of his tribe, his bloodline. With Rahani's aid, he had watched his son grow, fall in love, father children, nurture them and their mother—and, sadly, grow old and die. He had not had the heart to watch his grandchildren long, but had reached down to them with help now and then—by Rahani's aid. It had been many generations since he had watched his descendants, though, and wondered if he had the courage to do so again.

But it was so far to the west, his homeland! He had always thought of the Land Between the Rivers as being to the south and east—but here it was, southerly, yes, but very much to the west of the steppes overrun by the centaurs! Very far west indeed, but the rippling tide of charioteers had flowed through the great mountains to the south of the vast grasslands to engulf all the lands to their west, stopped only by the western ocean. Everywhere, the teeming horde of the Vanyar triumphed—and slaughtered, raped, and burned, plunging the world into darkness and barbarism.

"Can nothing stop Bolenkar's rampage?" Ohaern whispered.

"Of course." Rahani passed her hand between themselves and the cloud bank, and the vision disappeared. "The events you have seen will take a century and more to triumph, for they are only now beginning."

"Even now beginning! What will happen to the descendants of my son? To the descendants of my friends, of Lucoyo and Dariad?"

"They live, they still live—but many will be butchered by the onslaught of the Vanyar, if this vision turns real."

"It must not! How may I stop these Vanyar?"

"Only by stopping Bolenkar," Rahani answered.

For a moment, Ohaern was dismayed. "Stop Bolenkar? Stop an Ulharl, a creature half human and half god?"

"You know we are not gods, Ohaern," she reproved.

"No, but superhuman! It is no man we speak of felling, but a superman! Oh, he cannot change his form, like a full-blooded Ulin, but his natural body is twelve feet tall and four wide! He has the strength of twenty men and the brains of five, and has been learning subterfuge and wily ways of cheating for half a millenium!"

"As you have been learning magic," Rahani reminded him sternly, "more and more every day. What, my love! Have you no faith in my teaching?"

That restored Ohaern to calm and some measure of self-assurance. "Of course, it is even as you say. With Rahani's wisdom, skill, and power to strengthen me, how can I fail?"

"Too easily," she said tartly. "Remember caution, for Bolenkar is, as you have said, ancient in evil and deception, and many times more powerful than any man. But he can be killed."

"Then I shall slay him for you!"

Rahani went misty-eyed and swayed close, reaching out to caress Ohaern's cheek. "I fear not, my love—for, while your spirit-body has tarried here with me and learned so much of magic and of wisdom, your mortal body has lain asleep in the depths of the chilled cavern into which you went to seek me."

Ohaern stared, a veil lifting from his mind. Suddenly he remembered the tortuous path up into the mountains, the twisting and harrowing journey deep into the bowels of the earth, not overly reassured by the guidance of the taciturn dwarves, until at last he had found the cavern, its walls glittering with crystals of ice, the bier laid out and waiting for him. He had lain down; the cold had made him shiver, then penetrated to his very marrow; a curious feeling of warmth had stolen over him, and he had lulled himself into a trance.

In that trance, he had assumed the form of a bear and climbed the World Tree into the shaman's land—but the Tree rose higher still, and he followed it to this luxurious realm, where he took on human form again, and found Rahani waiting. Every morning thereafter, he awoke lying next to her on cushions of silk, beneath perfumed trees, beside a brook that filled the air with freshness, and it was her caresses that wakened him . . .

His pulse quickened at the memory, so he put it firmly from him; there was work to do, for Rahani and for his own humankind. "My body is dead, then?"

"Not dead," she corrected, "but sleeping very deeply—and aging very slowly, as men judge time. Aged it has, though, and is now old. Its muscles are shrunken, its skin wrinkled, and its hair and beard long and grizzled. You can no longer fight for me by yourself, my beloved, for your body will not bear it."

Distress seized him. "Then how *can* I do what you ask of me? How can I confront this monstrous Ulharl and slay him for you?"

"You must find the fragment of Lomallin's spear that fell to Earth during his ghost-battle with Ulahane's spirit, and forge it into a magical sword."

"Well, that I can do," Ohaern allowed, "for was I not a smith before I was a shaman? And was I not a warrior before both? Surely with a magical sword, I can slay this terror, aged body or no!"

"Surely you can *not!*" She swayed closer, body to body, sympathy filling her eyes. "You do not know age, beloved, but I have seen it in too many men to doubt it. Besides, the Star Stone was tainted by Ulahane's weapon, and that taint will poison your mortal body. You will be too weak even with a magical sword, but even more important, you will be too slow." She pressed fingers over his lips to stop his protest. "I know, you do not believe, for you were swift as lightning when you dwelled on Earth—but trust me in this. You must place the magical sword in the hands of a hero who *can* slay Bolenkar, for only thus may you forestall the fall of darkness."

"But how shall I find this fragment of Lomallin's spear?" Ohaern cried. "It was no mortal thing, but a weapon forged of the stuff of stars by mightier magic than men have ever wielded!"

"You will find it far to the north, where the ice never melts and a man must wear the skins of animals to keep his body's warmth, or die. You will see the Star Stone from afar, for it glows by its own light and casts dancing shadows into the sky. You must forge it by magic—but the power that emanates from it is so great that it will weaken your mortal body, as if the strength within you will go out to it. However, it will be the most perfect work that ever you have forged—and the most mighty."

"But where shall I find the hero?"

"I shall lead him to you," Rahani said, "and you to him by signs in the sky and in the trees and the water—and you will think me a maddened goddess, for he will be anything but a hero; he will seem the most corrupted and mean-spirited of men. But there is greatness within him, and you must bring it out."

"Just as there is strength in a lump of iron ore?" Ohaern muttered.

"Even so. You will have to forge him into a hero, even as you forge the Star Stone into a sword. When you are done forging them both, you must direct them toward Bolenkar and loose them to find his heart."

"Can I no longer be your champion, then?" Ohaern asked, still muttering.

"You can and you will always be." Her hand caressed his face, and her body churned in slow and demanding rhythm against his. "You shall always be hero and champion for my heart, as true as any steel and twice as pure—and when you have forged both Star Stone and wolf's head into sword and hero, you shall come back to me in the prime of your life, in fullness of youth and vigor—for no matter the age of your body, your spirit will always be young."

Then she silenced any further protests with a kiss, and her fingers played upon him as upon a harp while her body made clear its demands. In a few minutes his arms came up about her, his fingers stroking, caressing, as if she were a living tree that he must shape by love alone, and they sank together into the hill of cushions beneath the perfumed tree, sealing themselves in faith to one another, in both promise and prediction, and assurance of triumph.

Something cold and wet stroked his cheek. Culaehra's eyes flew open; he shouted in anger and lashed out. His fist struck something, and he sat up in time to see someone small go flying backward into the leaves, something pale-colored flying from his hand.

No, *her* hand, now that he looked—she wore a plain blouse and skirt, though with borders of elaborate embroidery. Was that gold thread he saw? Then why not take it? After all, she was plain enough—coming to her knees, pushing herself to her feet one-handed, for the other was pressed to the side of her head, where his fist had struck. Her eyes were huge, far larger than any woman's he had known, but she squinted, as if the dim light under the trees were too much for her. Her head was hairless, her hands and feet also huge; she was unshod—and as she straightened, Culaehra saw that she was less than two feet tall. With a shock of fear, Culaehra realized he had struck one of the Little People.

No, wait—those huge eyes, slitted against daylight . . . this was no elf-woman, but a gnome! His confidence returned somewhat— everyone knew that gnome-magic was no match for that of the elves. It *was* magic, though—and no one could be sure what the gnomes could and could not do.

Control it, then! Control *her*, Culaehra thought, as he had always controlled everyone who might have been a danger: by fear. He pushed himself to his feet, ignoring the hammering in his head, and stepped close, towering over her as he demanded, "What were you doing to me, vixen!"

"I—I only sought to soothe your head, to heal you," the gnome-woman protested. She reached for the pale thing before he could stop her and held it up. "A cold wet cloth for your forehead, to reduce the swelling."

Culaehra narrowed his eyes, automatically suspicious of any seeming kindness—it had never been more than a ruse to make him lower his guard, so that he might be more easily hurt. "Why should you wish to aid me?"

"I cannot stand to see any creature in pain," the gnome explained, "and . . . and when I beheld your face . . . I wished to heal you even more . . ."

She looked away, and Culaehra stared in amazement that was quickly followed by soaring elation and triumph. She was in love with him! A gnome-maiden, in love with a human man! And why not, seeing how ugly she was? True, he was no paragon of beauty himself, with his crooked nose and thin lips, and the layer of fat that smoothed over his great muscles was enough to make any fool who met him think he was *only* fat—but he was human, and must therefore look amazingly handsome to her! He swelled with the sense of power the knowledge of her infatuation gave him, his aches and pains seeming to recede, even the stabbing in his side. "What is your name, gnome?"

"L-Lua, sir," she stammered.

Culaehra sat down again, snapping, "Get busy, then! And mind my ribs—one is broken, I think."

"I—I shall go gently," the gnome quavered, and took up her cloth again. She washed his bruises with slow, gentle strokes, using water from a clay pot that had miraculously escaped tipping. He gasped with pain at every touch and cursed her newly at each bruise. At last she knelt back and said, in faint tones, "Pardon, master, but—you must take off your tunic if I am to see to the bruises on your chest . . ."

Master already! Elation thrust again, and Culaehra untied his tunic. He gasped and spat a curse as she probed his ribs. She shied away at his anger, but he snarled, "Fix it, wench!" and, trembling, she came back to touch his ribs ever so gently.

He winced at the pain, and she said apologetically, "The bone is not broken, master, but it is badly cracked. You must keep it still until it heals—not move your arms much, nor breathe deeply."

"Fair enough! Then you shall be my hands. Gather wood and build a fire to warm me—and find something to cook!"

She did, for a wonder—began to move in and out among the trees picking up sticks. Didn't the little fool realize she could run off among those trees, that he was too lame to follow her?

Of course not—she was in love. Culaehra grinned again at the thought of the power that love gave him, then noticed that, gnome or not, there was a certain femininity to her movements, a grace, even a trace of contours. It reminded him of Dinecea, the girl who awaited the birth of his baby, and at whom he had laughed when she told him they must wed. The thought raised the ghost of desire, but raised also the memory of his humiliation and shame at the hands of the gang who had beaten him and hauled him in front of the elders. Cowards! He could have beaten any one of them, even any five of them, but not ten of them together. Anger built, and he looked at the gnome-maiden anew—the perfect receptacle for his wrath: too much besotted to flee, too weak to fight back, too small . . .

Small! And the memory was on him again, the forest about him dimmed by the image of the grove with the screams tearing from it, and he was lost in the vision of the past.

CHAPTER 2

The screams tore from the grove, and Culaehra was a boy of ten running toward it, knowing some girl-child was in danger, then bursting through the screen of underbrush and seeing Borli, huge and hulking and ugly, so ugly that even his wife would have nothing to do with him, and little Culaehra had seen what he was doing to Kerlie, five years younger than he, had seen her skirt already torn aside and Borli laughing with lust as he held her shoulders pinned against the sodden leaves, lowering himself. Culaehra had cried out in rage, boy or not, and kicked at Borli's midriff, but his foot had gone lower, come up and caught him in the loins. Borli howled with pain and rolled aside, and Culaehra cried, "Run, Kerlie! For the life of you, run!" For suddenly he knew it would have been her life; stupid though he was, even Borli would have known better than to leave a witness.

Even himself! For Kerlie was up and running now, stumbling away without her skirt, but away and still whole in body at least, and Borli was pulling himself to his feet, eyes wild with rage, lip lifted in a snarl of wrath, and he snatched up a fallen tree limb and ran at Culaehra, swinging.

White with fear, Culaehra ducked under the blow, snatching his dagger out of its sheath. He leaped in too close for Borli to strike with the stick, stabbing with the dagger. It sank between Borli's ribs at the side, and the lumbering fool screamed with pain. Culaehra leaped back, dagger poised to thrust, hoping Borli would fall back, give him time to run . . .

But Borli only swung the stick again, leaping forward, and Culaehra didn't duck low enough. It cracked into his head. He fell, dizzy and sick, the world dim about him, but he held onto the dagger, somehow knowing it meant his life. He heard Borli's victory yell as if from a distance, then felt the impact of the man's body atop his own, felt the clumsy hand fumbling at his trews, realized with sick horror that what Culaehra had prevented Borli from doing to Kerlie, Borli was trying to do to him instead. He stabbed with the dagger, up and as high as he could, heard the scream but stabbed again and again even after the scream began to bubble, then finally realized that Borli had gone silent and the weight on top of him was still. He pushed against it, forcing it up enough to roll out from under; then, gasping and crying, making sure his knife was in his hand, Culaehra stumbled away, glancing only once at the horrid thing behind him. Tottering out of the grove, he leaned against the assurance of a huge oak's rough bark, drawing strength from the tree until his breath was nearly even and he could begin to hobble out across the stubble of the field, to call for help, any grown-up help . . .

But the men had come to meet him, running to meet him, in a panic from Kerlie's incoherent sobbing, Culaehra's father foremost among them. He had taken the boy in his arms, crushed him to his chest, thanking the gods for his safety, then loosing him as he looked up at the other men's yells from the grove. He had started toward them, but Culaehra had pulled away, crying, so his father had stayed with him until one of the men came back to tend the boy. But there was some reserve about the man, some strange distance as he talked, trying to reassure Culaehra that all would be well—and when Culaehra's father came back from seeing what the grove held, there was something of the same distancing about him, too, a shunning, even a hint of fear as he asked, "Did you do that?"

"I had to!" little Culaehra had protested. "He was trying to . . . trying to . . ."

Warmth came back as his father had pressed him against his side. "There, there, boy, we know you did what you had to do, and saved little Kerlie from the worst of it, too. There is no blame for you, but only a hero's honor."

And the villagers did honor him as a hero that night around the great central fire in the meeting lodge, while Borli's wife and mother turned away their faces in shame, though no one laid any blame on them. A hero's honor, yes—for one night. But even the next morning, Culaehra realized that the other folk were beginning to shun him, to greet him with politeness but no warmth, and wondered why—wondered more and more, hurt and perplexed, and his parents couldn't explain it, told him it was all in his mind, wasn't real—but it was in them, too. He couldn't help but wonder until the next week, when he went hunting, and the biggest boy in the village caught up with him, and a dozen behind him, challenging, "You think you're such a great fighter, eh? Let's see if you can beat *me!*" and leaped in, punching.

Anger surged, all the confusion and hurt behind it, and Culaehra fought back like a madman, fought back until the bigger boy finally ran with blood streaming from his nose and his cronies with him, running from the berserker. Culaehra followed them a dozen yards, then slowed and glared after them, chest heaving, realizing that everyone was afraid of him because he had slain a grown man . . .

And all the boys would fear him now, because he had beaten their biggest and scared the rest.

Later, when he was mostly grown, he realized that it was partly fear and partly revulsion because of the deed he had stopped Borli from committing, which was nonetheless associated with him—revulsion and fear. A deep well of contempt built up in him, contempt for people who would honor a boy for saving a little girl and killing to defend himself, then shun him for having done it at all—contempt and anger, always anger never far from the surface, ready to lash out at anyone who gave him insult. He grew to despise them and their rules, even their gods, and began to think that only the wicked one, Bolenkar, might be devoid of hypocrisy, for at least he stood for wickedness openly.

Culaehra grew up as a man without a god he would honor, without any faith except faith in himself, in his own wit and strength and skill in fighting—for he had to fight the other boys again and again, and when they finally left him alone, he knew that it was only the fear of a beating that stopped them. He became the best fighter and most despised man in the village, and showed his contempt for his fellows by bullying them and breaking their silly rules whenever he could . . .

Such as the rule that said he had to marry the woman he bedded and got with child.

But never the rule against rape.

So revulsion came up in him as he crouched over Lua, came up as soon as he felt the stirrings of desire, self-contempt and nausea intensified because the gnome-maiden was smaller than a five-year-old. Instead he showed his contempt for her professed mercy and the sickness she called love by commanding, "Unlace my boots, so my feet may feel the warmth of the fire."

He was still amazed when she did it. He sat back against a tree trunk, let her spoon hot broth into him, and set himself to healing . . .

And to contemplating his revenge.

Ohaern woke shivering—but worse, he woke aching. Before he even moved, he ached in every limb. He lay absolutely still, afraid even to open his eyes for fear the effort would hurt.

Coward! he scolded himself. *Churl and swine!* He nerved himself to stir at least a little, at least his eyelids . . .

Light seared through to his brain, and he narrowed his eyes to bare slits, telling himself the light was really dim, that it was only his five-hundred-year-old eyes to which it seemed a glare. When it had become bearable, he opened his eyes a little farther—and could have sworn he felt sand beneath the lids. Had his eyeballs gone dry in five centuries?

Fifty years, he told himself. Surely by his body's time it had only been fifty years, or less! But fifty years or fifty decades, he felt as if his body were iron that had rusted solid, and that he must break free again.

He opened his eyes farther, waited till the dazzle ceased, then opened them even more, and saw—a dazzle indeed! The flecks of ice that had coated the cavern when he was young had grown to sheets and columns now! He lay in a hall of ice, lighted by a foot-high flame from a crack in the rock at his feet. The reflections danced all about, refracting, reflecting, and surrounding him with light.

At least Rahani had given him a tomb worthy of a hero—but, no, say a bedchamber, not a tomb! For he had slept, not died—only slept, while human history flowed by. And it was time to waken.

Ohaern turned his head—slowly, slowly, and it felt as if he had to break through a layer of rust. There by his bier sat a small, round table of ebony, and on it, in a silver bowl, fruits of many shapes and colors. The mere sight repelled him, but he knew this body needed nourishment. He moved a hand—but it stayed still. Frowning in puzzlement, he willed it to move, looked down at it, lying over the gray blanket that covered his chest. Slowly, the hand moved, feeling heavy with the weight of centuries—but move it did, and Ohaern managed to hold it up as the arm moved behind the hand, farther and farther until the palm reached the table. There Ohaern let it rest, breathing heavily, feeling as if he had just moved the earth. Alarm stirred—how was he to forge a sword if he could scarcely move his hand? But before that alarm could take hold, a new one shoved it aside:

Blanket?

He had pulled no blanket over himself, had indeed lain down in only the cloak, tunic, and leggings that the villagers at the foot of the hills had given him. There had been no blanket, certainly not a gray one. He had a dreadful suspicion what the fabric was, but shoved the issue aside, telling himself that strength was more important. His weakness was only that of muscles wasted from inaction, he assured himself, and slack from lack of food. He knew he needed nourishment, so he took a yellow globe from the bowl on the table and hefted it, though it seemed as heavy as any boulder he had ever managed to lift, and brought it back to his mouth, a distance that seemed as wide as a river. He forced it to his lips, bit, and felt the juice seep over his tongue—but with almost no taste. What! Had his body forgotten how to register the sweetness of food?

But that sweetness coursed through him, spreading strength and warmth. He bit deeper and felt a fly-bite twinge, tasted something flat—and realized it was hair. He, who had always shaved his face clean, now felt his own hair in his mouth, for his beard and moustache had grown while his body slept—and he knew what the gray blanket over his breast was. Slowly, he forced the other hand up, over, then let it collapse onto his beard, feeling the chest labor beneath. His fingers twitched in the grizzled mass, feeling the texture—softer than it looked. He would have to cut it back to a manageable length—and his hair! How long had *it* grown? And what was he to cut it with?

Painfully, he turned his head, looking about the cavern. On the floor beside the ebony table lay a leather rucksack, and on top of it, a hammer, tongs, chisels, all the tools of a smith's trade—and shears! Well, he could trim his hair and beard, then—if he could move his hands.

That struck him as an excellent place to begin. Slowly, he began to squeeze the fruit as he ate it, feeling the strength flow into him. Then he began to flex his hands. It took an immense amount of effort, but at last they moved fairly easily, and with almost no pain. He rewarded himself with another piece of fruit—difficult, because his arm still moved like a bough in winter. Then he began to flex his arms, finally managing to touch his shoulders. From that, he went to working his upper arms, resting his hands on his breast. When he could do a reasonable imitation of a bird flying— though no bird ever flew so slowly!—he ate another piece of fruit, forcing himself, because he still had no appetite. Then he began to work his legs.

By the time he swung his feet to the floor, he had finished the fruit, and sweat beaded his forehead. He didn't try to stand, only turned over onto his stomach and put part of his weight on his legs, then leaned back on the bier, then back on his feet again until he could do it without feeling that his knees were about to buckle. At last he achieved the colossal feat of getting himself back up on the bier again, and was about to reach for another piece of fruit when he remembered that the bowl was empty. But it didn't matter, because he had already fallen asleep again.

The bowl was full again the next morning. His achievement for the day was standing, even walking a few steps—enough to discover that wood was laid for a fire, at the foot of his bier. He kindled a stick in the flame that jetted from the crack in the floor, then lit the fire. He warmed himself at its flames, glancing apprehensively at the ice about him as he did, but it never melted. Indeed, the warmth from the fire seemed to radiate only a few feet before it was swallowed up in the constant chill of the cavern. The heat helped him to begin bending and stretching, though.

By the end of the day the fruit bowl was empty again, and it was all he could do to climb back on his bier once more. As he drifted to sleep, the thought crossed his mind that fruit was all very well, but to rebuild muscle, he would need meat.

Rahani must have been watching his every movement and caring for him as much as she could from the spirit realm, without more outright magic. How else could he explain the piglet that wandered into the cave, or the fact that its mother never came after it? How else explain that his muscles grew from that meat to reasonable resemblance of their former strength, if not their bulk? How explain the partridge that flew in, or any of the other small animals that made up a virtual parade, until his limbs moved easily, though they still ached, and he had stitched together enough chewed skins to cover his loins?

One morning, he woke to find a new cloak and tunic lying on the ebony table. It was time to begin.

Culaehra may have put aside thoughts of rape, but he still enjoyed having someone to order about and to cuff if she didn't obey him quickly enough. He ordered her to fetch him some meat, and she asked, "How?" wide-eyed.

"Kill it, you little fool!" Culaehra roared, and gave her a slap.

She cowered back, gasping and shaking her head, almost a shudder. "No, master! A poor little squirrel? I never could!"

"It had better be more than a squirrel, or I'll beat you sore!"

And beat her he did, but kill she never would, only wept and wept as if her heart would break, so he beat her for that, too. Even when he killed a partridge himself, she wept as she plucked its feathers, and he had to beat her to make her gut and clean it. Did these gnomes know nothing of cooking meat? Well, this one learned, for he browbeat her into setting up a spit and roasting it for him. She would have burned it, too, if he hadn't told her when to stop. He could have done that himself, of course, but it gave him a singing elation to force someone else to do it.

After a few days he was healed well enough to begin his journey away from his village. "We go," he told Lua. "Take the food and walk ahead of me."

She gave him a huge-eyed, frightened glance, then wrapped up the remainder of the meat and stumbled after him. He caught her up and shoved her ahead of him, giving her a slash with a leather thong every now and then, barking "Faster!" He could feel the strength returning in him, having someone to bully again.

So they went through the afternoon, Culaehra driving and snarling, Lua stumbling ahead of him, weeping and squinting, for her eyes hurt from the brightness of daylight. Inwardly, Culaehra exulted in her pain, and if something much deeper in him felt wrung out in agony, he ignored it.

That night, he glanced at her eyes glowing in the firelight, and took a savage delight in no longer seeing any vestige of love—only fear. But there was no hatred in that look, only a weary resignation, and that galled him.

In revenge for that, he pretended to close his eyes and regulated his breathing so that he seemed to be asleep, but watched through his eyelashes. They almost sealed themselves in real sleep, but at the last moment Lua stirred, then knelt up and began to creep away into the forest, stealthy as a stalking cat, silent as a gliding bird.

Culaehra leaped up and threw himself after her with a shout, caught her ankle and slapped her again and again, crying, "Desert me, would you! No one leaves me unless I wish it! Oh, you vile creature, you slime-coated rock-heart! Run away from me, would you? I'll see that you don't!" But he stopped the beating short of leaving her limping—after all, who would carry his burdens if she were lamed?

The next day, he tied a leather thong about her neck, and held the other end as he drove her before him with a switch. It felt good, but whenever he looked at her eyes, he grew angry all over again, for he still saw no hatred there—and, worse, no despair, only that same old resignation. It was almost as if she expected someone to rescue her!

That someone fell upon Culaehra at dinner that noon. A small body dropped from a tree to kick at his belly and stab at his eyes, shouting, "Run, Lua! Flee for your life!"

"Flee, and I'll whip you raw!" Culaehra thundered, angry and alarmed. He rolled away from the kicking fury, then snapped upright suddenly and caught the blasted creature by the neck, holding it at arm's length. It wriggled and squirmed, windmilling tiny fists and kicking diminutive legs, trying to screech curses and threats, but only making a strangling noise through Culaehra's grip while its pale blue skin grew darker. Culaehra stared at it in amazement.

"Oh, Yocote!" Lua gasped in tones of mourning.

Culaehra grinned, suddenly understanding. He threw back his head and laughed loud and long. "So her swain has come to the rescue, eh? Much good may it do her! What could you rescue her from, mannikin? A squirrel?" And he laughed again.

"Do not shame him!" Lua pleaded. "O Master, please do not shame him!"

"Why not? He looks so amusing as he turns purple!" Culaehra gave the gnome a shake, grinning at him, then laughing yet again.

Yocote emitted a gargling noise, face contracting in fury. He raised his arms, hands moving and writhing in strange abstract gestures while his gargling turned into incomprehensible syllables. Culaehra laughed and laughed—until he realized the little gnome was working magic! Then he squeezed the creature's neck hard, cutting off talk, but it was too late—Yocote made fists in a gesture of finality, and the spell struck.

Something popped under Culaehra's nose with a bright light, loosing a puff of foul-smelling smoke. He was so startled that he nearly dropped the gnome—nearly. But he held on and forced a laugh. "Is that the best you can do? Oh, I fear your magic, little one! So vastly do I fear your magic!" And he dropped the little man indeed—but planted a foot on him, or on his skirts, rather; the gnome wore a robe that seemed too big for him, though his kicking had showed leggings and buskins beneath. What manner of race was this, Culaehra wondered, where the men wore robes and the women did not? Yocote looked so dispirited that Culaehra thought it best to rub it in. "You were better off fighting me with your fists than your spells, mannikin!" And to demonstrate how useless either was, he bent down and clouted the gnome.

Lua cried out, hands to her mouth and eyes wide, but the gnome only picked himself up off the ground, glaring. "It's true, my magic is weaker than that of most gnomes . . ."

"And gnomes' magic is weak, compared to elves!"

"It's strong enough when it comes to things of the earth!" Yocote snapped.

Culaehra backhanded him so hard his head rocked. "Talk nicely when you talk at all, gnome—and don't speak unless I tell you to!"

Yocote shook his head and stared slit-eyed up at the bully. "I'll talk as I please, and as you *don't*, suet face!"

Culaehra stared a moment in surprise and outrage, then roared without words and waded in, kicking and punching. When the spasm of anger was spent and the gnome lay moaning on the ground, he spat, "Talk *now*, fool!"

Yocote groaned; Lua whimpered.

"Now!" Culaehra kicked him again.

"Noooo!" Yocote groaned.

"What!" Culaehra struck again.

Yocote managed to push out words. "Why did you . . . do that? I talked . . . didn't I?"

Culaehra stared; then anger grew as he realized that in some way the gnome had managed to make a fool of him. He yanked the little man up by the scruff of the neck, gaining savage strength from Lua's whimpering. "None of your tricks, you lump of dough! You're a failure as a magus—and a failure as a man!"

Yocote's voice was thin, strangled by the weight of his body against the collar. "As a man ... perhaps ... but a success as a gnome!"

"Will nothing stop your prattling?" Culaehra dropped him, then caught him with his toe before he hit the ground. Not too hard, of course—he wanted another underling to bully, not a corpse. "I'll teach you to mind, and to speak only when you're spoken to!"

"You can't ... teach what ... you don't ... know," Yocote gasped.

"You'll learn it, then! And you'll learn it hard!"

"I'll speak when ... I wish, and ... flee when ... I please!"

"Oh, will you, then?" Culaehra snarled. He drew his dagger and seized the little man. Lua screamed, but Culaehra only sliced a long thin strip from the gnome's robe and tied one end around his neck. "You'll not flee at all!" He yanked the gnome to his feet as if he were a puppet. "Now, pick up that pack!"

Yocote stood immobile, his face stone, and Culaehra began to worry that he might actually have to kill the little man, and what good would the gnome be to him then? But inspiration struck. "Came to rescue your maiden fair, did you? Well, you can rescue her from carrying the burden! Up with it, now, and off with you!"

Yocote stood immobile a moment longer, then slowly picked up the pack and slung it over one shoulder. He winced at the contact of the strap.

"Oh, Yocote!" Lua mourned.

"None of your whimpering!" Culaehra felt a savage exultation—he had made the gnome do his bidding. "Up, now, and off!"

Staggering under the load, Yocote moved away in the direction Culaehra pointed. Lua reached out in distress as he passed by, but he turned his face away from her, ashamed.

Ohaern knew he was as fit as he was ever going to be, staying by his fire in the chill of his tomb. He was astounded to feel a thrill of fear at the thought of going into the outside world, but he mastered it sternly, telling himself how ridiculous he was, for he knew the form of the world even after five centuries, had watched the ebb and flow of tribes and nations across its face. Still, he was going forth into uncertainty; sheer pain and death could meet him, whereas for five hundred years he had been safe in Rahani's bower.

Too soft, he told himself. *You have lived in luxury and safety too long.* It was time to learn to fight again. He loaded his tools into their pack, shouldered it—and was amazed at the weight. In his youth he would scarcely have noticed it!

Time to rebuild wasted muscle. Leaning against the weight of his pouch, he turned his back on the fire and the bier and went into the tunnel from which the little animals had come. Even now his bones creaked with the unaccustomed movement; the rust was gone, but his joints ached, his muscles pained him with every movement. He felt a surge of anger at the cruel joke Time had played him, a feeling of outrage at the stolen years, at having been robbed of the chance to grow old with dignity, to keep this wasted body in some echo of its former strength. But the surge crested and passed; he reminded himself that he had gained instead five hundred more years of youth, and what ancient would not willingly have traded slow aging for centuries of ecstasy, and gladly accepted this catapulting into old age?

Still, his body did not understand, and screamed at him for failing it.

Darkness closed around him, and he stifled a feeling of panic. He stopped, lowering his pack to the floor, and waited for his night sight to return. It did, even after five hundred years, and he saw faintly by the distant light of the jetting flame—saw two dark holes ten feet in front of him, branching off to either side. Who knew what other turns and branchings there might lie ahead? And surely there would be no light at all!

CHAPTER 3

I t was a pretty problem, and Ohaern found his old limbs would no longer take the weight of standing still to decide. He lowered himself beside his pack, then sat contemplating the tunnels, puzzling out how to choose which led up to the earth's surface and which led downward into a farther and more tangled maze with—for all he knew—a fathomless pit of dark water at its end.

But as he gazed, a flutter of whiteness appeared within the tunnel. He stared; the fluttering grew, until a white bird flew out of the tunnel, a huge white owl. Ohaern stiffened, recognizing the bird for Rahani's messenger, even if the fowl itself did not—as surely it could not have, for it fluttered about in the passage, dashing itself from side to side, but not daring to go past Ohaern into the cavern beyond. Realizing that, Ohaern rose with a shout, rose slowly and with great effort, but shouting still, waving his hands in their long flapping sleeves. Alarmed, the bird turned and flew unerringly back into the passage from which it had come. A trace of fresh air that it recognized? Or an impulse from Rahani? Ohaern neither knew nor cared—he caught up his pack, swung it up to his shoulder and staggered under its weight, but staggered into the tunnel, following the owl. The light dimmed and surely must have been gone, but still that ghostly flutter went on before Ohaern, as if it glowed of itself in the gloom. Hurrying as fast as his stiffened limbs would let him, he hobbled after, somehow managing to keep it in his sight. On and on he went, tripping over stones and bouncing off rocky walls, swearing and cracking his head on sudden dips in the ceiling, but forcing himself on and on, in a panic lest that white dancing flit from his sight.

He managed to keep it in view until the darkness began to pale, to wash away under light coming from ahead. Then he rounded a bend, and true daylight lanced his eyes, dazzling him. He squeezed his eyes to slits, then opened them a little at a time as they adjusted to the glare . . .

And the owl was gone. Had he missed its passing out from the tunnel? Or had it melted into thin air? Ohaern threw off a shiver and breathed ardent thanks to Rahani as he forged ahead.

Out into the light of the world he came, then lowered his pack to the ground with a crash and all but fell beside it, trembling with relief and exhaustion in every limb.

Long he sat beside that cave, till the trembling eased and he began to think of fire again. The day was light but held no sun—overcast, but early summer, to judge by the leaves about him. He glanced at the sky, wondering about rain, but not overmuch, for hadn't he a cave behind him?

Yes, but one without fuel. Ohaern used the roughness of the rock about the cave mouth to pull himself to his feet and, leaving the pack, moved slowly into the forest ahead of him to gather wood—but before he picked up a single stick for the fire, he selected a fallen branch, almost completely straight, longer than he was tall, and thumped it against a nearby tree. Satisfied that it was sound and had no rot, he used it to lean upon as he bent to gather stick after stick—and roots and berries, too. Then he returned to the cave's mouth, laid a fire, drew his great knife from its sheath and the scrap of flint from his pack. He struck sparks into tinder and breathed on the coal, slowly blowing a flame alight. Then he sat by his fire under a lowering sky, nibbling on berries as the roots roasted in the coals, and began to carve runes and mystic symbols into the wood of the fallen branch.

For three evenings he carved by the fire; for three days he exercised, turning and twisting, striking a boulder with his great hammer, first the left, then the right, then the left again, changing the hammer back and forth between hands as it rebounded. At first he could scarcely lift it for the first stroke; three days later he could hammer for an hour. He could kneel down and stand up five times without resting; he could pull himself up to a tree limb; he could hurl a javelin he made from a straight stick and a piece of chipped flint. Most important of all, he had taught his body to hunt again, refreshing skills it had not practiced for hundreds of years.

He finished the staff on the third night, then pointed it at a dead and distant tree and chanted words of power. The dead trunk groaned, then broke with a loud report and fell to the ground. Ohaern nodded, satisfied, and lay down to sleep.

In the morning, he buried his fire, shouldered his pack, then looked up at the clear sky, murmuring, "Where would you have me go, O My Beloved? Show me where he lies, this lump of clay that can become a hero, and I shall find him!"

For a moment he thought Rahani had not heard him. Then, slowly, trails of white appeared against the blue dome of sky, streamers of cloud that joined together to form a plume, a long sweep of arrowing streamers meeting—and pointing to the west.

Ohaern gazed up at the mile of arrow with a smile, reassured that he was remembered—and not alone. He set off toward the west.

As he walked he stayed alert for other signs, and, days later, found the next—a stunted pine, its branches all pointing to the southwest. By itself this was nothing exceptional—on a windy hillside; but in the middle of a forest of full-branched trees, it was unmistakable, especially since the branches of the pine all joined together to point. Two days after that, as he was coming out of a high mountain pass, a white stag burst from cover and sprang away across his path. Recognizing an emissary of Rahani, Ohaern hurried after the beast, but the smith's tools grew heavy upon his back, and within a hundred yards his legs ached and his breath came in hoarse gasps—and the stag was growing smaller and smaller in the distance. But it looked back, saw Ohaern laboring, and slackened its pace. In relief, he slowed to a walk, wiping his brow—then realized that he would lose the stag that way! He started to run, though his limbs were leaden—and saw that the stag, too, was walking. He slowed again and followed the animal toward the north, until it rounded a ten-foot-high boulder. When Ohaern came behind the boulder, it was gone. Alarmed, he looked about him, then remembered his hunter's lore and looked down at the ground. There he saw its hoofprints, curving around the stone—and disappearing.

He stared a moment, not believing, then saw the magic of it and smiled. He settled his pack more firmly on his shoulders and trudged away toward the north, wondering if he would find another sign, or the reluctant hero himself.

Kitishane had known her father, but had never spoken to him if she could help it, nor did he speak to her. He never acknowledged by word or gesture that she was his daughter, for his wife was not her mother. It would have been bad enough if only they two had known of it, and Kitishane's mother, of course—but the whole clan knew, and never let her forget it.

"Do not worry, my dear," her mother crooned to her, rocking her when she was young. "We both know your worth, and it has nothing to do with his."

Nothing indeed—but the other children did not know that. They mocked her and struck at her—until she taught herself to block their blows, then even strike back. Most of the boys her age were smaller than she, so they learned to give her a wide berth. The girls did, too, muttering that she couldn't really be female if she struck at them.

When she came of age, though, and the young men all sought to bed her as her father had bedded her mother—well, then she learned to fight in earnest. Not just as women were supposed to fight, with tooth and nail, but as men fought, too, for she had watched them at their wrestling practice, admiring the sheen of sweat on flexing muscles. She discovered some new movements, too—that her hips worked well as fulcrums for her arms to lever a man off his feet, and that if a woman was weaker in arms, she was quite strong enough in the legs. She learned to kick, and where; she learned to block with her legs as she blocked with her fists. It was a hard school, and the first time a boy struck her, fear shot through her, sapping the strength of every limb—but she realized what he would do if she did not fight back, and struck at him in panic, then struck and struck and struck until he ran.

She watched them practice with sword and dagger, then practiced herself with sticks, but thankfully never had to use them—until young Cheorl was found dead.

"Murderess!" Cheorl's father howled, pointing a trembling finger at her, there in front of all the villagers assembled, and the village elders nodded.

"Where were you last night?" Goreh the chieftain demanded, eyes flashing from beneath his bushy white brows.

"At home, helping my mother weave, then sleeping!" Kitishane answered.

"It is true," her mother said. "She—"

"Of course she will say Kitishane was at home!" Cheorl's father snapped. "Of course she will make excuses for her daughter!"

He should know, Kitishane reflected bitterly. She didn't doubt that he had done so a score of times and more, for Cheorl.

"We know she can fight," one of the boys put in, eyes gleaming at the prospect of revenge.

"We have seen her practicing with sword and dagger," another added.

"A wooden sword!" Kitishane cried. "A stick for a dagger!"

"So you would know how to use Cheorl's dagger when you wrested it from him," Goreh inferred. "Did he seek to rape you, maiden?"

"I was never there!"

"I saw her going into the wood with her bow last night," Shchambe said loudly.

"A lie!" Kitishane said hotly, turning on her accuser. "I went inside my mother's house at dusk, and did not come out!" She had learned the hard way to stay indoors at night—it needed less fighting, and she never knew when two or three of them might gang up on her.

"*I* saw her go into the wood, too," Alluye said through her tears. Kitishane turned to her, words of anger on her tongue, but she bit them back—Alluye had been Cheorl's betrothed, and was deep enough in grief. She had always treated Kitishane with scorn, and had hated her for not accepting that contempt meekly—but Kitishane's heart went out to her nonetheless. To have found a love, and lost it!

Then she remembered the hot looks Shchambe had given Alluye, not in the last week alone, but for years—and she knew who had slain Cheorl. "Ask him!" she cried, pointing at Shchambe. "Ask him where *he* was last night!"

"Why, at home with me, where he should be," Shchambe's mother said quickly—and since she had been wed, no one called *her* a liar, even though her husband was dead.

"Shchambe is not on trial here," Goreh said. "*You* are. All who think she is guilty, say 'aye.' "

"Aye!" all the villagers chorused.

"Those who think her innocent, say 'nay!' "

Only Kitishane's mother said 'Nay.'

"The punishment for murder is death," Goreh said heavily.

"No!" Shchambe cried. "Let her be no longer a maiden, then cast her out!"

A chorus of voices agreed with him, both male and female. "Aye!" "Yes, that is a fit punishment for being so unwomanly!"

"I would rather die!" Kitishane braced herself. It would be only tooth and nail at the last, then—but she would take at least one of them with her as she died.

"There has never been such a punishment in our village!" Goreh spoke sharply, and the tumult died. "But casting out has been done, and shall be done now. Give her a pack, and a bow for hunting—then send her out!"

There were shouts of disagreement, but more of delight. They ran to bring her a pack of food, ran to fetch her bow, then chased her out then and there, running after her, throwing stones, but she ran faster than any, and only one or two stones struck her. So she left her village, leaving her poor mother alone and weeping in the village square.

In the darkness of the night wood she slowed, hearing the yells of the mob dwindle behind her. When they were silent, she collapsed against a huge old elm and let herself weep. The tears poured and poured, but finally began to slacken.

That was when she heard the laugh, low and menacing.

She stiffened, tears drying on the instant. She knew better than to ask.

"So you'd have sent me to the noose, eh?" Shchambe stepped into a patch of moonlight, shadows painting his face into a mask of evil.

Kitishane leaped to her feet, snatching an arrow, frantically trying to string her bow.

Shchambe stepped in to strike it aside with a snarl. "Goreh's a weak old fool not to give you the punishment you deserve!"

"*You* deserve!" Kitishane shouted. "*You* slew Cheorl so that you could have Alluye!"

"And you were there to watch it, were you?" Shchambe growled. "Well, I'll give you the punishment Goreh should have! Oh, I'll have Alluye, when she's done mourning—but first I'll have you!" He seized her with one bearlike arm, pawing at the fastenings of her tunic with the other, then reaching for the neckline—but he had forgotten that she still held the arrow. Kitishane drove it up as hard as she could, and Shchambe gave a strangled yell, falling back from her, doubled over, the arrow sticking out just below his rib cage. Kitishane stepped in, yanked his dagger loose, then stabbed with it, stabbed again and again, feeling no guilt or compunction, for as Goreh had said, death was the punishment for murder—and, as far as she was concerned, should have been the punishment for the rape Shchambe had tried to commit.

When his body had stopped moving, even the slight rise and fall of breath, Kitishane tore his swordbelt loose and turned away into the wood, appalled at what she had done—but within her elation formed and grew. She was alive! Alive, and he who had sought to slay her lay dead!

Ohaern woke from sleep and lay taut, waiting to discover what had waked him.

An owl hooted.

Ohaern's eyes flicked from tree to tree till he found it—the huge white owl again! It stared back at him, eyes glowing from the light of his fire, and hooted again, demanding.

"As you will, my love," Ohaern muttered, and rolled to his feet. He buried his fire quickly, shouldered his pack, caught up his staff, and went toward the owl. It was off in a flurry of wings, but landed on another tree fifty feet away. When Ohaern was only halfway to it, the bird flew on again.

It was urgent, then. Was the hero-clay passing soon? Or facing a monster that might slay him? Ohaern picked up his pace, hurrying as much as he could with the weight of his pack and the awareness that he might have a long way to go.

The owl perched and waited impatiently until he came near, then flew on.

Bone-weary, Kitishane let her pack drop and began to gather kindling for a fire. She had wandered through the wood for three days, not caring where she went so long as it was away from her village and the horrible bloody thing she had left behind—and surely they would hang her for its death, if they found her! While the sun was up, she had glanced at the shadows frequently, making sure they stayed before her in the morning, behind her in the afternoon. She had stopped to pitch camp only when it was too dark to go any farther, slept lightly and poorly, then waked and begun marching again before the sun was up. Now she was about to pitch camp once more—when she smelled wood smoke! She went rigid, heart bounding in panic. But she fought down her fear, strung her bow, and crept silently through the darkened forest. They might be harmless travelers, perhaps even women lost in the wood—but if they were not, she intended to strike while she still could. She hastened toward the scent of smoke until she began to hear voices. Then she slowed, creeping toward the sounds, and crouched watching the people through a screen of leaves—a big man and, by Heaven, two gnomes!

"Be done with that stew, Lua, and bring it!" the big man snarled.

"Yes, master!" The gnome-maiden snatched the kettle off the fire—and dropped it with a cry of pain. The stew went running out over the ground.

"You clumsy get!" The man leaped up. The gnome-maiden

turned to run, terrified, but he caught her by the neck and yanked her off her feet, then began to strike her with the other fist.

Kitishane stared through the underbrush in outrage, then raised her bow.

"Let her go, Culaehra!" The other gnome leaped up from the shadows and sprang at the big man, clutching his belt and leaping up to strike at his face with a tiny fist.

"Let her go? As you please, Yocote!" Culaehra dropped Lua and seized Yocote by the neck, pummeling him instead. Lua cried out in pain as she struck the ground, but rose to strike small, ineffectual blows at Culaehra's legs.

"Let them both go!" Kitishane cried in rage. She stepped from the underbrush, drawing the arrow back to her cheek.

Culaehra dropped Yocote indeed, turning to Kitishane in surprise, then slowly grinned. "Let them go? Aye! You're more my size!" He stepped toward her, ignoring her arrow.

Kitishane had seen the same sort of look on the young men who had tried to bear her down. Without the slightest tremor of conscience, she loosed the arrow.

But Culaehra leaped aside, and the dart flew past him into the trees. With a howl of triumph, he sprang at Kitishane; there were no memories to bar him from a woman full-grown.

No time to draw another arrow, or space to fire it. Kitishane dropped her bow and drew her sword, slashing at the big stranger. He hadn't expected it; he tried to reverse direction, jumping aside, but the blade scored his arm and blood welled. With a snarl of anger he drew his own blade and came at her.

He had all the finesse of a bull in heat, which was nearly what he was. Kitishane snapped her blade up to parry—but the sheer power of his stroke bore her back. She retreated, parrying frantically, but Culaehra followed closely with lumbering strokes that sent pain shooting up her arm. The lust in his eyes, the greed in his grin, waked enough fear for her to try desperate measures. She ducked under a blow and thrust, but the big man leaned aside, and her blade ripped nothing more than his tunic. "Clawed cat!" he snapped. "You'll mend that for me!"

"Only for your funeral!" she spat, but his next stroke drove her back even farther; she tripped on a log and fell. With a cry of victory he was on her—but the gnome Yocote dove for his leg, wrapped both arms and legs about it, and bit.

Culaehra howled, kicking violently, and the little man went flying—but Kitishane rolled away and up, then threw herself into a lunge, sword tip aimed straight at the big man's heart.

At the last second he spun aside and seized her wrist. "Let go!" she raged, and kicked at his groin. "Let go of me!"

He blocked the kick with his thigh, then yanked hard on the wrist, pulling her up against him. "Let go? Aye, when I've had my fill!"

Kitishane swung her dagger at him left-handed. He dropped his sword, moving his head aside enough so the dagger missed, then caught her left wrist, too, and twisted both. Kitishane cried out in pain, dropping both sword and dagger—and the vile man forced her wrists down behind her back, where he caught them both in one of his huge paws even as he pressed his lips against hers, wet and wide. Disgusted, she shoved him away—but he caught at her neckline, and she couldn't strike his hand away, he was holding both of hers behind her back . . .

"Hold!" a deep voice bellowed, but Culaehra only snapped, "Be done with your tricks, Yocote!" and yanked at the neckline, but the leather held, only pulling Kitishane up close, into a stench of sweaty, unwashed body, and unclean clothing . . .

Something cracked, and Culaehra howled, letting go of Kitishane as he swung about—to face an old man in black robes, with short grizzled hair and beard. He also had a long, hard staff that was swinging high to strike again.

Culaehra stooped to catch up his sword, then lunged at the old man's midriff—but the staff swung down, cracked again, and Culaehra dropped his blade with a yowl of pain. He lashed out with a kick, and the old man stepped aside—but he stepped too slowly, and the kick caught him on the hip. He grunted with pain even as his staff moved in a blur, the butt coming up to catch Culaehra under the chin. His head snapped back and he fell. Lua cried out in fright—Yocote flashed her a glance filled with surprise and pain—but Culaehra rolled and came up in a wrestler's crouch, shaking his head to clear it, growling, for all the world like a bear.

Kitishane finally realized she could do something again—and what chance had an old man against a bear in the prime of his youth? She caught up her sword and stepped toward Culaehra.

"No!" the old man barked at her, even as he laid his staff aside. "He is mine to fight—and with no more weapons than he has!" He, too, dropped into a wrestler's stance, though it looked quite different from Culaehra's. He began to move around the outlaw, east to west.

CHAPTER 4

Culaehra gave a gloating laugh and charged the old man, stooping to catch up his fallen dagger on the way. Kitishane and Yocote shouted in alarm as he swung his arm high, stabbing down—but the old man blocked his stroke. There was a brief flurry of movement, swirling robes and flapping black sleeves—then Culaehra shouted with pain as his dagger dropped on the ground. The old man released him, almost throwing him back. For the first time a glimmer of fear showed in Culaehra's eye—but it submerged quickly under anger, and he bellowed as he charged the old man, arms outspread to grapple. The stranger stepped aside, but again too slowly, and Culaehra caught him with one outstretched arm, sweeping him into a bear hug. Kitishane heard the old man's ribs creak and cried out in alarm, and Culaehra gave a gloating laugh. Then, suddenly, he was falling backward, the old man falling with him, and the two of them seemed a single churning mass until Culaehra gave a shout that verged on a scream, and the old man shoved himself back to his feet, backing away, breathing hard—and waiting, ready. Very ready. Culaehra pushed himself up, panting and clumsy, blood in his eye, growling low in his throat. He advanced on the old man, but slowly now, feet wide apart, almost waddling, arms uplifted, until only a yard separated the two men. Then Culaehra lunged.

What the old man did, Kitishane couldn't have said—but Culaehra went whirling through the air to land heavily on his back. He scrabbled at the forest floor, breathless, the wind knocked out of him, and finally managed to turn himself over onto his stomach. Breath rasped in his throat at last, and he pushed himself up again, feet spraddled, arms low and circling, head down, glowering and gasping for breath.

The old man stepped in, feinted with his left fist, swung low, and as Culaehra tried to block, stepped in, smashing his right fist into Culaehra's jaw. The big man straightened, his eyes glazing, then toppled and crashed into the underbrush. Kitishane and the gnomes stood frozen, breathless, waiting—but Culaehra lay still.

"Have no fear," the old man wheezed. "He will not . . . rise again . . . till he wakes." He moved toward his staff, but Yocote was there before him, dashing to pick it up and present it to the old man in outstretched hands.

The movement broke Kitishane's trance. "Thank you from the bottom of my heart," she said, breathless. "I cannot thank you enough—but why did you save me? You do not know me at all!"

"I have some reason of my own to punish this man," the old man said, leaning heavily on his staff now. His face was grim as he said, "He is my affair—so I would prefer that he do no more harm."

"It is for all of us to thank you," Yocote said.

Lua nodded, eyes wide. "Yes, thank you for freeing me from this tyrant!"

"Tell us who you are, that we may praise your name," Yocote implored.

"Call me Illbane," the old man said. He took a deep breath, heaved a sigh, and rubbed his side.

"Are you hurt?" Kitishane was by him in an instant.

"Bruised, nothing more," Illbane assured her. "Cursed we are, that we must grow old! If I had taken better care of this body, I could have whipped this cub in three blows!"

"It seems a miracle that you won at all!" Lua said, eyes wide.

Kitishane agreed. "He is so huge, so strong!"

"Strength and youth, he has," Illbane agreed, "and the quickness and endurance that go with it—but he has very little skill, and is so clumsy that I should have had him half a dozen times before I finally did. Yes, and without his even touching me, too!"

Kitishane stared. "Is it true? Can people learn such fighting skill as this?"

"I stand victor, in testimony to it," Illbane said with irony. "Believe me, there is greater skill than I have shown you today, far greater!"

"Teach it to me!" Kitishane pleaded.

"To you?" Illbane looked up at her, frowning. "No, for I must take this bear in hand and make a man of him."

"Bear?" Yocote studied the unconscious Culaehra with a frown. "They say that bear cubs are born without form, and that their mothers must give it to them by licking them."

Illbane laughed. "Do they truly? What marvelous tales people have made up in these centuries! I can see the source of it—the newborn cubs *do* look like shapeless masses, and the mothers lick them to dry them and warm them."

Kitishane stared. What manner of man was this, who talked as if he had been midwife to a bear and seen the new cubs at arm's length!

"And will you, like a mother, give this bear form?" Yocote nudged Culaehra with his toe.

"I shall lick him into shape, yes—but not like a mother." The old man lifted his head to look around at the three. "You may go now—you are free. Or, if you wish justice, you may wait until he wakes, this lump of clay, and beat him as he beat you."

Yocote's eye gleamed as he looked at the supine form, but Lua shuddered.

Illbane noticed. "What troubles you, gnome-maid?"

Startled and frightened that he should talk to her, Lua stared up.

Illbane saw; his voice became much more gentle. "Come, you need not fear to tell me. He has wronged you, he has caused you pain. Why not take the chance to give him as much agony as he has given you? I assure you, he will never retaliate!"

"But—it is wrong!" Lua exclaimed. "To beat another, to hurt someone else for your own pleasure—what a horrible notion!"

Illbane nodded gravely. "I see that you are too gentle to seek revenge." He turned to Yocote. "What of you, gnome-man?"

But Yocote's eyes were on Lua. "It is wrong, as she says," he said slowly, "and would serve no purpose. Besides, if I beat him when he were helpless, I should be no better than he, and—" His lip curled. "—be sure, he is the most loathsome of creatures! Would he have sought to fight me if I were three times his size, as he is to me? I think not! A bully and a coward!"

"A bully surely, but perhaps not a coward," Illbane said slowly, "and if he would run from one three times his size, it would be because he found nothing worth the fight or the risk." He turned to Kitishane. "What of you, maiden?"

Kitishane regarded Culaehra's unconscious bulk with disgust. "I would love to beat him as he did the gnomes, Master Illbane, but I fear I would not stop until I was exhausted—and by that time he might be dead."

Low-voiced, Illbane asked, "Do you care?"

Lua's gaze snapped up to him, appalled, and Kitishane's eyes widened; she seemed unsettled. "Care about him? No! But care that I not be a killer of people, yes! I have slain rabbits and pheasants with my bow, slain deer, even slain a man who sought to rape me—but I am no murderer!"

"No killer of your own kind." Illbane nodded, and though he still looked grim, Kitishane sensed approval; it reassured her. "And, though we may not think of this hulk as our kind, he is nonetheless human." He prodded Culaehra with his staff. "Up, son of infamy!"

Culaehra sat bolt-upright, as if something had yanked him straight. *Then* his eyes opened—and squinted with pain. He moaned and rubbed his jaw, then saw the gnomes and the maiden watching him. Memory struck, and he swiveled his head to look up at the tall old stranger.

"Yes, I have beaten you, lump-face, and shall do so again if you seek to disobey me! Up, now, and shoulder the pack!" He nodded at Culaehra's makeshift sack.

Kitishane fought to keep her face impassive in spite of her surprise at the change in Illbane, from the understanding protector to the tyrant—and at his choice of insults. She surely wouldn't have called Culaehra "lump-face." In fact, she would have called him handsome—quite handsome, if he hadn't been such a brute.

"My head hurts," Culaehra grunted.

Illbane's hand struck like a snake, rocking Culaehra's temple. With a roar the big man surged up—but Illbane sidestepped, struck Culaehra's head as he blundered past, then kicked his legs out from under him. "You had better learn something about fighting, lumbering ox, before you try to strike me again!" Illbane dropped down, one knee on Culaehra's spine, the other pinning his arm. Culaehra tried to roll, then yelled as the bony knee dug into a nerve. He whipped about and tried to roll from the other direction, then howled as the other knee dug in. He lay frozen for a moment, and Illbane whipped an iron chain about his neck, holding the two ends together as he chanted some words that seemed mere nonsense syllables—but fire flashed from the two ends, and when it died, the chain was seamless. Illbane shoved himself to his feet, stepping back. Culaehra howled from the heat of the links as Illbane dropped them. He shoved himself up, pawing at the steel collar—then freezing as his hand found the small iron ball at his throat.

"It is an amulet," Illbane told him sternly. "It is magic. If you so much as *think* of doing something wrong, it will grow cold, and the more you think of wrong deeds, the colder it will grow. Think of right works, and it will grow warm."

Culaehra roared, clasping the chain with both hands and pulling. The muscles of his arms bulged, his face reddened—but the chain held.

"You shall not break it, no matter how hard you try," Illbane told him, "for it is magic that holds it, not the strength of iron alone. It is the collar of a slave, and a slave you are indeed! Now rise, and take up the pack!"

"I am no man's slave!" Culaehra bellowed. "Especially yours!"

"Oh, yes you are, as rightfully as you enslaved the gnome-woman!" Illbane kicked Culaehra hard in the side. The big man

yelled, but cut it off short, pressing his hand to the hurt—and Illbane swung the staff against his buttocks.

Culaehra clenched his teeth, keeping the shout down to a grunt,
and Lua cried out in protest. Kitishane agreed. "You do not need to
cause him so much pain, Illbane!"

"If he thought it right for him to hurt you, then he cannot deny
that it is right for me to hurt him!"

"Or," Yocote pointed out, "if he thinks it wrong for you to hurt
him, then he must admit that it was wrong for him to hurt us."

"Never!" Culaehra snapped, and Illbane struck again, leaning
down to slap Culaehra's head—but Culaehra saw the blow coming
and, quick as a scorpion, rocked back to catch the old man's wrist
with a cry of vindication.

Illbane planted a foot in his belly.

The cry turned into strangling as Culaehra curled around the
pain. Illbane stepped back and spoke with contempt. "Yes, you
cannot rise to your work if you cannot breathe, can you? Very well,
I will wait a few minutes."

Lua started to speak, but Illbane waved her to silence, and Kitishane laid a sympathetic hand on her shoulder. She felt she should
not watch a scene of such brutality, but morbid fascination held
her—and the creeping satisfaction of seeing the bully being bullied.

Yocote had no such scruples. He watched with shining eyes.

Culaehra drew a long, shuddering gasp, and Illbane dug the butt
of his staff under the man's belly to jab. Culaehra howled and rolled
away from the pain, then scrambled to his feet, glaring in fury—
but Illbane followed him every inch and was waiting to clout him
as he stood. Culaehra's head rocked; he straightened, bringing up
his hands to guard, but Illbane struck them aside with a sweep
of his staff, then slapped Culaehra, forehand and backhand, one
cheek, then the other. Culaehra struck out, but Illbane caught his
arm, stepped sideways, and twisted it up behind Culaehra's back.
The big man gave a shout of pain, then clamped his jaw. Sweat
stood out on his brow.

"Understand," Illbane grated. "You have only one choice—obey
me, or suffer pain at my hands until you finally die."

"I'll kill you for this," Culaehra ground out.

"Turn those words around." Illbane shoved and twisted, and Culaehra bellowed with pain. Lua winced. Illbane lectured. "You have strength and swiftness, more than I—but you are clumsy, and an ignorant fool when it comes to fighting. No, an ignorant fool in all matters, or you would have known it was wrong to beat and enslave those weaker than yourself! Well, you will learn it now, because I will teach it to you, or you will die from my trying!"

"Everyone does it," Culaehra said between clenched teeth. "What's wrong about it?"

"Many things, and if you weren't so determined to be ignorant, you'd know them! But for the moment, this alone will do—that no matter how strong you are, there will always be someone stronger! So if it is right for you to enslave those weaker than you, then it is right for someone else to enslave you—and just now, that someone is me! Now *pick up that pack!*"

He gave one final twist and shoved the big man away from him. Culaehra stumbled, but turned to glare at him, feet spread wide, shoulders hunched, arms up. Illbane glared back, though, pure venom; his contempt and disgust and, yes, hatred for all that Culaehra represented, daunted even the bully. He froze, his glare glazing, the tiniest shred of uncertainty coming into his eyes.

Illbane swung his staff high, then held it poised.

With a snarl of defiance, Culaehra turned away and caught up the sack.

Lua heaved a sigh of relief, but Yocote's breath hissed out in victory.

"The other one, too!" The staff jabbed at a dark shape lying at the edge of the clearing, then swung back up, ready to strike. Culaehra glared hatred at Illbane, then slowly stepped over to pick up the pack—and froze in surprise.

"Lift it up," Illbane jibed, "or are you not so strong as an old man? I have walked fifty miles with that load on my back! Come, are you so weak after all?"

"What is in it?" Culaehra grunted.

"Smith's tools. Be glad I did not bring the anvil! Now hoist it to your back, or your shoulders will know a heavier load!"

Red with shame, Culaehra lifted the pack and slipped his arms through the straps. Illbane nodded slowly, lowering the staff. Then he turned to the watching three and said, "Go, now. You have done your part; you have witnessed his shame, and thereby gained your revenge—or imposed justice." He nodded to Lua. "Go where you will—you are free."

"But the poor man!" Tears filled Lua's eyes. "How can I leave him, when he is so degraded?"

"By moving your feet!" Yocote cried. "Lua! He whipped you, he beat you, he degraded *you!*"

"He did," she said, tears welling over, "and therefore I know how it feels. I cannot leave him now!"

"You are too good," Yocote said in disgust, then raised his head in horrible suspicion even as Illbane said, "No one can be too good," and Kitishane contradicted, "This is not goodness, Lua, but another form of evil, to be so loyal to a man who has hurt you, and would again if he could!"

"Could it be you are still in love with him?" Yocote burst out. "In love, after all he did to you—all you saw him do to *me?*"

Lua hung her head in shame.

"No, there is nothing good in this," Illbane said heavily, "though good might come of it. I will not drive you away, gnome-maid, if you do not wish it." He turned to Yocote. "And you, gnome-man?"

Yocote still stared at Lua in outrage and hurt, then turned away in disgust. "Oh, I am as bad as she is—bound by some sick form of love to one who loves me not, and who I know will bring me hurt by it! But I'll go where she goes anyway, old man! I will come with you!"

"Oh, Yocote!" Lua reached out toward him, but he twitched aside, turning away, his face thunderous.

Illbane lifted his gaze to Kitishane. "And you, maiden? Will you not go forth in freedom?"

"I would rather go with you, in freedom," Kitishane said slowly, "if you will have me—and if you will teach me to fight as you do."

Illbane regarded her with a steady gaze for a few minutes, then said, "I may, or I may not. Why do you wish to learn?"

"Why!" Kitishane looked up in indignation. "Why, so that I will never again need to fear a bully! Is there another reason?"

"Many," Illbane told her, "but that is better than most, though not so good as some. Well, you may come with us, though I make no promises of teaching. Come, then!"

He turned away. "And start marching, you!" His staff swung in a blur; Culaehra yelped, then started off into the forest with Illbane close behind. Kitishane and the two gnomes had to hurry to catch up.

They marched all that day. During the morning, Culaehra balked frequently to match glares with Illbane, but each time a lash from the old man's staff sent him on his way again. Finally, near the middle of the day, he dropped the sack and kicked at Illbane—but the old man was ready. Slower than Culaehra, he collected a few more bruises, but for each, he struck the younger man three times, until Culaehra raised his arms in surrender, took up the pack again and stumbled ahead, the very picture of baffled misery. Lua went to him, reaching up to comfort, but he shrugged her off, and would have kicked her had not Illbane's staff hissed down between them. Illbane blocked the kick with a shrewd rap on the shin, then struck the thigh for punishment. Culaehra cursed and went hobbling on, while Kitishane gathered in the trembling Lua, and Yocote glared daggers at the human beast of burden, flexing his hands and clenching his fists in impotent anger.

They pitched camp after sunset, Culaehra and the gnomes dragging together a shelter and kindling a campfire while Kitishane hunted and Illbane stood guard—over Culaehra. As he watched he took up bits of wood and whittled, his huge knife very much in evidence.

When the wild pig had been shot and roasted, they ate with their knives, and the others were surprised that Illbane let Culaehra keep his. As they ate, Illbane told them of distant lands he had seen and the strange folk who lived in them. Their eyes shone as they listened, all except Culaehra's. Then, when the fire was banked and each person had rolled up in whatever cover they had, Illbane went aside, sitting alone and brooding—though in clear sight of Culaehra, and not so far from him that he could not leap beside him in seconds.

Yocote looked up and saw the old man sitting alone, frowned at him for a few minutes, then with sudden resolution threw off his covering of leaves and came slowly to the stump where Illbane sat. He stood still for a while before the old man turned to him, nodding. "Good evening, Yocote."

"Good evening, Illbane." As if they had not been traveling together all day! The gnome clenched and unclenched his hands, his face growing darker, eyes glowing in the night.

"What troubles you?" Illbane asked.

Yocote stood poised a moment longer; then the words erupted. "You are a wizard, are you not?"

Illbane regarded him, a faint smile curving his moustache, and nodded gravely. "I can work magic, yes—though I am more properly a shaman than a wizard, or was. I have learned much besides shaman lore since then, and am now more a sage than a mage."

Yocote frowned. "Mage? What sort of word is that?"

"A made-up one," Illbane told him. "The proper word is 'magus.' "

"What is a 'magus'?"

"A priest in the Land Between the Rivers. If you speak of more than one, call them 'magi.' They read the stars to foretell the future and the wills of their gods."

"Do they work magic?"

"Yes, but not my sort. I began as a shaman, and my magic is built on that."

The gnome stood trembling, then burst out, "Could I be a shaman, too?"

Illbane sat studying the little man for a time, then said slowly, "I cannot tell. Certainly you could learn some magic, at least a few simple spells, and being a gnome, you could probably learn more than most men."

Yocote hung his head. "I have very weak magical powers, even for a gnome."

"Perhaps," Illbane allowed, "or perhaps your gifts are different from those of most gnomes."

Yocote looked up with sudden hope.

" 'Perhaps,' I said," Illbane cautioned. "It may be, or it may not. I must watch you for a time. If you have the makings of a shaman within you, I will know it."

"*How* will you know it?"

"By certain signs." Illbane frowned, irritated. "One is a great curiosity about the world all around us—one might almost say an intrusive curiosity, perhaps to the point of plaguing those about you."

Yocote took the hint and shied back.

"But another is a sense of balance, which is the core of politeness," Illbane said, relenting. "A shaman has an inborn feeling of the world about him, its objects and the forces that reside in them, as well as the forces that reside only in oneself—though few ever think to put it in those terms before they learn shaman's lore. They simply *know*."

Yocote's shoulders sagged. "I have no such sense."

"Perhaps not—but perhaps so. You would not know it, if you have had it all your life, for you do not know how folk without it feel." He pointed his staff at the glow of the banked fire. "Why does it burn?"

Yocote turned, puzzled at so obvious a question. "Why, because it breathes air and eats wood."

"If you can say 'breathes' and 'eats,' you may have the sense I speak of," Illbane told him. "Most folk would not even mention the air."

"Not mention?" Yocote turned back, incredulous. "Everyone knows that you smother a fire by heaping dirt upon it, or drown it by throwing water on it!"

"Yes, but they never think why it goes out—they only know that if you heap earth or pour water, it will." Illbane smiled. "There still is hope, Yocote. I cannot say that you do have the shaman's gift—but I cannot say that you do not, either. Sleep now—or, like the fire, your energy will flicker out in tomorrow's march."

"I will." The gnome's eyes were wide in the darkness, seeing more than Culaehra could have, perhaps as much as Illbane did. "Thank you, sage—for hope."

"You are welcome. But remember!" Illbane held up a forefinger. "A woman will not necessarily love a man simply because he is a shaman!"

Yocote went back to his bed, deep in thought, and covered himself in leaves again. Illbane watched, a half smile on his lips, and was amazed to feel the faint sting of tears trying to invade his eyes. He blinked against them, and the thought soared from him: *Ah, Rahani! There are still folk of good heart upon this earth! What might I not do with this brute Culaehra, if he had half the goodness of this gnome!*

It seemed that the night wind brought him answer, that owl calls and leave-rustling formed into words, and that the breeze itself wafted sentences to his ear.

CHAPTER 5

The night spoke, saying, *There is that much good in Culaehra and more, though it is hidden.*

Was it Rahani who had spoken, or his own deeper thoughts, not yet surfaced as words in his mind? *Are you certain, beloved? For surely, a man who beats small folk and women for pleasure must be the scum of the earth!*

Again, the words breathed in his ears—or were they there inside his head? *The scum of the earth is composed of lichens, which breathe out the good air that sustains the greatest beasts. Even so depraved a specimen as Culaehra can be salvaged from the mold into which he has slumped, and the good within him freed to shine forth. Then his strength and his courage can be fashioned into the determination and qualities that make a hero among men.*

If you say it, Illbane thought with a sigh. *But if there is hidden good in Culaehra, then there is hidden goodness within all men and women.*

But Rahani rebuked him sharply. *Not all, O Sage. Most, perhaps, but by no means all.*

What man would be so foolish as to argue with a goddess?

Soothed by this contact with Rahani, the sage Illbane—who was, of course, really Ohaern—let her reassuring presence within his mind lull him into the trance that served him as well as sleep serves most men. His body was at rest, though it still sat propped against a tree, and his mind at peace, though he still perceived the glow of the campfire and the slowly breathing forms of his companions. They seemed distant, like a painting upon a cavern wall lit by the reflection of firelight. He heard owls call, saw a bat swoop low over the fire, heard a night bird cry—then saw Culaehra rise in the middle of the night. He brought his consciousness closer to the surface as the big man came cat-footed through the night to stoop, frowning, to peer into the sage's unblinking eyes. Still Ohaern sat motionless, waiting, wondering how much courage the man had—and Culaehra raised a huge fist. But as he swung, Ohaern's staff leaped up to block, then whipped about to crack into Culaehra's head. Without even crying out, Culaehra slumped to lie unconscious at Ohaern's feet—and the sage, satisfied that the rogue had enough courage to attack a sleeping man, but assured that he would not have so much bravery again, let himself sink back into the stillness that refreshed his mind and soul.

When sunlight dappled the clearing, Ohaern let it warm his body slowly, then began to move his arms and legs in small motions, clenching and unclenching his fists, unpleasantly reminded of his waking in the cavern. When he felt that he could move easily enough again, he rose, being careful to step over the sleeping Culaehra; moved about a little; then straightened and squared his shoulders, ready once more to become Illbane.

"Wake, back-stabber!" He jolted Culaehra with his staff.

The big man stirred and rolled up on one side, blinking film out of his eyes. Then he closed them, rolling over and growling, "Go away."

Illbane dug harder with the staff. Culaehra shouted with pain and leaped up, crouched and ready—but he stared into a bearded face with a staff poised beside it, and hesitated.

Illbane waited.

Beyond them, Kitishane and the gnomes sat up, waked by Culaehra's shout.

The big man said, "I had a dream in the night . . ."

Still Illbane waited.

"I dreamt that I waked and saw you . . ." Culaehra's voice ran out as he realized where he stood. He glanced at the ground, but quickly back up at Illbane, not trusting him for a second—then flashed another glance at the watching companions.

"Yes," Illbane said. "That is where you fell asleep last night."

Culaehra's eyes widened, and Illbane could almost see the thoughts connecting in his head. If he had fallen asleep there, and waked here, the dream must have been real! "Do you never sleep?" he cried in outraged protest.

"Never, while you are as you are," Illbane returned. "No, it is not fair at all, is it? That I will never be vulnerable to your treachery. You will have to face me waking, Culaehra, or not at all." Then his voice snapped like a whip. "Stir up the coals, now, and set a kettle to boiling! We must break our fast!"

Culaehra jumped in surprise. Then his eyes narrowed and he stood glaring at Illbane, tensing himself, working himself up to fight . . .

Illbane waited, the staff at guard, watching.

There was no overt sign, no slumping of the shoulders or lowering of the head, but he knew when the fight went out of Culaehra. The big man snarled a curse, but turned to do as he was told—and carefully kept his eyes away, so that he could seem not to notice the staring of the gnomes and the woman.

When breakfast was done, Illbane commanded Culaehra to take up the whole company's baggage, what little of it there was, "For," said he, "you have a broad back." The others were astounded that Culaehra only cast Illbane a look of hatred, but obeyed without any other protest. Slowly, Yocote started to bury the fire as Kitishane shouldered her quiver—but Illbane stopped them with a word. They gathered around, and he gave each of the gnomes a curved slab of wood with leather thongs tied to the corners.

"So this is what you were carving!" Yocote held the object up, marveling. "What is it, Illbane? Some sort of mask?"

"But how can we see through such narrow slits?" Lua asked.

"Far better than such huge eyes as yours will see at midday without them," Illbane said.

Yocote held his up with a cry of delight. "The slits keep out most of the light! We will no longer need to squint!" He tied his goggles on swiftly and nodded. "It works, it works marvelously, Illbane! Thank you, thank you twenty times!"

Lua donned hers more slowly, with Kitishane tying the thongs. "Yes, they are marvelous," she said. "How can I thank you, Illbane?"

"There is no need," he told them, "and so small a gift certainly does not oblige you to travel with me, if you do not wish to."

"We wish to," Yocote said quickly. Then he glanced at Lua and added, "Or I do, at least . . ."

"I, too," she assured him.

Illbane nodded. "You have said you wish to, and you are welcome to do so—but you must understand that there are certain principles we must all agree to if we are to thrive in this wilderness. If you find them too hard, you are free to go—except for this lout." He shoved Culaehra with his staff. The big man glared at him, but didn't speak.

"What rules are these?" Kitishane asked, feeling somewhat hesitant.

"First, that if you stay with us, you learn what I have to teach," Illbane said. "There is much Culaehra will have to learn, if he wishes to live, and anyone resisting my teaching will slow him down."

"Gladly!" Yocote's eyes glowed.

Kitishane, though, frowned and glanced at the captive. "Are we all here because of Culaehra, then?"

"He is why we met," Illbane replied. He turned to Lua. "Will you learn, gnome-maiden?"

"I will, sir," she said slowly.

"Good enough, then." Illbane looked up at Kitishane.

"What will you teach?" she asked.

"Wholeness of mind, heart, and body, and as much of fighting as each can be trusted with—perhaps even some magic, for those who have talent."

"Gladly!" Her eyes fired.

"What other rules will you lay down?" Yocote asked.

"Not I, so much as the nature of our journeying," Illbane replied. "If one is in trouble, all must seek to aid—and if all but one are in trouble, that one must aid the others."

"There is sense in that, for if we do not, we shall all die," the gnome said. "What else?"

"None of us must steal from another. None must fight with another, save for the practice bouts I will give you—and that will be hard when two disagree, but we must find ways to work out agreements without fighting." He went on and told them several more rules, each of which made excellent sense; they nodded acceptance.

When he had finished, Illbane nodded with satisfaction. "If you are agreed, then, come with me, and welcome. Let us march." He started to turn away, but Kitishane stopped him by asking, "Will you not tell us we must obey you?"

Illbane turned back, smiling in amusement. "There is no need to say it, maiden. If it stops being plain for all to see, you will no longer wish to travel with me." He turned to prod Culaehra with his staff. "Go, wolf's head!" And off he went, driving his captive before him.

The gnomes followed, and Kitishane behind them, more slowly; she found she resented Illbane's words, but even more resented their truth.

Twice during that day Culaehra turned on Illbane. The first time, Illbane came up right next to him—he was never far away, but this time he almost seemed to be taunting the outlaw. Culaehra suddenly threw off the packs and whirled, left fist slamming at Illbane's midriff while his right was drawing his knife.

Illbane took the blow with only a grunt of pain, then clouted Culaehra behind the ear. The big man rocked back, off balance for a moment, and Illbane leaned on his staff while his foot swept out to kick Culaehra's feet from under him. Even as he fell, though, the outlaw turned to slash at his tormentor with the knife. The butt of the staff cracked on his hand as Illbane shouted, "Wood for steel!" Culaehra clamped his jaws shut, and the sage leaned on his staff, saying, "Yes, I *can* blame you for trying. Now take up your burdens, Culaehra, and march north."

In absolute silence the outlaw slowly stood, took up his knife and sheathed it, then swung the packs to his back and started off.

Illbane followed, and Yocote caught up beside him, muttering, "You goaded him into that."

"He learns what he must," Illbane told him, "and so do you, Yocote. Be glad your school is not as hard as his."

The second time was in midafternoon, and this time Culaehra deliberately lagged, though to Lua it seemed that his steps dragged with weariness. She hurried up beside Illbane and said, "You must not drive him so hard, sir! He is ready to fall from sheer exhaustion!"

"Do you think so?" Illbane said. "Then watch, Lua—but step farther away from me as you do, please. I do not wish you to be endangered."

Wide-eyed, Lua stepped away—back to Kitishane, trembling.

"Don't be frightened, little one," the huntress said. "Any blows he receives, he deserves."

"Illbane doesn't deserve to be hurt!"

"I wasn't speaking of Illbane," Kitishane said dryly.

Just then Culaehra did drop, facedown in the grass. Lua cried out and started toward him, but Kitishane caught her shoulder, holding her back.

Illbane stepped over beside the fallen man. "Up, lazybones! We have yet a long way to go before—"

Culaehra jackknifed, his feet sweeping out in a half circle, knocking Illbane's feet out from under him. "Hah! How does it feel when it's done to *you*, dotard?" Then he threw himself on top of Illbane—but the sage, amazingly, caught him by the front of his shirt and pulled him closer.

"The sage is using his own shirt to choke him!" Yocote cried.

"By all the stars, he is!" Kitishane stared.

Red in the face, Culaehra nonetheless managed to seize the sage by the robe and yank him up, then slam him down. Illbane held him too closely for the outlaw to rise to his knees for better leverage, but he managed to yank the old man up, then fall as heavily as he could. Illbane held on grimly while Culaehra turned magenta, then purple, then finally went limp. Illbane shoved, pushing the inert body off. Lua let out a cry and ran to him—then past him, to kneel by Culaehra.

Yocote wasn't far behind her, but he stopped to help Illbane up—sparing a hate-filled glance for the unconscious man. He forced himself to look back at the sage. "Are you hurt, Illbane?"

"A few bruises, perhaps, but I've many for them to join." Illbane glanced keenly at the gnome as he came up to his knees. "You are hoping I have killed him, are you not?"

"Would that be so bad?" the gnome returned.

"For him to be dead? Yes, for my purposes. For you to *wish* him dead? A little bad there, but nothing you can avoid. It would be far worse for you to pretend you do not."

"It is no fault of his, I suppose, that Lua is once again in love with him."

"No, and no fault of hers, either, though it is a failing in her that she must seek to remedy. We shall have to help her in that, Yocote."

"*Can* we?" The gnome's goggled face turned up to him, and Illbane knew his eyes were wide behind the mask.

"In some measure, we can," Illbane assured him, "but only a little at a time. As to Culaehra—no, I have not slain him. He will wish I had, though. Not yet, but soon."

Kitishane had approached, and stood by, frowning. "Do you enjoy tormenting him thus?"

"No," Illbane said instantly. "I hate it, and despise him for making it necessary. Lua we may heal with gentleness, but Culaehra only with the same measure of cruelty that he metes out to others—for only thus will he come to know the wrongness of what he does."

"Will he truly?" she asked.

"If there is enough goodness buried within him, yes." Illbane sighed. "But if there is, I cannot see it—though there is one who can."

"Who?"

"Rahani," Illbane answered.

Kitishane stared, her face blank with incomprehension. So did Yocote.

Illbane sighed again, reflecting that five hundred years seemed far too short a time for a goddess to have been forgotten—but perhaps it was only her name that had faded. He determined to ask them about their gods—but slowly, and subtly. Now was certainly not the time, the more especially because Culaehra was hacking and spitting, forcing himself slowly up. Lua reached out to him, but he struck her hands away with a snarl. Yocote started forward, face blazing, but Illbane withheld him, then went over to Culaehra, leaning on his staff, watching and waiting. The big man glared up at him, rubbing his throat.

"It will still work," Illbane told him. "Say your name."

Culaehra spat a curse.

"Yes, that is it. Rise now, rebellious one, and take up your burden once more." Then with chivvying and nagging and prodding with his staff, Illbane brought Culaehra to his feet again, decked him with packs, and shoved him on his way.

Yocote and Kitishane followed, faces glowing with delight at Culaehra's humiliation. Lua followed in distress, moisture pooling where her mask did not quite fit her nose.

Culaehra slogged along, cursing under his breath—but in the core of him an old emotion was coming to life again: fear. It was coming to life, and growing. Who could have thought that a weak old man could outfight a warrior in the pride of his youth!

But then, this old man was anything but weak—not as strong as he by far, Culaehra thought, but still far from weak. And he was skilled; the younger man tasted bitterness at the thought, but had to admit it—the old man was amazingly skilled. He would have thought him a wizard, but everything the old man had done in fighting could be explained by knowledge—and a very hard staff.

He *was* old, though—a graybeard—and certainly could not be so fast as a man as young as he. Even in fighting, the old man could not match him for speed of movement. The outlaw felt a surge of satisfaction at the thought. True, the old man's skill more than made up for his slowness—but all the skill in the world could not make an old man run as fast as a young one! He could outrun him, Culaehra decided, and should be able to do so easily, even if Illbane were a wizard!

Culhaehra bided his time, waiting for his chance. The amulet that had fairly chilled him to the bone last night, when he had struck at Illbane in his trance, was now surprisingly still, only a weight at his throat. There was nothing wrong in seeking to escape, then. Culaehra plodded along, letting his shoulders slump, doing his best to appear defeated and docile—and watched for a clear run.

It came when the sun was low in the sky at his left hand. The road rose up before them; they climbed a small incline—and found themselves in the middle of a pine forest. The trees stretched away to left and right, tall, dark, and serene—and straight. There were few low branches, and no underbrush—only a carpet of needles in long avenues.

Culaehra dropped his packs and charged away into the wood. *Then* he gave a shout of joy at his freedom. He dared not stop, though—only ran pell-mell through the wood, turning and twisting around the great trunks. Behind him someone shouted, but he kept running, his heart singing. He had bested the old man after all!

But the old man wasn't even trying to follow him.

"You must stop him, Illbane!" Yocote cried. "He will sneak up on us at night, he will slit our throats!"

"Only mine." Illbane drew a circle in the dirt with the tip of his staff.

"Yes, only your throat!" Kitishane cried. "Then he will beat the rest of us, and use us for his pleasure! Can you not stop him, Illbane?"

"I can, if you will be silent long enough for me to cast a spell." Illbane set his staff in the center of the circle and began to chant in a language that none of them recognized, but that sent chills up their backs. After a few minutes he lifted the staff, nodding with satisfaction. "That should serve. Come, young ones—*now* we will follow."

"As you say." Quickly, Kitishane strung her bow. "But for myself, if I go to hunt a bear, I go armed."

Lua hung back, afraid, but Yocote took her arm, speaking gently. "Do not be afraid, Lua. If the sage does not fear, neither should we."

Reluctantly, Lua came with him. As the gloom deepened under the trees, she took off her mask. So did Yocote, and saw that her eyes were wide with fright.

As for Culaehra, he lost the companions in a few minutes. He had better sense than to slow down, but he did begin to caper and leap with delight, shouting with victory. He didn't notice that the limbs of the trees were drooping lower, or that their sap was beginning to run, thickening into resin—didn't notice until a low branch blocked his way, thick with stickiness that gathered in a lump. Culaehra didn't give it a thought, only ducked beneath it—but a gust made the branch dip, and sudden pain ripped at his scalp. He bellowed in agony and surprise, twisting about to find his hair thoroughly tangled in the lump of resin. He stepped toward it to stop the pressure and the pain, then reached up to try to break the branch—but it was green and limber; it bent but did not break. He wrestled with it, cursing, then finally grasped his hair with both hands and pulled. A few strands broke, but the tree held the others fast.

That was how he was when the others came on him, wrestling with the tree, cursing at the branch that would not break. "Enough!" Illbane commanded, and enforced it with a swing of his staff. Culaehra left off wrestling and lunged at the sage with a shout of fury. Illbane only stepped aside, then reached out with his staff to tangle the outlaw's feet. Culaehra tripped and howled with pain as his full weight swung from the lump of resin. A gnarled old fist swung to crack into his jaw; dazed, he subsided, but heard Illbane saying in disgust, "What a mess we have here! You have done a fine job of tangling your long hair in this resin, oaf."

"How shall you loose him from it, Illbane?" Kitishane asked.

"Why bother?" Yocote said sourly. "Let us leave him here to starve!"

Even dazed, Culaehra managed a hoarse growl of anger.

"Oh, no!" Lua cried. "That would be too cruel! Free him, sage, I beg you! There must be a way!"

"The simplest in the world," Illbane told her, "one that he would have thought of himself, if it had not been for his vanity." He drew his knife, and Lua cried out—but the sage only began to saw at Culaehra's hair. Realizing what he was doing, the outlaw came out of his daze with a bellow of protest, but Illbane only clouted him again, befuddling him. The knife hacked and ripped; a sinewy black-clad arm wrapped around Culaehra's head. He struggled and fought, but Illbane held him still as he cut through the last few strands, then let go. Still struggling, Culaehra blundered away, tripped on the old man's foot, and fell heavily to the ground.

"Up, wolf's head!" Illbane's toe caught him in the stomach. "Vain fool, get up! You have packs to carry!"

This command, at least, Culaehra could disobey. He lay burrowing into the carpet of needles, hating them, hating the pines. Were the very trees conspiring against him, conspiring with the old wizard?

They were, he realized—and shuddered.

Steel fingers pinched his leg. Pain tore through him, sudden and more intense than ever he had felt. Culaehra screamed and rolled onto his back, knife coming out to defend—but the tip of the staff hovered over his face, and he didn't doubt that the old tyrant would strike downward at the slightest excuse. He froze.

"Hurt?" Illbane barked. "Yes, it did—but you can still walk. Up, and step back to the road—or your leg will sear agony all through you, and you will not be able to walk again until morning." He waited, but Culaehra lay frozen, eyes locked on the staff tip. Illbane shrugged. "I will not march again until dawn, and this is as good a place to camp as any. Rise and walk back to the packs, or stay here all night with fire in your leg—I care not." He withdrew the staff and bent down, fingers poised over Culaehra's lower leg. "Rise—or lie in agony."

Culaehra snatched his leg out of the way with a curse, but the old man followed closely and rocked his head with a slap. Culaehra snarled in outrage, but those horrible talons were poised over his leg again, and Illbane snapped, "Get up!"

Culaehra rolled up to his knees, glaring pure hatred at the sage. Illbane only smiled, straightening, staff in both hands before him. Growling low in his throat, Culaehra climbed to his feet and went limping back toward the trail.

He didn't realize just what the old man had done until they had pitched camp and he went to dip up water in a bark bucket. Then he saw his reflection in the dark pool.

His proud locks were gone—his head was nothing but ragged stubble! He stared, appalled, scarcely even recognizing himself. Then he threw back his head and howled.

"Yes, Culaehra."

He whipped about, staring.

The old man stood there, his staff before him, nodding. "Yes. You are as much of a slave now as you had forced Lua and Yocote to be."

With a howl of dismay Culaehra surged upward, charging the old man.

That demon-born staff tripped him again. He fell flat on his face, then rolled up to his feet with blazing speed—but the fist cracked into his jaw and the world went funny. Through the slipping and the sickness in the belly, the voice echoed in his ears: "A slave, and only a slave, until you learn to be a man. Now fill the bucket with water, slave, and take it back to the fire."

His vision cleared; Culaehra glared up at Illbane, but the sight of those flinten features made his heart sink. He turned away and took up the bucket, dipped it full, and went back toward the campfire with Illbane right behind him.

He was *not* a slave! He would not let himself be! He was still a man, a powerful man, and would prove it! There must be a way . . .

Then he came in sight of the camp, saw Kitishane turning a spit, and knew how.

CHAPTER 6

The amulet lay cold at the base of his throat, but as the hours passed, Culaehra became so used to its chill that he scarcely noticed it. From that time on he watched his chance to catch Kitishane alone.

It came the next evening, when Illbane set him to pitching camp with the gnomes, and Kitishane had set off in search of game. Culaehra bided his time, gathering wood for the fire, though his pulse quickened with the first excitement of the hunt—and the amulet grew cold and colder at his throat. It grew colder still as he took up the bucket and left the camp, seemingly seeking water—but actually hunting Kitishane. The amulet grew colder still, a biting chill that shortened his breath—but it was short anyway, with anticipation. The grim old man might thrash him for it later, but he would have proved that he could still bend others to his will—and would do so again and again whenever he wished, ignoring the punishment.

As soon as he was out of sight of the camp, he dropped the bucket and set off through the trees, moving with the silence of a lifelong woodsman. He knew which direction Kitishane had taken at first, and circled around the campsite, being careful to keep a thick enough bulk of trees between himself and the ominous old man until he found her tracks, small footprints in a patch of moist earth where the wind had blown leaves aside to show the ground itself. He followed in the direction her track pointed and soon found another such bare patch with a footprint so delicate that it quickened his pulse. Of course, he reminded himself, she had a bow. He must not forget that.

The amulet grew still colder at his throat.

He did not. He came upon her as she drew, aiming at a fat hare. His amulet was so chill now that it fairly burned, but he clamped his teeth against the pain, waiting for his moment. The bowstring thrummed, and Culaehra struck. He rushed across the fifty feet or so of leaf mold between them, still as silently as he could.

She heard him twenty feet away and turned, then screamed even as she whipped another arrow from her quiver, screamed again as she fumbled it frantically to the string; screams of fear and anger that made Culaehra's heart exult with the feeling of power.

Kitishane saw him bearing down on her and raised the bow, but he struck into her before she could aim, struck and bowled her down, the bow flying from her hand. She screamed and fought, but he pinned her with his weight, too close for her to hit anything but his back. He was fumbling at the waistline of her breeches, and she screeched with rage, bucking her whole body to try to throw him off, drumming her fists on his back as hard as she could—but over his shoulder she saw the old man step out of the trees and she screamed again, screamed for help, but the bear-man only laughed deep in his throat, and Illbane wasn't rushing to her aid, only sawing the air with one hand and flourishing his staff with the other, only watching . . .

A shimmer began, thickened, warped the sight of him like a heat haze—and a unicorn sprang from thin air, screaming in rage, bearing down upon the would-be rapist. Its horn gored Culaehra's buttock, and it danced back. Culaehra threw himself upright with a howl, hand pressed to his hip, his half nakedness ominous and absurd. He grabbed for his leggings with one hand, turning to defend with the other, but the unicorn feinted with its horn twice, then lunged, and a long gouge ripped the side of his hip. He bellowed in rage and threw himself upon the beast, but the unicorn was no longer there, dancing lightly about him. Culaehra managed to tie his breeches again and turned with the unicorn, drawing his knife, hands raised to guard. The unicorn was between him and Kitishane now, and she cast about, found her bow, snatched it up, and scrambled back into the safety of the trees. Culaehra saw her escaping and lunged after her with a roar, but the unicorn leaped to block him. He dodged and tried to run around it, but it followed his every movement while his quarry slipped away. He bellowed in baffled anger, then had to leap aside as the unicorn thrust and thrust again. He followed, parrying with his knife, snatching at the horn whenever it came near, but always it evaded his grasp.

Then, suddenly, the unicorn leaped aside—and Culaehra saw that terrible old man advancing on him, staff raised. His stomach sank with dread; terror weakened his limbs, but he raised his hands to guard anyway . . .

Kitishane ran through the woods, breath ragged with unvoiced sobbing—but she only went a few yards before she saw Lua, standing there with her arms outstretched. Kitishane dropped to her knees, all but collapsed, sobbing with terror and relief. The gnome-maiden wrapped small arms around her head, murmuring softly, words Kitishane did not recognize—but finally realized were gnome-magic. Surely it was a charm to shield, to protect—but it also soothed, and Kitishane was just beginning to find calmness again when the shouting broke out behind them. She whirled, frightened again, but Lua assured her, "It is only Illbane, giving Culaehra the punishment he deserves. Be of good heart, Kitishane—you are safe."

Cold water slapped Culaehra in the face; he coughed, sitting up, and realized he had been unconscious. He had fought back as well as he could, and knew he had struck Illbane half a dozen times, but the old man had struck him far more frequently, and far harder, with that abominable staff. Culaehra's head ached; his ribs ached; his legs and hips ached . . .

His hips! Culaehra suddenly realized that he lay naked as a skinned buck. That foul old man had stripped him while he lay unconscious! He struggled to rise—then froze as the horn came down, aimed between his eyes. Behind it the unicorn pawed the ground and nickered a threat.

"Yes, hold still indeed," said Illbane's voice, and Culaehra felt hands on his hip and buttock. For a moment the horrible thought sickened him, that Illbane and the unicorn meant to do to him what he had tried to do to Kitishane . . .

But no, the hand was pinching and the voice was chanting. Then the pressure eased, and Illbane said, "There. The wound is closed and shall not bleed more. It will ache like fury for a day or two, and well you deserve it—but the pain will fade." He stood, stepping into Culaehra's vision, towering, threatening in his glare. "You deserved to have bled to death, but I have plans for you."

Culaehra's blood ran cold. What kind of plans did he mean?

"Your other wounds are healed, too, so let us have no nonsense. Rise and dress, and go fill your bucket."

Slowly, Culaehra dressed, muttering, "I did not fool you for a moment, did I?"

"I shall always know where you are, Culaehra, and I can guess quite easily what you mean to do. You are an intelligent man, but a very simple one in your wants and needs, so there is no difficulty in discerning your actions. Yes, I followed from the moment you went out of sight, and when I saw you drop the bucket, I guessed what you intended. I will say this, though—you move very quickly and quietly in the woods. I was almost too late in catching you up."

Strangely, Culaehra felt a glow at Illbane's praise, even so faint a sample as this. That glow crashed as Illbane said carelessly, "Of course, that hardly mattered. If I had not found you in time, I would have cast a spell that froze you in mid-stride."

"You are a wizard, then," Culaehra said thickly.

"There! I knew that you were intelligent! Now back to your bucket, oaf, and do not try to deceive me again until you have learned a gram of subtlety!"

The words stung the harder for the small compliment that had gone before them. Culaehra turned away with a growl of defiance—but it was all show. Inside, he was sick at heart, knowing any resistance was useless—no matter what he did or where he went, Illbane would be there before him.

Kitishane and Lua were already back at the camp by the time he returned, but they moved to the other side of the clearing as they saw Culaehra come—and the unicorn was there, too, quietly cropping grass, but deliberately between him and them. Yocote turned the spit where Kitishane's hare roasted, but lifted his head to give the outlaw a malevolent look as he passed. Culaehra returned it with interest, thinking how he would avenge himself on the little man when the chance came—but the amulet chilled his throat, and his resolve suddenly faltered, weakened by fear. He had to think a moment to realize why, then discovered the cause: when the amulet turned cold, a beating from Illbane followed. What was wrong with him? Pain had never mattered to him before!

But then, always before, he had been sure of winning, of inflicting more pain than he received. Now, he was helpless to stop it. Oh, he fought back surely enough—but it did no good, and it was he who received more pain than he dealt! Mortification burned within him at the thought of the unfairness of it, but there it was, and he could do nothing about it.

To make it worse, the chill of the amulet lessened until it was only dead metal again. It was almost as if the sage had outfaced him in person, then sneered with contempt at his retreat. Sick at heart, Culaehra knelt to hang the bark bucket over the fire.

It was a very silent dinner, punctuated only by Illbane's occasional question and Yocote's laconic answer. But as they were finishing their meat, the gnome frowned and asked, "Who puts the evil in men's hearts, Illbane?"

"There are many answers to that," the old man said slowly. "What have you heard, Yocote?"

"That there are good gods and evil gods," the gnome replied, "and the evil gods find ways to make men wish to do as they do."

"And you, Lua?" Illbane asked.

"I, too, have heard of the gods," the gnome-maiden said slowly, "and I believe it, because I cannot help but think that all people are truly good, and only an evil god can make them otherwise."

"Why, what a stock of nonsense is that!" Culaehra burst out. "People are born evil, look you, and what they call 'goodness' is simply following the rules they make up to protect their wickedness!"

The others stared at him, shocked, but Illbane asked, "What of those who seek to help others, even those they do not know at all?"

"They delude themselves," Culaehra said bitterly. "They cannot stand to face the fact that the world is a brutal place, and the people in it all self-seeking and cruel—so they pretend to kindness and unselfishness, and soon begin to believe their own lie, forgetting that it was all just a pretense!"

"It was no pretense!" Lua cried, eyes filled with tears. "I sought to help you because I pitied you, not because I wished anything for myself!"

"I do not want your pity," Culaehra snarled, "and I did not ask for it, though I would have been a fool not to take advantage of it. And you *did* want to believe yourself to be good and noble, and helping me was what you had to do to make yourself believe it!"

Kitishane stared at him, rigid and pale, a protecting arm around Lua—but Yocote, strangely, only frowned in somber interest. "What horrible things did people do to you, Culaehra, to make you believe such lies?"

Culaehra's arm flashed up to strike, but the amulet turned cold against his throat, and Illbane's staff intervened. The outlaw lowered his arm slowly, but growled, "They are not lies, but only the truths of the world that others are too craven to face!"

Yocote stared at him a moment longer, then looked up at Illbane. "I think he truly believes that."

"What reason have you to believe otherwise?" Culaehra fought to keep his anger from showing—not very successfully, but the attempt was new to him.

"Experience," Yocote told him. "Others have helped me for no better reason than that I lived in their village—some of whom did not especially like me. I helped them in turn."

"That is selfishness there!" Culaehra jabbed a finger at him. "They only helped you in case they needed your help some day, and you them!"

"There is some truth in that," Illbane said. "A village in which the people do not help each other will not last long—they will die one by one. But that in itself means that only those who are willing to help one another will live."

"Yes, or that those who the villagers are not willing to help will be cast out!" Anger was hot in Culaehra—but he was amazed to see it reflected in Kitishane's eyes. What could she know about being cast out? Instantly, he wondered why she had been hunting alone in the woods when she found him beating the gnomes. Strange that he had never thought of it before.

But Illbane was nodding slowly. "Perhaps—but even so, as time passes, the people who live together will be those who do feel the urge to help anyone they see in trouble—and those cast out will die childless, for the most part, so the race of humankind will become more and more they who are born to help one another."

"What old wives' tale is this?" Culaehra asked in contempt.

"Not an old wives' tale, but a legend of the gods." Yocote was proving obstinately hard to anger tonight. "Have your elders never told you of the hero Ohaern and how he led the jackal-heads and nomads against the armies of the Scarlet God?"

"What has that to do with why men work evil?" Culaehra demanded.

"Then you have not heard it?"

"I have, and I have no wish to hear it again! Start that tale, little man, and I shall—"

Illbane cuffed him, silencing him for a few moments while the world wobbled around him and the sage's words echoed in his head. "Tell the tale as you know it, Yocote. Perhaps it will do him some good."

Culaehra barely bit back a hot retort. A picture flashed in his mind, of Illbane stretched out naked under the hot desert sun and he there to torture the old man with a knife—but the amulet's chill bit deep into his throat, making him gasp and banish the image. Of course—it was Illbane's amulet!

"Ohaern was only a man, then," Yocote began. His voice took on the singsong cadence of a tribal tale-teller. "But that was 'then.' His wife lay on the point of death, and Ohaern prayed to the god Lomallin for her life—and Lomallin sent Manalo, a wandering wizard, who healed her. Later, though, she labored in a hard birth, again at the point of death, and again Ohaern prayed—but this time the wizard came not, and the wife died. Ohaern was furious with Lomallin—until he learned that Manalo was held prisoner in a city dedicated to Ulahane, the god who hated humankind—and all the races of the world, save the gods alone."

"There are some who say he hated even them," Lua reminded.

"Even so," Yocote agreed. "So Ohaern led a score of men against that city, but on the way, the half-elf Lucoyo joined him, burning with fervor to destroy the works of Ulahane and those who dedicated themselves to him."

Illbane raised his eyebrows at that, but did not interrupt.

"They freed Manalo—this is not the full tale, my friends, but only as much as you could put in a cup. Ohaern had been a smith, but he used no tools to break the bronze and copper that held Manalo, only the strength of his hands and arms. They freed the wizard and took him back to their homeland—where Lucoyo met a beautiful daughter of Ohaern's clan and fell in love with her, and she with him. They courted, lost in their own world of dreams— until they were wakened most rudely when the Vanyar struck and devastated their village."

"Yes, the horse barbarians on the steppe, to the east!" Culaehra snapped. "They still ride there, and train themselves to wreak mayhem! What did your Ohaern gain after all?"

"He drove them away from us for five hundred years. Is five centuries not enough for you?" Kitishane asked with withering sarcasm.

Culaehra glared at her, anger filling him—but the unicorn raised its head and moved silently to stand behind the woman, then lowered its horn. Culaehra throttled his anger back, but watched the beast with narrowed eyes. Lua, misunderstanding who was threatening whom, reached up to stroke the unicorn's nose. Surprisingly, it accepted her touch.

"Still, it was not the Vanyar alone whom Ohaern overcame, but he who stood behind them," Yocote reminded them, "dread Ulahane, the god of evil, who had sent forth his Ulharls—half-human children of the women Ulahane had raped—to suborn human agents, then send them out to seduce the barbarians to his worship."

"Others, too," Lua murmured.

Yocote nodded. "Other Ulharls he sent to overawe the jackal-headed folk and command them to do his bidding. Indeed, some of his emissaries bribed whole cities to Ulahane's worship and became high priests, rivaling the kings in power. But Ohaern journeyed through those cities while Manalo wandered the land to raise other folk to fight the human-hater. Ohaern exhorted the city-folk and swayed them back to Lomallin, then taught them how to fight off the Vanyar when they attacked. With Lucoyo, he went to one city after another, and was safe—but in a farming village where the folk had been swayed to worship Ulahane in the guise of a hag, they were nearly slain as sacrifices, and would have been, had not the goddess Rahani appeared to Ohaern in a dream to warn him. He struck aside the priestess who sought to slay Lucoyo, and the two of them fought back-to-back. Still, what are two against a whole village?"

"But Manalo came back." Kitishane was hanging on every word, almost hungrily.

Yocote nodded. "Manalo came back. The wizard appeared to save them, then led them out into the desert and disappeared again. There, in the center of a ring of standing stones, the god Lomallin came to earth, to fight Ulahane in personal combat—and was slain. Ohaern and Lucoyo fled, grieving, and Ohaern sank into a death-like sleep, wishing to die indeed—but Rahani appeared to him again and bade him live. He came back to life, but even then, he and Lucoyo would have died in that desert, had they not been saved by a band of nomads. Thus they met Dariad the Defender, the chieftain who gathered an army of nomads to fight at Ohaern's command. Then those whom Manalo had raised came to them— the homunculi made by the wondersmith Agrapax; renegade jackal-men who had fled the harsh rule of Bolenkar, eldest of the Ulharl, Ulahane's sons; and tribes of hunters, each few in number, but together, a mighty army. They marched on Ulahane's capital city—but Ulahane sent his Ulharls out to murder them, each leading a band of monsters. Ohaern, Lucoyo, Dariad, and their people fought and bled mightily—but they persevered, slew the Ulharls, and drove the monsters away. So they came to the walls of the city, where Ulahane himself confronted them—but Lomallin's ghost sent down lightning and slew the evil god, whose soul sped to the sky to fight Lomallin again. There they battled, forging stars into weapons—and there Lomallin's ghost extinguished Ulahane's completely. Seeing, the folk who had worshiped the human-hater cried out in despair and turned to the worship of Lomallin.

"Then Ohaern and his friends marched victoriously through all the cities of the Land Between the Rivers, freeing them from bondage to the Ulharls whom Ulahane had left to rule them, and preaching Lomallin's kindness. The hard task done, Dariad led his nomads home, where the desert folk heaped honors upon them. The desert folk would have honored Ohaern and Lucoyo all their lives, but those two were lonely for forests and streams, and yearned for their homeland. Back to the north they went—and found that some of Ohaern's tribesmen had lived after all, though in hiding. Among them was the woman Lucoyo loved. They wed, and lived to see many grandchildren about them—but Ohaern could not stay; the presence of his homeland wrenched his heart with memories of his dead wife. No, he wandered away into the wastelands, where the spirit of Rahani could console him. She led him to a magical cavern, where he fell asleep, and lies dreaming of Rahani."

Illbane stared in shock. How on earth had people come to know of that? *Beloved, have you been telling tales in people's hearts?*

He thought the breeze answered, *Do you not wish to boast?* but Yocote was saying, "Now and again, the soul-cries of human misery disturb Ohaern's slumbers, but the trials of his people pass, their cries die down, and he sleeps again. The day will come, though, when too many people dwell in misery, too many suffer from the tortures that the strong and cruel wreak upon the weak and gentle."

Culaehra's head snapped up, his eyes smoldering.

"When the cries from the hearts of the oppressed echo too loudly within Ohaern's head and do *not* die down, they shall wake him, and he shall break forth from his cavern and stride out to free all slaves and smite all the wicked."

"Why, what a stock of nonsense this is!" Culaehra scoffed. "The strong shall always rule, and the weak shall always suffer!"

"Ohaern will free the weak and bring them to rule," Yocote said with massive tranquility.

"If the weak rule, they shall cease to be gentle! Indeed, when enough weaklings band together, the first thing they do is to turn on a strong man and torture *him*!" Culaehra's eyes glowed with anger and bitterness. "Speak not to me of the virtues of the weak— I know them for what they are and know that only their weakness prevents them from showing the cruelty that is buried within them!"

Kitishane stared at him, appalled. "I think you really mean that."

"Do not seek to tell me differently," Culaehra said, quietly but with such intense bitterness that Kitishane and Lua recoiled. "I have lived it too much, seen the weak turn on the strong too often!"

Yocote's eyes flared, but he only said, "How often is too often?"

"How often is too often when the strong smite *you*?" Culaehra returned. "Once is too often, then—but when it is you who do the smiting, there is no limit!"

His head rocked with a sudden blow. He whipped about with a roar, starting up to fight.

CHAPTER 7

❀

But the amulet bit his throat with coldness, and Illbane's eyes burned down at him with such ferocity that Culaehra hesitated, feeling his spirit quail—and in that moment of hesitation, Illbane demanded, "Was that too often?"

Snarling, Culaehra lunged at the old man—but even seated, somehow Illbane leaned aside, and Culaehra blundered past, tripped, and fell. He rolled over to shove himself up—and found that blasted staff pointed between his eyes again. "If you truly believe that for the one who strikes the blow it is never too often, then Ulahane's spirit is not fully dead!"

With sudden elation, Culaehra realized how he *could* strike back at this magically invulnerable dotard. What matter blows, if he knew he had hurt Illbane with his words? "There never was an Ulahane—nor a Lomallin, nor a Rahani! They are nothing but tales the slaves make up to give themselves enough hope to slog their way through the next day, through all their days to their graves, where there is no afterlife nor any thought nor virtue, but only dirt and worms!" He trembled within at his own audacity, his blasphemy, but stood crouched and ready for the blows of Illbane's rage.

But the sage only frowned, turning grave—and the probing of his eyes spoke of an understanding so deep that Culaehra shrieked again, "Dirt and worms! There are no gods, none, for if there were, no one would suffer!"

"You believe that so that you will be free to hurt others," Yocote snapped.

But Illbane waved him to silence and said, "You would not speak so if you had not suffered in your own turn, strongman."

"You have seen to that!" Culaehra had to turn away from the understanding, the compassion in those eyes, had to make it sink under the weight of anger.

It would not founder. "Think!" Illbane commanded. "Before the first hurt that was given you, before those weaklings of whom you spoke first banded together against you, there was a stranger who stayed awhile in your village!"

Culaehra froze, staring into the vortex of those eyes, turning pale.

"Before the first great cruelty of your life, there was a stranger!"

Suddenly the memory crashed through the barrier in his mind. Culaehra sank down with a high, keening cry, clutching his head in his hands.

"He came, he stayed, he talked!" Culaehra went on inexorably. "All liked him, all respected him, even when he began to talk to certain of the villagers one at a time."

How had he known? Culaehra himself had forgotten. In all his memories of that awful childhood day, he had forgotten the stranger who had come a fortnight before, who had stayed a fortnight after, whose words had swayed the other children against him, made the adults fear and shun him. "You could not know!" the outlaw cried. "You could not ever have known!"

"I need know only that Ulahane's evil lives after him," Illbane told him, "lives in the body of his eldest Ulharl, Bolenkar. He it is who has sent his own corrupted minions throughout the lands, through all the lands, from his stronghold in a southern city!"

Culaehra's head snapped up; his eyes locked on Illbane's. "Bolenkar? But he is a tale, a lie!"

"He is as real as you or I, and he lives," Illbane told him. "He dwells in Vildordis, a city of evil and cruelty, where slaves are brought only to be tortured, and where the miasma of corruption overhangs the whole citadel like a cloud. Oh, be sure, he lives, doughty hunter—lives, and seeks to do his father's work, but do it even better, to succeed where his father failed, for only thus does he feel he can revenge himself on the blasted ghost who raised him in humiliation and brutality."

"Has it come again, then?" Yocote looked up, his huge eyes tragic, his whole face wan. "The time of devastation?"

"It nears," Illbane told him, "for there are far too many who hearken to Bolenkar's promises of wealth and victory and pleasure, who turn to worship him by bloody sacrifice in his temples and worship him even more in their actions—in wars upon the weaker, in conquest and rapine and slaughter and destruction. But Bolenkar's agents go before him, to seduce good folk to his ways and, after they have learned to enjoy depravity and cruelty, to his worship."

"And my village saw such a one," Culaehra groaned, head still in his hands—so that he could not see the paleness of Kitishane's face, see her trembling as she, too, remembered. "Have I, then, become a finger of Bolenkar?" Abruptly, Culaehra shook himself, then looked up at Illbane with maddened eyes. "I cannot believe that I swallowed your lie whole! What am I saying? A finger of Bolenkar? He is a myth, a legend, like these gods you speak of, like this dead Ohaern and his more-dead Lucoyo!"

"Lucoyo is dead; his blood lives on," Illbane confirmed. "But Ohaern lives, and Rahani, too."

"Oh, and no doubt he has spent five hundred years in her embrace, and it was that which kept him alive!" Culaehra braced for the blow again.

But the wretched old man only nodded slowly, gaze still locked with Culaehra's. "But Rahani is not a goddess, nor were Lomallin and Ulahane." He raised a hand to still the protests of the others. "They were Ulin, members of an older race, a magical race, a race that could not be slain by any but one another—a race that could have been immortal, for none of them died unless they wished it or were slain by one another. Still, they did murder each other in a war over the younger races, and the few left did pine away and wish to die—save for Rahani and a few others, who dwell alone, solitary and morose. Their half-human children, the Ulharls, are not immortal, but they live long, very long."

"Can they be killed?" Culaehra whispered.

"They can, and by human beings—but they die hard, very hard, and the chance of a human living long enough to finish that slaying are very poor, the more so because they are huge, half again the height of a man, and very, very powerful, both in muscle and in magic." He shook his head slowly. "No, my friends. The hour of Bolenkar's dominion approaches, and if Ohaern does not rise again to lead good folk against him, all humankind will sink beneath his yoke and die by the strokes of his lash."

"Cannot this Manalo help us?" Culaehra jeered. "If Bolenkar still lives, why not Manalo?"

"Manalo *was* Lomallin, in the disguise he adopted to walk among men. He did not abandon Ohaern and Lucoyo in that circle of rock—he transformed himself, took on his natural shape, and swelled into the god he was. When his ghost fought Ulahane, the sword he forged from stars broke, and a fragment of it fell to the earth, far to the north."

"How could you possibly know these things?" Culaehra scoffed.

"Yes, how?" Lua asked, her voice trembling, her eyes wide.

"How indeed?" Yocote frowned. "Our wisest elders, our priests and wizards, have not heard this, O Sage. How could you?"

"I have lived longer than they," Illbane returned, "and the knowledge that was lost through generations of telling and retelling, I still hold."

"How old are you?" Kitishane whispered, but Culaehra turned away, stalking out into the darkness alone, and Illbane turned to watch. "I must guard him, my friends. Do you speak with one another, then sleep." He rose, leaning heavily upon his staff, and started out into the night.

He followed Culaehra more by feeling than by tracks or sound or scent—the outlaw moved with the born woodsman's automatic silence, slipping between branches rather than bending them aside, and only occasionally treading on a patch of ground soft enough to hold his footprint. Illbane knew he would not even have done that if he had really been paying close heed. No, Illbane followed as a shaman follows, by an inner certainty as to which direction his quarry has taken, as much a matter of reading a host of different signs without realizing it as of magic.

He came out of the woods to a small lake, dark in the moonlight. Culaehra sat on a boulder beside it, shoulders slumped, head hanging. For a moment Illbane felt compassion, the man looked to be so miserable—but the sage reminded himself that the brute had to pass through just such misery as this if he were to become as much of a hero as Rahani thought possible. To stiffen his resolve, he remembered the degradation Culaehra had forced on the gnomes and would have forced on Kitishane, then imagined the crimes that had led to the outlaw's tribe casting him out. Saddened but certain, he sat on a cushion of fallen pine needles, folded his legs, straightened his spine, and settled himself for the long vigil. Slowly, his mind stilled, his emotions became tranquil, and Illbane passed into the waking trance that gave him as much rest as sleep would have. His eyes held Culaehra, his mind and body were ready to move if the outlaw did—but only ready; in all else, they rested.

His mind was still as a sheltered pool, but in its depths, memories moved and twisted. He saw again the battle between Lomallin's ghost and Ulahane's, marked in memory the flashing fragment of star that streaked away to fall in the north, remembered Rahani coming to him, glowing with praise and delight, as he stepped from the World Tree in the form of a bear, then the desire that beat in waves from her as, with a gesture, she changed him back into his own form, that of a man in his prime.

He remembered the long centuries of loving and delight, let himself dwell on them for minutes, for he needed that promise to raise himself from the utter weariness that accompanied age and the discovery that human beings were still as brutal in their desires and their behavior as they had ever been, needing only the slightest of temptations from Bolenkar to induce them to abandon the ways of helping one another, of comradeship and tolerance. He remembered her caresses, her words of love and encouragement—and of reassurance, as together they had watched the growth of the cities.

Then they had watched the poor, heart-twisted children and grandchildren of Bolenkar come into the cities and the villages, to corrupt and control and rule and enslave. Appalled, the Ulin and her consort had watched the degradation of humankind begin.

Ohaern sat behind the leaves and watched, but his mind's eyes saw more vividly than his body's. He was suddenly alert when Culaehra rose, looked longingly at the trail before him, then back to the camp, but at last lay down where he was, and was soon asleep. Then Illbane relaxed, losing himself in memories again, to stiffen his resolve for the course that lay before him—because truly, cruelty did not come naturally to him, and his anger at Culaehra was nearly worn-out.

At last Ohaern came out of his reverie to see that Rahani's star had risen clear and bright over the lake before him. He hoped it was an affirmation. He shook off the lingering dread of memory, held fast to the determination to undo Bolenkar's work, aligned his heart to the beacon of the promised reunion with Rahani and, strengthened and renewed in spirit, rose to work the stiffness and chill of the night from his limbs. Then he took up his staff and strode over to Culaehra, to begin the next stage in his campaign to reform the outlaw.

"Wake up!" His staff whizzed down and struck Culaehra's rump. The outlaw bawled in surprise and outrage as he leaped to his feet, one hand pressed to the wounded anatomy, shaking his head to clear it. Illbane roared merrily, "Will you lie abed all day? Come, blow up the flames to cook breakfast!"

"It's still dark!" Culaehra protested.

"It will be light by the time we are done eating! Come, slug-abed! To work!" He swung his staff like a switch, and Culaehra leaped back with a cry of surprise. Then he turned and stumbled back toward the campsite, too much amazed and too groggy to work up enough anger to resist.

The fire was bright and food frying as they came out of the wood. Kitishane looked up, her face anxious, bereft. "The unicorn is gone, Illbane!"

"He is not." The sage lowered himself to sit by the fire with a sigh. "Your unicorn will be by you until he is sure you no longer wish a guardian against Culaehra, maiden. He will watch from the wood and from the roadside, but you will not see him. Warm your heart with the certainty of his presence."

She did.

When breakfast was done and the campfire drowned, Illbane's staff cracked across Culaehra's shoulders again. The man yowled with anger. "What have I done now?"

"It is what you have not done," Illbane said sternly. "You have not washed your body for as long as I have known you. Off with your clothing, now, and into that lake!"

"What, here and now?" Culaehra glanced frantically at the watching gnomes and woman.

"You were eager enough to strip and show them a part of your own body before!" The staff struck Culaehra's buttocks. "Off with those rags, now, and wash!"

Mutiny showed in Culaehra's eyes, but only activated in his hate-filled voice. "Someday, old man, someday!"

"If I live long enough to see it!" Illbane snapped, and so did his staff. A half cry escaped before Culaehra clamped his jaws shut on it and turned his back to strip his clothes.

"Gather branches," Illbane directed, and Lua turned away to find soft leaves—but Yocote, with a wicked gleam in his eyes, broke off spruce. Kitishane only watched Culaehra with amusement.

Blushing furiously, Culaehra rushed back along the trail to the pond. Illbane followed closely, roaring merrily and swatting him with boughs. Culaehra dived into the lake to escape him, but whenever he came up, coughing and spluttering, Illbane was there to strike and swat him with the branches. Finally Illbane tossed him a square of cloth and sat down on a rock, saying, "Scrub your hide with this, and I'll let you out of the cold. But you'll do this every morning from this day forth, or I'll do it to you!"

Culaehra didn't doubt that he could. He scrubbed.

They had been out on the trail only an hour before that carved staff struck his shoulders again. "What *now*?" Culaehra bawled.

"You should have turned left where the trail forked! What kind of idiot are you not to know?" Illbane demanded.

"Idiot?" Culaehra protested, outraged. "How *could* I have known?"

The staff whizzed down again. Culaehra yelped and leaped aside, but that served only to let the wood score the side of his hip. "Woodsman, do you call yourself?" Illbane roared. "You could not see that the tracks of the beasts led off to the north? You could not tell from the sides of the trees on which the moss grew?"

"How was I to know you wanted to go north?" Culaehra replied hotly.

"I've only said it every day!" The staff whizzed through the air, but Culaehra leaped inside its arc and blocked Illbane's forearm with his own as he drove a fist into the old man's belly—and shouted with pain.

"Hard, isn't it?" Illbane said with a twinkle in his eyes. "Almost as if it were frozen, wouldn't you say?" His own fist hooked up hard, and Culaehra doubled over as his belly muscles locked in pain.

Lua made a soft noise and stepped forward, reaching to heal.

Illbane put out an arm to stop her. "He'll breathe again soon enough—and then he'll go back to take the right trail."

But later in that day, when they came to a fork and Culaehra stopped to study it for signs, the staff struck again across his buttocks and Illbane bellowed, "Lazy knave! Walk, and keep walking! We've only two more hours of light left, and I've no wish to waste it standing about!"

"But you told me to study the signs to find the way north!"

"I said no such thing! I said to go north, and the main path does!" And Illbane drove the baffled man before him.

Kitishane followed with a small smile, but it faded quickly. Lua came up beside her and said, "Sister, I think he has suffered enough."

Kitishane looked down, surprised by the term—but they had indeed become sisters in shared pain, imposed by the same "brother." "Not enough yet, little sister," she said, returning the affection. "He hasn't even been punished enough for what he did to me, let alone you—and certainly not enough for what he would do to us if he could, nor for the pains he has caused to people before us."

"But Illbane does not punish him for those sins! Indeed, he punishes him for none!"

"Without immediate cause, yes," Kitishane said slowly, eyes on the trudging outlaw, every muscle of whose body was tense with suppressed outrage. "Still, let us trust Illbane; I do not doubt that he knows what he is doing—and why."

Nonetheless, around the campfire that night she contrived to sit near Culaehra—though not too near, and warily. Curiosity overcame fear and revulsion, though it might not have if she had not been certain the unicorn was watching from behind the leaves. As excuse for her closeness, she ladled the stew out of the pot and onto his plate. "Eat well, big man. You will need all the strength you can gain."

"What good will it serve," Culaehra said bitterly, "if an old man, weaker than me by far, can defeat any power I exert?"

"You will endure," Kitishane said, her voice no longer hard. "You will outlast him."

Culaehra looked up at Illbane, glowering. "Yes. There is that, isn't there? I'm much younger than he—I have only to wait." He stared, brooding, and began to eat. Kitishane watched his profile and began to see some signs of humanity there. Surely it must have been her imagination!

Suddenly Culaehra turned to her, frowning. "Why would *you* offer me comfort?"

Kitishane recoiled, taken off guard. Why indeed? But even more questionable—why would he resent it? "Perhaps because I've been foolish enough to begin to see you as a man!"

"As a man?" Culaehra frowned. "How else could you have seen me?"

"As a beast!" Kitishane snapped, and rose to take her bowl of stew elsewhere. But throughout that meal, whenever she glanced at Culaehra, his gaze was on her, and there was no lust in it, only puzzlement.

It made her shiver.

At breakfast the next morning Illbane snapped at Culaehra for not bringing enough water in the bark bucket, then snarled at him again for bringing too much. He chivvied him for grilling the meat too long when Kitishane thought it done to perfection—then suddenly praised Culaehra for having boiled the eggs perfectly. How much skill did it take, Kitishane wondered, to hard-boil an egg?

Still, she had to admit that for Culaehra, that was probably the first time he had ever done so.

On his part, Culaehra was amazed at the upwelling of satisfaction he felt at the old man's compliment, even gratitude—and cursed himself for a fool, reminding himself that Illbane had cut a long, slender wand and peeled the bark from it as they were setting breakfast to cook. He was vindicated when Illbane yelled, "I said to bury the fire, idiot, not raise a cairn over it!" and struck the backs of his hands with the wand. Culaehra cried out in anger and felt the welcome upwelling of the old, familiar anger and hatred. It was almost a relief—gratitude and satisfaction made him nervous.

But they felt good.

He put the thought out of his mind as he swung the packs up onto his back. Yes, Illbane's praise had raised a pleasant feeling within him—but his scolding and insults raised a bitter anger that he could not discharge, and he had no idea which actions would bring praise and which punishment. The old lunatic was completely incomprehensible—there was no way to predict what he would do or say next. Culaehra was beginning to go in constant dread of the old man's whims—a dread he had not felt since he had been a boy and unsure how the men of the village would treat him because he had slain one of them, even though he had done so as much by luck as skill, and done it to save one of their daughters. Illbane was very like them, he thought with hatred—telling him he wanted one thing, but punishing him when he did it, then praising him for something else he had never even mentioned!

As they were bedding down for the night, Culaehra heard Lua daring to speak to Illbane in mild reproof. "The outlaw deserves as much pain as he has given others, sir, but no more—and certainly for reasons that can be understood!"

Illbane sighed. "Ah, but when you grow old, you can scarcely understand your own angers, Lua. The aches and pains of age make us suddenly angry when we would otherwise be able to keep our tempers—and the regrets and bitterness that come from a life less than perfect make us liable to sudden changes of mood."

"Are there no signs by which we may see if you are in pain or in sorrow?"

"There are, but you should not have to trouble yourselves to learn to read them." Illbane laid a hand on her head. "Sleep peacefully, Lua—and be assured, if I grow surly or angry, it is Culaehra on whom I shall vent it, and none others of you."

There must have been magic in his touch, for the gnome-maid's eyes closed immediately, and within minutes her breath was the slow and even respiration of sleep.

But Culaehra lay awake, staring with triumph into the night. Signs, were there? Then he would learn to read them indeed, would learn to see when Illbane was in good humor and might be pushed or even insulted a little, and when he was in a fell mood and must be obeyed on the instant! He lay awake awhile longer, reviewing the day's events in his mind, then the events of the days before, trying to detect signs that should have told him a blow would be coming at the slightest infraction—or signs of a good mood that would have led to praise. And, remembering, he fell asleep.

Sometime after his breathing had steadied, Kitishane rose, drawing her cloak around her shoulders, and came to sit by the fire, gazing into the flames. Cloth rustled next to her, and she started with fright, then saw it was Illbane settling by her, his staff leaning back over his shoulder, a look of concern, even gentleness, on his face. "What troubles you, maiden?"

Kitishane looked away. "I cannot tell, sir. I only know that my heart beats slowly, and that I feel hollow within my breast."

"Has it anything to do with this outlaw?"

Kitishane looked up at him in surprise, recognizing the feel of rightness within that his words brought. "I believe it must be. How did you know, sir?"

"Call me Illbane," the old man said absently, turning to gaze into the fire. "I know that young men trouble young women's hearts, maiden, even though there may be no love between them. Does your heartache stem from my forcing him to strip naked before you this morning?"

It was a novel idea. "That may have had something to do with it, si—Illbane." Kitishane, too, turned to gaze into the fire. "But I think there is something more."

"I have driven him to confusion, Kitishane, and in those moments of consternation, he lets us see more deeply into him. Is it that which troubles you?"

"Perhaps . . . Yes, it lies therein." Kitishane felt the comment strike home. "Am I so tenderhearted as that, Illbane, that I melt at the slightest sign that he can be hurt in his heart?"

"Yes," Illbane said at once; and, "I wish you were not, maiden, for he has been hurt, often and deeply, and that is why he has grown so thick a skin and hidden his soft heart under a hide of spines."

"Is his cruelty, then, nothing but a shield?" she asked, low-voiced.

"No. His cruelty began because he enjoyed the sense of power it gave him, then grew because no one punished him for it. Still, he had a sense of fairness—but I think that something happened when he was very young, something that made him believe that no one else really tried to deal fairly with him—no, neither him nor anyone else. Then, convinced that justice and mercy were lies, he had no reason to hold back from cruelty."

"Is that what you are trying to do?" Kitishane stared up at him, unbelieving. "Trying to show him that someone will really give both justice and mercy?"

"That is a part of it—but before I can show that I will treat him fairly, I must show that I do not have to, or he will only believe my justice is a sign of weakness."

"And as it is for justice, it must be ten times so for mercy." Kitishane frowned. "So your cruelty to him is necessary?"

"Necessary for that, and to make it clear to him that there is one who will not permit him to be cruel to those weaker than himself. There will be time for mercy, and for more." Illbane frowned at her. "And yourself, Kitishane—do you believe people can be fair? Do you believe in justice?"

She turned away, eyes on the fire again. "Believe in it, yes," she said slowly, "though I've more often been treated unfairly than fairly. Still, I've seen other people given justice, so I know it is possible."

"But that the strong will exploit the weak if they can?"

"If they can, yes." Some bitterness entered her tone. "Culaehra was no surprise, in that."

"Is that why you learned to fight—and wish to learn to fight better?"

"It is," Kitishane said slowly. "I do not want to have to depend on a man for justice—the more so because I do not believe any man will defend me."

"You have been used, then."

"No," Kitishane replied, "but only because I could fight, at least a little."

"And because of that, they cast you out?"

Kitishane whirled to stare at him. "How did you know that?"

"Because you are here." Illbane spread his hands. "Here, with Culaehra and Lua and Yocote and myself. I do not know why the gnomes left their homes, but I suspect that you will find that Lua fell because of injustice or exploitation, and Yocote followed her. Then, too, this is a harsh world, maiden, especially out here in the wild. No one would choose to go about in it alone, not without good reason—and most especially a young woman who feels the need to learn more about defending herself."

Kitishane flushed and turned away. "I would rather take my chances with a wild bear than an overbearing boy."

"The bear would kill you."

"Better death than life-in-death."

Illbane concluded that she had not yet seen death, at least not wanton death. "Well, then, Kitishane, I am glad that you travel with us. We all, it seems, have some stake in proving that justice is possible, and in helping it triumph."

"Even Culaehra?" she asked, looking up again.

"Culaehra more than any," Illbane affirmed, "for he has the need to feel justice triumph within him, whereas we others only feel the need to see it triumph without." He smiled gently at her. "I think you see that in him, maiden—and I think that is what troubles you."

She looked into his eyes and, after a moment, began to smile, too. "Not anymore, Illbane," she said. "Not anymore."

CHAPTER 8

Thwack! went the wand, and Culaehra bolted up, bawling like a calf under the prod. "Be still, unruly child!" Illbane bellowed. "Up with you, now, and march!"

"March? Where? Why?" Culaehra cried.

"Where and why are my concern, runny-nose! Haul up your pack and march!"

"But it is the middle of the night!"

"Closer to dawn than that, but deep enough, yes. What troubles you, swaddled babe? Do you fear the dark?"

"I fear nothing, you doddering dotard!" Culaehra shouted. "Now be off and let me sleep!" He turned back to his bed.

Thwack! The wand struck his legs again. "Up, I tell you!" Illbane cried. "Or shall I use a stouter stick?" He thrust the wand back in his belt and hefted his staff, glaring menace.

Culaehra met his gaze, and they held glare for glare for minutes. Then Culaehra broke the lock, turning away with a snarl to take up his pack.

Illbane nodded brightly to the others. "This need not trouble you. Go back to sleep; we shall see you at daybreak." And off he went into the darkness, driving Culaehra before him.

They watched him go, wide-eyed. Finally, Yocote said, "Do I dream it, or is there actually a tone of humor under Illbane's insults?"

"If you imagined it, I did, too," Kitishane told him.

"Could there be some affection there, even?" Lua asked.

Yocote frowned. "How could there be?"

Kitishane thought Lua might have a point. All she said, though, was, "There is no reason for us to lose sleep over it, friends. Let us find our beds again."

"Well said," Yocote agreed, and they all lay down. But Kitishane lay awake after the gnomes had begun to breathe deeply and evenly, wondering about Culaehra—and almost feeling sorry for him.

They came back at dawn indeed, and Kitishane already had three pheasants turning on the spit. Culaehra staggered into the camp, dropped the packs, and sat down heavily by the fire, head hanging, breathing in deep, hoarse gasps. Kitishane felt sympathy spring and held out a cup of water brewed with herbs. Culaehra stared at it in surprise, then took it with a nod of thanks—but not, of course, a word—inhaled its vapors gratefully, then slurped.

"Where did he take you?" Kitishane asked, keeping her tone gentle.

"Nowhere," Culaehra said in disgust. "He drove me onward and onward all night, and would not tell me where we were going or why. If I dared to protest, there was that blasted wand, and that accursed staff beside it! Then, as the sky lightened, I saw your campfire, then finally saw the camp itself!"

Now Kitishane stared, and the gnomes with her. "Marched half the night only to come back to where you started?" Yocote asked. "Why?"

"Why?" Culaehra snarled. "Ask some demon, if you wish—or ask Illbane; it comes to the same thing!"

Yocote frowned. "To you, perhaps." But even he seemed unsure.

Kitishane frowned, too. "He does nothing without purpose, Culaehra."

"Oh, I do not doubt that! But his purpose won't do *me* any good, I assure you!"

Kitishane eyed him, noticing that in their time with Illbane, Culaehra had lost fat; she did not doubt he had gained muscle—and surely this was the least unpleasant conversation they had ever had! He was actually talking to her, not snarling or blasting orders or shouting. She began to realize what Illbane's purpose might be—or some of it, anyway.

From then on Illbane repeated the exercise two or three times a week, always forcing Culaehra to carry all the baggage with him, never with the same number of days between, never predictably. Culaehra could never guess when, could only know that the wand would strike him in the middle of the night with Illbane roaring, "Up, slugabed!" and they would be off into the darkened wood—or plain, or mountain. He found himself going to bed already planning to be rousted out in the middle of the night, and began to take sleep whenever he could, to be ready for the next midnight excursion. This was fortunate, because Illbane never allowed Culaehra more than six hours' sleep a night, and frequently only two or three.

Finally, when Culaehra was weaving on his feet as he climbed a slope and Illbane struck him with the wand, Culaehra turned about, dropping the baggage and bawling, "How am I to manage when I am half asleep on my feet?"

Illbane stilled, looking up the slope at the big man.

"It isn't really fair, Illbane," Kitishane said, softly enough so that she hoped the outlaw could not hear. "He cannot work for you without sleep."

"Well, then, we'll teach you how to fall into the shaman's trance. Sit down, since you've dropped your packs already."

"What—right here?" Culaehra looked about him in disbelief.

"Some places are better than others, but any place will do. Sit with your back against a rock—there, that's good enough."

"Where's the rock behind yours?" Culaehra grunted.

"I no longer need it, Culaehra; my back knows it is there even when it is not. Now fold your legs and sit with your back straight. Think of a string of beads, hanging straight down from a hand. Let your backbone be like that string . . ."

"What are we doing, anyway?" the big man groused, even as he imitated Illbane's position.

"We are bringing your mind into calmness and stillness, so that the energy that is all about you can flow into you, and revive you as if you had slept. It will not renew your body as fully as real sleep, but it is better than nothing."

"Is that its only purpose?"

Illbane turned to see the source of the voice, and saw Yocote sitting cross-legged beside him, back straight against a slab of rock, legs folded. Illbane smiled. "No, Yocote, that is only the most obvious of its effects, and the only one that a man of action will truly need, or understand. Even for that, it will not serve in place of sleep if you do not also cast a spell, but it is so simple that anyone can cast it—if he has the favor of a deity who will work it for him."

"More a prayer than a spell, then," the gnome said, frowning.

"If you wish. My prayer is, 'Rahani is in my heart, and I in hers.' "

"But Rahani is dead!" Kitishane protested. "All the old gods are dead!"

Illbane sat very still for a few minutes, and her heart rose into her throat for fear she had offended him. At last, though, he said only, "Rahani, at least, is very much alive, I assure you."

"Shall we say her prayer, then?" Yocote asked.

"Only if she is your goddess—and if you did not know she lived, then she is not. Recite a prayer to your own god—but be sure it is short, only one sentence, so that you may recite it over and over."

Slowly, Kitishane sat cross-legged, hands in her lap.

"I thought this was to be *my* magic!" Culaehra protested.

Illbane gave him a long, level look, then said, "There will be other magics for you alone, for not everyone can cast a warrior's spells. This, though, is open to everyone. Come, now, recite your prayer, and calm your mind."

There was more, quite a bit more, but soon enough, all of them sat still as statues, their eyes unfocused, the mountain path silent. Slowly, Lua, too, came to sit down among them, and even more slowly fell into the trance with them.

After a dozen minutes Illbane began to move again. Slowly, gently, he waked each of them, brought the rhythms of their bodies back to a faster tempo. They sighed as they came to their feet once more, amazed how refreshed they felt.

"Remember, this will not do in place of sleep," Illbane cautioned them, "but it will refresh you when your mind is weary and you cannot take the time for rest. Take up your packs, Culaehra! You have the energy now!"

"Illbane," Lua called softly.

"What troubles you?" The sage turned—to see Yocote still sitting cross-legged, eyes glazed.

"He has fallen back into the trance," Lua explained.

"Then he was never truly roused from it." Illbane knelt, peering closely at the gnome-man.

"But he rose! He walked!"

"Yes, but he walked entranced." Illbane began to sing in a strange language, clapping his hands in an irregular rhythm.

Slowly, Yocote lifted his head. Suddenly, his eyes came back into focus. "Illbane! Must I leave, then?" he protested.

"You must," Illbane said gently. "You have not yet enough knowledge to go wandering in the shaman world alone, little brother. Come now, rise and walk with us, for we have several miles to go before we camp for the night."

Yocote stood up, staring at the sage. "Why did you call me 'little brother'?"

"Because there is no question of your talents now," Illbane told him. "If you love the shaman's trance so much as that, you shall most definitely be a shaman someday. But come, we must march!"

Off they went, with Yocote bringing up the rear—and his eyes were shining.

Illbane began to teach Yocote in earnest then, that very night. He taught him the first few words of the shaman's tongue and warned him of the perils of the shaman's trance. He told a tale that all of them listened to with rapt attention. As he told it, he beat one stick against another, and before long they found themselves clapping in time to his taps. The tale was fascinating but simple, about a man who went to seek a treasure, and the monsters and demons he encountered on the way. Finally, he began to be able to turn himself into the forms of the animals he confronted, whereupon they turned themselves into men and women, and helped him to find the treasure.

"But what *was* the treasure?" Lua asked, perplexed.

"Knowledge," Illbane said.

Culaehra spat an oath of disgust.

"But knowledge is not a treasure," Kitishane said.

"Oh, but it is," Yocote said softly, and his eyes shone with so eerie a light that even Culaehra turned away with a shudder.

The next night, Illbane conducted Yocote into a deeper trance than he had undergone before, and stood guard over him while he sat entranced.

Culaehra didn't like the idea of one of his former victims learning more than he knew. "Will you not teach me this magic, too, Illbane?"

"If you wish." Never taking his eyes from Yocote for more than a minute, Illbane showed Culaehra a series of gestures and recited a phrase in the strange language. Culaehra imitated them as best he could, but nothing happened.

"No, no!" Illbane said. "Like this." He repeated the gestures, then told Culaehra, "Try that much, without the words." The outlaw did, but Illbane shook his head. "You have missed the curlicue in the first circle and the helix in the thrust, like this." He demonstrated again. "Try it once more."

Culaehra did, brow furrowed in concentration as he tried to remember Illbane's every movement.

"Well, perhaps you need to learn the words first," Illbane temporized. "Here they are . . ." He spouted a stream of incomprehensible syllables. Culaehra repeated them as best he could, brow furrowed again. "*Woleg sabandra shokhasha . . .*"

"No, try no further," Illbane interrupted. He seemed almost alarmed. "You nearly blundered into a spell that would have made the ground cave in beneath you." A sudden thought occurred to him. "Try the gestures again, only this time instead of a curlicue, think of binding an opponent's blade, and instead of the helical thrust, think of turning a blade as you stab."

This time Culaehra repeated the movements perfectly. "I've mastered it!" he cried jubilantly.

"Yes, so long as you think of it as fighting, not magic," Illbane sighed, "and of course, there is no way to disguise the words as a bully's insult or a hero's challenge. No, Culaehra, I fear that your talent for magic is as slight as your gift for combat is great." Seeing how crestfallen the big man was, he added, "It should not trouble you. True excellence in combat is as much a matter of brain as of brawn, just as the shaman's gift relies as much upon the body's co-ordination for mime and gesture as it does upon memory for the words, or intuition for understanding. Different talents are given to different men."

"Aye, except that you were given all of them!"

"Those of a warrior as well as those of a shaman, yes." Illbane nodded, unruffled. "But I was denied the joy of home and family. Be content with your own talents, Culaehra, especially since they are huge."

The outlaw looked up, startled.

"Is it so surprising to hear me say something good about you?" Illbane smiled, amused. "I shall tell you the truth as I see it, wolf's head, and not trouble myself to soften it, whether it be good or bad— for surely you are strong enough to take both. Yes, you are most exceptionally gifted in combat, and will someday have as much skill as I, but with the speed and strength of youth added to it." He saw the calculating look on his pupil's face, and hastened to add, "By the time you can beat me, though, you will no longer wish to do so."

"No longer wish to!" Culaehra exploded. "I have many revenges to take on you, old—" He finally caught himself, forcing his jaws shut on the words, for a gleam of anger had appeared in Illbane's eye.

"Revenge will not be worth your while when the day comes, Culaehra, for you will be far too busy staying alive. Besides, even when you can best me as a warrior, you will still need to fear me as a wizard."

"Am I not to have a second talent, then?" Culaehra demanded, barely managing to hold back his anger. "You are both wizard and warrior! Will I be only a man of arms?"

"You will also discover a gift for governance," Illbane prophesied, "but you must learn how to live in harmony with other people before you will be able to realize that. Until then, Culaehra, develop the aptitudes you do know of, such as brawling, and leave the more subtle arts to those who have the gift for them."

Yocote moaned.

Illbane turned away to him on the instant, leaving Culaehra to fume alone, seething at the notion of being inferior to a gnome in any way, and swearing to himself that he would someday astound Illbane with his expertise.

"Up!" Illbane cried, and the wand slapped down. Culaehra came awake cursing—then stopped when he realized that the others were rolling out of their cloaks and leaf blankets, too, and the dawn was showing. Why had that blasted old man roused them all out? Of course, he did so every morning, but why with all the extra vigor?

"On your feet!" Illbane barked. "All of you! Yes, you, too, Lua. Mind you, any of you three who wishes to leave may do so—but by Rahani's hem, if you stay, you'll work your bodies into proper shape!"

Yocote grumbled as he rose and shuffled a few paces forward of his bed, but the two women rose with lithe turning, puzzled.

"All in a row, now! Take a step forward on your right foot! Bend your knee! Raise your hands like this!" He held his own up to demonstrate, elbows bent, one hand straight, stiff, and upright, the other a fist.

"Fighting!" Yocote cried. "He teaches us to fight!"

Kitishane's eyes kindled; she was suddenly fully awake; but Lua dropped her hands, stepping back, eyes wide in revulsion.

Culaehra spat an oath and straightened up. "I already know how—"

Illbane's fist shot toward his face. Startled, Culaehra dropped back, snapping his arms up to block—and the sage kicked him in the belly. He doubled over, knotted with pain, hearing Illbane's voice through the roaring in his ears: "You more than any need lessons! Fighting is more than strength and quickness of reflex! Straighten your back!"

"Illbane, he is in pain!" Lua protested, but the sage stepped behind the outlaw, seized his shoulders, and put a knee to his buttocks. "Straighten up, I said! Yes, like that! Now hold up your arms as I showed you!"

Struggling for breath, Culaehra did the best he could to raise his arms in imitation of Illbane.

"Crook the elbow like this! Hold the fist up like this!" Illbane adjusted the outlaw's arms and hands with his own. "Well, good enough!" he grumbled, stepping around in front of the line again. "Now draw your right fist back! Punch with it, hard! Do it again, but step forward with your right foot as you do! Again! Again!"

From that time on, every day began with an hour of such practice movements, before they journeyed onward. Culaehra lost patience with it quickly, especially since Illbane always found fault with his postures and movements, though he fairly rained praise on the others for the slightest improvement. But when they actually began to strike at one another, the situation changed. Oh, Illbane was scarcely a fountain of compliments, but as Culaehra kicked at him, he shouted, "Good!" Of course, he diverted the kick with a swing of his staff, but he went on to say, "Well aimed, and with each limb in exactly the right position! Now, strike with strength!"

Reassured and cocky, Culaehra laughed. "With strength, old man? I've no wish to maim you!" Which, of course, was far from the truth.

"Do you not?" Illbane frowned. "Then you are a very turtle in speed, a sapling in strength! One blast of my breath and you will bend!"

Angered all over again, Culaehra lashed a kick at him.

Illbane bent to parry it with an arm. "Ah! There is the strength I spoke of! But you let anger distract you, lost awareness of your body! Your knee locked, your arms went stiff! If I had caught and pulled your foot, you would have toppled!"

"*If* you could have caught it!" Culaehra cried, and lashed out another kick—but not quite so strongly this time, for he was minding his posture, keeping his arms and knees flexed.

He forgot that the old man could move quickly enough when he wanted. He caught Culaehra's ankle and pulled. Taken off guard, Culaehra jerked forward, but managed to push against that bent knee and stay upright.

"Better than I thought!" Illbane cried, and pushed on the foot. Culaehra gave a squawk of surprise even as he hopped backward. Illbane grinned with delight. "See! *Now* a simple thrust or pull can't fell you! Well done!"

"Not well enough," Culaehra grunted, but he still felt a warm glow inside as Illbane turned away to spar with Kitishane.

The next day it was Culaehra who sparred with Kitishane, though Illbane warned him, "Mock blows only, wolf's head! Hurt or harm her, and I'll shave your head anew!"

Kitishane faced Culaehra with an angry glare, trying to conceal her fear. She well remembered the last time they had fought and how it had ended—or would have, if Illbane had not intervened. She had not learned that much more about fighting! Why was Illbane making her do this?

"Half speed," Illbane commanded. "Culaehra, attack!"

The outlaw's fist shot toward her face. Panic shot through her, and Kitishane blocked as fast as she could, managing to duck aside at the last instant. "He said half speed!"

"That is half speed!" Culaehra snapped.

"*Her* half speed, if you will," Illbane told him.

"*Half* speed? Perhaps a quarter!"

"Very slowly indeed, then," Illbane said sternly.

"Oh, very well," Culaehra grumbled, "but what good will that do *me*?"

"It will teach you precision—and humility, Culaehra. You cannot always do things solely because they benefit you!"

"Can I not?" the outlaw snarled. "Prove to me that others do not!"

"I am your proof, for only the good of others would bring me to lumbering myself with you! Strike, now, but slowly!"

This time Culaehra's fist moved slowly enough so Kitishane had time to raise her forearm to block slowly, though scarcely at half speed. Nonetheless, his forearm struck hers with numbing force. She fell back, clamping her jaw shut to hold back a cry of pain. Fear clamored inside her, but she glared at him all the more angrily for that.

"Gently, Culaehra!" Illbane snapped. "Gently, I said!"

"That *was* gently!"

"You pulled your punch, but there was still far too much force left in it!"

"Aye, if I struck at a rabbit!"

"You do not know your own strength," Illbane told him, "and that is the first step toward disaster. Do you see that dead tree by the spring?"

Culaehra looked up. "Yes. What of it?"

"The darker spot on its trunk is rot. Go strike at it with the same force you used on Kitishane."

Frowning, Culaehra went. He aimed the blow, he struck—and rotten wood crushed under his fist, cascaded down around his arm. He stared at it, amazed.

"Kick at it with all your force," Illbane told him.

Culaehra wound up a huge kick and lashed out. The tree groaned, its groan swelling, then fell. Culaehra stood staring.

"A green tree that size would have only hurt your foot," Illbane told him. "Do you understand why you must strike with no more than a feather's stroke when you deal with Kitishane?"

"But she can strike with all her strength?" Culaehra said sourly.

"Let us see." Illbane held up a palm. "Hit, Kitishane!"

Kitishane stared.

"Strike, I tell you! Do not fear for me!"

Kitishane shrugged and swung at Illbane with all her strength. He wrung his hand, smiling sardonically. "No, not *all* your strength—not in mere practice. Now kick at Culaehra."

She kicked, aiming for the groin, and had to use all her powers of self-restraint to keep the blow from full strength, or full speed. She need not have worried—Culaehra's thigh was there well before her foot, blocking, but she pulled back too quickly for him to catch her ankle, even going at half speed. Still, she reminded herself grimly, if this had not been mere practice and Culaehra not moving so slowly, he would have pulled her off balance then and there.

So Culaehra learned exactly how powerful he was, and how to control his vast strength, while Kitishane and the gnomes developed the muscles of their arms and shoulders to their fullest extent. Their reflexes became almost as fast as Culaehra's, and all of them became much more skilled in unarmed combat, until Illbane pronounced them able to defeat three opponents at once, and to disarm a man equipped with sword and shield.

Then he set them to practicing with staves. Their deftness without weapons quickly lent itself to the use of them, and they gained the new skills quickly. Then, and only then, did Illbane let them begin to practice with wooden swords. This they learned quickly, too, but there was more of it to learn.

Here, at least and at last, Culaehra finally excelled, though Illbane was rarely satisfied and only expressed approval when Culaehra had not yet executed the movements perfectly, and Culaehra began to think he would never be able to sense the old man's moods well enough to avoid disaster.

CHAPTER 9

So the days passed in slow travel, for they spent as much time in practice as in walking—and in Illbane's exacting insistence on Culaehra's cleanliness afterward, which the others began to imitate from sheer boredom in waiting at first, then from pleasure later—though Kitishane was always careful to find some sheltered pool where she and Lua could seek privacy. Illbane also insisted on stopping the day's travel while the sun was still well above the horizon, for he tutored Yocote in magic while Culaehra cooked dinner.

There were whole days when they had to wait in idleness, while Illbane sent Yocote off on errands by himself. When Culaehra asked what they were, Illbane told him curtly to attend to things he could understand. Simmering with anger, Culaehra imagined extravagant revenges on the sage, until the bite of the amulet grew too painful to ignore.

So northward they went, but their progress was very slow, with Culaehra bearing the burdens and forced to behave by Illbane's staff and wand. They came out of the woods into open, rolling land and found that streams were smaller and farther between. Kitishane fashioned water skins from the stock of pelts she saved from the meat she shot for meals. Northward they marched, with Culaehra continually kicking against the goad of Illbane's stern discipline, and trying to sneak chances to beat or intimidate the others. Illbane frustrated the worst of them, though, and Kitishane was instantly defiant, lashing back with words that held no hint of mercy, both for herself and for Lua; and she was quick to call for Illbane if Culaehra threatened to strike. As for Yocote, he gave worse than he took in insults, for his were always barbed with wit, and Culaehra could only simmer about them for hours after, unable to forget the gnome's sallies, for there was always some kernel of truth to them that smarted. No one had dared tell him the truth about himself for a dozen years, and having to face all his flaws was a new and very unpleasant experience. He spent most of his marching time trying to think up excuses for his behavior, and counter-insults to throw back in Yocote's teeth—but he rarely had a chance to use them.

Then, one evening when they were finishing their meal, such a chance came. They had dined on roast boar, and Culaehra pointed out the resemblance between the gnome's face and that of a pig—though truthfully, there really was very little. Yocote replied, "I would rather look like a swine than behave like one. Don't bother trying to shape insults, Culaehra, for you really are a bore."

The pun rankled, and Culaehra grinned with anticipation as he picked his teeth with a sliver of bone and said, "Do you not feel like a cannibal, Yocote, when you eat the flesh of a swine?"

"No, Culaehra," the gnome retorted, "for I would never bite into you; you are scarcely a man of good taste."

With a roar, the outlaw leaped up and kicked at the gnome.

He was fast, moving with almost blinding speed, but Yocote had learned from the same teacher and started falling backward before the foot struck him. Even then, it was his leg that caught the blow, for he had raised his thigh to guard. He yelped with pain, but the kick sent him rolling faster and farther, and he uncurled to dodge behind a tree as Culaehra followed him with another kick.

"Stop him, Illbane!" Kitishane cried, but the sage only shook his head, standing stiffly, taut, his face pale.

Kitishane turned back with a cry of pain, drawing her sword, but before she could leap to intervene, a shower of sparks burst from the tree as Culaehra's kick lashed out.

"Not the salamander!" Kitishane would have thought Illbane were giving instructions to his pupil, if his voice hadn't been so low. "Only its skin!"

Culaehra shouted with pain and hopped around behind the trunk—and Yocote came backing up into sight, following the curve of the tree, hands miming strange actions, mouth droning incomprehensible syllables. It was a yard-thick trunk, so he was almost out of sight again before Culaehra came hopping around the bole, face dark with rage. He threw himself forward, hands outstretched to catch the gnome's neck. Yocote's words shut off with a gargle—but the earth suddenly gave way beneath Culaehra's feet. He shouted in alarm as he fell into the pit—and let go of Yocote. The little man hopped back away from the edge, rubbing his throat.

"No time!" Illbane whispered. "There is no time, little shaman! Hoarse or croaking, speak the spell!"

Almost as if he had heard, Yocote began to chant in a cracked and reedy tenor, hands sawing the air. Then he scrabbled in the dirt, coming up with a handful of fallen acorns, and began to juggle them as Culaehra's arm slammed over the edge of the pit. Then came his head, face swollen and dark with anger. He clambered up and went for Yocote, hands outstretched to throttle.

The gnome gestured, and hailstones rained down upon the outlaw. He squalled in surprise, then clamped his jaw and ran at Yocote again—but the hailstones rolled under his feet; he slipped, bleated as he windmilled his arms, striving for balance before crashing to the ground as the hard rain fell about him.

Kitishane stared in surprise, then gave a shout of mirth, a shout that turned into loud and long laughter.

Red with embarrassment as well as anger, Culaehra staggered to his feet, fell again—but threw himself forward as he did and seized the gnome's ankle.

"Oh, Illbane, help him!" Lua cried, but the sage only shook his head, lips pressed thin.

Yocote had been preparing another spell as Culaehra had been trying to catch his balance. He shouted a last phrase as Culaehra managed to find bare grass and struggled up, holding the gnome hanging upside down—but the air thickened about him, thickened into a fog so dense the watchers could not see him. "You'll have to do worse than that, little man!" he shouted, and Yocote came arcing up out of the cloud as Culaehra swung him high to dash him against the ground. But Yocote shouted a phrase in the shaman's tongue, and the fog suddenly lightened with a brilliant flash. A thunderclap drowned Culaehra's bellow of shock and pain as he tumbled out of the cloud and lay still, Yocote flying from his grasp.

Lua cried out in fright and ran to him.

"He is only stunned." Illbane knelt by the big man, felt at his throat, then nodded with satisfaction and turned to grasp Yocote by the hand and set him on his feet. "Well done! You called upon the elements—all, earth, air, fire, and water—and they gave answer! Well done indeed—shaman!"

Flushed with triumph, Yocote grinned up at him. "I thank you, Teacher!" Then he turned to see Lua rising from Culaehra to run to him, and a shadow darkened his face.

Lua saw and slowed abruptly, but still came on toward him. "Praise the gods you are well, Yocote!"

"I thank you for your concern, Lua." Yocote inclined his head with grave courtesy, and if there was a tang of irony to his words, it was slight enough to pass unnoticed. He turned back to Illbane, and his eyes began to shine again. "Am I truly a shaman, then?"

"You are," Illbane told him. "One who has a great deal more to learn, of course—but yes, a shaman you are." He let the grin show again and clapped his small pupil on the shoulder.

Culaehra groaned.

"Lie still." Kitishane knelt beside him. "Roll to your back if you wish, but no more."

Culaehra rolled over, then moaned with pain. "What . . . happened?"

"You fought with Yocote."

"I remember." Culaehra lifted a hand that virtually fell to his forehead. "The fog, and then . . . with what did he hit me?"

"Lightning." Illbane knelt beside him, across from Kitishane.

"Fire, from the water in the air. You were foolish enough to pick a fight with a shaman, Culaehra."

The big man squinted up at him. "When did the gnome become a shaman?"

"While you were brooding in your misery."

"But how?" Culaehra struggled up on one elbow. "When I first caught him, he could scarcely manage to conjure up a puff of smoke! How has he come to be a wizard?"

"Not a wizard yet, nor even a powerful shaman, but certainly one who is strong enough to defend himself," Illbane said, musing. "However, he was born with a strange talent. Most gnomes are born with the knowledge for working earth-magic and are mighty in that, for they live by rock—but Yocote was born with an affinity for all four elements, not earth alone, so his instinct for earth-magic was diminished. His talent needed training—and with that, he gained power over not merely earth, but also over air, fire, and water, even so much as to make air and water conjoin to produce hail, or to make them both join with fire to produce lightning. Oh, he shall be a most puissant shaman when he is fully trained, I assure you, mastering not only the elements, but also the trees, the flowers, the fish, and the beasts—all manner of living things."

"Including men," Culaehra muttered. He looked down the length of his fallen body, still filled with tremors from that blaze of light. "The wheel has turned now, has it not? Yocote has been raised up, and I am now the lowest of the low."

"Far from it." Amazingly, Illbane's tone was sympathetic. "You are a strong and courageous man, Culaehra, one who has learned some skills of fighting, and you will become truly mighty when you have learned them all."

Culaehra looked up at him in surprise. "But even a gnome can beat me! I might as well kill myself now, for if I don't, someone else will surely do it for me!"

"A *shaman* beat you," Illbane corrected, "and only a fool fights a shaman. When you are done with your training, Culaehra, you will be so mighty a fighter that few will be able to stand against you—few other warriors, that is. You will never again be so foolish as to go up against a shaman if you do not have to."

Culaehra sat still a moment, looking at the ground. Then he said, "Do you tell me truly?"

"I do," Illbane assured him, "and I am a master warrior as well as a sage. When I tell you what you can be, I speak from knowledge. As to truth, have you ever known me to lie?"

Culaehra was silent a moment, then admitted, "No."

"Nor will I ever," Illbane assured him. "Criticize you, yes, even insult you—but lie to you? Never."

Now Culaehra looked up at him. "What must I do to become the best warrior I can, then?"

"You must train as hard as I push you," Illbane told him, "and you must live by my rules."

"Your rules!" Culaehra glared at him. "What have your rules to do with . . ." His words ran down as comprehension came into his eyes.

Illbane met his gaze, nodding gravely. "Yes, Culaehra. This defeat was not due only to Yocote's magic."

"You mean," Culaehra said slowly, "that if I had not broken your rule against picking fights, I would not have been defeated."

"That is part of it." Illbane's tone was neutral.

"And that it is my own bullying that has undone me."

"Yes!" Illbane's satisfaction showed in his tone and his eyes. "There will always be a stronger one to bully the bully, Culaehra."

Culaehra stared incredulously. "You cannot mean the rule was there to protect me as much as Yocote!"

"It protected you both," Illbane confirmed—but did not explain. He only sat, watching and waiting, a great stillness about him.

The stillness was almost as frightening to Culaehra as Illbane's anger. The warrior bent his brain to the riddle, frowning. "If I had not been cruel to the others when I was the most powerful one, they would not be cruel to me now?"

"Not these three, no."

"But I have known men who were!" Culaehra burst out. "And women, too! I had been cruel to only one or two, certainly no more than any child—I even gave help and protection! But they were cruel to me nonetheless!"

"They were not folk who knew how sharply such cruelty bit," Illbane explained. "They had not suffered it themselves."

Culaehra gazed at him a moment, then said, "But Kitishane and the gnomes have."

Illbane nodded.

"From me."

"Even before you," Illbane told him. "I have gleaned the odd remark here and there, the comment in passing, and bound them in sheaves to yield sense. Each in his or her own way knew as much cruelty as you did, Culaehra, in their own home villages. That is why you could have been sure of them, when you could be sure of few others."

Still Culaehra gazed at him. "*Could* have."

Illbane nodded.

"Before I was cruel to them."

"Yet still may," Illbane told him, "if they come to believe you will not be cruel again, if you ever gain the power."

Culaehra's gaze drifted. "I am not sure that I would not be." Then, with great reluctance, "I cannot be sure that I would not *want* to be."

"Then wait until you are."

Culaehra looked up at him again. "You mean that it is not too late to gain the protection of the rules, by living them."

"There is still time," Illbane said, "but I must tell you that my rules are not merely my own inventions. They are laws that govern any band of people, and there are more of them than I have taught you. Without them all villages, all tribes, either fall apart or kill one another off."

"What other laws are these?" Culaehra asked, but Illbane only shook his head, smiling.

"You must discover them for yourself, Culaehra. I will tell you, though, that there are not very many of them."

"Not even all of yours make sense." Culaehra scowled. "What is the purpose of ruling that the strong should protect the weak? Does that law arise so that those who live by it will protect me when I become weak?"

"That is one of its effects," Illbane said.

•　•　•

The next day everyone was very quiet—oddly, Yocote most of all, marching with brows knit, eyes downcast. Now and again he stopped to pick up something—a pebble of unusual shape or hue, a few stalks of grass that he braided into a cord, a limber rod that he thrust into his belt, a tubular reed—but Lua recognized an excuse when she saw it; collecting such scraps gave him a reason for downcast eyes and a solemn, almost grim, air. Lua's eyes filled with tears as she watched him, but whenever she made a move toward him, Illbane caught her eye and shook his head.

All these weeks, they had been marching steadily northward, through land that bore no sign of people except the charred ruins of villages and cattle roaming wild, with pigs and dogs who had quickly reverted to the ways of nature.

When first they came to such a village, Lua stared in shock, Yocote began to look angry, and even Culaehra felt a chill at the postures of some of the skeletons they found.

"What has happened here?" Kitishane cried.

"Bolenkar's agents have come among these villagers," Illbane told her grimly. "They have found cause for war between neighbors, then between hamlets, and finally between villages. The victorious villagers then fought one another, and this country now is stripped to a few small cities that live in an uneasy truce, each waiting only for some advantage over the others before it strikes."

"Is there no remedy?"

Illbane shrugged. "Destroy the agents of Bolenkar."

"Then let us do so!"

But the sage shook his head. "We are not yet strong enough. Meanwhile, more of his emissaries work among the cities of the south and the nomads of the steppe, and in time both will march to conquer this land. Their armies will chew one another to bits and strew these plains with the dead and dying."

Even Culaehra blanched at the thought of death on such a scale, but he said stoutly, "They will all deserve it."

"They will *not* deserve it, for they would have been peaceful enough without tempters to puff them up and tell them that each of them deserved dominion over all the others." Illbane glanced keenly at the outlaw. "Would you not stop it if you could?"

Culaehra started to answer, then bit his tongue, remembering to gauge Illbane's mood. Carefully he said, "They are nothing to me, Illbane, and would probably cast me out if I had been born among them. Why should I care?"

The sage never took his gaze from the outlaw's face, only nodded and said, "You must discover that."

He would not say why or how, only led them away from that village and on toward the north. All Culaehra's pestering would not draw an answer from Illbane, and when the outlaw perceived that the sage's mood of the day was patience, he grew bold, even to the point of hectoring. "You seem to think that I should take another person's troubles upon me, let them become my troubles! Why ever should I do that?"

Illbane stopped and gave him a long, penetrating look, his face so grim that Culaehra's heart sank and he readied himself to fight even though he knew he would be beaten and punished. However, Illbane merely said, "Only experience can teach you that." He turned away, and Culaehra followed slowly, dying to ask what he meant, but too wary.

He found out when they came to the cliff.

The cliff happened at the end of their path. They were following a faint animal trail toward a line that they took for a ridge, a trail that suddenly veered aside to a spring that jetted from a crevice, then ran to splash off the side of the ridge. Illbane halted and held out a hand to stop them. Glad of any rest, Culaehra dropped the packs with a sigh, but Yocote peered through his goggles. "Why did the animals who made this trail turn away? The stream runs to the ridge." Then he frowned. "Come to that, if it is a ridge, why does the spring run over it without pooling first?"

"A good question." Illbane leaned on his staff, watching Yocote intently. "Seek the answer carefully, you who are now a shaman."

Yocote glanced up at him, frowning, then turned to follow the animal trail, dropping to all fours at the spring. He crawled as he followed its course.

Culaehra snorted. "Yes, Yocote, crawl like the worm you are!"

"Do not make your ignorance march where all can see, Culaehra!" Illbane snapped. "He mimics the deer who made the trail so that he may take in their thoughts."

The outlaw glared at him. "Take in their thoughts? You mean

think like them, do you not? Oh, I do not doubt that Yocote thinks like a timid antelope!"

"He takes in the thoughts of the animals who made the path!" Illbane strode over to him, his voice dropping to an angry mutter. "It is shaman's work, to bring the memories buried in the stone and the earth into his own mind, that he may know what they know! Do not speak of what you cannot understand!"

Culaehra's head snapped up as if he had been slapped, and within, he vowed revenge on Yocote for Illbane's insults. The amulet at his throat chilled him, but he shook off its spell angrily.

Yocote stiffened, then shied away. "It is no ridge, Illbane, but a cliff's edge!"

"Is it truly?" Illbane sounded quite interested, but Culaehra felt sure he had known it all along, and silently cursed him for making them go through this game. The sage strode up to the edge of the cliff and nodded. "Indeed it is, and we can see an amazing distance from it! Come up, my companions, and look upon your path for the next sennight—but come carefully."

Slowly, they came up, Yocote to one side of him, Kitishane to the other, dropping to their knees for the last pace or two. They gasped in awe—and Lua, finally curious, crept forward to join them.

None stood right next to Illbane, of course; they maintained their respectful distance—and Culaehra suddenly realized that now, even now, he could run at the sage's back and push him off the edge. His blood quickened even as the amulet turned so cold that he almost yelped in surprise—but it reminded him to be cautious. For all he knew, Illbane might sprout wings and fly! And, come to think of it, Illbane had stepped up quite close to the edge, turning his back on him, ignoring him quite deliberately—almost as if he were inviting the assault. Illbane was angry at him; Culaehra knew that, and he also knew the old man must have eyes in the back of his head. He wouldn't put it past Illbane to sense when he was rushing, and step aside at the last second, to let him go hurtling over the edge of the cliff. Culaehra's blood chilled at the thought—or was that only the amulet's effect running through him? No, he decided, the risk was too great. He went forward after all, but slowly, moving up beside Yocote and fighting down the urge to kick the little man off the precipice instead.

Then Culaehra saw the view and forgot all thoughts of revenge or assault.

The plain stretched away to another range of mountains far in the distance. It was grassy, with three lines of trees winding across it. One had deep curves, even an oxbow. He wondered why the trees grew in lines, then caught the glint of water from the oxbow. The trees showed the courses of rivers! Was water so scarce in this land that trees could grow only on the banks of streams?

It would seem so, but the grass was lush green with the summer rains—summer, and Illbane had caught him in early spring!—and the sky arched huge above all, almost awing him with the depths of its blueness and the streams of clouds that streaked it like rivers in the sky.

He stood spellbound by the vista until Yocote's voice brought him out of his daze. "How are we to climb down there?"

A good question! He glanced at Illbane—and saw the sage watching him with a thoughtful, weighing look, almost as if he were suspecting there might be some good in him after all. Culaehra flushed and turned away—to find Kitishane watching him with a look that was much the same, but held some difference in both kind and intensity. Culaehra turned quickly back to the vista before him. "Well asked, Illbane. How *do* we climb down?"

"There is a broad ledge some twenty yards below us," the sage answered, not even looking. "It runs down the face of the cliff like a ramp, switching back on itself three times."

"I see it!" Yocote lay on his belly, looking down over the edge.

"All well and good, once we come to the ledge!" Culaehra replied.

"There is a coil of rope in my pack. I shall lower you down one by one."

Culaehra's blood ran cold. Lua whimpered. If it hadn't been for his slender stock of remaining pride, he would have joined her.

"You need not carry the packs while you descend," Illbane told him. "I shall lower them to you."

"To *me?*"

"Of course. You do not think I would trust you behind my back while my hands were occupied, do you?" Illbane stepped over to take the packs from Culaehra's back. "Besides, you are the largest. If any of the others slip, you will cushion their fall."

"Oh, how very considerate of you!" Culaehra brayed. "How if *I* do not trust *you* to hold the other end of the rope from which I hang?"

Illbane looked up from rummaging in the pack. "Why, you have no choice," he said. "I do."

Culaehra stared into his eyes and thought they were the coldest he had ever seen. He licked lips gone suddenly dry and said, "I could flee."

Illbane spread an arm, bowing. "Attempt it."

Culaehra knew just how far he would be able to flee. True, there were no resin-laden pines here, but he did not doubt that the sage would find some other magic trick to bring him down.

"You are going over that cliff, Culaehra." Those frigid eyes held his again, breathing the chill of glaciers into him. "With or without that rope."

"You've said you need me for some purpose of your own," Culaehra croaked.

"Perhaps it is to be a sacrifice to the goddess," Illbane told him. "Perhaps this is the place of sacrifice."

Culaehra didn't believe that for a second—but he would not have put it past the sage to let him go through all the pains of death, then haul him back to life for his own nefarious purposes. He spat an oath of disgust and held out a hand.

Illbane took the rope from the pack and held it out to him, his eyes glowing—with amusement? Or triumph? Or something else? Culaehra couldn't be sure, but whatever it was, he hated Illbane for it. The sage told him how to arrange the rope about him so that he could lower himself. Illbane would only need to anchor his end of the cable.

"You have great faith in the strength of my arm," Culaehra grumbled, stringing the strand.

"On the contrary—I have great faith in the strength of the rope." Illbane wrapped his end around the trunk of a stunted pine that grew nearby, then took a firm hold on the six-foot length of rope that was left. "You see? You have this tree holding you, as well as me!"

"Aye, provided you do not let go of your end," Culaehra said sourly. He sat on the edge of the cliff, took one brief glance down-ward—and felt his heart sink. Fear filled him, bawling within him to run, to fight, to do anything but drop off that mountainside—but greater fear held him still, fear of Illbane's staff and his magic. He took a deep breath, said, "If I die, Illbane, my ghost will haunt you," then took another deep breath and shoved himself off the side.

Somehow, he did not think Illbane feared ghosts.

The rope jerked on his arm but held firm. Culaehra planted his feet against the face of the cliff, resolutely not looking down. His heart hammered in his chest, reverberated through his head.

He wondered if Illbane liked him that day.

CHAPTER 10

"Walk down the cliff face now," Illbane called cheerfully. "Let the rope slip about you as you do—but make sure you let it out, handhold by handhold."

"*Very* sure," Culaehra assured him. He started down the cliff face, his heart hammering like a dozen blacksmiths. Illbane's good cheer could be a good sign—but Culaehra remembered the harsh words he had just now spoken, and swallowed against a thick lump in his throat. He looked up resolutely, even though all he could see was Yocote's goggled face peering over the cliff's edge, and pure sky beyond—anything was better than looking down. He felt mildly surprised that the gnome wasn't grinning at his discomfort—in fact, Yocote seemed genuinely anxious. Why should that be?

"Too fast!" Illbane called, and sure enough, the slipping rope burned his palm. How could the old demon have known without looking? But Culaehra forced himself to move more slowly, even though all he wanted was for this nightmarish descent to be over.

"Only a few yards more!" Yocote called, and relief almost made Culaehra go weak—but why should the gnome be helping him, even in so slight a way? He clung to the rope for dear life, letting it slip about him slowly, walking step by slow step down the cliff face. Finally, his reaching foot struck a horizontal surface. Scarcely daring to believe, Culaehra lowered both feet, let out another foot of rope—and felt it go slack. He ignored the spurt of panic that raised, and stamped his feet to make sure the footing held. Then, at last, he looked down, and saw solid rock beneath his feet.

"Unwind the rope!" Illbane's voice was thin with distance.

What if Culaehra did not?

They would be stranded up there, and he could escape down the ledges! The amulet stabbed his throat with coldness, but Culaehra rapidly considered the idea. He couldn't run away without letting go of the rope—but he could tie it to a huge boulder, if he could find one . . .

And Illbane would slide down that strand and catch him with that blasted staff. Culaehra heaved a sigh of regret and unwound the rope. At least Illbane seemed to like him today; perhaps he should do nothing to lessen that. He stood waiting, watching as Yocote's legs dropped over the edge, the rope wound around him just as Culaehra had worn it. He crept down the cliff face like a snail—or had he himself gone so slowly? Culaehra wondered.

Suddenly, he realized that he would be alone with the gnome for at least a few minutes. What was there to keep him from throwing the little man off the ledge? His heart leaped at the thought, even as the amulet chilled his throat—and that spreading numbness made him remember Yocote's magic. A bare beginner in shamanry, Illbane had called him, but Yocote was still able to counter all Culaehra's strength and size. Of course, he probably couldn't work much magic while he was falling to his death . . .

But perhaps enough to save his own life?

Then, surely, enough for revenge—all the more potent because, as Yocote's spells sped upward, Illbane would be falling upon him with his own vengeance. It probably would not be fatal, Culaehra thought, not judging by all Illbane's claims that he needed him for some nefarious purpose of his own—but it was likely to be very painful. Not that he minded a little pain, or that he could not endure a great deal of it, if he might gain victory thereby—but fighting Illbane had proved to be a guarantee of defeat, so what purpose was there in pain?

With regret, Culaehra held up his hands and caught Yocote by the waist. Even so, the urge filled him to hurl the little man over the edge—but it faded under fear of Illbane by the time the gnome had unwound the rope. Culaehra sighed and lowered him to the ledge.

Yocote looked up and slowly said, "Thank you, Culaehra."

The words surprised Culaehra—no one had thanked him since he was twelve, and he found out how much truth there was in *their* words! Old anger rose, and he snarled, "Did I have a choice?"

"Several," the gnome said, still slowly, "the least of which was to stand aside and let me step onto the ledge without aid, though I'll admit it was a huge relief to feel your hands about my waist."

"Yes, I could have done that," Culaehra conceded, and wondered why he had not thought of it.

Yocote studied him a moment longer, then turned back to the cliff face. "Now who comes?"

It was Kitishane, and watching from below, Culaehra found that he had something left to enjoy in life. Clad in breeches though she was, the woman was still very pleasant to watch; her leggings were laced tight, and their form was very pleasing. He let his imagination wander until the sharp bite of the amulet made him rein it in—the amulet, and the dangerous closeness of Kitishane's feet as they stepped down the cliffside. Culaehra grinned and held up his hands to clasp her waist, but Kitishane snapped, "I'll land on my own two feet, thank you!"

"As you wish." Culaehra tried to sound nonchalant as he stepped aside.

Kitishane dropped the last foot to the ground and stalked aside, red-faced. It was hard to stalk when you were only going two steps, but Kitishane managed it. As Culaehra raised his eyes again, she snapped, "Don't you *dare* watch!"

"I have to catch her if she falls," Culaehra pointed out. "How can I, if I do not watch?"

Kitishane's face closed even more tightly, but she made no answer.

Really, there wasn't much pleasure in watching the gnome descend. She wore so many underskirts now that no one could have seen the shape of her legs, only her feet—and Culaehra could not feel more than the faintest stirrings of desire in so small a female anyway, without it evoking memories that somehow still had the power to strike fear through him, even though he was a grown man and easily half again the size of the brute he had slain.

He heard Lua's whimpering twenty feet above him, and somehow felt both exasperation and pity. Quickly, he concentrated on the exasperation, not liking the pity. Still, he reached up and caught her waist as she came within reach. She gave a start and cried out, letting go of the rope, then crying out again in fright.

"Do not fear, little sister!" Kitishane leaped forward, holding out her arms, and Culaehra released the gnome into her hands with a grimace of distaste. Kitishane glared daggers at him, but Lua had not seen; she only clung to Kitishane, sobbing.

"Yes, I know, it was a harrowing ordeal," Kitishane soothed, "but you have come down to us without letting go of the rope, and Culaehra would have caught you if you had fallen."

That only made the little woman cry more loudly. Culaehra found room to feel indignant. Yocote watched her anxiously, so Culaehra was the only one glancing up when Illbane swung himself off the cliff's edge. His robe billowed about him so much that Culaehra could only catch an occasional glimpse of his legs, and they weren't anywhere nearly the sticks that he expected in a man of that age.

Then it occurred to him to wonder who was holding the other end of the rope.

He leaped forward, arms outstretched to catch. Kitishane noticed and glanced up, then said, "Never fear, hunter. He holds the rope securely."

Culaehra kept his arms spread, even though his heart ceased racing—and he cursed himself for a fool, to have worried for his enemy's safety. Why, if Illbane fell to his death, these other three would be his slaves again! If it weren't for Yocote's magic . . .

But Illbane swung down to a safe landing and acknowledged Culaehra's spread arms with a small bow. "I thank you, woodsman. I might indeed have missed my grip, and been slow to recite a flight spell."

So, Culaehra thought, I have been promoted from wolf's head to woodsman, have I? He wondered why.

Then he wondered why Illbane had not merely pronounced the flight spell in the first place. Perhaps he really could not, perhaps it was all a lie . . .

Looking up, Illbane pulled, and the loose end of the rope shot upward. He kept pulling, and it disappeared over the edge. Then Illbane gave a sharp tug, and the rope's end sprang loose from the top of the cliff. "Step aside!" the sage commanded. Culaehra stepped back quickly; so did Yocote and Kitishane. Even Lua finally managed to stifle her sobs enough to look—just in time to see the rope cascade down into a heap at their feet.

"Coil it," Illbane told Culaehra, "and we will go."

Culaehra heaved a sigh and bent to start coiling the rope.

Kitishane found herself stealing glances at Culaehra as they marched along. She could scarcely believe he was the same man who had assaulted her several months before. Illbane's insistence on bathing had shown him to have a fair, clean complexion, and his hair was actually blond, not light brown. Perhaps it was the exercises, perhaps the lessons of humiliation and pain, but the big man's skin almost seemed to glow. The pudginess had melted away, revealing the hard muscle underneath. His face was leaner, and she noticed that his eyes were very large for a man, his nose straight, and the fullness of his lips sent strange shivers through her.

But those shivers reminded Kitishane of the way he had attacked her before, and though he had shown no aggression toward anyone since Yocote had beaten him with magic, she knew he might well try again. Whenever she paused to admire him, those memories rose, making her turn away with a shiver.

For her part, Lua was noticing the changes in Yocote. He seemed different to her since he had defeated Culaehra—stronger, more confident. However, he also seemed to be darker, more silent; she missed the old cheerful jibes and sarcastic thrusts at Culaehra—

not that they had ceased, but they became rare. He had grown in bulk, laying on even more muscle than gnomes usually built through their cleaving of rock. In the evening, when he took off his goggles, she began to notice that he was quite handsome.

She found, to her surprise and delight, that she was no longer in love with Culaehra. It gave her a feeling of relief and freedom that amazed her—but she also felt the beginnings of such an obsession with Yocote. The gnome, though, seemed almost to shun her. Could it be that he misunderstood her compassion for Culaehra when he was hurt? But she felt compassion for everybody! In confusion, she was well on her way to misery again.

Culaehra, for his part, found himself thinking more and more about the rules Illbane had so extolled, and he began to work at finding objections to them. Chief among them, he doubted that he truly would meet a man who was stronger than he, a bully for a bully. Four or five bullies together, yes—but one? He had never seen a man as big as he was, nor as strong, and Illbane's skill did not deter him, for if it was only skill, he could gain it himself someday. Magic, no—he was willing to accept that rule, at least: never pick a fight with a shaman, which meant never try to bully one. But he remembered that Illbane had said, "Unless you cannot avoid it," and began to try to develop a strategy for fighting magicians. Strike fast, before they could pronounce a spell? But how would you come close enough for one quick strike to end the matter? He mulled it over in his mind.

Illbane had begun to trust him out of sight now, and one day, while Culaehra was out gathering firewood, he saw a big stranger coming toward him through the wood. He realized that he was about to test the question of a bully stronger than himself.

The other man looked to be a little taller than Culaehra, with brown hair and a wide face with large eyes. He was dressed in woodsman's tunic, breeches, and boots, and was fleshy, with a soft look to him. Still, Culaehra knew from his own experience that a layer of fat could hide quite a deal of muscle, so he did not put much faith in it. He braced himself to dodge quickly, though, for the stranger carried a bow, and a quiver filled with arrows on his back.

Sure enough, the stranger nocked an arrow, grinning. "Come

along, fellow! I'm off to shoot deer, and could do with a slave to carry the carcass."

"Come along yourself!" Culaehra's heart sang at the prospect of a blameless fight. "I'm no slave, and certainly no friend to a man who shoots more than he can eat!"

The arrow rose to point at his face. "Oh, but you are—or you're a dead man."

"Kill me, then," Culaehra invited.

The bowstring thrummed, and Culaehra whipped aside to his left. Sure enough, the arrow passed far to his right—the hunter had planned on his dodging that way. Then Culaehra dashed straight at the man and caught him with the next arrow not yet to the string. The hunter dropped his weapons just in time to block Culaehra's punch, but the impact of Culaehra's body sent him tumbling to the ground—with a fistful of Culaehra's tunic. It jerked Culaehra off his feet, but he slammed a fist into the hunter's belly as he fell. Sure enough, there was hard muscle under the fat, and not that much padding at that—but the man grunted, and his hold loosed just enough for Culaehra to strike his hand aside, then roll to his feet. The hunter came up as quickly as Culaehra did, though, rising in a crouch, arms spread to wrestle, a grin on his face.

Culaehra struck hard at that grin, hard and fast.

The stranger's arm flashed up to deflect the blow, then his own fist struck back at Culaehra's belly. Culaehra blocked it, then blocked the punch that came at his face right after it, but the third punch caught the other side of his face, and he leaped back, head ringing, shaking his head to clear it. A roar of delight echoed in his ears, and he saw a blur as the stranger followed up his advantage. Culaehra blocked and gave ground, turned and ducked just enough to take a punch meant for his belly on his arm—then tripped and fell backward over something hard. The stranger whooped with glee, leaping over the log and swinging a kick at the fallen man.

Culaehra caught the ankle, pushing it up above him, and rolled. The stranger squalled as he fell. Still holding onto the foot, Culaehra struggled up, managing to push the hunter's leg from side to side as the man struck at him with kick after kick. Culaehra grinned and shoved it high—and the hunter caught him in the ribs with the other foot. Culaehra dropped the ankle with a breathless curse and tried to keep his guard up as his lungs clamored for air. The hunter leaped up, striking at Culaehra's face with three quick blows; Culaehra blocked two and rolled back in time to take most of the force out of the third. He retreated quickly, dancing backward, blocking punches—then suddenly ducked under the stranger's guard and slammed a fist into the stranger's gut. The hunter folded over with a grunt, keeping his guard up as he glared at Culaehra while he struggled for breath. Culaehra could sympathize; the fight had been going on long enough so that he was almost winded himself.

But it went on longer, punch and counterpunch, kick and block, retreat and advance, till finally both men stood shivering with fatigue, glaring at one another with their guards low from sheer weariness, heaving great gasps and striving for enough energy to aim another punch.

"We are too well matched!" Culaehra finally wheezed—but he kept his guard up.

"True," the stranger said, with massive reluctance. "If we fight on, we shall both lose, and neither win."

"Truce, then?" Culaehra held out an open hand, ready to clench it into a fist and strike if need be.

"Truce," the stranger agreed, showing an open hand in like manner.

Culaehra stepped back and dropped his guard—ready to raise it again in an instant. "You are the strongest man I have ever fought, save one."

"One?" The stranger straightened, dropping his guard. "Do you mean to say there is a better fighter than I?"

"Well, yes, but he is a wizard, so it is no matter."

"It is a great *deal* of matter!" the stranger said indignantly. "Can he best you without using his magic?"

"Most of the time," Culaehra admitted.

"But for the rest? Oh, there is no trusting them, shamans, sorcerers, or sages! They are all alike, nothing but the bullies they so claim to despise, intimidating and enslaving all with their magic!"

"It would surely seem so, by my experience," Culaehra agreed.

The hunter sat down on the grass. "Come, sit by me and tell me of it—sit, sit, for after fighting you, I am far too weary to stand!"

"I, too," Culaehra confessed. He sat down. "What has been your experience with the magic brotherhood, hunter?"

"Only the shaman of my native village, woodsman, who had the audacity to lead them all into casting me out only because I did by force of arms what he did by force of magic! And the shaman of the village I went to, who invited me in, then sought to overawe me with his ceremonies, and when I would not kneel, led *his* people in casting me out. Thereupon I decided to hunt alone, and prey upon the weaker as they deserved."

"Aye, for being weaker!" Culaehra said with heartfelt indignation. "Is it not the way of the world? Is it not right that we do as the animals and the trees and the elements do?"

"Surely it is! But tell me, what has been *your* experience with shamans?"

"Much the same as yours." Culaehra told him the story of his adolescence and outcasting, of being shunned by his own people until he had attained his full growth, then excoriated for responding by bullying them, and finally being cast out. That led to childhood reminiscences, and the occasional upstart lad who had gone against the way of rightness by trying to fight back.

Culaehra was amazed to discover a man so like himself, whose opinion agreed with his on almost every point, and whose experiences had been so like his own—but he did not tell of the pivotal event of his childhood, that had begun his fellow villagers' fear of him. The hunter, as far as he could tell, had no such turning point to relate; he had merely grown as the biggest of his generation, and taken it as his right to beat those smaller, enjoying the heady sense of power it gave. Something about that struck a note of wrongness in Culaehra, but he ignored it, so glad was he to meet someone who would not condemn him for being what he was. He even unbent enough to tell of his encounters with Lua and Yocote—which set the hunter to guffawing with appreciation. Then he told of Kitishane's interference and his subjugation of her—or the subjugation that would have been, if Illbane had not interfered.

"What right had he?" the hunter said indignantly—and with the heat of a man who has been deprived of a lurid tale. "She was your meat, not his! He did not even want to use her!"

"Unfair indeed, and so I thought it," Culaehra agreed. The anger and frustration woke in him all over again. "But he was not content merely to drive me off and free them." He went on to tell of Illbane's subjugation of *him*, of the scores of humiliations the sage had heaped on him, of the hopeless fights and unavenged blows and insults—and as he told it, his anger built higher and higher.

"The gall of the man," the hunter cried, "to degrade a warrior so!" He wrapped his fist in the throat of Culaehra's tunic and yanked his head close. "He deserves death, woodsman! He deserves worse than death!" He let go, pushing the outlaw back. "Why do you suffer him?"

"Because I have no choice," Culaehra admitted, though the words were gall on his tongue.

"You do now." The stranger grinned at him. "There are two of us."

Culaehra stared back at him, then slowly smiled. For a second his heart soared at the thought of freedom—but he remembered Illbane's talk, and damped his spirits enough to say, "Perhaps I should not, though. I chafe under Illbane's rules, but I cannot deny that they make sense."

"Rules?" the stranger frowned. "What rules are these?"

Culaehra explained the rules to him, which certainly did not take long.

"And you obey him?" the hunter asked incredulously.

"I begin to see the sense in them." But with the hunter staring at him as if he were an idiot, Culaehra was no longer so sure.

"It is an outrage!" The hunter leaped up and began pacing. "A strong man being bound by a wizard's rules? What right has he? What right?"

"Illbane says that these rules are not of his making, really, but are those that bind all groups of people, for without them, such groups tear themselves apart." But the words no longer sounded so true as they had when it had been only Illbane and himself talking, and the defeat by Yocote so recent.

"Illbane says, Illbane says! You are a *warrior*! Who is this Illbane to say what you shall do or not do? Who is *any* man to tell a warrior what to do?" The hunter spun, finger stabbing out at Culaehra. "And who are you to obey him? Come, let us set this situation to rights!" He sat down by Culaehra again, his body tensed with eagerness. "I shall help you with it! I shall creep into your camp at night and hold the dotard down while you slay him!"

Excitement flared in Culaehra, and he was amazed at the strength of his own longing, a desire for revenge so strong that it made him shake. Even so, he could imagine what Illbane would do to any who tried to kill him—especially if that "any" were Culaehra himself. "There is always a sentry posted . . ."

"I shall wait until that sentry is you!"

"He may not need his hands or his staff to work magic, only his mouth . . ."

"I shall kneel ready to stifle him and hold his arms if he should waken, but he will not!"

Culaehra stared. "You mean to kill him in his sleep?"

"How else can you kill a wizard?" the hunter demanded impatiently. "If you let him wake, he may work magic by the power of his mind alone, for all we know! Who kens the ways of wizards, or how they work their magic? Of course we shall kill him in his sleep!"

Even to Culaehra, that sounded particularly vicious, certainly cowardly.

"It is the only way to counter that huge and unfair advantage that the wizard has over you!" the hunter exhorted. "Give him a chance to fight back, and you will have no chance at all! Slay him in his sleep, for there is no other way! Slay him in his sleep and be free!"

Cowardly indeed, and terribly wrong—but so anxious was Culaehra to regain his freedom that he felt himself attracted to the notion.

"Then you and I shall enslave the gnomes and the woman again." The stranger grinned.

The thought of Kitishane in his arms sent the blood roaring through Culaehra's head. To see if she really was as beautifully

formed as the contours of her leather breeches and tunic hinted
. . . to examine and admire those contours at his leisure, taking as
long as he wanted . . .

Of course, to take his time, to caress lingeringly, she would
have to be willing . . . well, he would find a way around that one.

"Will you do it, and have the woman?" the hunter demanded.

"Yes!" Culaehra leaped to his feet and clasped the hunter's forearm. "I should be sentry in the three hours before dawn! Come
then, and we shall do it!"

"Stout fellow!" The hunter grinned, thumping him on the shoulder. "Go, then, and gather your wood as you go! Tonight, whet your
knife!"

"I will! Come in the darkness before the dawn!"

"I shall!" The hunter stooped to take up his bow and quiver.
"Look for me in darkness!"

"In the darkness, then!" Culaehra punched his arm, then turned
to go—and he glanced back, ready to jump aside in case the hunter
loosed an arrow at his back. But the man only waved the first time
Culaehra looked, and was gone into the undergrowth the second
time. Culaehra relaxed and set himself to gathering a convincing
stack of wood as he went. Really, the hunter was a fine fellow!

Culaehra came swinging into the camp with an armload of
sticks, whistling between his teeth, amazed at how well he felt.
Why, his heart had not sung like this since the day he was cast out
of his village!

Yocote looked up from the small fire he had kindled, frowning.
"What brings you in such good spirits, Culaehra?"

"The smell of autumn in the air, Yocote! The feeling of well-
being it gives a man!" The lies came easily again. He dropped the
wood next to the gnome. It felt so good to plan, to believe he could
once again be free and be able to bully, to plan on beatings or
worse without that dratted amulet burning cold into his throat . . .

Culaehra's hand flew to his collar as he realized he had been
planning to slay Illbane in detail, and not once had the amulet
even cooled his skin.

It wasn't there.

For a moment he groped frantically, thinking surely the chain must have broken, the amulet fallen beneath his shirt—but no, it was gone, chain and all! Suddenly, he remembered the hunter's hand gathering the cloth of the tunic at his throat, hauling him near, then thrusting him away. "That snake! He stole my amulet!"

"What snake?" Lua stared up at him wide-eyed.

"The one who struck at me in the forest! The swine! The vulture! Steal from *me*, will he?" Culaehra turned about and charged back into the trees.

Kitishane and the gnomes stared after him, dumbfounded, as Illbane came up beside them, watching Culaehra go.

"Why should he be angry if someone took the amulet?" Lua asked. "He has hated it so!"

"Yes," said Kitishane. "He claims it is the badge of subjugation!"

"As indeed it is," Illbane confirmed.

"Then why would he be angry at having it stolen?"

"Because," Illbane said, "it is his."

CHAPTER 11

Culaehra ran through the woods, cursing as he went. How dare the thief steal from him! Worse, how dare he claim to be an ally and scheme with him to achieve his fondest desire, all the time knowing it was only to distract him from the theft! Thank heaven, Culaehra thought, that he had not tried to slay Illbane, depending on the man's help!

It was dark now, but moonlight filtered through the branches here and there. Culaehra ran stumbling, back to the clearing where he had met the hunter. Moonlight filled it; he cast about quickly for the stranger's trail, found it, then plunged into the trees, searching.

As he went he calmed a little, enough to remember the folly of making a huge amount of noise when chasing quarry. He slowed a bit, placing his feet carefully if quickly as he followed the hunter's trail. Oddly, it was quite clear, as if the man had made no attempt at all to hide it.

There, through the trees! The light of a campfire! Culaehra slowed, moving quietly, but there was murder in his heart as he stepped into the clearing.

Not quietly enough. The stranger turned from the fire, grinning as he stood. "So, woodsman! You could not wait for me to come join you!"

"No one could wait that long," Culaehra retorted, "for you would never have come." He held out a palm. "My amulet, if you please."

It glinted at the stranger's throat. "Come and take it," he taunted.

Culaehra stalked close, then leaped, lashing out with a kick.

The stranger dodged, snatching at Culaehra's leg but missing. He leaped forward even as Culaehra landed, slamming a fist at his midriff, then a right at his face, then a left at his belly again—but Culaehra had learned that was the hunter's favorite combination by now, and blocked all three, then stepped in with a quick uppercut. The stranger blocked and cracked a fist into Culaehra's jaw. His head swam, and he grabbed at the stranger even as he turned away, almost losing his balance—but hearing a heavy thud as the stranger hit the ground. Then Culaehra stepped back, his balance almost restored, shaking his head, clearing it—to see the stranger uncoiling from the ground fists first. But it was too crude a movement. Culaehra sidestepped easily, slamming a blow into the stranger's head as it passed. The hunter shouted in anger and lashed a kick even as he hit the ground. It took Culaehra off guard, caught him in the belly, and he doubled over in pain, backing away quickly. The stranger took a minute coming to his feet, though, clearing his head, then came at Culaehra hammer and tongs.

They went at it again and again for what seemed like hours, deflecting most of each other's blows but landing some, ducking and dodging and kicking and being kicked, until finally they stood at arm's length, knees bent and shoulders hunched, gasping for breath, exhausted and weaving.

"I think you would have come to the camp after all," Culaehra wheezed, "but not to slay Illbane—to kill me!"

"Think you so?" the stranger said, and suddenly his face seemed to soften like a tallow candle in the sun, then to slip strangely. It firmed again, much leaner than it had been, the brown hair bleached to blond—and Culaehra found himself staring at his own face!

He must have gaped like a landed fish, for the stranger gave a mocking laugh. "Oh yes, I am Culaehra, I am yourself! You cannot escape me, woodsman—woodsman and wolf's head, for who should know so well as I! You cannot escape me, cannot flee from me, cannot slay me without slaying yourself—for I am you, and am in you, and will always be, for I am indeed you and no one else!" He threw back his head, laughing loud and long. Culaehra cursed, but the stranger laughed all the harder, even as he seemed to lighten, even as the moonlight seemed to show through him, then through the campfire and the trees till he was only an outline filled with vapor that lost its form and churned in the night breeze, churned and arrowed straight at Culaehra. He tried to dodge it, cursing and shouting, but it shot back into his torso—chest, belly, and groin—and was gone.

The night was still—still, but for the night air stirring in the branches of the trees, and Culaehra's hoarse breathing where he knelt, shaking, swearing, and sweating.

"Take heart, Culaehra."

The outlaw's head snapped up; he stared upward, fear striking deep—then saw it was Illbane, and sagged with relief.

Then it occurred to Culaehra that the sage might know of his conspiracy to murder him, and he tensed again. To hide his fear, he spoke roughly. "Take heart! How can I, if I am truly so treacherous and despicable a snake as that!"

"Because he is not *all* of you," Illbane said, "nor even the essence of you—he is only the outer husk of you, not the whole nut nor even the kernel. He is the outer husk, and you can peel him away and leave him behind—if you wish."

Culaehra stared with sudden hope, and caught at the sage's robe. "How!"

"Think," Illbane said. "Was he truly the spit and image of you?"

Culaehra lowered his gaze, frowning, thinking over everything the stranger had said and done. Finally, he grimaced with self-disgust. "He did nothing that I had not done—or would not have done, given the chance."

"Did you never think there was anything wrong in what he said?"

Culaehra frowned, remembering.

"Did you never doubt the rightness of what he urged you to do?"

"I did," Culaehra said in self-contempt. "I felt reluctance, hesitation. I put it down to fright."

Illbane did not ask of what he had been frightened. "You never thought it might be a sense of right and wrong?"

"I have never believed what people preach about that!" Culaehra snapped.

"Perhaps not," Illbane said, "but that does not indicate you have no sense of rightness or of justice. It only means that what people tell you is right goes against your innate sense of the word."

Culaehra sat very still, frowning downward.

"Since you did not agree with your shaman and your chief and your elders," Illbane said, "you thought you were wrong. Worse, you thought you were bad—and if you were bad anyway, you decided to do a good job of being bad."

"How could you know that!" Culaehra glared up at him.

"Because you are not the first young man who has let others make his face for him," Illbane responded.

Culaehra bridled at the notion that he had let anyone control him so much. "Have you known any others?" he demanded.

"What if I told you that the first was Lucoyo?"

Culaehra sat staring up at the old man for a minute. Then he said, "What! Are you the demigod Ohaern, then?" and laughed. "I would say you surely seem old enough!" But he became serious again. "I see. You mean that Lucoyo is the example for all of us who have turned to the wrong. But he reformed!"

"Or was reformed by the trust and liking of Ohaern and his men," Illbane said, "a reformation sealed by the love of his wife."

"I should sneer at such a statement," Culaehra said.

"Then why do you not?"

"Because I would not believe myself," Culaehra confessed, then stopped and frowned, gazing inward. "There has been a great change in me, hasn't there?"

"Inside yourself, yes," Illbane told him, "but you persisted in believing the outside."

"I will never believe in him more!"

"I hope not," Illbane said, "but it will be difficult, Culaehra. You have believed in him for so long."

"Not now that I have seen him as others do! I swear that I shall never again be such a louse and a snake as this treacherous hunter!"

His face turned thoughtful. "But how can I become a better person, Illbane? I am what I am, and there is no changing it."

"No, but there is the wearing of a mask," Illbane told him, "which is what you have done—and that hunter was the mask. You do not need to change what you are, Culaehra—you need to discover it."

"What am I, then?" The young man looked into the old one's eyes with a terrible intensity.

"You are a good man, and an honest one," Illbane said simply. "You are a strong man who can become a mighty warrior; you are a courageous man who can become a hero."

A few months before, Culaehra would have laughed in his face, then spat. Now, he only said slowly, "I am not sure that I want to become that."

"When last comes to last," said Illbane, "it is not a matter of what you want to be, but of what you are—and of becoming all that you *can* be."

"How shall I do that?"

"You have the amulet back." Illbane pointed at Culaehra's throat. He put a hand to it—and sure enough, it was there! The sage said, "Use it well, and strengthen your spirit, as these months of toil and practice have strengthened your body."

Culaehra ran his finger over the clasp—and it came loose. Amazed, he held the amulet out where he could see it. "What *is* it, Illbane?"

"Only a hollow drop of iron," Illbane told him, "but inside is a broken arrowhead that was forged by Lomallin himself, forged to fly straight and true with an Ulin's magic—so if you ask it right from wrong, it will still fix straight upon the truth, and you will feel its answer within you."

"But all I have felt before is its chill!"

"You were not open to feeling within," Illbane said. "You may be now—or you may have to rely on its turning cold while you listen for some answer in your heart. But given time, you will begin to feel that answer, and over the months, you will become more aware of it." He clapped the outlaw on the shoulder. "Come now, clasp it back around your neck, and let us return to the others."

Culaehra fastened the amulet and rose to go with him.

Halfway back to the camp he stopped abruptly, staring at Illbane.

The sage nodded. "You have just discovered where the hunter came from, then?"

"How did you make him?"

"Just as I told you," Illbane replied. "He is your spit and image."

Culaehra tried to remember when Illbane could have gathered up his spittle, but he had spat so often that he could not say. He resolved never to spit in the future. "Need I ask why?"

"Do you?" Illbane returned.

"To show me myself, so that I might be disgusted."

"Of course." The sage laid a hand upon his shoulder. "But remember, Culaehra—I only showed you yourself as the world sees you. The rest you did yourself—both of you."

Even now it rocked him, but Culaehra found that he was no longer devastated to realize that he appeared to be so treacherous and self-serving, for he remembered that Illbane had told him there v as a better man buried deep.

As (ulaehra went to sleep that night, he realized Illbane must have k iown about his murderous plan but did not hold it against him,] ad not even mentioned it to him. This, perhaps, was the most humbling realization of all—that the sage had known he would plot to slay him, given the chance.

How could Illbane say that he had the soul of a hero?

Illbane slowed the pace even more, taking whole days for lessons in fighting and magic, then telling them tales of the Ulin around the campfire.

Finally, they began to be able to fight without thinking about their movements, more or less automatically. Illbane approved, explaining that their discipline had yielded spontaneity.

That night, he told them once again that the Ulin were not gods, but only an older and more powerful race than their own.

"Then who made the Ulin?" Yocote asked.

Illbane smiled, glad the question had finally come. "The God who always was and always will be—the God of Dariad and his people."

Culaehra frowned. "What does he look like?"

"No one knows," Illbane told him. "He has no face or form, and is as likely to appear as flame or smoke as in human guise. In fact, He probably is neither male nor female, but more fundamental than either."

"You mean this god is an 'it'?" Culaehra's skepticism was clear—but Kitishane and Lua stared in amazement.

Yocote, however, only frowned and nodded. "What else is known of this First God?"

"That, and little more," Illbane told him. "He created everything that exists from Himself; everything exists within Him."

"If He is neither male nor female, why do you call Him 'him'?" Kitishane asked.

"Because I am a man, and it gives me the illusion that I can understand Him better if He, too, is male," Illbane said frankly. "He has power over everything that exists. He helps those who need help and call upon Him, if the help will aid their souls in coming back to Him when they die. Those who displease Him will never come back to Him—"

"And probably will not want to," Culaehra said sourly. This talk of a supreme God was bothering him strangely.

"He is the beginning and end of all life, and there is no lasting happiness except in Him," Illbane concluded.

Culaehra gave a short, ugly laugh. "I have known many who were happy enough."

"Then they lived in Him, and within His laws, whether they knew it or not," Illbane said.

"If so, He has very strange laws! I speak of men who robbed and cheated those weaker than themselves, and beat them into submission if they would not obey!"

"If they were truly happy," Illbane countered, "why would they have been constantly trying to gain more wealth and power?"

Culaehra stared, taken aback.

"Because they enjoyed the gaining as much as the having," Yocote said slowly.

Illbane nodded. "But if they constantly craved pleasure gained from outside themselves, there was no pleasure inside, no abiding feeling of joy that did not need constant replenishing from some outside source."

"Are you saying those who worship your Creator do not need constant replenishment?" Culaehra's skepticism neared the point of anger.

"They do, but they gain it from Him," Illbane told him. "They draw from a never-empty well, and their happiness is not only in the afterlife, but also in the present."

Lua and Kitishane gazed at him, their eyes wide and their faces thoughtful, but Culaehra said flatly, "I will not believe it!"

"*Will* not," Illbane noted. "Not *can* not."

"Will or can, what matter?" Culaehra was angry now. "You say the Ulin are not gods, but they can kill us at their whim, they can blast mountains into gravel, they can fight wars in the skies! Whether you call them supermen or subgods matters little—they are what they are, and if they are not gods, they are certainly so close as to make no difference! Gods' powers they have, so gods they are!"

"They are dead," Illbane said, "most of them. Only a few still live."

"So you say!" Culaehra jumped up, pointing at the sage. "You say they are—but no one ever saw the Ulin more than once in a lifetime, and most never saw them at all, so how would we know if they are dead or not? Myself, I will refuse to believe they are not gods, or are truly dead, either!"

"I will, though." Yocote still sat, eyes glowing. "I will believe they are only an older race, giants endowed with magical powers, created by the same Creator who made us, the younger races."

"You will *believe* this old wives' tale?" Culaehra spun to stare down at Yocote.

"I will," the gnome confirmed, "for magic makes so much more sense if all its power proceeds from a single Source."

"Only one?" Culaehra scowled. "What of evil magic, eh? What of necromancy, what of the raising of demons?"

"Anything good can be twisted to a bad use by bad people," the gnome replied, unruffled. "That does not change the fact that it was good at the outset." He nodded. "Yes, that even makes it clear how such evil magic can be untwisted, can be defeated."

"And just incidentally will make your own magic stronger," Culaehra accused—but he shivered inside at the thought.

Especially because Yocote nodded placidly. "Any increase in understanding will make me a better shaman, yes."

"So you will believe Illbane," Culaehra said in disgust and turned to the sage, his sarcasm heavy. "Is there anything you do *not* know?"

"Too much," Illbane told him, "far too much," thus beginning the cry that would echo down the ages, and that scholars would repeat ever after.

Northward they went, as the autumn grew colder and the altitude higher. At night Kitishane brought out her collection of animal pelts and showed the others how to stitch them into coats. Illbane told them that the people who lived in the northern countries attached hoods to their collars, much as southern people wore cowled robes.

"The nights have not grown longer, Illbane," Yocote pointed out. "How can that be? It is high autumn!"

"Yes, but we are traveling northward," Illbane told him. "The farther north you go, the longer the days—so as the autumn lengthens, the days do not."

It made no sense to Culaehra, but Yocote seemed to understand, nodding and smiling, pleased. The big man's hatred for the gnome had been receding, but this brought it back full-force.

The land rose beneath them; in two days' travel they looked back and saw the plain spread out below them, the trees already small enough to seem like curving lines of weeds. Looking ahead, they saw mountains rising up to fill the sky.

"We have to *climb* those?" Yocote stared up, appalled.

"Someday, you will be able to sit cross-legged and rise from the ground in your shaman's trance, Yocote," Illbane told him. "Then you will be able to fly over mountains such as these. But for now, you must climb, yes."

Lua shivered, staring. "We shall fall off!"

"No, it is only walking," Illbane told her, "for there is a pass between peaks, high above. There is only walking, but a great deal of it."

Culaehra was tempted to ask how he knew, but thought better of it.

Climb they did, and it was heavy, wearying work. The sky was overcast more often than not, and with the shadow of the mountains, the light was gloomy—but the gnomes still wore their goggles—until they met the stranger.

Now it was Lua who occasionally stopped to pick up a rounded rock and admire it, and a very few of them she saved. Yocote watched her, frowning, but said nothing. But it was quite a surprise to all of them when one of the rocks said, "Ouch!"

Lua leaped back, staring, and Yocote was by her side in an instant. The others stopped, frowning, but Culaehra and Kitishane could see nothing other than rock.

"Your pardon, Old One," Lua stammered. "I did not realize that was your toe!"

"Are you blind, then?" a gravelly voice said, and some of the rocks moved. Kitishane gasped, because that movement suddenly revealed a human form!

Not completely human, of course. It stood only as high as a man's waist, and was the color of the rocks around it, even having skin of the same texture—but the shoulders, arms, and head were the size of a grown man's, a very strong man's. The torso was short and the legs shorter.

It was a dwarf.

"Of course you are blind." The dwarf answered himself. "You are gnomes, and you wear masks that block out most of the light!"

Lua yanked her goggles up to her forehead and winced at the sudden brightness. "Yes, now I see you—and the daylight is dim enough that it does not pain me. Foolish I was not to raise them sooner!"

"Foolish indeed," the dwarf grated. "What do gnome-folk do in the company of humans?"

"We learn from a sage," Yocote answered, lifting his goggles. "What do *you* do abroad in daylight? I know dwarfs gather minerals from the surface now and again, but always at night!"

"*Our* eyes can bear the daylight," the dwarf growled. "Get along with you now, though if you had sense, you would stay with your own kind."

Yocote's face darkened; he readied a scathing retort.

Illbane forestalled it. "He will say anything rather than ask for help."

"Help?" Lua looked the dwarf up and down—and gasped. "His foot is caught!"

Culaehra looked, then stared. "A wonder that it is not flattened!"

"You do not know how hard dwarfs are," the stranger returned, but his eyes were on Illbane, and he showed no surprise as he said, "So you are awake, are you? The world must be in far worse condition than it seems!"

"Only the part of it that lives," Illbane assured him. He nodded at Culaehra. "Take the crowbar from my pack, lean it over a small stone, and lift that boulder enough for the dwarf to free himself."

Culaehra reflected that the dwarf would thereby scarcely be freeing himself, but was wise enough not to say so. He took off the pack, found the crowbar, and pushed its flattened end under the boulder, placing a small stone for a fulcrum, reflecting that perhaps he really had learned something about people, after all.

He leaned down as heavily as he could, and the boulder vibrated.

"A spell, Yocote," Illbane said.

The gnome began to chant, and the dwarf stared. Culaehra redoubled his efforts, and the front of the boulder lifted two inches. The dwarf yanked his foot free, then lifted it to rub with a hand, making a rasping sound. Culaehra let the boulder drop and was glad to pull the crowbar loose.

"I thank you," the dwarf said slowly.

Yocote and Lua stared.

Kitishane understood. To the sage, she murmured, "Illbane— the stories say dwarfs are never grateful."

"The stories lie," he murmured back.

Lua had recovered. "We were glad to aid you, Old One."

"Yes, glad indeed," Yocote agreed, still staring. "*Weren't* we, Culaehra?"

"Absolutely delighted," the big man agreed. He put the crowbar away and tied the pack.

"I shall repay," the dwarf said, "or another dwarf shall. Call by Graxingorok. Dwarfs honor debts."

"There is no debt," Lua protested. "We have done what we have because it is right!"

"It is a debt," the dwarf insisted. "Farewell." He stepped back against the bare rock wall and disappeared.

The humans stared, but Yocote pointed out, "He could still be right here, and us unable to see him."

"He could indeed," Illbane agreed. "You have done well, my friends."

"Any excuse to take off my pack for a few minutes." Culaehra lifted the rucksack again with a grunt. "Of course, that excuse is worn-out now, isn't it, Illbane?"

"Satisfied, I should say, rather than worn-out," the sage replied, amused. "But you are right, Culaehra. We must go on."

For the rest of their travels in the mountains, though, the gnomes wore their goggles up on their foreheads. They needed them only once, when the sun shone for a few hours.

Fortunately, even here Illbane put them to only half a day's travel; the other half, he insisted on their practicing their fighting skills and learning new ones, chiefly how to breathe when the air was so thin. They grew dizzy at first, but became used to it. "Be wary when you come down the other side," Illbane cautioned them. "The air will seem like broth."

Culaehra wondered irritably why the old man forced them to learn to fight at such an altitude. Did he expect them to meet an army in a high mountain pass? But he held his tongue, reflecting that a true warrior must be ready for attack at any time, in any place.

Then they came to the pass at the top of the trail and were glad of Illbane's drill, for a monster came hopping out to bar their way.

The women gasped and recoiled in disgust, and even Culaehra expelled an exclamation of surprise. "Illbane! It is half a man!"

It was—a monster with only one huge, broad foot at the end of a single leg. There was no cut-off stump beside it; it had grown that way, molding smoothly into the torso; if there were a hip, it could not be discerned. It had a head with a spiky thatch of hair, but only one eye square in the center, a snub of a nose with a single nostril, and a wide, thin-lipped mouth below it. Its chest and belly were lumpy with muscle, and a long, thick, sinewy arm grew out between the massive pectorals that moved it. A single hand slapped up, palm out and stiff, as if to bar their path. The creature uttered a threatening guttural bark that communicated the same message. It wore no clothes, and all could see that it had no genitalia.

Lua shuddered.

"What is it, Illbane?" Yocote asked, eyes wide.

"It is called a fuchan," Illbane told him, "and there is no going around it."

"What!" Culaehra stared. "Must we stand and await its convenience, then?"

The monster uttered another harsh and threatening bark, and Illbane said, "It will never be convenient. Bolenkar has stationed it here to keep folk from penetrating farther into these mountains."

Culaehra frowned. "Why? What difference does it make to him?"

"If the way is closed," Illbane told him, "there can be no escape from the Vanyar hordes he is pushing west."

It struck Culaehra as odd phrasing, but this was not the time to consider it. "Let us at least test the creature." He moved to the left, keeping his face toward the fuchan and his guard up. The fuchan hopped even as he moved, always facing him, its eye unblinking. Frowning, Culaehra leaped up on a crag, and it imitated him, hopping high—but landing at the foot of the crag, clearly waiting for him to leap down.

Yocote dashed for the pass.

The fuchan sprang high, its broad foot falling straight toward the spot where the gnome would be when it landed. Yocote veered aside, but the fuchan, incredibly, changed its trajectory and landed squarely in front of him.

At the far side of the defile, Culaehra leaped down.

The fuchan was on him in an instant, springing to lash out with a huge fist. Culaehra fell back, raising an arm to block—and the fuchan spun, its fist opening to scoop up Yocote as he tried to dash past. The broad hand hurled the gnome high. He squalled in fright, but Illbane reached up to catch him. "It has chosen its ground well, Yocote. The pass is too narrow for more than two people to confront it at once, and it can deal with two."

"But can it deal with one?" Culaehra sprang straight toward the fuchan, hunching over and slamming three quick blows at its belly.

It was like pounding oak.

Culaehra sprang back with an oath of surprise to cover his pain—and the fuchan's fist caught him halfway, sending him sprawling. Lua was beside him in an instant, but he shoved her aside with a snarl and pushed himself to his feet, glaring at the fuchan to keep his world from tilting too badly.

"Remember the arts I have taught you!" Illbane barked, and Culaehra fell into a guard stance without even thinking about it—because he was realizing that, whether or not his teacher had intended it this way, this was a test.

"I had not thought it would be so strong," he said.

"Strong enough to chip rock, if it holds a stone in its fist! Go warily!"

Culaehra moved around the monster in a chain step. Instead of merely pivoting to follow him, it hopped bent-kneed in a grotesque parody of his steps. Culaehra timed his kick to catch the fuchan in midair. He lashed out at what should have been its groin—but the fuchan lifted its knee, deflecting the blow. Then its foot blurred with speed, and Culaehra went smashing backward into his companions with a howl of pain. He doubled over, retching, for the kick had caught him in the stomach. Lua was beside him instantly, rubbing at the small of his back, and he was too weak to bat her aside. Through the ringing in his ears he heard Kitishane say, "It mirrors your movement."

When the haze cleared from his eyes, he saw her moving toward the monster. "No!" he cried in sudden fear. "It will kill you!"

"I will not go that close," she assured him—and, incredibly, began to dance!

Left foot over right, right swinging back, leaping in the air to click her heels—and the fuchan mimicked her, springing to one side, then the other, then leaping up and flexing its leg, mirroring her movements as well as it could with only one leg. She began to move in more complex patterns, faster and faster, and the fuchan kept imitating her, but began to fall behind. Its forehead wrinkled in concentration, its foot began to move so quickly that its body seemed to hang in midair—but the single steps were behind Kitishane by several seconds, and grew more and more clumsy as the fuchan began to try to execute two or three steps at a time.

"You're confusing it!" Lua breathed, wide-eyed.

Kitishane nodded, panting, eyes bright, and drew her sword. The fuchan suddenly went still, staring warily, but Kitishane laid her sword on the ground, crying, "Illbane, Culaehra blade!"

Illbane stepped forward, holding it out to her. She took the hilt and laid the blade over her own sword in an X, then began to prance in the quarters formed between steel edges, toes pointing, springing lightly. Her eyes glowed, her cheeks were rosy, her bosom rose and fell with quick deep breaths—and Culaehra stared spellbound, forgetting his pain in awe of her beauty.

The fuchan began to imitate her movements again, hopping about in a parody of her light-footed steps, faster and faster, falling behind and becoming confused again, trying to catch up, to execute two or three figures at once.

Kitishane swooped down, caught up a sword and lunged.

The fuchan's fist blurred, knocking her blade aside and striking her breastbone.

"Kitishane!" Lua cried, and ran to her as she struck the ground—but Culaehra was there first.

He cradled her head in his hand, and there was alarm in his voice. "Kitishane! Do you live?"

Her eyes opened, to stare at him in amazement. "Alive . . . yes." Then she went limp, and Lua was there to stroke her forehead, murmuring.

Culaehra left Kitishane to her ministrations, rising to glare at the fuchan. "Vile monstrosity! To strike at so gentle and fragile a being!"

Kitishane's head cleared enough for her to realize what he was about to do. "Culaehra, no!"

"It deserves whatever it gets," the big man growled, pacing toward the fuchan.

"Not in anger!" Kitishane waved weakly. "Lua . . . tell him . . ."

The gnome laid her friend's head down and dashed to Culaehra's side. Her little hand touched his big one timidly, but she said, "Do not strike for revenge, Culaehra, not if . . . you love her. Strike only to accomplish."

Love! The word rattled Culaehra—but it amazed him even more that Lua could speak of his loving another, and that without bitterness or anger.

"She speaks wisely," Yocote said stiffly. "We must trick the thing—it has proved we cannot defeat it by force of arms alone."

That was the last thing Culaehra wanted to hear, but he slowed reluctantly, glaring at the monster. It waited, impassive and patient—and ready.

"She has shown you the way," Yocote reminded him.

A gleam came into Culaehra's eye, and slowly, clumsily, he began to mimic the steps he had seen Kitishane execute. Slowly, yes, but faster and faster, his steps wove her intricate pattern, making it wider and wider, taking him farther and farther to each side. Warily, the fuchan began to imitate him, hopping out the pattern as well as it could with its one foot. Culaehra began to move forward and backward as well as from side to side, and each bend forward brought him closer and closer to the fuchan.

Yocote began to beat on his thigh and chest, making a rhythm to match Culaehra's dance; Lua joined in, with a lilting, fluting, wordless tune. Faster and faster the music went, faster and faster Culaehra danced, faster and faster the fuchan hopped, growing more and more clumsy, trying frantically to keep up with Culaehra. He began to leap high between steps, the fuchan leaped high—and Culaehra lashed out with a kick, straight at its "hip."

It was a brave try, but fast though he was, the fuchan was faster. It hopped out of the way, even as it swung its single foot high, kicking back in imitation—and Culaehra, landing, caught that foot and shoved it higher. The single arm flailed, the fuchan let out a caw of alarm and struggled to swing its foot down—but Culaehra held it up, and the monster slammed down onto the ground. Its head cracked against the stony path and it went limp.

"Foul beast!" Culaehra growled, and stepped in to kick where it should have had a groin—but Lua threw herself onto his leg, wrapping arms and legs about it, crying, "No, Culaehra! Not for revenge! You have beaten it; that is enough!"

He shook his leg, snarling, but she held on long enough for Kitishane to come up and throw her arms about his chest. "Yes, enough and more, O Brave One! You have rendered the poor thing unconscious; have pity on its empty life! Let us pass it quickly now."

Culaehra stared down in amazement and saw only her eyes, huge and brown, staring up at him. Then, a moment later, the whole of her face registered, seeming small and fragile, chin little, forehead high, nose a temptation that he suddenly ached to kiss, even more than the moist, full lips below . . .

She saw her effect on him and smiled as she stepped away. "Come, then!" She held out a hand, even as she turned away to pass the fuchan.

She did not see Lua's face, a strange mixture of sorrow and tenderness, tasting the sweetness of seeing love begin as well as the bitterness of seeing one whom she had loved now discovering another.

Yocote saw, though; his face went hard, impassive, as he felt the blow of knowing she loved another—but his love for her overcame the hurt, and he stepped to her, saying softly, "Don't you dare tell them, Lua, or they'll say you're wrong and start a fight just to prove it!"

She turned to him in surprise, then managed to laugh even as her eyes filled with tears. "Oh, Yocote! Must you taste all of life?"

For a moment the longing was naked in his face, and he touched her hand. "All that I can—but the sweetest is denied me."

Lua stared, then blushed and turned away. Yocote gazed after her a moment, face somber, then pulled down his goggles and followed.

They passed the prostrate fuchan, harmless now that it was unconscious. Lua almost tarried to tend to it, but Illbane reached down and urged her along. When they were a hundred feet farther along the pass, he let her pause to look back.

Kitishane turned to gaze, too, and shivered. "It seems as if it should be so helpless, yet it is lethal! You did amazingly to best it, Culaehra."

"Only because of the example you set me." It was hard not to take all the credit, but the hunter would have done that, so Culaehra did not. "Yours was the insight, gentle one."

Kitishane stared at him, amazed, but he did not notice; he had turned to Yocote. "You were right, gnome," he said grudgingly. "We could never have defeated it by force alone."

Yocote stared in surprise, but Illbane nodded, smiling in his beard. "Well said, and very true, Culaehra! No one of you could have defeated the poor thing alone, but together, you were easily a match for it."

His praise made Culaehra uncomfortable. He turned to glare at the old man. "Why did you not aid us, Illbane?"

"Because," the sage said, "there was no need."

Culaehra stared at him, amazed, then whipped about to stare at his companions—and found them all staring at him.

Illbane saved them all from embarrassment. "It stirs, it wakes! Quickly, we must be out of its sight, or it will pursue us!"

None of them wanted that. They turned to hurry away. Culaehra stood staring at them a minute, struggling with unfamiliar feelings, then realized that Kitishane had recovered her sword, but Illbane had left his blade lying there in the path. Culaehra scooped it up, feeling a surge of triumph and a great relief, stuck it through his belt and hurried after them. Time enough to recover the scabbard later.

As he caught up, Kitishane was asking, "You called it a 'poor thing,' Illbane."

"Would not you call it poor," the sage returned, "if you had no sex nor companionship, and your whole life was spent in waiting to stop folk who might never happen by?"

"Then how did it come to be?" Yocote asked.

"I shall tell you when we sit about the campfire, but let us first come to a place where we may light one in safety! Hurry—the monster even now crawls to the rock face to pull itself upright!"

Culaehra glanced back, but they had begun to descend; the path sloped downward, and its rising behind them hid the fuchan from sight. How could the old man know what it did?

Illbane called a halt when they were a mile farther down the path. By that time, it had darkened enough so the gnomes led them, their goggles up. They chose a wide, flat area with a rock face at its back, and small, stunted trees that yielded enough dry cones for a fire—though Culaehra found himself wondering if Illbane really needed wood for a blaze.

There was little or no game so high up; dinner would be jerky, stewed to soften it, and hard biscuit. As they waited for the water to boil, Illbane explained, "Bolenkar, being an Ulharl, is half human and half Ulin, so he was born with magical powers, though nowhere nearly as strong as those of his father Ulahane. The human-hater taught all his halfling children the use of those powers, and they are strong enough to work a great deal of mischief."

"But how could he make so warped a creature as this fuchan?" Yocote asked.

"Even as you have said—by warping one that the Creator had made. In this case, he took an unborn child, divided it in two, removed any glands that might have given it desires of its own, and wiped its mind of all but the desire to please him. When it was grown, he taught it fighting of a limited sort, then set it to guard the pass, making sure the sole thought in its mind was to gain his pleasure by stopping any who sought to come by."

"And that it would earn his displeasure if any came through?" Lua asked softly.

"Regrettably, yes—but Bolenkar is no Ulin, and may not know."

"If he learns, we might have been kinder to slay the thing," Culaehra grunted.

Lua cried out in protest, but Kitishane seemed unsure.

Yocote, however, had another question. "Why did Bolenkar wish to keep folk from coming through that pass? It cannot be only to ensure that they would not escape the Vanyar and the other marauders!"

"I cannot say with any certainty," Illbane said reluctantly.

"Certainty?" Culaehra sat bolt upright in indignation. "Give us your best guess, then! Surely we have earned that much—and your guess is so close to knowledge that it makes little difference! Why did Bolenkar set a guard on that pass?"

Still Illbane was silent, his lips pressed hard and thin as he stared at the fire.

It was Yocote who asked it. "He knew we would be coming, did he not?"

"I think so," Illbane told him. "I think he has guessed that much, yes."

There was a numbed silence around that fire, so small in the vastness of the mountain night.

At last Lua asked, her voice small, "How can we be so important?"

"Because," Yocote answered, "it is Illbane who leads us."

The wind blew cold indeed around their shoulders.

CHAPTER 12

Strangely, they slept well that night—so well that Illbane's shout of warning yanked them from so deep a sleep that they were all thick-headed as they leaped up, looking about frantically, trying to clear the fog from their eyes. "What is it, Illbane?"

"Where is the danger?"

"What?"

"Into the trees, quickly! An ogre comes!"

They needed no chivvying. Lua and Yocote scrambled up the nearest oak while Culaehra caught Kitishane about the waist and fairly threw her up to catch the lowest branch of an elm. He ran around to clamber up the boughs of a large fir, crying, "Stop him with your magic, sage!"

"He works," Yocote called, "but the defense could be as devastating as the attack!"

Sure enough, Illbane stood by the fire, sawing the air with his hands and chanting—but not quickly enough. A hand the size of a knapsack swung out of the shadows and sent him careening into a tree. Culaehra almost shouted with rage, but throttled it as the monster itself stepped into the firelight, grinning and drooling. It stood ten feet tall or more with hunched shoulders that were balks of muscle, arms like the limbs of a century-old oak, and legs like its trunk. Its torso was blocky and lumpen, swag-bellied and hairy; its head was so low-slung that it almost seemed to grow out of its broad, hairy chest. It was so hairy that at first Culaehra thought it wore a tunic and leggings of fur. Then the light flared up; he saw the moth-eaten hide that served it for a loincloth, and could see how it contrasted with the creature's own pelt. Lua gasped with horror at the sight, and the ogre turned its head to look up, catching the firelight. Its head was like a huge melon with a gash of a mouth, foul and with wide-spaced, blackened stubs of teeth, its nose scarcely more than a shelf with nostrils beneath, its eyes small and glinting with malice under a very low brow. Even Culaehra had to repress a shudder.

High in his tree, Yocote gestured and mumbled with frantic haste.

The ogre apparently decided the sound had come from a night bird or something equally beneath its notice, for it turned to waddle to the campfire, yanking the spit from the flames and running it through its mouth, cleaning off the roasted fowls in one bite. It sniffed, following a scent to Kitishane's pack, which it tore apart, jamming the store of rations into its maw, then caught up the wineskins and tossed them in, too. It bit hard, swallowed, then spat out the empty skins. After that, it battered down their tents and swatted packs flying, grunting in disgust as it found no more food. Finally it turned to go—but as it went, it bumped into the oak, and Kitishane let out a small cry as she clung to her swaying branch in fright. The ogre looked up, saw her, and grinned its widest. It reached up to pluck at her, but Kitishane clung all the tighter, crying out. Culaehra shouted in alarm and scrambled down from his fir, but the monster merely broke the limb off the tree and stripped Kitishane from it as if she were a flower. She screamed as the ogre lifted her toward its mouth.

Culaehra hit the ground, bellowing, "Put her down, fiend! That morsel is mine to take or leave!" He leaped high, lashing a kick into the monster's negligible buttocks.

Negligible, but tender; the ogre howled like a whole pack of wolves, dropping Kitishane and turning on the outlaw. Huge fists swung at Culaehra, so huge that he could have seen them coming a mile away and had no trouble dodging. He sprang aside from the left, then from the right; then both hands slapped the ground beside him, and Culaehra jumped on one with his full weight. The ogre bellowed and tried to swat him with the other hand, but Culaehra leaped aside, and the ogre roared as he slapped his own hand. Thinking the monster was distracted, Culaehra leaped high and grabbed hold of a huge ear. The ogre went on roaring, but one huge hand swung up and knocked him away as if he were a gnat.

Culaehra flew through the air, trying to somersault, to get his feet under him; but he only succeeded in landing flat on his back. Pain wracked him; he could not breathe, and he saw the ogre towering above him as it straightened up, then turned toward him, lifting a huge foot—

An arrow struck its nose, an arrow that bounced off but made the monster roar with pain. He turned toward the source just as another arrow lanced up and struck his forehead. Culaehra would have admired the marksmanship—it wasn't a very large target—if the monster hadn't been advancing on the archer with blood in its eye. And the archer was Kitishane! He scrambled to his feet and dove at a huge knee.

He struck behind it like a boulder, and the monster shouted with surprise and fright as the leg folded under it. It sat down hard, and for a moment Culaehra was squeezed so tight that he felt his head must burst—but the ogre fell onto its side, and the pressure eased enough for Culaehra to wrestle himself free.

The ogre was roaring in baffled rage as it pushed itself back to its feet, trying to swat aside the arrows that stormed upon it. Culaehra saw, with surprise, that some of them were only half the length of the others, then realized they were flying from two different directions. Somehow one of the gnomes had gained a bow, too!

None of them struck a vital spot, though—the ogre's eyes were so small that only luck would send a shaft to them, and he was batting most of them out of the air with his horny palms. But the few that struck through seemed to hurt enough; he roared with pain as well as anger as he advanced on the biggest archer.

Culaehra couldn't let the monster reach Kitishane! He dashed in and launched another flying kick at its knee. He struck it on the side, then leaped back as the joint bent and the ogre roared in anger, turning to flail at him even as it fell.

The ground gave way beneath it; it fell into a pit.

"Well done, Yocote!" Culaehra cried, then picked his place and waited. A huge arm slapped down over the side of the hole; then a huger head followed—

Culaehra spun, kicking it right in the eye.

The ogre bellowed again, but the other hand came up and caught Culaehra, drawing him toward its mouth even as it fell.

An arrow struck from the side, straight into the monster's maw.

It howled with pain, dropping Culaehra, who leaped up and lashed a kick at its nose, then turned and ran a dozen paces. He turned back as the ogre finished climbing out of the pit. It roared and thundered down on him, huge fist swinging around to crush him. Culaehra leaped aside, but too slowly; the blow glanced off his arm and side, sending him staggering. His arm and shoulder flared with pain, but he managed to stay on his feet, turning to face his foe—and saw Yocote at the end of a limb, gesturing furiously, while Kitishane stood by with a drawn bow.

He hoped they liked him tonight.

The ogre pivoted, fist swinging out like the limb of a whirlwind, but Culaehra ducked under it easily and drew his sword, managing to get the point up just as a great foot came swinging at his belly. He jabbed and stepped aside. A roar of pain shook the forest as the ogre limped around the campsite, then turned back to him with fiery eyes. It started toward him, claws hooked to seize and hold— then whirled aside, clenching its fists, and slammed a blow that sent Kitishane flying. Culaehra bellowed with anger and charged, sword first, all finesse forgotten. The monster whirled back, grinning now, a huge ball of a fist swinging straight toward him—but the campfire suddenly roared into a towering flame that singed the back of his leg and hip. The ogre gave a yelp of pain and scurried away, then turned back with an ugly look. It scanned the trees . . .

Realizing what it was looking for, Culaehra ran, sword first, to distract the monster, but too late—it saw Yocote on the end of his branch and swatted at him as if he were a fly. The gnome cried out and went tumbling a dozen feet, to land in a thicket.

"All right, Illbane!" Culaehra shouted, hating himself. "I admit it! An ogre is more than we can handle by ourselves! *Now* will you help us?" Then he had to leap back, for the ogre turned to charge at him.

It was unkind, really—the sage was just managing to get back on his feet. But he strode up to the ogre without the slightest sign of fear. His staff whirled, and the ogre doubled over, clutching its belly in sudden pain. The staff whirled again, catching the monster right behind the ear. It stumbled forward and fell, then pushed itself up, roaring and shaking its head.

Yocote crawled out of his bush, climbed to unsteady feet, and began to gesture and chant. Illbane turned, saw, and took up the same gestures, the same chant, in unison.

The ogre climbed to its feet with a bellow of anger, stepped toward the two magicians, stepped twice before its legs gave way and it collapsed to the ground with a roar of agony.

Lua, gentle Lua, dashed in brandishing one of Kitishane's arrows like a spear and drove it into the ogre's eye, through the orb and deep into the brain. The monster's bellow cut off; its body convulsed once, then went limp.

So did Lua. She sank to the ground, head in her hands, weeping.

Yocote dashed to her, putting an arm around her shoulders, Kitishane right behind him. "Don't mourn, little one, don't be frightened," the gnome said in a soothing tone. "Poor thing, you did what was best!"

"I had to!" Lua sobbed. "It was in so much pain!"

Culaehra stared, dumbfounded.

"And I couldn't try to heal it," the gnome-maiden wailed, "or it would have slain *us!*"

"Yes, we know, we know, brave lass," Yocote said, his voice a caress. "You have done the kindest deed for all of us. You could not have done otherwise."

"Sometimes kindness means giving the lesser pain, sister," Kitishane said, her tone soothing, too. "You have saved us all."

"Yes, you have," Culaehra said, amazed, "but most remarkably of all, you have saved *me!*" Sheer relief flooded him, and bore "Thank you!" with it on the flood. "Thank you most extravagantly, from the bottom of the hide that is whole because of you! But you had no cause to aid me, Lua—if you had reason to do anything to me, it would have been to return hurt for hurt!"

She looked up at him, appalled.

"So had you all." Culaehra looked from one to the other, still unbelieving. "Yet you fought to save me, and I thank you most earnestly, for without you that monster would have slain me! But I have beaten you, demeaned you, insulted you, and . . ." He glanced at Kitishane, reddened, and glanced away. "I would have done worse, if it had not been for Illbane. So why would you save me now? *Why?*"

Kitishane, Lua, and Yocote looked at one another, and from the looks on their faces, he could almost hear their thoughts: *He has a good point. Why* did *we help him?*

Yocote tried the first answer. "Perhaps because you fought to save us, Culaehra—or Kitishane, at least. Why did you do that?"

But Culaehra chopped the implied thanks away with impatience. "There is no virtue in that, for I fought to save what I regarded as mine!"

"Perhaps we did, too," Kitishane said, and the gnomes looked up at her in surprise.

Culaehra stared in amazement. "You cannot mean that *you* think I am *your* property!"

"Not property, no," Lua said, "but I think I know what my sister means. It is not a question of owning, but of belonging."

The consternation on his face was answer enough.

"Yes, belonging." Yocote nodded with firm understanding. "It is not that you belong *to* us, Culaehra, but that you belong *with* us now."

"Yes," Kitishane agreed, with some relief of her own. "We have shared hardships, Culaehra, and have fought the fuchan together. Whether we like one another or not does not matter as much as that."

Culaehra's face went impassive as conflicting emotions warred within him.

Lua saw, and said quickly, "That is not to say that we do *not* like you."

"You have every reason to hate me!"

Yocote's face turned thoughtful and he shook his head. "Odd, but I find that I do not, Culaehra—not anymore."

"You have, after all, helped us all at the cliff face, and against the fuchan," Kitishane reminded him.

"And you?" He turned with an intense stare. "Do you no longer hate me?"

She blushed and turned away, muttering, "Certainly not."

His gaze lingered on her, then turned back to Lua. "And you, gnome-maiden—you have more reason to hate me than any!"

"Oh, Culaehra, of course I do not!" Lua cried with a huge outpouring of sympathy. She flung herself high to clasp him about the chest, then fell because her arms were far too short.

He caught her and lowered her to the ground again, smiling. "No, you would not, would you? You are far too good for that."

"Aye, too good for a rogue like him!" Yocote stepped up beside Lua, pain showing in his face for a moment, then as quickly masked. He glanced up at Culaehra, puzzled by his own emotions. "Your pardon, Culaehra."

"None needed," the outlaw assured him. "I *am* a rogue."

"Were," Kitishane corrected.

"No, *is*." At last Illbane stepped forward. "A rogue is one who goes apart from the herd. In men, rogues are usually regarded as being dangerous, for they do not live by the herd's rules, and are therefore as apt to turn on their fellows as to aid them."

"But are therefore as apt to save them as to harm them," Yocote said thoughtfully.

"They are unpredictable." Kitishane's gaze lingered on Culaehra. "Yes, I could say that of you."

Culaehra returned that gaze till it made him uncomfortable, then grinned. "Unpredictable *now*. Not so long ago, you could be quite sure of what I would do next."

She returned his grin. "Aye—beat and bully."

Culaehra was amazed to realize that was no longer true. He was not sure he liked it.

"Good, bad, likable or detestable, we had to save you so that you might someday save us," Kitishane went on. "What matters to me is that you were trying to save me—never mind the reasons."

"Why never mind them?" Culaehra demanded with intensity.

"Because they are as likely to be good as bad," Yocote retorted, "and none of us are sure what they are anyway, least of all you!"

Kitishane smiled, amused. "You are part of our little herd now." Then she turned to the gnomes in surprise. "So are we all, come to think of it." She pivoted to Illbane. "When did that happen?"

"Over the last six months," he told her, "but you need not think of yourselves as a herd—rather, as a very small army."

Yocote grinned. "Very small indeed! But why did you not aid us sooner, Illbane?"

"Do not tell us there was no need this time!" Culaehra said forcefully.

Illbane shook his head. "For a time I thought there might be none—that you might manage on your own. Even when I did aid, I only struck a few blows, then added the strength of my own magic to Yocote's spell."

"It is you who have done it!" Culaehra accused. "You have welded the four of us into your own little army! But for what battle?"

"Why, to save humankind, of course," Illbane said lightly, then nodded to the gnomes. "And all the other younger races, too."

"Don't jest with us now, old man!" Culaehra snapped. "Against what foe shall we fight?"

"Bolenkar," Illbane said.

They stared at him, appalled, and the wind blew chill about them again.

Kitishane said slowly, "Bolenkar is in the south. You are leading us north."

"I did not say you were ready to fight him yet," Illbane replied.

"Then where do we march?" Culaehra demanded.

"To find the Star Stone," Illbane told him.

That night, around the campfire, he told them of the Star Stone.

"You have heard me speak of Lomallin and Ulahane," he said, "and of the War Among the Ulin."

"Yes, and we heard it often enough from our shamans as we grew," Culaehra grumbled.

Kitishane nodded. "Lomallin was all that was good and right, and Ulahane all that was evil and wrong."

"Ulahane was all that, and more," Illbane agreed, "for it was his determination to slay all the younger races that brought Lomallin to lead a band against him."

"All the younger races?" Lua looked up in surprise. "But Ulahane is called the human-hater!"

"He hated all the younger races; the humans were only the most numerous of them," Illbane assured her. "He would have slain the gnomes, too—when he had finished with the humans and the elves and the dwarfs."

Yocote, too, stared in shock. "The shamans were wrong, then?"

"They were right so far as they went," Illbane told him, "but they did not know all of the story."

"What of Lomallin? Was he truly the human-lover? Was he truly the Shaman of the Gods?"

"He loved all the younger races, as he loved everyone, even the wicked," Illbane answered. "As to being a shaman, though—no. The Ulin had none—and in any case, Lomallin's knowledge went far beyond the catalogue of shamanry. He was more a sage than a warrior, though he could fight at need."

Yocote frowned. "But he fought the scarlet god and slew him!"

"Not while he lived," Illbane told them. "In life, he met Ulahane the human-hater at a stone ring, an ancient temple humankind had raised to the Ulin, and fought him there."

"But our shaman told us that Lomallin slew the Scarlet One!" Lua cried.

"His ghost did, when Ohaern and Dariad pursued their hopeless war against the human-hater," Illbane told them. "When the Scarlet One was about to strike them down, Lomallin's ghost appeared between Ulahane and Ohaern and slew the Scarlet One. But Ulahane's ghost sped into the sky, and there the Ulin fought, shaping stars into weapons. Ulahane broke Lomallin's spear, and a fragment of it sped off to the north, falling to earth as a shooting star. But Lomallin forged another weapon and slew Ulahane's ghost, obliterating it."

"So not even a ghost is left of Ulahane?" Yocote asked, eyes huge.

"Not even that—but his memory lives on in his half-human son Bolenkar, who seeks to finish his father's work."

"You mean that Bolenkar truly seeks to destroy humankind?" Kitishane asked.

"He does indeed, but he lacks the power—he is only half Ulin, after all—so he works to pit one breed of humans against another, one nation against its neighbor, one tribe against its kin-tribe. In this he has enlisted all the other Ulharls that Ulahane begot, who work to turn gnome against elf, dwarf against giant, all the younger races against one another—and humanity against them all. His plan is easy to read: let them slay one another in a frenzy of blood lust. Then, if any survive, he will doubtless lead the Ulharls to slay them all."

"But he cannot bring back the Ulin!" Yocote exclaimed. "He cannot raise the dead! . . . Can he?"

"No, but it is yet possible for the few Ulin left to beget more of their own kind—if Bolenkar can stimulate their interest in the project." Illbane frowned, then repeated, "If. It is far more likely for him to save out a few human women for breeding stock, and persuade the male Ulin to make more Ulharls. Many more," he said darkly.

"And there shall be no more humans, only Ulharls?" Culaehra cried. "No, Illbane! We must not let that happen!"

"It is for you to say," Illbane said, locking gazes with him.

Culaehra stared back at him, realizing the import of his words, and turned chill inside—but he searched his heart, and found that his determination did not lessen; it was no mere bravado. He would not surrender the world to Bolenkar and his kind! "How can I stand against one so mighty?" he whispered.

"With a magical sword in your hand, and a brave band of companions by your side," the sage told him.

"Where shall I find a magical sword?"

"I shall forge it for you, for I was a smith before I was a sage, or even a shaman."

Yocote started, and stared at Illbane with sudden dread.

"But I must have magical iron from which to forge that blade," the sage said.

"The Star Stone," Yocote breathed.

"The Star Stone?" Kitishane glanced from him to Illbane. "Is *that* the fragment of Lomallin's spear that fell to earth in the north?"

"It is," Illbane said quietly.

"A fragment of a god's spear!" Even Culaehra stared at the enormity of it. "By all the heavens! That *would* be iron of power!"

"It would indeed," Illbane agreed.

"And that is why Bolenkar set sentries to keep us from it!" Kitishane cried.

"The fuchan?" Lua asked.

"The fuchan," Illbane confirmed, "and this ogre that you have just slain. It was one of Ulahane's nastier pastimes, to see to the forceful begetting of such monsters, to encourage their birth by magic, and to warp and distort them as they grew. It is a depraved game that his son has learned, and still practices; his magic is by no means equal to an Ulin's, but he can manage this much, though I believe it stretches his powers to their limits. There is no race of ogres; I would guess Bolenkar forced the begetting of this one by a giant upon a human woman."

"How could a woman live through such a nightmare?" Kitishane cried in disgust.

"Most likely she did not—but the embryo did, and Bolenkar kept it growing by magic, birthed it by enchantment, then raised it with distorting spells and set it upon our trail."

"So that is why it came upon us!" Culaehra cried. "It was set to hunt us!"

"And found us," Illbane agreed. "It will not be the last—but there are still lands ahead where people dwell, and the hunters there may be more subtly disguised."

"Not monsters, you mean?" Kitishane asked.

"No," Illbane agreed. "We must look for his agents among people, my friends, and among other races. They will set up obstacles to ensnare us, they will seek to strike from hiding."

They traded glances filled with trepidation, and only Lua seemed to have noticed that the sage had called them his friends.

"How do you know all this, Illbane?" Culaehra frowned. "How do you know that this fragment fell from Lomallin's spear?"

"Because I saw it," the sage answered.

"You have visions?" Kitishane breathed, but Yocote stared at him in awe.

"I do," Illbane admitted.

"You did not say that this was one of them, though," Yocote pointed out.

Illbane turned to him with the ghost of a smile. "No, I did not," he agreed.

Two days later they came to the edge of a lower pass and saw no more mountains before them.

"Open land!" Lua breathed. "I had almost forgotten the look of it!"

"Surely not." Yocote smiled as he came up beside her. "It is simply that we who were reared underground have less need of such spaces, Lua."

She glanced at him, smiling, and he returned the smile, but the goggles hid any other expression their faces might have held.

They all came up along the ledge and stared out over the valley. The foothills rolled away below them to a verdant plain cut into segments by three rivers, one flowing from the mountains behind them, another from a distant range that towered on the far side of the valley, and another that ran more or less down its length. All three met in the distance to the east, and buildings clustered at the junction, with a castle rising from a headland between the northern stream and the eastward-flowing one. The valley floor was cut into a crazy quilt of cultivated fields, in varying shades of tan now that the harvest was in. Where fields intersected, collections of huts stood.

Perhaps it was the chill, perhaps that the day was overcast, but Kitishane shivered. "I like not the look of that castle, Illbane."

"Neither do I." Culaehra scowled and hitched his pack a bit higher. "Let us go down and discover why."

He started down the trail, but Yocote stopped him, holding up a hand against the rogue's knee. "Hold, Culaehra, and think! Could this not be one of the traps that Illbane warned us against?"

The warrior frowned down at him, but Illbane nodded as he came up. "It could indeed, Yocote. That was well thought."

"Yes, it could," Culaehra told him, "but Illbane said 'obstacles,' not 'traps.' Let us go and overcome this one!"

He pushed on past. Yocote looked up at Illbane in astonishment. The sage could only shrug. "What can I say? He is right; I did say 'obstacles.' If we cannot go around them, Yocote, we must go through them—and these mountains prevent us from the roundward journey. Let us go."

The gnome sighed and followed the sage, who followed the impatient warrior rushing to meet his war. The others advanced as well, without quite so much zest.

They descended through two levels of foothills that day, then camped for the night. The next morning, they gained the summit of the lowest hill and found themselves looking down on a village.

It was very poor. The thatch of the roofs was old, dark with streaks of rot, and the daubed walls were cracked. The few trails of smoke rising were thin and small. The village "green" was bare earth—packed hard now, under the boots of a troop of soldiers who stood, pikes at guard, glaring at the cowering villagers as if angered at thoughts of rebellion. A man on a tall horse waited in their midst, wrapped in a fur cloak against the chill, watching as soldiers loaded grain from each hut into a wagon and led pigs into another, which also held coops into which they stuffed the chickens they took from trembling villagers. Two cows stood by that wagon patiently; soldiers were driving a third to join it. Another dragged a girl screaming from a hut; an older man cried out and charged the soldier, but two more leaped forward and felled him with quick blows.

"The swine!" Kitishane cried, and turned to Illbane. "Can you not stop them?"

"Yes, but it would mean a war," the sage told her. "Have we time to fight it?"

The soldier shoved the girl up and into the wagon with the pigs, then tied her wrists to the side; her screams slackened into sobs. The man in the fur cloak gestured, and the teamsters whipped their teams into motion. The wagons pulled out of the village green, soldiers falling into place before and behind. They moved out along the town's one road, which led to the hill where stood the castle.

As they went, light winked off a golden band around the temples of the man in the cloak.

"A crown!" Yocote hissed. "He is a king!"

"If you must needs call him so," Illbane said, with scorn. "In the cities of the south, they would scarcely call him a royal steward—certainly not a governor, when he rules only a few barbarian tribes. Belike they would call him a chieftain and let it go at that."

Culaehra frowned. "Be that as it may, in this northern country and among *us* barbarians, he is a king!"

"Yes, and the land over which he holds sway is vast enough to merit the title," Illbane admitted, "though the number of people is not—and here, in the marches of the civilized world, he and his army are all that stand between civilization and the wild peoples of the wasteland."

"King or not, he is a villain!" Kitishane fumed. "How dare he take a maiden against her will! And look at the size of that heap of grain! He can scarcely have left the folk of that hamlet enough food to survive the winter!" She turned on Culaehra. "Can you do nothing to stop them?"

"Yes, but not by a direct attack." The big man stood hard-faced and spoke through thin lips. "There are forty of them to our four, and all heavily armed into the bargain."

"Then how *can* we save her?"

"Let us search for information before he answers that," Yocote said. "The soldiers will be far along the road by the time we come to the village. Let us seek, my companions." He started off down the hillside path, not waiting for the rest of them.

They fell in quickly enough. Lua glanced back, then looked again in surprise. "Why do you smile, Illbane? Surely it is a horrifying sight!"

"Yes, but 'companion' is a good word," the sage replied. "Let us see what the villagers can tell us, Lua."

The people told them a great deal by hiding at first sight of them. As they came into the circle of beaten earth at the center of the cluster of huts, Culaehra glanced around, frowning in puzzlement. "Why do they flee, Illbane? We are only four!"

"Four, but armed, and strangers," the sage replied, "and gnomes by daylight are never seen; who knows what magic they might work? You must earn their trust, Culaehra—at least, enough to hear their tale."

"Let me." Kitishane touched his arm, and he stared down in surprise, but she had already turned away and was calling out to the silent huts, "Ho, good folk! We are strangers, angered by the events we have just seen transpire here! Come out, and tell us if there is more to it than there appears!"

The village still stood silent.

"Oh, come!" Lua cried, and whipped off her goggles, squinting painfully even under the overcast. "I shall not hurt you, nor shall any of my companions! Yocote, unmask!"

Reluctantly, Yocote took off his goggles and stood squinting.

"See! We have rendered ourselves nearly blind to show our faith!" Lua cried to the silent huts. "Our archer has unstrung her bow, our sage waits to hear and advise! Oh, come, and tell us what has happened here!"

The distress in her voice must have touched a heart, for an older woman stepped out of a hut. "My daughter has been taken to satisfy the king's lust. What else matters?"

"Nothing," Kitishane said instantly, "but it might—"

"Revenge!" Culaehra said, his eyes smoldering.

The woman stared. So did Culaehra's companions. Then the woman spoke, her voice hushed and awed. "How can you have revenge upon a king?"

"He is as human as any other man," Culaehra replied, "and can be slain or punished just as easily."

"Will that save my daughter?" The woman's eyes brimmed over. With a cry of distress, Lua ran to her, arms open. The woman recoiled in surprise, stared—then opened her arms, too, dropping to her knees to embrace the gnome, sobs racking her body.

Culaehra looked around and saw faces at every doorway—wary, frightened, but watching, and here and there the fire of anger in an eye. He turned back to Kitishane. "If not revenge, what?"

"An ending," she said slowly, studying his face. "Perhaps we can prevent his doing such a thing again."

"Is that all?" Culaehra cried in exasperation. "A quick death? Is he not to suffer for all the suffering he has imposed?"

"There are other walls than death," Kitishane said, still studying him as if puzzled. "For a man who has wielded power, prison would be punishment indeed—but we must be sure he merits such treatment."

Culaehra turned away with an oath of disgust, but Kitishane called to the villagers, "We may find some means of action, good folk, but we must know more about your king before we go against him. Come out, and tell us of him."

Slowly, they came.

CHAPTER 13

"What more do you need to know?" a man asked. His weather-beaten face could have been anywhere between thirty and fifty years in age; his shoulders were thick and broad as a beam, his hands callused to a horny hardness, his tunic and hose patched and ragged. "He has taken our food—all the produce we have labored the year to grow, and taken, too, the meat animals we raised from calves and piglets."

"Has he left you nothing?" Kitishane asked.

The man shrugged. "Enough to keep us alive till spring, if we eat sparingly."

"Very sparingly," a woman said, her face hard.

"That brings illness," Illbane said. "How many of you die every winter?"

They looked up at him in surprise, and here and there someone shivered. "It is the dying season," the man said simply.

"Has he always been so hard and grasping, this king of yours?" Kitishane asked.

"Not always," one old man rasped, and the people stepped aside so that he could come to Kitishane. He hobbled up, leaning on a staff.

"How did he begin, then?" she asked.

"When his father died and he became the King of the Northern Marches in the old man's stead, he told us all he would work for our good, and we rejoiced, though some of the older folk said they would wait and see, for they had heard his father speak so when he was young. But King Oramore began well, seeking for ways to protect us."

"Protect you?" Culaehra frowned. "From what?"

"From ogres and trolls and raiders out of the east, young fellow," the elder told him. "The land was beset by them twenty years ago. Folk say it is because Ulahane still twists the unborn into monsters in his stronghold in the ice mountains far to the north."

"But Ulahane is dead!" Yocote protested.

"So said our young king, with great bravery, and he rode alone into those mountains, heavily armed and well-armored."

"He *sought* Ulahane?" Culaehra said, unbelieving.

"Did I not say but now that he claimed Ulahane was dead? No, he went to seek the god Agrapax, to whom we all pray here—but he might have found Ulahane instead."

"Agrapax, the Wondersmith?" Yocote asked, eyes huge.

"Even he. King Oramore found the god and asked Agrapax to grant him the means to protect his people. He swore he would give every year's first fruits to the god."

"Agrapax must have been intrigued by so unselfish a request," Illbane said.

"The god was pleased indeed," the oldster said with a quizzical glance at the sage. "He gave the king magical armor and told him what strategy and tactics he must use."

Yocote frowned up at Illbane. "I had not thought Agrapax was a general."

"He was not, but any Ulin could see the ways a battle could be won against humans or monsters."

"Are we younger races such bumblers as that?" the gnome asked.

"No—the Ulin are so vastly more intelligent." Illbane turned to the old man. "Your king triumphed, then."

"Aye." The man was eyeing him strangely. "He gathered his men and led them to battle against an ogre. They slew the beast, saving the maiden it had stolen. Heartened, the men followed him with a will to his next battle, where they slew a dragon. Only one or two soldiers died—"

"But never the king." Culaehra's lip curled.

"Certainly not; he wore enchanted armor. One by one they slew the monsters or drove them out of this valley, and when next the barbarians came driving down from the mountain passes, the king tricked them into an ambush and slew many of them; the others fled for their lives." His eyes shone. "Oh, we were proud of him then. It was ten years and more before the bandits rode this way again, and he fell upon them as well then as he had before."

"A bright beginning indeed," Illbane said. "When did he change?"

"At the first harvest. As they were bringing in the sheaves, a stranger came to the castle and rebuked the king for giving so much to the god when the people were nearly starving. He challenged King Oramore to put on a peasant's tunic and leggings and go among us, to witness our suffering with his own eyes. The king was never one to turn aside from a challenge; he came among us in disguise and was stricken to the heart when he saw how gaunt we were, how poorly fed and how frequently ill. He went back to his castle, thanked the stranger profusely and appointed him steward, then broke the bargain, keeping the first fruits in his storehouses to protect us against famine. When we people learned what he had done, we trembled with fear of the god's revenge." His mouth twisted. "Now we long for it, to end our suffering! Agrapax could hurt us no worse than the king's greed!"

"Perhaps that *is* the god's punishment," Illbane said quietly. "Perhaps it will last until you take it upon yourselves to find a way of keeping the bargain on the king's behalf—after all, he struck it on *your* behalf. But how did this king, who thought only of the welfare of his people, come to think only of himself?"

"His new steward advised him to take all our harvest into his granaries and storehouses, then dole it out to us as we needed—but to give back far less than he took, for thus would the king be ready to provide for us if drought struck, and prevent famine. King Oramore did as he was advised, and for the first few seasons we were well-fed and well-clothed, though we lived always in the shadow of fear of Agrapax's anger."

"Only the first few seasons?" Illbane asked. "Why did hardship come?"

"Because Malconsay the steward said that it was his office to see to thrift, and bade the king save more, always more. He bade him, too, to sell grain and buy steel for his smiths to make weapons and harness for his soldiers, to ward against the bandits. He increased the number of days we serfs had to give in labor, to make the king's castle higher and stronger. Then he found a wife for the king, and she wanted comfort and brightness in her quarters, that she might rear her children in safety. She gave him five children, and he proved a doting father, wanting more, ever more, for them; he sold grain to buy it. Then she wished to go to the court of the high king and take all her brood with her, that they might grow in culture and meet others of their own station; King Oramore sold more grain to send her there, and ever more to keep them all, then to take himself there twice a year . . ."

"So the steward planted the seed of greed, then found a queen to nurture and encourage it," Illbane interpreted.

"Even so," the old man agreed. "Every year the king took more and more and kept it for himself and his family, until we suffered as badly from his taxes as we had from the raiders and monsters."

"The caitiff!" Culaehra cried. "The thief, the knave! An oath-breaker and a serf-miller, who grinds up those for whom he should care? Nay, he is worse than any bandits that haunt the highway, for they only take what people have with them, but this robber king also takes all that you ever will have!"

The villagers shrank from his wrath. Kitishane and the gnomes stared at Culaehra, amazed, for his face had darkened and the veins stood out on his throat and his forehead. "Nay, friend, ease your heart," Yocote urged. "It is not you from whom they steal, nor your belly that is empty from this king's greed."

"Hurt to any peasant is hurt to all!" Culaehra stormed. "If we let this forsworn grasper steal from his own, we imperil all who labor in the shadows of the lords! Oh, believe me, my friends, if it was wrong for me to beat you and shame you when I had the strength, it is just as wrong for this King Oramore to treat his people as muzzled oxen! What farmer would abuse his plough team as this corrupted king has abused his serfs?"

"To treat them as his cattle, his kine, when he should think of them as his own kind?" Yocote's smile was hard. "I think there is truth in your words, rogue."

Culaehra scowled at him, unsure whether he had been complimented or insulted, but Illbane nodded with approval. "Well said, Yocote, well said indeed! Yes, Culaehra, it is wrong, very wrong, for a king to treat his people so. However, there is no point in punishing the king unless you free him from the steward who has corrupted him."

Culaehra turned to him, frowning. "Why, how is that?"

"Chastise the king, and the steward will only corrupt him again when you have gone your way. Slay the king, and the steward will corrupt his heir—if the mother he chose has not already done so."

"How now!" Culaehra faced him, hands on his hips. "Must I slay both the steward and his master to free these folk?"

The serfs drew back with a gasp of horror.

"You must not slay the king, or his heir will be worse," Illbane instructed. "But you must slay the steward and warn the king against his kind, for I doubt not that both he and the queen were agents of Bolenkar, sent to turn the king against his own people, and the people against the king." He turned to the serfs. "Has there been none among you who have counseled rebellion?"

They glanced at one another nervously; then the elder said, "Aye . . . there is a soldier who comes alone to bedevil our daughters, then harangues us all for cowards when they turn him away."

"He, too, is an agent of the hating son of the human-hater," Illbane told them, "but it is the steward whom you must fear most, for he is the chief of these corrupters. Without him, the king has only to come among you again as one of you to realize what he has done, what he has become."

"Then I shall slay the steward!" Culaehra turned on his heel and marched off toward the castle.

"Culaehra, wait!" Kitishane cried, running after him. "Go straight into that den of thieves, and you will be slain straightaway!"

"None need come with me who does not wish to," the big man tossed back over his shoulder. "As for me, I go to fight for the right!"

Kitishane stared, then ran after him again. She had only gone a few paces before she realized that Illbane was right beside her. "What have you done to him?" she gasped. "When I met him, he scarcely believed anything was wrong and only what he wanted was right!"

"He knew better," Illbane said, smiling. "I had only to bring it out in him."

Behind him the gnomes ran flat out, goggles bobbing, breath rasping, though Yocote managed a few curses.

They caught up with Culaehra and gratefully slowed to a fast walk or, in the gnomes' case, a slow trot. One look at the warrior's face and they put aside all thoughts of asking him to slacken his pace.

Halfway to the castle, soldiers suddenly rose from the hedges that lined the road, halberds at the ready. Half a dozen of them leaped into the road before the companions; half a dozen more closed the gap behind them. "Fools!" the sergeant sneered. "Did you think the king has no spies among the villagers? The sentry on the castle battlements saw you come into the village green and sent a runner to tell the king. He went on with half his bodyguard and left this other half here to greet you—and a villager ran to tell us what you have said of him! Now, state your business, for we'll not hang you without giving you a chance to deny it."

Yocote was mumbling and gesturing; even Lua was clearly trying to nerve herself to fight. But Culaehra's eyes narrowed; he gathered himself to charge.

"Hold!" Kitishane cried. "We wished to go to the king, did we not?"

Culaehra looked up, startled, and the tension seemed to bleed out of him as understanding came into his eyes. He gave a wolfish grin, and Yocote stopped mumbling, staring in surprise. Illbane nodded slowly, smiling approval, and Culaehra turned to the sergeant, still grinning. "Our business? Our business is with the king, soldier! Take us to him!"

"Oh, we'll take you to him, right enough," the sergeant answered. "We'll take you to him alive, but we'll take you *from* him with your death warrants in our pockets! Come along, then—but you should have been more careful in thinking what you wanted!"

The rest of the soldiers stepped from the hedges onto the road, surrounding the prisoners in a hollow rectangle, and the sergeant marched them up the hill toward the castle.

Lua tugged at Illbane's robe. He looked down with an inquiring smile, then reached down and swung the gnome onto his shoulder. "Illbane," she whispered in his ear, "I'm afraid of what Culaehra will do when he sees the king!"

"But not of what the king may do to him?"

Lua frowned, considering the matter, then shook her head. "No—I had only thought of what Culaehra might do."

"Such confidence in your companion is much to be desired," Illbane told her, "but you might give a thought to the fact that he is vastly outnumbered."

Lua did, pursing her lips in thought, then said, "That still does not worry me. Why?"

"An interesting question," Illbane replied. "Let us watch and see if Culaehra has an answer."

The king's great hall was luxurious, its paneling glowing with wax and constant polishing, the tapestries new and intricately worked. The king's huge carved chair stood on a high dais, and he wore a coronet about his brows. He may have been young and burning with zeal once, but now he was middle-aged, paunchy, and cynical. There was a hint of cruelty in his smile as he said, "So you have business with me? The business of slaying my steward, perhaps?"

Behind his chair a lean man in brocade gave a mirthless smile.

Culaehra gathered himself, eyes narrowing, but Kitishane stayed him with a hand on his arm, and Illbane said, "You are well-informed. Still, Sir Malconsay, we will leave you your life if you quit this kingdom at once, never to return, and go home to your true master."

Alarm flickered in Malconsay's eyes, but King Oramore said, "I may leave *you* your life, if you do not attempt to escape my dungeon. How now, wanderer! Do you accuse my steward of spying?"

"No, king, I accuse him of subversion—of subverting you from the course set by your bargain with Agrapax. Expel this tempter and seek your peace with the Wondersmith! Honor your bargain with him before your bad faith dooms you!"

Oramore laughed, and the sound must have restored the steward's composure, for he added his own thin chuckle and said, "Foolish vagabond! Surely the god would have stricken the king down before this, if he cared at all!"

"The wills of the gods work slowly, but when they have set all in readiness, they strike with devastation," Illbane told him. "Moreover, this Ulin may have other matters that capture his attention—Agrapax was ever single-minded—but when he grows bored, he may remember you, and strike!"

The king frowned. "Who are you, who speak of the gods as if you know them as one to another?"

Foreboding came back into Malconsay's eyes.

"One who has studied them long and intensely," Illbane returned. "However, I did not say that Agrapax would strike you down—though he may, he may—but that your own bad faith would doom you!"

"Indeed?" King Oramore smiled thinly. "And how could my own faith, good or bad, doom or save me?"

"Because if you act in bad faith, you will tear your own spirit apart bit by bit until you die a victim of your own excesses, and die in misery, no matter how much wealth you have hoarded, no matter how much luxury you have bought!"

Oramore frowned. "I like not this manner of speech."

"Aye, because you hear truth in it! Bad faith will also turn your peasants and serfs against you, for they will never know whether or not they can trust your word!"

Oramore tensed. "Do you insult my honor? Do you say I am not a man of my word?"

"Ask Agrapax," Culaehra snapped.

The king glared at him, turning pale—but Illbane pressed the issue. "Surely you cannot be a man of your word if you speak in bad faith—and if your peasants cannot trust you, surely they will someday turn against you!"

Oramore gave a bark of laughter. "The peasants? Those crawling feeble ones? What need I fear from them?"

"Your life, if you anger them so much that they march!" Culaehra barked. "Where do you find the men who make up your army?"

The king turned a stony gaze on him. "You do not know how to address your betters, *peasant.*"

"I do when I find them," Culaehra retorted. "I will not acknowledge any man as my better until he has proved it by his own body—and I will not acknowledge any man as noble who steals bread from the mouths of his own people!"

"Seize him!" Malconsay called to the guards. They started forward, but the king held up a hand to forestall them.

"Let it be as this arrogant clod says—let him meet me in personal combat."

"My king, no!" Malconsay cried in alarm.

But Oramore would not be deterred. "Let him meet me in the courtyard with his sword. And though he may not acknowledge me his better, his comrades will—when they see his dead body." He grinned with anticipation. "I enjoy slaying those who are foolish enough to challenge me."

Kitishane looked up at Culaehra in alarm, but he only nodded with grim satisfaction. She turned to Illbane, but he was gazing at Culaehra with pride and approval. In desperation she turned to Lua. "Is no one sane here?"

"Men never are." The gnome trembled with agitation. "They must do manly things now, and hack at one another till the end." She turned to Yocote. "Can you do nothing to stop them?"

"What, me? Save the life of that monster who was so cruel to you?"

"That is past! He would never do so now! Oh, Yocote, I beg—"

"Do not." He cut her off with a curt gesture. "The braggart has saved my life, and I his—that is all that needs saying. I will save him if I can—and if he needs it."

The soldiers marched them out into the courtyard, Kitishane hurrying alongside Culaehra to cry, "Are you mad? A warrior, a woods-runner, to meet a king in pitched battle? He will have armor and a shield! What will you have?"

"A sword," Culaehra returned, "and the skill Illbane taught me. Have you no confidence in our training, Kitishane?"

"Well, yes," she said, "but not against armor!"

"I am in the right, for once." Culaehra smiled, fairly glowing. "It is a strange feeling, Kitishane, but a very pleasant one."

"Being in the right will not shield you from a sword forged by a god!"

"Perhaps it will." Culaehra gave her a wild look, one that showed a man reading his weird. "Surely the god who forged that sword is displeased with him. Perhaps he shall make me the instrument of his punishment."

"And perhaps he doesn't care a pebble's worth! Agrapax never cared for anything but his art, if the legends speak truly!"

"Then let us hope that I am about to become a work of art."

"What, by being carved? Culaehra, come to your senses! Kneel to the king and beg his forgiveness, and he may let you live!"

"Then what of the peasants in the valley? What of their children?" Culaehra gave her that weirded look again. "Will *they* live when winter comes and the cold strikes through their threadbare cloaks, chilling them to the bone because they are faint with hunger?"

"I care nothing for the peasants!" Kitishane cried, though her heart wrenched within her. "It is for you that I care!"

Culaehra stopped so suddenly that the soldiers behind him collided with him. They snarled, but he ignored them, his eyes boring into Kitishane's. "Do you? Do you really care for me?"

She stared at him, then dropped her gaze in confusion. "Of . . . of course I do, Culaehra! We are comrades, we have fought side by side!"

"Is that all?" he demanded with a strange intensity.

"What more should there be?" she protested, still with lowered gaze.

"Yes," he said softly. "What should there be, indeed?"

She looked up in alarm, but there was no hurt in his eyes, only a fervor, a dedication that had never been there before.

The soldier behind him snarled at him to move, and Culaehra glanced at the man in irritation. "Yes, surely, let us go! For I must see to it that there should be more, a great deal more, and thus I begin it!" He turned away and strode on down the steps.

Kitishane followed in a welter of confusion—but with a strange glow rising in her heart.

They came out into the courtyard, and Illbane stepped up to counsel. "You will think to use your sword two-handed for greater strength, but that would leave your left side unguarded. Use your dagger in your left hand, and evade the cuts of his broadsword. Do not fear, your own blade will cut quite well enough."

Kitishane thought the old man must have lost his wits. How could Culaehra's very ordinary sword cut through the king's armor?

For there he came, resplendent in a plumed metal cap, breastplate, gauntlets, kilt, greaves, and shield that glowed with the luster of the finest bronze. To make it worse, the sun came out at that moment, striking golden highlights from it—but Illbane said, "I know that armor," and reached out to touch the king's breastplate with his staff.

The metal screamed, and the king froze, eyes wide in horror. The scream grew louder, and its pitch swooped down to a groan as the breastplate cracked from neck to waist, then fell from the king, leaving him only a padded shirt for protection. As the pieces fell they struck his greaves, and they, too, shrieked, then groaned and split. Illbane touched the gauntlets with his staff in a swift movement that took the king by surprise, and the gauntlets, too, fell to pieces. At last the king turned with an angry shout, bringing up his sword—but too late; the foot of Illbane's staff touched his helmet and it cracked with a sound like thunder.

The king reeled, and Malconsay shouted, "Seize him!"

The soldiers started forward, but Illbane turned to them, his staff up and ready, and they halted in uncertainty—so as the king's head cleared, he heard only Malconsay's curses and saw Illbane leaning upon his staff, watching with interest.

The king cried in anguish, "Agrapax's gift! The enchanted armor that no sword could pierce!" Now it was not the steward, but the king himself who roared at his soldiers, "Slay me that upstart magus! No, seize him and hold him, that I may flay him alive!"

The soldiers still hesitated, and the king raved, "Do you dare disobey? Then it is you I shall skin, while you live and scream! Seize him now, or die in anguish!"

The soldiers started forward, but Illbane called out some ancient words as his staff spun, and where its tip traced, fire sprang up. In seconds all the companions were surrounded by a ring of flame. The soldiers shrank back, moaning in awe.

Yocote watched it all with shining eyes.

Malconsay whipped a long wand from his robes and waved it in a circling sideways sweep as he shouted a phrase in unintelligible syllables—and the ring of fire died.

Illbane turned to him slowly, his eyes lighting, a small smile kindling in his beard. "So, then. Not a councillor only, but a magus! Did you know that, king?"

Oramore looked up at Malconsay in surprise, then sudden distrust. Quickly, the steward said, "You need not fight this duel, my lord, not when you face a magus as well as a warrior!"

"But you have a magus beside you," Illbane pointed out, "and though he has no staff of power, yet he has a wand." He nodded at Yocote. The gnome held up his hands, waving and chanting, and the wand grew amazingly, thickening in Malconsay's hand as it stretched out to twice its former length. The steward dropped it with a curse.

"Now your staff is as long as my teacher's," Yocote said helpfully.

"But you know it has lost its power, now that another magus has exerted his strength over it!" Malconsay cried.

"Has it really!" Yocote looked up at Illbane, and the sage nodded. The soldiers shrank back, moaning.

"Then you have two magi," the king said, watching Culaehra warily, "and I have none."

"But you have fifty guardsmen hard by," the warrior replied.

The king seemed to gain a little reassurance from the reminder.

"Your men will avail you naught, king." Illbane spoke as an equal in station. "If they do attack, they shall force me only to use greater spells that shall render them all unconscious. Let them stand aside, and go you to the duel you have accepted."

The king eyed Culaehra, hesitating. The big man grinned and lifted his sword to guard.

"What, do you hold back?" Illbane chided. "Surely you are not afraid only because your magical armor is gone and your guards can no longer leap to your defense! Admittedly, my champion is half your age, a head taller, and has the strength and speed of youth—but you claim that you are his better, for you are noble and he is not! Surely your nobility alone will assure you victory! Go, king, and prove your boast!"

"He *is* afraid!" Lua whispered to Kitishane, her eyes round with wonder—but her whisper carried; the king heard it, and advanced on Culaehra with a snarl.

The warrior grinned and raised both sword and dagger.

CHAPTER 14

The king swung a huge downward blow with his two-handed sword. Culaehra stepped lightly aside, then lunged. The king pivoted, bringing his great sword up barely in time, and Culaehra's blade glanced off it. Whatever else he might have been, the king was no weakling; in fact, his arms, chest, and shoulders bulged with muscle, and he handled the heavy sword as if it were weightless—which perhaps it was, in his hands, for it had been crafted by the Wondersmith.

But he was also gone to fat a little, carrying spare flesh around his middle. His reflexes had slowed since his youth, and already his breath was rasping in his throat as he swung the great sword like a scythe, coming up from below. Culaehra sidestepped again, but the king's blade followed him as if he were a magnet; he had to drop his dagger, taking his sword by both hands, to turn it aside. Metal clashed, striking sparks, but Culaehra's sword did deflect the king's. Culaehra's whole left arm went numb and he shook it frantically as he gave ground, trying to regain feeling. The king gave a shout of satisfaction and followed hard, the huge blade sweeping from side to side. Culaehra backed and backed again, but the king caught the rhythm of his movements and leaped farther forward; his sword tip traced a red line across the middle of Culaehra's tunic. The big man shouted in anger, then remembered Illbane's teaching: that anger only slowed a man and tempted him to foolish strokes. He cooled his rage and gave ground again and again, but moved in a circle, then stooped to snatch up his dagger again.

The king shouted in anger and swung at Culaehra's head, but the blow was so low that Culaehra leaped high, pulling up his feet, and the king slashed air beneath him. The warrior landed lightly and kept giving ground, even though his left arm was restored enough to bring up the dagger again. Sure enough, the king's breath rasped harder and harder, then began to come in gasps; he cried in bursts, "Hold . . . still! Cow . . . ard!"

"Do not, Culaehra!" Yocote called. "Why should you risk your skin when you have but to keep retreating until he falls from exhaustion?"

The king spun in a rage, slashing at the gnome, but Yocote leaped behind Illbane so quickly that he disappeared before the blade could touch him, though his grin seemed to linger after him for a moment.

Culaehra saw his chance and lunged. Even with the distraction the king was almost quick enough—he spun about, and his broadsword slashed the space where Culaehra had been. The big man gritted his teeth against sudden pain in his leg, but felt a savage delight as he saw the crimson blossom on the king's padded arm. The king shouted in anger and pain and leaped forward, swinging again and again—but his swings were off balance now, for one arm was weaker than the other, and Culaehra, backing quickly, was able to choose the instant to strike down with his blade, beating the king's sword to the earth for just long enough to slash with his dagger, then leaping back as the king swung the magic sword up one-handed even as he cried out in anguish, his left arm hanging limp at his side.

His guards shouted in anger and started forward, but Kitishane whirled to send half a dozen arrows into their ranks, and though they glanced off boiled leather armor, the soldiers slowed, uncertain. Lua lifted the little bow Kitishane had made her and shot a dart into a soldier's cheek. He shouted and fell back just as Yocote called out the last line of a spell, and serpents rose up from the dust, hissing, tongues flickering, waiting for a bare leg onto which to fasten fangs. The soldiers moaned in superstitious fear and held their ranks.

Illbane nodded, eyes glowing with approval.

King Oramore roared in anger and charged Culaehra, huge sword windmilling. The younger man retreated swiftly until the king ground to a halt, heaving hoarse breaths, sweat streaming down his face, glaring, his blade wavering. Then Culaehra leaped in, sword and dagger flickering in a dizzying dance, licking out of their maze with death on their tips.

Malconsay shouted a phrase and swung his staff. In mid-swing it bent, flexed, and lashed out as a whip that wrapped about Culaehra's blade, its tip cracking against his hand. He shouted in pain, barely managing to hold onto the hilt, and the king cried triumph as he swung his huge sword.

But Illbane spun his own staff, crying out words in the Ulin tongue, and the whip became a steward's staff again, whirling back at its master. Malconsay dodged aside, crying words that seemed to be gibberish until the name "Bolenkar!" rang clear and the staff spun back toward Illbane.

But Illbane shouted in plain speech, "O Ghost of Lomallin, strike down this overweening emissary of hatred!" and swung his own staff. It cracked into Malconsay's; fire erupted, and the steward's staff exploded into bits. One shard shot toward Malconsay to strike his head. He toppled like a duck to a sling-stone as Culaehra fell backward to escape the king's broadsword. He landed on his back; the king roared in triumph and raised his sword for the death-blow.

Culaehra shouted and lashed out with his foot. The king stumbled over that boot; his roar of victory changed to a cry of surprise, which cut off into a grunt as Culaehra's other boot came up to catch him in the stomach, then propel him tumbling past the warrior's head to somersault and slam into the earth. The king thrashed about on the ground, struggling for breath, while Culaehra leaped to his feet and kicked his opponent's hand. The great sword flew clear, to land glowing on the ground.

The soldiers shouted and started forward again, but Yocote gestured, and the snakes rose high to hiss, even as Kitishane and Lua sent another half-dozen arrows into their ranks. The soldiers halted.

The king finally managed to catch a huge gasp of air and shoved himself upward—and froze, staring at the sword tip that trembled before his eyes, as if with eagerness to strike. Culaehra dashed sweat from his eyes, panting. "Now . . . give the . . . people back . . . their food! . . . And take . . . the first fruits . . . to Agrapax!"

The king gasped for breath and used it to say, "I sold the . . . first fruits . . . long ago."

"Of course, but . . . this season's . . . firstlings . . ."

"Them, too . . . I have . . . sold."

"Then take the gold you gained from them!" Culaehra commanded.

"I dare not . . . Surely the god . . . would kill me!"

"Choose your executioner, then," Culaehra said, "for I will kill you if you do not go."

The king levered himself up on one elbow, scowling at the ground, chest still heaving. Culaehra drew back the sword enough for that. Finally, the king seemed to collect himself and said, "It was I who broke the promise; it is my doom. Yes, I shall take the gold to the god."

But Kitishane said, "We cannot trust him so long as Malconsay stands beside him."

The king turned a bloodshot glare on the unconscious form of his steward. "Have no fear. He has betrayed me by persuading me to forswear my pact with Agrapax; he has led me bit by bit into Bolenkar's work, and into abusing my people. He shall be my steward no longer."

"What do you mean to do with him?" Lua asked with trepidation.

"I shall deal with him; that is all you need know."

Culaehra exchanged a glance full of doubt with Kitishane, who gave an almost imperceptible nod. The outlaw turned back to the king. "You shall have more than enough to deal with here, then, between disposing of Malconsay and seeing to the needs of your people. We shall take the gold to the god for you."

Lua gave a cry of distress, and Yocote looked up in alarm, but

Kitishane only nodded openly, though her eyes were filled with foreboding.

"I should thank you for that," the king said slowly, "but how do I know you will not take the gold and go your own way?"

"Be sure." Illbane's voice rang so true that the king turned to him in surprise, and the sage looked him directly in the eye with a gaze that penetrated to his core. "Be sure we shall bring the gold to the Ulin. Be sure."

"I shall be, then," the king said, unable to tear his gaze from Illbane's. The sage nodded and turned a little away. The king broke the stare with relief and turned to Culaehra. "And, strange as it may seem, I thank you indeed." He gazed at him a moment more, frowning, then said, "You must be noble."

He wondered why Culaehra laughed.

As a treasure chest it wasn't much—only a large box a little more than a foot wide and a little less than a foot high, and perhaps nine inches deep, covered in leather and bound with brass strips—but two soldiers grunted effort as they brought it to set between the king and Culaehra. The outlaw stared down at it, scandalized. "*This* is the first fruits of many years?"

"A single piece of gold is worth all the firstlings of our fields," the king told him, "and another is worth all the firstlings of all the flocks and herds. You see before you the first fruits of twenty-six years."

Culaehra cast a glance of disbelief at Illbane, but the sage nodded. "Gold is very dense, Culaehra. A single coin holds much value." He turned to the king. "But that is only the first fruits, leaving the great bulk of all your people have raised. You must have a vasty store of gold indeed."

"Not so much as you might think," the king said. "Most of it has been transformed into luxurious appointments within my castle, armor and arms for many soldiers, and the court life of my wife and children."

Culaehra frowned. "What shall you give back, then?"

"The grain, fruit, and meat I took from them this fall, even as you bade me—and I shall take much less from them in the future."

"You shall have to bring your wife and children home from court, then," Kitishane said, frowning.

The king smiled with little mirth. "Oh, there is enough gold left to keep them there, and they have very little desire to come back here."

Kitishane looked into his eyes and realized that he wasn't terribly eager to have them come back. No doubt, to those refined court-dwellers, he seemed an uncultured bumpkin, and the life of the kingdom boring and isolated. She could sympathize with both king and queen, and hoped Culaehra would not insist on all the gold being given to the people.

He did not. "So much for the food. What of their clothing, their houses?"

"We can see to that without gold. I shall leave them most of the cloth they weave, and when they discover that, I doubt not they shall weave more. As to their houses, if I require fewer days of labor on my own fields and castle, they shall have more time to re-pair their cottages."

"Hovels" would have been a better term, but Kitishane wasn't about to discourage a worthy goal.

The king turned to Illbane. "How shall I protect them now, though? My enchanted armor is gone."

"Your people must become your armor," the sage said sternly, "and you must work your body back into hard readiness. As to the rest, you still have the knowledge of strategy and tactics the Ulin gave you, and his enchanted sword. Build loyalty from your peas-ants again, and you shall be still the scourge of bandits and barbar-ians both, the terror of the marches."

"There is hope there," the king admitted. "With Malconsay gone, there is hope."

"And what of the wife he chose for you?" Lua asked, her voice low.

"Aye." Culaehra lifted the chest—and stared, amazed at its heaviness. The two guardsmen who had brought it stared at him in amazement considerably greater, though, then began to eye him with fear. Culaehra shouldered it, grunting with annoyance, and said, "Your wife will be wroth when she discovers this is gone."

The king gave a mirthless smile. "She will not wish to return to this provincial kingdom when she can dwell at the court of the High King. If you come this way again, look to see the lot of the folk much improved."

But when they were out on the road again, Kitishane said, "His wife will not remain at court if Malconsay is dead or discarded."

Illbane looked up, eyes glittering with approval. "Truly said. How do you know it?"

"I do not know it, I guess it," she said tartly, "and the reason is simple: the wife is Bolenkar's creature as much as Malconsay was, or the steward would never have chosen her."

Lua gave a cry of dismay. "What will be the king's fate?"

"If we come this way again," Illbane said somberly, "we shall discover that he is either a widower, or she a widow."

"Then let us not come this way again!"

Yocote looked up at a sudden thought. "Might not the captains of the soldiers be Malconsay's creatures, too?"

Illbane nodded with a slight smile.

Yocote whirled about, gesturing and chanting, and only just in time, for flowers of fire blossomed in the air as the arrows fired at their backs burst into flame.

"I thought you would never guess it," Illbane said, and to Culaehra, "You really should go armored in this world."

"Yes, I should," Culaehra said, shaken, then to Yocote, "I thank you, friend."

"My pleasure," Yocote said dryly. "Let me see, now—you have saved my life twice, and I yours twice."

"I shall have to work to get ahead again," the warrior grunted. He glanced at Lua, then gazed at Kitishane as he said, "And I thank you, too, my friends."

"But we did nothing," Kitishane protested, and Lua echoed, "Nothing."

"No, only held off a score of armed men long enough for Yocote to cast a spell that stopped them," Culaehra said. "Be sure, you strengthened me amazingly, if for no other reason than that I knew you were there to guard my back."

"Accept his thanks," Illbane advised, "for you have all done well, even better than you knew." He looked from one to the other, his smile broad enough to part his beard. "Yes, you have done very well."

Kitishane felt her spirit glow within her at the praise, and scolded herself for letting a man's opinion matter to her. To hide it, she said tartly, "What of you, Illbane? Why did you do no more than speak to the king and his steward, and counter Malconsay?"

"Because you were quite able to do all the rest yourselves, as you proved," Illbane told her. "As to Malconsay, you were not yet proficient enough to deal with him—but now that you have seen the way of it, you will be, if you let Kitishane speak the words and Yocote work the spells."

Kitishane suddenly felt much less sure of herself, but Yocote said, "You have an uncommon amount of faith in us, Illbane."

"Why yes," Illbane said. "I do, do I not?" But he could not keep the pride from his voice.

Culaehra's breath came hard; he leaned against the straps Yocote had rigged to hold the treasure chest, and his face was pale.

"Let us take a turn bearing it, Culaehra," Kitishane urged for the tenth time. "Illbane and I can—"

"No!" Culaehra sounded angrier than he meant; the weight was a constant irritation. "It is my burden, and I shall bear it!"

Lua's eyes filled with tears behind her goggles; she lifted up a hand, but Illbane forestalled her. "He shall bear it himself no matter what we say, gnome-maid. Do not fear, he shall not need to carry it much longer."

"Why?" Culaehra demanded, frowning.

"You shall see at the crest of this hill." Illbane strode ahead of them to forestall any more questions. Culaehra glared at his back, at his ease of movement unencumbered, not noticing the stiffness of his joints.

Illbane gained the top of the hill only a few minutes ahead of them and stood waiting, leaning on his staff. As they came to the crest, he pointed, and they looked, then stared, for none of them had ever seen a body of water so big that they could not see the other side.

"How huge is that lake?" Kitishane asked, awed.

"A thousand miles across, and its water is salty," Illbane told her. "It is an ocean, not a lake."

Yocote's nose twitched. "What is that tang to the air?"

"The salt I spoke of, scattered to the air and borne by the breeze," Illbane told him. "We need not go a thousand miles, though—only across the bay that lies before us, a journey of a hundred miles."

"I must carry this chest so far as that?" Culaehra cried.

"No, Culaehra—you need only carry it down to the ship that we will board." Illbane pointed and, looking, they saw boats with tall masts beside a collection of houses along the shore. "It will take us to a town behind which mountains rise. We need only walk a dozen miles from that farther shore—but nine of those miles are uphill, and steep."

Culaehra groaned at the thought, but said stoutly, "I will be glad of the rest aboard ship."

"We must guard this chest closely, then," Kitishane said, frowning.

"We must indeed," Illbane agreed. "Yocote, it is time you learned how to do without sleep."

"About time indeed," the gnome returned. "Culaehra had to learn months ago!"

The big warrior gave him a whetted glance, but the gnome didn't notice—he had already started on the downward path.

Illbane found an inn, and left Culaehra in a private room with Kitishane and Lua while he took Yocote out to find a ship. The big man glared blackly about him the whole time, as if he expected the walls to erupt thieves or the door to burst open to admit a dozen bandits. The women did the best they could to distract him with lighthearted talk, but it was a losing battle—so, what with one thing and another, they were very glad when Illbane and Yocote returned to summon them aboard ship.

"We must hurry, for the ship sails on the tide, whatever that is," Yocote told them.

Illbane took a large, empty leather pack from under his cloak. "Large enough to hold the chest, Culaehra, and then some, though we shall have to pack spare clothing around it to hide its shape."

"An excellent thought!" The big man hefted the chest. Lua

quickly folded some cloth into the bottom of the new pack, and Culaehra set the chest in after it. He straightened up with considerable relief. "That will be easier to carry."

"Yes, and well-disguised," Kitishane pointed out.

Culaehra nodded as he swung the huge pack onto his back. "Aye. No sense in announcing to one and all that we have a small, very heavy chest, is there?" The pack settled into place, and a look of surprise came over his face. "It is lighter."

"Only a mild little spell," Yocote said uncomfortably. "Walk braced for sudden weight, Culaehra—I am still quite new to this."

"The relief is vastly appreciated," Culaehra assured him, "even if it does grow heavy again."

But he remained moody as they walked the streets of the little port with the tall masts ever before them. Kitishane eyed him uneasily and finally asked, "What troubles you, companion?"

"Your forgiveness!" Culaehra blurted. "How can you overlook what I tried to do to you, Kitishane? How can any of you?"

Kitishane shivered as the memory returned and drew a little away from him. "I do not think of it, Culaehra. You have changed so much that you scarcely seem to be the same man. I think of you separately from the stinking woods-runner who brought me down."

Culaehra winced at the words, but did not even feel an urge to retort. "Then I am a fool to remind you of it. You are too good for me to understand, Kitishane—you, and Lua, too."

"But not Yocote?"

Culaehra shrugged. "He is a man, like me—and I have no illusions. He would cheerfully summon a tree to fall on me if he did not think he would need me to save his life again."

But the gnome heard, and his head swiveled about to stare with eyes hidden by his goggles. "Do you truly think so, Culaehra?" he asked with a frown. "Well, so." He turned about and strode beside the sage again.

Following, Culaehra watched him, frowning. He had to admit that the gnome had not *had* to make his load lighter; it would not ensure his being able to help Yocote when needed. He fell back a pace so that he could watch all his companions from the back as he followed them, pondering the riddle of human goodness. By the time they reached the ship, he had almost begun to believe in it.

"Quickly, board!" The captain waved them up impatiently. "Quickly, ere we miss the tide!"

They hurried, though Culaehra's stomach roiled at the way the gangplank swayed beneath his weight. Two sailors hauled it in the second he was aboard. "Settle yourselves against the side of the pilothouse," the captain ordered, then turned to stride away down the deck, yelling something about casting off, though he didn't say what they should cast, and something more about cracking on sail.

Culaehra lowered his pack to the floor gratefully and sank down beside it. "Do you understand one word of what they are saying, Illbane?"

"I understand 'off,' 'on,' and 'the,' " the sage told him. "The sailors have their own language, and I have never been to sea long enough to learn it."

Culaehra looked up, interested to hear the old man admit to not knowing some definite thing.

Kitishane leaned closer and muttered, "Do not sailors think it is unlucky to let a woman on board?"

"The deep-water sailors do," Illbane told her, "the ones who sail out of sight of land for a stretch of weeks or even months, when there is time for them to work up fights over a woman's smile. But these coasters, who are out of sight of land for only a day or two at a time, have no such dread. Indeed, they make too much money carrying passengers to be able to afford such beliefs, for many of those passengers are female."

The wind filled the sails above them, and the ship began to glide out toward the horizon. Yocote hopped with excitement. "Bear me up on your shoulder, Culaehra, I pray you! I can see so little down here!"

"I wish to see less," Lua moaned, burrowing against Kitishane— but her human friend only gathered her close as she, too, stood, looking out at the vast sheet of water with shining eyes.

"Do look, Lua!" Yocote cried from his perch on Culaehra's shoulder. "It is amazing! I never even thought to see nothing but water and sky! There is so *much*!"

Lua lifted her head for a quick peek, then stilled, staring through her goggles. The sight was amazing indeed.

"Drink it in while the daylight lasts," Illbane said. "Brace your feet wide, and hold onto whatever piece of the ship comes to hand, for we will rock like a babe in a cradle."

Culaehra and Kitishane caught at the nearest piece of wood or the ropes that wrapped about them, and just in time, for the ship began to rock forward and backward like a trotting horse. Lua cried out in alarm, but the other companions only grinned with delight at the sensation.

"When the light fails, we must set watches," Illbane told them, "so that one will always be awake, even as we did in the forest."

Culaehra gathered that sailors were not entirely to be trusted. "I could not sleep anyway, Illbane."

"You must," the sage said firmly, "or you will not be able to fight if need arises."

Culaehra could feel his fighting readiness rising at the words. Illbane really did *not* trust the sailors—but who could trust anyone, with a chest of gold about? Especially gold that rightfully belonged to a god!

But no one tried to steal from them that night, though Kitishane and Culaehra took it in turns to stay awake and watch. Illbane and Yocote sat up all night, but sat in shamans' trances. Still, Culaehra knew from experience how alert they could be in such a state, and took comfort in the thought that of their party of five, there were three always on guard.

Strangely, Illbane had allowed each of them only a few mouthfuls of bread and a gulp or two of water. In the morning, though, he fed them properly. "Why did you starve us last night, Illbane?" Lua asked.

"Because I am new to shamanry," Yocote answered for the sage, "and he needed to be sure the spell I cast against seasickness would hold."

"Since it has held well," Illbane said, "you may all eat your fill," and they did.

They grew bored watching the sky and the sea that day, but Lua taught them games to play with the pebbles she had gathered. As the sun was lowering, though, an air of tension began to grow. Watching the sailors, Kitishane could almost see the apprehension thickening the air about them. As one passed near, she called out, "Goodman, is danger near?"

He stopped and stared down at her as if wondering how much to tell. Finally he said, "There may be, lass. Do you see that island ahead and to port?"

Kitishane looked. "Aye. What of it?"

"Peaceful people dwelled there centuries ago—but a wild tribe came to these shores and, not content with the mainland, built boats and invaded the island, slaughtering all the peaceful folk who could not run fast enough. Those who could, fled to the shore, but found the invaders had chopped their boats into kindling, and left guards upon their own craft. The islanders tried to swim the strait, but the wild tribesmen came running down to the shore and shot them with arrows, then took to their boats and rowed out among them, shooting as they went, even spearing the peaceful folk like fish. In despair, some of the islanders managed to grapple gunwales and overturn the invaders' boats, but they, too, drowned. At last, when all were dead by iron or dead by water, the invaders moved into the islanders' cottages and held their own drunken festival of victory. But the drowned bodies rose to the surface, blue with cold, and their ghosts reentered them. They swam back to the island, where they found the invaders all too drunk to stand, and slew them with their own swords. Then they went back to their graves at the bottom of the strait, but it is said that ever and anon they come up to test the virtue of sailors, and if they find them wicked, drive their ships upon the rocks to wreck them. Then they drag the seamen down beneath the waves, to drown."

Yocote and Kitishane shuddered, and Lua stared at the sailor in fright. "If you know this, why do you sail through this strait?"

"There is a riptide on the far side of the island; this is a far safer route, and a shorter one, if one wishes to sail across this bay to the harbors on the far shore. Besides, the Blue People rarely rise, and even then have been known to spare ships. It may be years, or even decades, between their last rising and the next."

Culaehra turned to Illbane. "Is this true?"

The sage shrugged in irritation. "It may be. There are many strange things in this world that I know not of, Culaehra."

Culaehra stared at him for a moment, then turned away, feeling gratified that Illbane was not infallible.

"What shall we do, then?" Kitishane asked.

"Hope the Blue People do not rise," Illbane said simply.

"What if they do?" Culaehra felt the beginnings of dread pooling within him.

"Hope that they declare us virtuous."

Culaehra had little hope of that.

The ship moved onward, but the wind slackened and the sailors began to mutter fearfully.

"To your oars!" the captain barked. "Have you never seen a wind die before?"

The men went to the six benches that lined the gunwales and unshipped long, long oars. They set them in thole pins and began to row. The ship moved on into the strait, but slowly, slowly. The wind died completely.

"They come!" A sailor shot to his feet, pointing; his mate caught his forgotten oar just in time to keep it from slipping away.

The companions turned to look. Behind the ship, all along its wake, dark heads were breaking the surface. A few had even begun to set up small wakes of their own, arms rising and falling as they swam after the ship.

"Row!" the captain howled. "For your lives, row!"

The sailors bent to their oars in a frenzy, but they lost the beat, and oars clashed and tangled. They lost precious minutes in freeing their blades.

"Together!" the captain bellowed. "One! Two! Three! Four! Bend! Push! Rise! Pull! Bend! Two! Three! Four!"

"They rise ahead, too!" Lua cried. She had climbed to the pilothouse rail and stood, pointing a trembling finger.

The ship rocked and came to a shuddering halt. Culaehra ran to the side to look down and forward. Blue faces looked back up at him all along the side of the ship; blue arms rose from the water, pushing against the side.

"Ship your oars!" the captain cried.

The sailors tried, but called back, "We cannot!" "They are stuck!" "The Blue People are holding them fast!"

Three sailors moaned, dropping their oars, and raised arms in prayer.

"Forget the oars and draw your knives!" the captain thundered, and strode among them with his sword raised—a long, heavy blade meant for cutting rope.

"What use, against those already dead?" a sailor groaned.

"It is better to die fighting than to wait to be slaughtered like oxen!" Culaehra drew his sword. "We may not be able to slay them, but if we can cut them into pieces, perhaps we shall live!"

The sailors took heart enough to draw their knives, but white showed all around their eyes.

"Is there no way to fend them off?" Lua wailed.

"Aye—prove your virtue!"

"How can we do that?" Culaehra cried in disgust.

"They will set you riddles that only the virtuous can answer!" the captain called back. "Is there any one among you who can puzzle out answers?"

"Perhaps!" Yocote's eyes lit. "We can try, at the least! Can we not, O Sage?"

Several of the sailors looked up at the word "sage," a sudden wild hope in their eyes.

"Perhaps we can," Illbane said thoughtfully. He strode to the side and called down, "Ho! Blue Folk! Why will you not let us go by?"

"You know why," answered a deep, gurgling voice.

"I do not know! I have only heard rumor!"

"Believe you so," answered a croaking rasp of a voice. "'Tis enough for to doom her!"

"Illbane!" Kitishane cried. "They answer in rhyme!"

"What 'her' does it speak of?" Lua asked, her voice trembling.

"The ship," Yocote explained. "I have heard the sailors speak of their ship as 'her.'" But his eyes were alight with excitement.

The sage stood still for a moment. When he spoke again, his voice was deeper, more vigorous. "Let me hear the answer from your own lip! Why do you seek to stay this ship?"

A voice hissed approval from below. "He answers in rhyme."

"Prove you are worthy to go your way!" the gurgling voice challenged. "There is one among you who went astray!"

Culaehra tensed. "He speaks of me!"

"Let Illbane speak to them." Kitishane caught at his arm to hold him back, but she was too late; he had already shot to his feet, and strode now to the rail. "Culaehra!" she cried, a wail of despair.

"I was outlawed from my tribe for seduction and breaking faith!" the big outlaw called down to the hundred blue faces below. "I bullied and despoiled everyone I met thereafter! If you have any quarrel, it is with me!"

CHAPTER 15

The sailors rumbled with surprise, then menace, but the gurgling voice called up, "We died from the work of Bolenkar. It was he who sent the wild tribe upon us. Should we not then seek revenge upon any whom Bolenkar sends?"

"Me, sent by Bolenkar?" Culaehra's face turned purple with anger at the insult. "I seek to defeat Bolenkar's agents, not to league with them!"

"Answer," the gravelly voice called up.

"I did answer!"

"But you did not make it rhyme." Little Lua came up behind him, goggles off and eyes dancing with excitement. She leaned over the rail of the pilothouse and called down,

> "Revenge is wrong because it
> Only destroys—your foe, aye,
> But at yourself gnaws it!
> Within, you begin to die!
> It wastes your strength and your heart,
> Wastes also your time and your mind!"

Put hurtful ones behind you!
Go on to build something new!"

A buzz of approval answered her. "Small heads may be wise," a voice that might once have been feminine screeched, and another replied, "Deep-seeing her eyes!"

The gurgling voice challenged,

"Have we no right to drown
Those who seek to strike down
Those weaker than they?
Are not brutes of less worth
Than those gentle at birth?"

Culaehra was amazed to feel the answer within him, and even more amazed to feel it rising unbidden to his lips. He had to let it out—but he tried to force some semblance of rhyme to it.

"The answer lies in the Creator,
For none can be lesser or greater
To Him.
All souls are of infinite worth
Therefore, every soul on Earth
Must be equal before Him!"

"It is well spoke," the gurgling voice admitted grudgingly.

"But is that worth not then broke,
If your Creator's a joke?
Who can prove He is there,
When all the world might be air?
For we can only know
What we see and feel,
But surely, in dreams,
What you see's just as real!
And if life only seems
To be real, then none did create it!"

Anger rose in Kitishane, and she rushed to the rail to call down,

> "If there is a dream, there is someone who's dreaming.
> Nothing unwilled comes from naught.
> If dreams can hurt, though they be only seeming,
> Those hurts can kill, though life be sought.
> If dream from waking can't be shown,
> Then waking dreams cannot be known.
> We must live as if the world were real.
> Or it will wound us sore, and never heal.
> But what is real, is really doom.
> No child is born without a womb.
> All is, All was, All will be,
> All is the Source!"

A murmur of appreciation passed through the blue faces.

"Where did you gain such a gift of poetry?" Culaehra asked, amazed.

"I—I do not know," Kitishane said, and glanced at Illbane. "Do you?"

But Illbane only smiled, and turned back to the Blue Folk as one with a voice like a tuneful crow called out,

> "You claim that since you cannot tell
> Dream from Real, you then must live
> Life as Real, though fine or fell.
> Why not believe that life can give
> Far greater pleasure if 'twere Dream,
> And do as you please, with no regard
> To others' pain, who only seem
> To live, so naught's untoward?"

"But folk *are* real!" Yocote cried, and leaped up beside Lua to call down,

> "Hear one whom others used as toy,
> Because I was too small to fight!

The seemers live, and can know joy
And pain, wherefore in their plight
They shall revenge if e'er they can!
Reality will turn and bite!
You can ignore, but cannot ban!"

"Errant nonsense," he muttered to himself, sagging in self-disgust, then slipping down to the deck again before Lua could speak. But the Blue Folk seemed satisfied enough, to judge by the pebble-rattling of their conversation. Finally, one with a voice like the dripping of mud called up,

"What's wrong is right, and right is wrong
Depending on the place and time!
One priest for worship orders song!
Another censures tune and rhyme!
One god demands, another bans!
One nation holds it wrong to slay—
Another murders all it may!
Do as you please, for on this earth
Someone, somewhere, will praise your worth!
Somewhere, someone will find no sin
In what you are, or what you've been!"

Now Illbane's brows drew down in anger. He stepped to the rail and thundered down,

"Hypocrites!
You don't believe the words you speak,
But tempt and taunt us all to seek
Our weakening, our self-damnation!
Some laws are lived by every nation,
Some sins condemned by every station!
The clan whose people kill at pleasure,
When they have all slain one another,
Ceases to exist. Which tribe, at leisure,
Lets each man steal from his brother

195

Will find each jealous and suspicious
Till none can trust his fellow, and
Strikes at hints of theft malicious.
Thus their tribe the tribesmen slay,
Or break their tribe and go away."

The rattle of approval deepened to a rumble. Illbane did not step back from the ship's side, but stood, staff in hand and glaring down at the Blue People, still indignant.

"You speak in circling contradiction," the muddy voice called out.

"Thus you earn our malediction.
You admit there may be tribes that do allow
Their folk to break the laws to which all others bow,
Yet say there are some rules that can't be broke!
Explain—or is your speech in vain, a joke?"

But Illbane's mouth drew tight in sarcasm.

"Vain tempter, speaking to confuse!
Do not think me to bemuse!
Paradox can be resolved!
Each broken ethic's self-enforcing—
Those who hold it mere discoursing
Perish if they dare to break it.
They're soon or late caught in the locks
Of tightening loops of paradox,
Which choke off breath as an affliction,
For it only *seems* a contradiction!"

The voices below rose to a roar, and its tone was uncertain.

"You have done it, wanderer," the captain moaned. "Now they will certainly wreck us. Sailors! Your oars as clubs!"

The sailors struggled to raise their oars as weapons, but before they could, Lua pointed downward, crying, "Look!"

They looked and, incredibly, saw the blue faces begin to move apart, to draw back from the ship's sides.

"We are saved!" a sailor cried. "They are leaving us! They will let us pass!"

It was so. In minutes they had vanished beneath the waves. A breeze sprang up, and the ship began to move forward again.

"This is all on your account." Another sailor glared darkly at Culaehra. "They came for you. If you had not been aboard, this would not have happened."

His look gave the big warrior a chill. But his anger was eclipsed by the captain's cry of triumph. "We have won! Our noble passengers have bested the Blue People! What a tale this will be to tell in the taverns—that the Blue Folk can be defeated by rhyming!"

Even Culaehra somehow felt that the captain had missed the point—twice.

The quay felt strange beneath their feet, after a week at sea— but as Culaehra carried the treasure chest off the ship, he looked up and saw the mountains, seeming so close that he could have sworn he would reach them by evening. He turned to join his companions in thanking the captain, then followed Illbane and Kitishane into the little port town. To his surprise, they slowed near an inn. "What are you about?" he demanded. "Let us strike out for the mountains! Surely we can reach them by evening, if we go at once!"

"It will be two days' journey, Culaehra." Illbane looked up at the mountains, the ever-present, looming presence over the town. "They are higher than they seem, so they are farther, too."

Culaehra studied the look on the sage's face, an expression at once bleak and nostalgic. Kitishane voiced his question: "What troubles you, Illbane?"

"There was no town when last I came to this shore," was all he said.

Culaehra stared, then looked about him at the town. It must have been there for a hundred years at least—sturdy little houses built of logs with the bark left on, two much larger, windowless versions of the same thing for warehouses, and another, almost as large, for the inn. How old was Illbane, anyway? He shook himself impatiently. "Let us be on the road!"

"Gently." Illbane raised a hand. "There may be little game in those hills; we would do well to bring food with us. Then, too, these mountains will be far colder than the winters of your homeland, and we must push even farther north beyond them. We will need warmer clothing, and cloaks of thick wool."

Culaehra stood rigid while anger built within him, then faded. Finally he said, "You are telling me we must spend another night in an inn."

So they did, with Culaehra sitting nervously on the chest the rest of that day and Yocote sitting atop it through the night. The warrior and Kitishane took the watch in turns, not trusting the trance-vigils alone of the shaman and the sage. At one point in the night, Culaehra felt a hand on his ankle, and woke to see Kitishane reaching out to touch him, her eyes on the door. He whipped about to look, just in time to see the portal ease closed and the bar fall back into its staple. Culaehra was up like a shot, catching up a stick of kindling wood to drive beneath the door. Then, breathing hard, he went back to his pallet, muttering thanks to Kitishane on the way. It took him a while to fall asleep again—he kept wondering how the landlord had rigged an unseen latch to raise the bar.

The next day, they broke their fast on bread that was only two days old, and fresh porridge. Fortified against the day's work, they left the village. Culaehra grumbled a little at the packs of fur clothing Illbane and Kitishane carried, but since the gold was his only burden, he did not feel he had the right to complain very strongly.

That night, they camped at the base of the foothills; the next night, they slept where the hills gave way to the true mountains. On the third day they began the long, slow climb. Culaehra had thought that Illbane had bullied him into excellent condition in the last six months, but by midday he was sweating and gasping under the weight of the load. He wondered how heavily it would have weighed without Yocote's enchanted pack, and felt an entirely irrational burst of gratitude for the gnome. Surely it must have been irrational—Yocote had certainly not done it out of love for Culaehra. Or even fellowship. Had he?

They halted to dine, and Culaehra thankfully lowered the pack—

then saw Illbane looking about him with the same faraway gaze they had seen on the dock. Before they could ask, the sage shook off the mood and said, "The mountains, at least, have not changed. Break bread, my friends, and rest."

They rested an hour. Then, with a groan, Culaehra shouldered his pack again. It was the king's sin, not his own, he thought with exasperation. Why was it he who must labor out the penance?

They were high among the crags when the mountaineers stepped out to block their path.

If the pack had not held gold, Culaehra would have dropped it to draw his sword. Even if it had been his, he would have let his load slide—but it was not; it was a sacrifice he had promised to take to Agrapax. He glared at the tall, rangy men and leaned into the load, readying himself to kick. But before he could challenge them, Kitishane smiled and said, "Good day to you, men of the mountains!"

They seemed a little taken aback, but the oldest said nonetheless, "It is a bad day for you. Open your packs."

"Why? Are you bandits?"

The man grinned. "I am Swiba. We are the clan of the Chamois, and these are our mountains. We demand a toll of any who pass here."

"Why? Do you maintain the road for us?"

"Because these are our mountains, and any who seek to pass through them must pay us!" Swiba flared, and his men stepped forward, their spears gleaming.

"How much is this toll?" Kitishane asked.

"Two parts in ten out of all you carry."

She frowned. "Rather steep, is it not? You are poorly clad for folk so well-paid."

That was true; the men wore woolen leggings and tunic, threadbare and patched. Their hair was greasy and unkempt, their beards untrimmed.

"One part for us, one part for our god!" Swiba snapped. "Show us your packs!"

"What god is this?" Illbane demanded.

Swiba turned, frowning at the sage's tone, but said, "He is called Wauhanak. Bow to him if you come here!"

"I know of him." Illbane's tone became even harder. "The sacrifice he demands is not in goods alone, but also in life. Which of us had you planned to sacrifice?"

The mountaineers muttered with foreboding, taken by surprise, and Swiba looked nonplussed for a minute before he shook himself and forced a scowl. "All strangers' lives are forfeit to the god. Since you have sprung the trap yourselves, put your wrists behind your backs for lashing; we would rather slay you on the altar than here in the pass, though we will do that if we must."

Culaehra's eyes narrowed. He slipped the pack from his back, holding it by its straps, leaving one hand free for his sword. The brass-bound chest would make a decent shield, and a better weapon.

Swiba's eyes glinted with approval—and relief. "Formil! Take that pack he offers!"

Before Formil could step forward to his doom, though, Illbane said, "You may not have the packs until we see your god with our own eyes. If we must die on his altar, we will view him first."

Culaehra's head whipped about; he stared at the old man, dumbfounded.

"As you will," Swiba grunted. "Your hands!"

"Our hands we will keep free for climbing, thank you. We will bear the packs ourselves, and you may hedge us about with as many spears as you like, but we will walk to your god as free folk and of our own will, not as captives."

The men looked uncertain, but Swiba grunted, "As you will; every man has the right to choose his own doom. Onward, then!" He gestured with his spear.

Illbane turned and stalked ahead. The Chamoyards had to hurry to close ranks and march before him. Others fell in beside the group, and Swiba brought up the rear with half a dozen more, all with spears leveled and frowns on their faces. "I do not know what trick you plan, graybeard," Swiba called out, "but it will not work!"

Why, then, was the mountaineer so nervous? Culaehra shouldered his pack again and hurried after Illbane. He almost wished the robbers had managed to take the gold, so he would have been free of the weight of it.

The route to the god went through the Chamoyards' village, if you could call it that—a collection of huts built of fallen branches and braided grass, as patched and worn as their clothes. Some were clearly little more than false fronts over cave mouths. The whole place stank of unburied garbage and open privies. At the sight of strangers, mothers called to their children sharply, and the little ones came running to hide indoors. They were scrawny and hollow-cheeked, mothers and children alike, and quite fearful.

Kitishane surveyed the scene with undisguised contempt. "Your god does not provide well for his people, Swiba. Why do you follow him?"

"Because he will tear us limb from limb if we do not!" Swiba snarled. "Walk!"

Kitishane did, but caught up with Illbane and muttered, "Why does this Wauhanak demand they sacrifice travelers to him? It means only that merchants will shun this route, and there will be less plunder for himself and the Chamoyards!"

"Indeed it does," Illbane agreed, "and one more road to the north will be sealed. Why did Bolenkar set the fuchan to guard his pass?"

Kitishane stared. "Then this Wauhanak must also be a creature of Bolenkar!"

"You reason well, and quickly," Illbane approved.

Culaehra had been close enough to hear the exchange. Frowning, he said, "Why did you not shun this route, too, Ill—" He broke off, staring.

So did Kitishane. "You knew! You knew what we would find!"

"Did you mean us to be sacrificed?" Culaehra hissed, then answered himself. "No, of course not. What is this, Illbane? Another test?"

"No," the sage said, "another task."

But Kitishane was frowning. "If you had inquired about the route, Lua would have mentioned it when she told me of your day's doings. How did you know?"

Illbane's eyes lost focus; he gazed into the distance, not seeing rocks and crags for a moment. "I saw many things as I waited until I would be needed . . . for this mission, maiden—and there was one who helped me to remember what I saw." He shook off the mood, but turned to her with a smile and eyes bright with desire—though she was sure she was not its object. "I know what Wauhanak is, and who sent him. That is enough."

"What is he, then?" Culaehra asked.

"An Ulharl," Illbane replied.

Culaehra's vitals went cold. An Ulharl! A misbegotten spawn of an Ulin upon a captive human woman! And Illbane thought of it as a task? Surely it was certain death!

He lowered his head and leaned against the weight of the gold, reminding himself that he was a brave man and, now, a trained fighter. If Illbane thought he could best an Ulharl, why then, he could.

But he did not see how.

Up they went, along an incline so steep that it left even the mountaineers short of breath, and Illbane, Kitishane, and Culaehra panted till their throats were hoarse. "Why would an Ulharl live atop so steep a slope?" the big warrior panted.

"So that . . . those who come . . . will be . . . weakened," Illbane wheezed.

Culaehra's stomach hollowed. The Ulharl had chosen shrewdly—and well.

But Yocote frowned. "If an Ulharl is so unbeatably powerful, why would he concern himself over such a strategy?"

Culaehra looked up, astounded. The gnome was right!

Illbane smiled. "Very good, Yocote—you have caught the flaw. Why indeed?"

"Because these mountaineers may be sure their god is unbeatable," Culaehra said, "but Wauhanak is not!"

Illbane nodded, his smile small but still, and Culaehra leaned against his load with renewed vigor. The Ulharl could be beaten!

Which was good to know, because there was his lair, a huge cave at the top of the incline—but it was more of a hollow than a cave, the inside glittering with inlaid gems around a great gilded chair, its seat as high as a man's shoulder. As they approached, a huge form rose from behind the chair, moving around to sit in it. Culaehra froze for a moment, staring, and fear clamored within him, for the monster man was half again his height and almost as wide from shoulder to shoulder as Culaehra was tall. Even his hips were four feet wide—but they had to be, since the legs that met them were two feet thick. His arms were each a foot across, and his chest was a vast and hard expanse under a mat of hair. He stood cloaked in purple, the color of kings, the color of might—but the cloak was gathered back at his shoulders to show his huge form, naked except for a golden loincloth. He stood a moment, glaring down at the group who advanced toward him. The mountaineers shrank back, cowering in fear, and Culaehra had to fight hard to keep from doing the same.

But Yocote was used to bracing himself against opposing height. He only smiled and said softly, "Very impressive."

His words pricked the giant's spell; it deflated like a blown bladder. Culaehra felt the fear diminish. Would the Ulharl really feel the need to overawe, if he knew he was proof against all assault? Why, he had used the same trick himself more than once!

And with that memory, Culaehra recognized Wauhanak for what he was—a bully, only on a larger scale than most. With that, the fear disappeared almost completely, for Culaehra knew now that the Ulharl could indeed be beaten.

But how? Bad enough he had so much physical strength. Worse, as the son of an Ulin—however unwillingly—he had magic!

Wauhanak stepped back and sat in the huge chair. Golden bands glittered on his arms, thick rings on his fingers. His hair was a black crest held by another golden band; his face was surly and glowering, with a thick nose, thick lips, heavy chin, and heavy lids over small eyes.

The Chamoyards gathered themselves again and prodded their "captives" on up the slope. When they had come within ten yards, Wauhanak boomed, "Why have you come, frail men?"

"W-W-With offerings for y-y-you, mighty Wauhanak!" Swiba stammered. "Five travelers, and all their goods!"

Wauhanak glared at them, his huge nose twitching. "A rich offering indeed! I smell gold!"

The Chamoyards stared at one another, then swung about to glare at the companions. Culaehra loosed the straps and lowered his pack to the ground.

"Your nose is sharp," Illbane told the Ulharl, "but the gold is Agrapax's, not yours!"

"How dare you speak so to a god!" Wauhanak thundered. "Down on your face, worm! Down, all of you, and pray that I may let you live!"

The Chamoyards crouched on the ground, moaning, but Cul-aehra stood all the straighter, fingering his pack straps—which kept his hands near the hilts of both sword and dagger.

"You are no god." Illbane spoke sternly. "You are an Ulharl, half Ulin and half human! But Agrapax is fully Ulin, with vastly more power than a mere Ulharl! Let us pass, or live in fear!"

Wauhanak threw back his head and laughed, a great booming that echoed off the rock faces and made the Chamoyards cringe in even greater terror than his anger wrought. "Fear, of Agrapax?" Wauhanak jeered. "Why, that absentminded gelding will not even notice your coming! I could eat you whole, and he would not care a bone!"

"Perhaps," Illbane returned evenly, "but every smith values gold, and he *will* notice that the metal is borne toward him. Dare you chance his wrath if you steal from him, Ulharl?"

"I am a god!" Wauhanak thundered in sudden rage. "You will address me as a god! Down on your faces, worms, or know the full lash of my anger!"

"It cannot be so strong a lash as all that," Illbane returned evenly. "Strike, charlatan—or bow!"

His voice cracked like a whip on the last syllable, and Wau-hanak roared in anger. From the folds of his cloak he snatched a huge broadsword, as long as a man was tall—but in the other hand he held a wand, with which he made a sweeping gesture that included all the companions while he shouted a verse in an un-known tongue. The rock cracked beneath them, and the companions cried out.

CHAPTER 16

The gnomes hopped aside, and Culaehra caught the straps of the pack, seeing a crack arrowing toward him. He leaped, landed on the far side, and the crack went past, yawning two feet wide. He started to pull on the straps, then heard Kitishane cry out.

Whirling, he dropped the straps and saw her clinging by clawed fingers to the edge of a crevasse that had not been there before. Culaehra sprang to her aid and caught her arm just as her hands began to tremble with the strain. He set his feet and pulled her up, clasping her in his arms while she shuddered, sobbing with relief. Another shock jolted their feet; they both looked around in a panic—and saw the new fissure speeding straight toward Culaehra's pack. He shouted, turning toward the gold—but the crack opened right beneath it and down it tumbled, down into darkness. Culaehra stood aghast, frozen—until he heard a splash far below, and knew he had failed in his trust.

He turned on Wauhanak with a roar of anger, but his noise was swallowed in the Ulharl's bellow as Wauhanak strode forth, sword swinging down at the biggest of the companions. Culaehra was too angry to be frightened; he snatched up his own sword and dagger and stepped out to meet the giant, Kitishane's wail ringing in his ears.

But Illbane, too, was shouting a verse and gesturing. The earth trembled again, the cracks closing as quickly as they had opened. Then Yocote shouted syllables, and huge shards of stone fell from the crags above, straight toward the head of the Ulharl. But the giant must have understood the words, for he stepped aside with only a brief glance upward as he shouted, "Chamoyards! Slay that vermin! Rend that gnome, or I shall rend you!"

The Chamoyards came out of their paralysis with a jolt and started for Yocote, their spears lowered to center on him. The gnome pulled the limber rod from his waist and chanted as he bent it double. The mountaineers' spears bent even as the rod did, till they pointed back at their owners. The men dropped them with curses and leaped back.

"Cowards and fools!" Wauhanak roared. "Will you let a mannikin's tricks afright you? Strike him—Ulahane!"

The curse in the old tongue brought all eyes instantly to the Ulharl, then to follow his stare. They saw the wand in his left hand drooping, bending back on itself.

"You struck better than you knew, my student," Illbane called with a grin.

The Ulharl dropped his sword and set both hands to the wand as he chanted; it began to unbend—and Culaehra, seeing his chance, shouted and charged.

Wauhanak heard and spun about, dropping the wand and catching up his sword barely in time to deflect Culaehra's blow. The warrior sprang back, cursing himself for a fool to have cried out and given warning—especially now that the huge blade was circling through the air with a hum so low that he felt it in his bones and saw the edge whirling toward him.

Kitishane, kneeling, loosed an arrow.

It struck the giant's shoulder; his swing went wide, the great sword clashing on rock. With a bellow more of anger than of pain, he plucked the arrow out of his flesh and hurled it at her. She leaped aside, but the Ulharl shouted a couplet, and the arrow swerved to follow its mistress. She dropped flat to let it pass over her, but it dipped and struck.

Lua leaped and almost caught it out of the air—almost, but only batted it aside. It pierced Kitishane's buttock, then fell off, for Lua had taken most of the strength from its flight. Kitishane shouted in pain, then ground her teeth to keep further shouts in—but Culaehra roared in rage to hear her cry, and ran back, swinging his sword up at the Ulharl's belly.

Wauhanak grinned, chanting a verse as he swept his palm up in a magical pass—but Illbane chanted, too, his voice a counterpoint beneath the Ulharl's, and whatever Wauhanak had intended to happen, did not. Culaehra's sword lanced into his stomach.

It bit into skin as tough as hardened leather, but stabbed through, for Wauhanak grunted and doubled over, his eyes almost starting from his head. When Culaehra pulled the sword back, its tip was coated with scarlet. The sight filled him with blood lust; he leaped, slashing at the giant's face with a howl of victory.

But the wound was slight in the Ulharl's great bulk. Wauhanak caught his breath and straightened, rising beyond reach of the sword, and swung his left hand with a roar of anger. The blow sent Culaehra spinning; he crashed against the rock face, and the world went dark for a moment. Something dinned in his ears; shouts came to him as if from a distance, dimly; tiny points of light moved and winked out against that darkness, and kept on appearing even as he began to see a blurred world again. He shook his head, trying to clear his sight, and felt a stabbing pain in his side. He held very still, and the pain ebbed—but his vision cleared, and he saw the Ulharl roaring as he swatted at Kitishane and Lua with his great sword. They were far beyond his reach, though, stinging him with arrows. His main concern, however, was Illbane; the rock was scorched in a long arc between Illbane and Wauhanak, pitted as though eaten by huge moths with iron jaws. As Culaehra watched, the air suddenly filled with a hundred glittering points speeding toward Illbane—but the sage swung his staff, and most of them disappeared. A few turned and shot back at the Ulharl. He shouted a curse and waved; the points melted away only inches from his chest.

Kitishane shot an arrow into that target.

Distracted by the magic battle with Illbane, Wauhanak failed to see the dart until it struck into his hide. He howled with pain and rage, leaping toward Kitishane, huge sword whirling up—

Culaehra shouted and charged in.

Kitishane skipped back out of harm's way, but Wauhanak saw Culaehra running toward him and turned his blow to slice at the warrior. Culaehra ducked under the swing; it struck the cliff face, chopping out a rock the size of his head—a rock that shot straight at Kitishane. Too late, she saw it coming and tried to dodge, but it grazed her hip hard enough to swing her about and slam her against the wall. Culaehra didn't see, saw nothing but the huge head hanging above him with the gloating smile, the maw opening to send a laugh between great yellowed teeth . . .

Culaehra leaped and thrust with all his strength, straight into that great yawning mouth.

Then something struck him; the world went dark again, and pain shot through his whole body. Dimly, he was aware that he was moving, flying . . .

And slammed into something hard. He must have lost consciousness for a minute, for when next he could see, forcing himself upright, the giant was kneeling, Culaehra's sword on the ground before him, blood gouting from his mouth, hands flailing about to strike anything he could.

Beyond the Ulharl's reach, Lua sent a dart speeding. Too small to notice, it stabbed into Wauhanak's eye, stabbed deep. He snapped upright, rigid for a moment. Then, like a tree chopped through, he leaned and began to fall, faster and faster, until his body slammed full-length onto the rock before his cave, jarring the whole mountainside. High above, a rock moved, slid, then fell; a huge boulder crashed down to crush the giant's torso.

For a moment the mountainside was still, everyone staring at the fallen Ulharl in disbelief. Culaehra stared, too, breathing in hoarse gasps. Then, warily, he stepped closer, and when he saw how deeply the boulder had struck, saw the glaze in the one still-whole eye, he knew without any doubt that the monster was dead. A grin he couldn't stop spread across his face, and he loosed a bellow of joy. The Ulharl was dead, but the warrior was alive! His enemy had tried to slay him, and lay slain himself!

Then the Chamoyards began to moan. They sank to their knees, throwing back their heads to wail. But Yocote turned away from them to run to Lua, who knelt with her face in her hands, weeping.

Swiba ran at Illbane, spear high, raving. "Our god! Vileness, evilness! You have slain our god!"

Alarm vibrated all through Culaehra. He ran at the mountaineer, to kick his legs out from under him. The pain in Culaehra's chest struck through to him again, staggering him as he brought Swiba down. The mountaineer fell hard, losing hold of his spear and flailing about for it as Culaehra, ignoring his pain, set a foot on Swiba's wrist. The man went limp, sobbing. "You have slain our god! What shall we do now?"

"You will become free men!" Illbane told him sternly. "Think, Swiba! If we were able to slay him, could he have been a god?"

Swiba stilled, the sobs catching in his throat.

"No, no god at all!" Illbane said. "Even his Ulin father was not a god, but only a sort of super-man! Even Ulahane the human-hater could be slain, and Lomallin's ghost slew him, then even slew his ghost! Surely this, his shamed and degraded half-human son, was even less!"

Swiba's head snapped up. "What was he, then?"

"An Ulharl, an Ulin's son begot upon a human woman by rape, by nightmare and terror. Only a slavemaster, nothing more. He was a younger half brother of Bolenkar, the heir to the human-hater, heir to his hate and his working of wickedness! I doubt not that Bolenkar sent him here to terrorize you, to slay and mutilate some of you until the others cowered in horror, vowing to obey—sent him here to grind you into a life of depravity and degradation!"

The other Chamoyards stared, awed by the revelation. Swiba stared, too, as he climbed to his feet, but asked, "Why us? Surely we are too small a tribe, dwelling in too remote a place, to be of importance to any of the great powers!"

"No human being is of too little importance to one who has sworn to slay all the younger races," Illbane returned, "and your tribe lives astride one of the routes to the north. Bolenkar wishes to keep us from that far land, and sent Wauhanak here to use you as tools to block our way."

"You?" Swiba stared. "Wauhanak was sent to stop *you?*"

"To stop whoever wished to go north on our quest," Illbane affirmed.

"A god, sent to stop mere mortals?"

"You see the need." Illbane gestured at the fallen Ulharl. "You have also seen that it was not enough."

"You are mighty indeed." Swiba looked from one to another in awe. Lua looked up, startled, then began to speak, but Illbane cut her off. "Even so. Yet we are only human, as are you. What we can do, you may learn."

"But how shall we fare without our god?" one of the Chamoyards wailed, and another cried, "Aye! What if the chamois come not, if the sheep all die? What if the rains fail?"

Culaehra frowned; even the pain in his side could not distract him from the senselessness of their worries. "How is this? Did you think Wauhanak kept the game within range of your spears, or kept the rain falling?"

"How do we know that he did not?" Swiba returned. "He may have berated us, he may have beaten us at his whim or taken one of our women for his pleasure when the urge came upon him—but he was always there as long as our grandfathers can remember, and we always knew what he would say or do if we erred in our duty to him!"

Kitishane stared in outrage, but before she could speak, Illbane said sternly, "But he did not control the weather or the crops. He gave you nothing and took everything, especially your pride and your manliness. Do you wish certain knowledge? Then be sure the rains will never fail here in the mountains, be sure that if you catch the sheep and breed and rear them, they will always be there. You are no worse off by his death, and greatly improved by your freedom. Go now to keep all you catch, all you raise! Go, to learn to defend yourselves, and to work out the confusion of choice!"

The Chamoyards looked uncertain, but Swiba went back to join them, then led them off down the mountainside. One by one they followed, glancing back uncertainly at the companions.

When the last of them disappeared around the curve of the path, Kitishane erupted. "The cravens, the cowards! To fear him dead, when he could harm them no longer!"

"But sister," Lua pleaded, "they feared only to go without his direction and protection!"

"Could they not see that he guided them only to their own

poverty and degradation?" Kitishane raved. "Could they not see that they needed protection only from him?"

"No," Illbane told her. "He had taken that sight away from them."

"Try to understand it, Kitishane," Lua pleaded. "People enslaved end by looking up to their master, to justify their own shame—it is not that they are so lowly, but that he is so high." She lowered her gaze. "Believe me, I know."

Kitishane stared at her in shock, then whirled to glare at Culaehra. He met her gaze and nodded slowly. "It is even as she says." He nodded at Illbane. "I, too, know—now."

That took some of the edge off Kitishane's wrath. She turned back to Lua with a frown. The gnome-maid gave her a tremulous smile. "Remember, too, that these men were born slaves, as their fathers were. To them, Wauhanak *was* the order of all the world."

"Blasphemy! And a mortal wound to the soul!"

"Not mortal—we recovered," Lua said, sharing a quick glance with Culaehra. "They will, too, though it will take them longer, since they were born to it."

"They will," Illbane assured her, "though it will take many years. Not only will they recover their independence—they will even come to rejoice in their freedom. But it will take time, maiden—it will take time."

Kitishane frowned up at him, brooding, then turned away with a shudder. "Slaves or not, they were lethal! I thought they would slay us sure!"

"What, a handful of ragged wild men slay you, when you have just slain their god?" Illbane turned to her, caught between amusement and annoyance. "Do you still have so little faith in yourselves? You have slain an Ulharl!"

"Surely that was a happy chance . . ."

"It was not! It was muscle and quickness, inspiration and strong magic, sure aim and shrewd fighting! It was all four of you working together against a giant and a dozen armed men! I could lead you to another Ulharl, and you would win again!"

"Oh, do not!" Lua wailed.

Instantly, Illbane softened. "Be of good heart, little one—I will not do so just yet."

Culaehra tried to ignore the chill raised by that "just yet" and said, "It was also because you were with us to counter the Ulharl's magic. We could not have won without you, Illbane."

"Well, no," the sage admitted, "not just yet. Yocote had never seen which spells to use against an Ulharl before, and the four of you might have been overawed if I had not been here beside you. But your shaman gnome learns more magic every day, and no Ulharl will ever afright you so much again by his mere presence. Be warned, though, my students—Bolenkar is huger still, and far more fearsome than any of his siblings, by the sheer intensity of his hatred and malice."

"Why do you tell us of Bolenkar?" Lua asked, her voice trembling.

"Why did you shoot at Wauhanak?" Illbane returned.

"Oh, I could not let him slay Culaehra!"

Yocote's face turned to stone; he turned away.

"Oh, do not be so, Yocote!" Lua cried. "Culaehra is one of our number, even as you are, even as Kitishane is my sister! Should I not defend him, too?"

"Even as he defends you?" The gnome turned back, and if his face was not warm, at least it had come alive again.

Culaehra forced a grin. "Why, shaman! Would you have her leave me to my fate?"

But he winced as he said it, and Yocote frowned at him. "Why do you press your hand to your side?"

"Stiff muscles," Culaehra grunted.

"Aye, with the sweat pouring from your brow and your breath so light it would not disturb a butterfly!" Yocote strode toward the warrior. "Lua, favor me by lighting a fire and boiling water! Kitishane, take him down! He has cracked a rib at the least, and perhaps broken it!"

"Can you sit without making it worse?" Kitishane stepped up to take Culaehra's arm.

"Why the devil should I?" he snapped, then winced again.

She stared at him a moment, then sank to her knees, reaching up to him. "Come, sit beside me, strong man!"

The posture sent desire throbbing through Culaehra with a strength that startled him.

"Please." Her voice was a caress, her arms beckoning.

Culaehra almost screamed within his brain, reminding himself that she was only luring him down to be healed, and for no other purpose. "You have no right to be so alluring," he snapped—but it came out as a groan, for he was trying to lower himself to the ground.

Illbane came up and planted his staff near. Culaehra grasped it to steady himself, carefully unfolding his legs as he sat. Broken ends of bone grated against one another, and he practically screamed with the pain, but managed to stifle it into another groan.

"Be brave, my friend," Kitishane said, her voice gentle, sympathetic. "Yocote, does he need to lie down?"

"No, only to be low enough so that I can reach him." The gnome stepped up beside the warrior, probing his chest.

Culaehra nearly screamed, then gasped, "What is this, gnome? Revenge?"

"Mercy," Yocote said dryly. "If I had wanted revenge, I would have let the Ulharl have you. You are fortunate—there is only the one rib broken. Grit your teeth, Culaehra—this will hurt like a demon for a moment, but after that, it will only ache abominably."

He set himself, fingers on the broken rib. Then his hands moved, not very much, but precisely, and enough to make Culaehra whinny with a suppressed scream. As his voice quieted, Yocote's rose, reciting a long string of syllables that seemed to have some sort of music buried in them, his fingers moving over the broken bone. At last he stopped, stepping away and saying, "Sit very still this while, Culaehra." He turned away to the little fire and the pot that boiled above it. "Thank you, Lua."

Yocote took small pouches from his belt, pinching powders from within and sprinkling them into the pot. He let them boil as he chanted over them, then took the little vessel from the fire and set it in front of Culaehra. "Sit still until the steam has ceased to rise," he said. "Then you may drink it—but drink it all, no matter how vile the flavor. Some while after that you may rise—and your rib should be as good as new. That is not to say it will not ache for a few days, but it will stand up to normal misuse."

"I . . . thank you, shaman," Culaehra said, as if not quite knowing how to pronounce the words.

"I shall delight to see you in good health again," Yocote said, inclining his head. "After all, it is to our benefit, for if you are laid low, who will carry that horrendous weight to Agrapax for us?"

"What horrendous weight?" Culaehra groaned.

Silence fell. Everyone looked about for the treasure chest. "Where is it?" Yocote asked softly.

Culaehra groaned again, not from the pain. Quietly, Kitishane said, "I was about to fall into a crevasse. He had to choose between the treasure and me."

"He chose well," Yocote said instantly.

"Oh, aye!" Lua said fervently. "Bless you, warrior, for saving my sister!"

Culaehra looked up in surprise. "*You* bless me?"

Lua could only smile beneath her goggles. "I forgave you months ago, Culaehra. Do you forgive Illbane?"

"Aye, if you wish it." But the warrior looked up at the sage, searching his feelings and finding only a lingering resentment of Illbane's bullying. The hatred was gone, and with it, the lust for revenge. After all, how can you keep hating a man who saves your life, who listens to your self-condemnations and never whispers a word of them to another soul, who nonetheless reassures you of your own worth? "I think I have already."

Illbane's smile was radiant. "What matters the loss of a mass of gold, against such discoveries as these?"

Culaehra's shoulders lifted and fell with the laugh he dared not yet let out, for fear of his mending rib. "It matters little to us, Illbane, but it will matter somewhat to Agrapax, and even more to Oramore. I find I have no wish to go to an Ulin and tell him I have lost his gold."

"Well, then, we must win it back," Yocote said simply.

"Oh, easily said!" Culaehra snorted. "But how shall we go down where the chest has fallen, especially now that the crack in the earth . . ." His voice trailed off as he stared at Yocote.

The little shaman smiled under his goggles, nodding. "Yes, Culaehra. We are gnomes—people whose natural home is far underground, to whom the seams and rips within the earth are as natural a playground as a tree's limbs are to you. Come with us, if you dare."

"I cannot let you go alone to mend my failure!"

"It was not a failure!" Lua's brows knit in a frown. "You saved my sister!"

Culaehra stared, wordless at hearing the gnome-maid speak sharply. Yocote took advantage of his silence to say, "You are a hero, Culaehra—accept it. Come now, drink your medicine, and when your rib is healed, we shall descend!"

"But how?" Culaehra managed to croak.

"Through there." Yocote jerked his head toward Wauhanak's cave. "Any cave is an opening into the earth, and my gnome's senses tell me that this opening goes deeper than most. Come, Culaehra—or are you afraid to go into a god's home?"

CHAPTER 17

Culaehra grunted. "A god's house I might fear," he said, "but what has that to do with Wauhanak?" Then, to Illbane, "Why are you smiling so?"

"Hear your own words," the sage answered. Culaehra thought back, then realized that he finally did believe the Ulharls were really not divine. Would he believe that of the Ulin, when he met their smith Agrapax?

He drank the brewed herbs, but Yocote insisted that he rest for an hour or two. He brewed another tea for all to share, and they sipped and chatted about the adventures of the last few months. They were amazed to discover how much they had all changed.

"Yocote has become a shaman, and Culaehra a man worthy of any trust," Kitishane said in tones of surprise. "Lua has turned from a timid sparrow into an archer who can slay if she must. Only I have changed little, save for becoming the trained fighter that I used to pretend I was."

"Oh, no, sister!" Lua protested. "You have changed far more than that! You are more quiet, you do not bluster or storm at those you perceive as a threat—and you are so much more sure of yourself that I might not know you if I had not seen the changes as they happened."

Kitishane stared. "Am I really?"

"You are," Yocote confirmed, but Culaehra only frowned and said, "You did not know?"

She met his gaze, her eyes still wide. He smiled, glowing within at her compliments, and vowing never, ever, to violate her trust.

"This is your doing, sage," Yocote accused.

"It is, and I rejoice in it." Illbane looked from one to the other, his smile radiant. "The ordeals through which I have led you, the enemies you have faced together, have put each of you well on the way to becoming all that you can be, a way that will go on your whole life, if you have the determination to follow it without me to goad you."

"All that we can be?" Culaehra frowned. "What is this?"

"It is most obvious in you, Culaehra, for your body, which was strong but running to fat from self-indulgence, is now hard and lean, and trained to true fighting skill. Your conscience is at last awake, seeking to tell you what is right, not finding excuses for doing as you please. This battle has shown that you have the spirit of a true warrior—" He looked around at them all, smiling. "—but so do you all. In Culaehra it is more apparent, for he had the furthest to go; in Yocote it is almost as much so, for he has changed from a gnome whose magic was weak into a shaman of formidable powers. But you and Lua have grown just as greatly, and the sign of it is that you have even more determination than Culaehra and Yocote in your chosen goal."

They all stared at him in surprise; then Yocote asked carefully, "What goal is that?"

"You see? You are not even aware of it yet." Illbane smiled upon Kitishane. "Speak, maiden. What do you seek to do?"

Her voice was hushed, almost as if she was afraid to be heard. "To destroy Bolenkar."

The men stared, then stared again at Lua, for she had not cried out in dismay. Instead she only nodded, slowly and with gravity. "So you have seen that, too, sister?"

"Yes, it is as you say!" Culaehra said, eyes wide. "It has been growing in me, but I had not yet put words to it!"

"Nor had I." Yocote frowned. "But it is true, is it not? The fuchan, the king's corrupter, the Ulharl grinding down these mountaineers—all were sent by Bolenkar, were they not?"

"Yes, and the man who sowed doubts of right and wrong in my village." Culaehra glowered at the memory. "Was there one among the gnomekind, too?"

"Was there? Why do you think they let Lua go wandering aboveground, and despised me for being too weak in magic?" Yocote spat.

"All is due to Bolenkar, is it not?" Culaehra asked.

"Not all humanity's woes, no," Illbane said, "for our kind is more than able to make one another miserable by rivalry for position and for mates, by greed and jealousy and the lust for power. But the suffering that has grown amazingly in this last hundred years, yes—it is far worse than is natural to humankind, and the gain is all due to Bolenkar's agents, playing upon our natural vices."

They were silent a moment, aghast at the magnitude of what they had said.

"It is audacity of the highest order, even to speak of overthrowing a god," Lua whispered.

"But he is no god." Culaehra pushed himself to his feet. "We know that now—Bolenkar is no god, but only an Ulharl, and can be slain, even as we slew Wauhanak."

"Can be, yes." Yocote frowned. "But Wauhanak dwelled alone, with only these mountaineers to do his bidding. Bolenkar surely must dwell surrounded by armies, all eager to win his favor by slaying his enemies!"

"That is very true," Illbane said, nodding.

"Then we shall have to amass an army," Culaehra said resolutely, "and we shall have to be devious in the extreme. What, little companion—can you not outsmart a lumbering hulk like that?"

Yocote's face split in a grin. "Why, surely I must! Come, big man, take up your sword again, and take a few brands for torches before you smother the fire. I pronounce you healed, and we have a treasure to find!"

He led them past Wauhanak's corpse and into his cave, where he and Lua took off their goggles. Around, behind the throne they led, then through the fine purple linen that masked the opening into the earth.

The Ulharl's dwelling was furnished in luxury. The walls were hung with precious cloths, the huge table and chairs and bed were carved from lustrous woods and ornamented with great care. Jewels winked in the cups and plates of silver and gold, and the stone floor was covered by furs sewn together to form one large carpet.

"The villagers may have lived in abject poverty," Yocote said sourly, "but their god did well enough for himself."

"Where did they find so many beautiful things?" Lua asked, eyes wide and wondering.

"From caravans that came here in the early years, before Wauhanak's 'toll' grew so great as to make them shun this pass," Illbane replied.

"It is so neat and clean!" Lua looked about her in amazement.

Culaehra grunted. "I doubt that was his doing. More likely the women of the village were summoned each day or week, to sweep and dust and cook for him."

Illbane nodded steadily, pleased at their reasoning.

"Enough of his dwelling!" Yocote began to thrash the wall hangings. "There is an opening to the world below; let us find it!"

"How do you know?" But Kitishane joined him in his probing.

"A gnome knows, sister," Lua assured her, flicking draperies aside. "There!"

They all turned to look, and saw a dark opening in the rock, perhaps five feet high, barred with a wooden grid of close-set rods. Culaehra looked upon it with a smile of irony. "He did not go through there himself, did he? It will be difficult even for me! But why the grid?"

"To keep out vermin, warrior," Yocote said dryly, "such as rats and bats—and gnomes! Come, take it aside for us!"

Frowning, Culaehra laid hold of the grid, twining his fingers through the rods, set himself and gave a hearty pull. The grid groaned, then came away—and they found themselves staring down into a lightless opening. Kitishane shivered, but Yocote rubbed his hands, pleased. "Now we go into gnomes' land! Follow, friends!"

Lua and Yocote stepped in boldly. Culaehra and Kitishane followed with somewhat less assurance. They held their torches higher as the darkness closed about them, leaving only a flickering light that reflected off the walls of the cave and disappeared into the darkness ahead of them.

They followed that light.

Lastly came Illbane, and down they went, into deeper darkness than Kitishane or Culaehra had ever known before. Children of the forest and the meadow, they were accustomed to the stars above even in the deepest night, or at least a little light diffused through the clouds to show sky from earth. Here, though, the darkness beyond their torchlight was total. Kitishane shivered and, without realizing it, moved a little closer to Culaehra with each passing step. The walls began to close in about them, turning a cave into a tunnel, but oddly, Kitishane drew comfort from that— at least her torchlight showed her what was on each side, even if it disappeared into the gloom before and behind. She glanced at it anxiously, wondering how long it had left to burn, for she had only three more sticks in her belt. Then she stared, amazed, for her torch had not burned any more wood than when she had taken it from the fire! She glanced at Culaehra's brand and saw that it, too, was no shorter. Amazed, she turned to stare at Illbane behind her, but he only winked at her and smiled. For a moment she could only stare. Then she found herself smiling, too, and turned back to the gnomes, oddly comforted.

Down they went, the sloping floor seeming to tug them forward— down and down, in a spiral, Kitishane thought. Then the floor leveled off and they went straight for a while. Glints of light began to appear in the walls, growing larger and larger until she could see jewels protruding from the stone. She gasped in delight and would have stopped, but the gnomes scarcely seemed to see the gems and would not wait. She followed, her heart torn with the loveliness of the space, especially as veins of pure gold began to show in the rock—but on and on the gnomes went, giving her no chance to tarry.

They came out into a grotto, and even Yocote had to stop and draw breath at the sight. Their torchlight winked back at them from jagged edges of quartz, but within and between and all about gleamed jewels of bright color and amazing purity, and runnels of gold all through both.

"How could such beauty happen by chance?" Kitishane cried, looking about her, enthralled.

"It could not." Yocote peered closely at the gems and gold. "This is the work of hands. Gnomes dwelt here once."

"Gnomes?" Culaehra frowned. "It could not have been dwarfs?"

"No." Yocote sounded rather insulted. "Dwarf work is altogether different—more square, more rigid. They are smiths; the models for their work are in their heads. Gnomes fashion curves and fluidity, modeled after water and light, brought about by gathering gems and persuading crystals to grow. Dwarfs scarcely notice our work, until centuries have gathered it to such a concentration as you see here."

"Centuries?" Kitishane looked about her. "To tend this garden of rock so long, and abandon it?"

"They left when Wauhanak came, I doubt not," Yocote said, his voice harsh, "and I do not wish to think by what magic he drove them out."

Lua laid a gentle hand on his. "Perhaps they did not wait to be driven."

Yocote nodded, still curtly. "Likely enough. They would have known when an Ulharl was near, and did not hesitate in departing. Yes, they would have fled, no matter how lovely their creations. Life is worth more than art."

"I have known some who would have said otherwise," Illbane mused.

"Then their art was their lives, but their lives were not art," the gnome-shaman said. "Gnomes' lives are. That does not mean," he added reluctantly, "that all of us succeed in art."

There was a note almost of despair in his voice. Lua gazed at him, eyes wide and moist, and slipped her hand into his. He did not thrust it away.

Out from the grotto they went, on down through another spiral, then into a cavern where the torchlight was swallowed by the darkness and diminished, where that darkness was absolute and their hushed footsteps set up thousands of echoes. Kitishane was about to ask if they were at all close to the treasure when Yocote held up a hand. "Hist!"

They all stilled, listening, and heard, ever so faintly, the susurrus of water, moving ever so gently.

"This is odd." Yocote scowled up at Culaehra.

The warrior was surprised to see the gnome's huge eyes in the light of the torch, then realized it was because he was unused to seeing him without his goggles. "What is odd?"

"The water. Underground lakes are not uncommon, mind you—but I fear the treasure may have been caught inside the rock when the cracks closed."

"With the chest splintered, and the gold spread to a foil within the stone!" Lua cried.

"No." Culaehra shook his head. "I had not thought, but now I remember that I did hear a splash."

"Why did you not say so!" the gnome said sharply, but with relief.

"But you said it was a lake!"

"Aye, which means it is deep enough so that the chest is probably not broken—and what is sunken can be raised. Come, let us see if this is a puddle or a sea." He turned away and went toward the sound.

They stepped through a huge irregular archway—and came out to see the most eerie sight they had ever encountered. The water rolled away from them in a cavern so vast they had no hint of its size, except for echoes. The waves, perhaps a foot high, washed the rocky ledge near their feet and receded—but they bore with them a strange light of their own, an eldritch glow that served to give the companions some notion of how vast a water it was. There seemed no end to it—the surface undulated into the distance until it disappeared.

"It fell into *this*?" Culaehra felt his stomach sink. "How shall we ever find it?"

Yocote shrugged. "One league or a hundred makes little difference, warrior. *It* will find *us*."

Culaehra turned a blank stare of incomprehension upon him—until the little man knelt by the water, took one of the spare sticks and laid a torch upon it to make a small fire, then took powders from his belt and sprinkled them into the flames, chanting arcane verses. In spite of himself, Culaehra's nape hair prickled; he stepped back, bumped into someone and spun to see it was Ill-bane. "What does he do?"

"He commands the waters to yield up what they have swallowed, and summons the chest to rise of its own accord." Illbane frowned. "It is a good thought, and he does the spell correctly, but I must tell him . . ." At the thought, his eyes widened, and he stepped quickly toward the gnome—

But not quickly enough. The water rose with a roar like a cascade, drawing together and swelling up to tower over the companions, parting and coalescing to form a huge, glowing, angry face. "WHO DARES COMMAND THE WATERS!"

A wave reached out, washing high, to fall upon Yocote's fire, and he leaped back, crying, "Illbane! What have I done?"

"You sought to command the waters, not to beseech them!" the sage called. "Their spirit has risen in anger! Calm it, shaman! Apologize!"

"WHO DARES SEEK TO COMMAND THE HIDDEN WAVES?" the huge face demanded. Slowly, its cavernous eyes turned toward the companions. "YOU DO!" It rushed toward them, looming above them, its vast maw opening wide, and within they saw a whirlpool about to fall on them and pull them in.

"Your pardon, Great One!" Yocote cried. "I had not meant to offend!"

"HAD NOT MEANT TO ANGER ONE MORE POWERFUL THAN YOURSELF, YOU MEAN!" But the face turned slowly toward Illbane. "WHAT SPELLS DO YOU WORK, SAGE?"

"Charms to calm the troubled waters, O Spirit—and I pray you, be calmed indeed! My apprentice does not yet know all the spells . . ."

"APPRENTICE?" The spirit turned back to stare down at Yocote.

"Less than fully accomplished, I fear," Yocote said in chagrin, hiding his fear. "I pray you, O Mighty Wave, let us recover what we have lost to your immensity!"

"What *I* have lost, he means!" Culaehra stepped forward, coincidentally between Yocote and the wave. "It was my carelessness by which it fell to your bosom!"

"Your good judgment, you mean!" For a moment Illbane was the stern disciplinarian again. "He had to choose between the gold and a comrade's life, O Spirit! He chose the comrade's life, and let the gold fall to you!"

Yocote stared up at the wave, trembling and aghast. Illbane had just told the spirit that it had missed the eating of a living person!

But the sage seemed to have judged well; the wave said, rumbling rather than thundering, "I dislike the taste of flesh, and must praise you for letting the only dead thing fall to me. Yet if you seek to command me, I shall take all the living together!"

"Forgive, O Mighty Water!" Yocote called. "I have only recently learned the shaman's language, and am still uncertain as to which voice to use with which entity! I did not know the waters have a spirit; I thought them devoid of life of their own."

The spirit peered more closely. "Of course—you are a gnome, so would think that only rock and earth have spirits. Do you know your mistake now?"

"I do," Yocote said fervently. "Oh, be most sure that I do!"

"Please, O Spirit!" Lua stepped forward, holding up her hands in supplication. "Take pity! Give us back what we have lost!"

"Pity!" the spirit boomed. "What would the flood know of pity?"

"Water is life," Lua replied. "We speak of peace and mercy flowing in imitation of it. Please relent, please give up what you have taken!"

"Give it up?" the water roared in a sudden upthrust, and skeletons danced in its flow, mixed in with waterlogged stumps, boulders, ironbound wheels, broken pottery, worn stone axes, chipped bronze spearheads, and all manner of other castoffs. With the voice of the flow, it thundered, "HERE IS WHAT YOU ASK! ALL THE SKELETONS OF THE DROWNED, ALL THE REFUSE THAT THE RIVERS HAVE BROUGHT TO ME FOR CENTURIES! SHALL I THROW YOU THESE?"

The gnome-maid shuddered, crying "No!" in tones of such distress that the upthrust subsided on the instant. "Thank you, O Water," she sighed with relief. "I do not even ask that you raise the drowned to the surface—only that you allow one of us to dive down to fetch it."

"Lua, no!" Yocote cried in alarm.

Culaehra cast him a puzzled frown. "It would not be her who dives."

But the spirit was demanding, "Give me reason!"

"Because the gold is not ours," Lua said simply. "It would not even suffice for us to dig up more gold to replace it; this very gold is the sacrifice we take to Agrapax the Ulin in fulfillment of a vow King Oramore made to him years ago."

"You bear it for the king?" the spirit asked. "How foolish! Why do you do his work for him?"

"Because he is twenty years late in the task," Lua replied, "and fears the Ulin's wrath."

"Wisely so!"

"And because we did not trust him not to change his mind and bring the gold back to his castle when we were gone," Culaehra explained.

"Did you not!" The spirit turned to regard him. "Why did you take others' burdens on yourself?"

"Because—it was right." Culaehra spread his hands, searching for words to explain it. "Because the same wicked councillor who persuaded him to forget his vow also persuaded him to grind his peasants down lower than his hounds. It would have been wrong to pass by, when we could bring about a change."

"Yes, that was our intent," Yocote said.

"Fair words, for one who sought to command a spirit!" the wave rumbled.

"I *said* I was sorry!" Yocote cried.

"Still, I cannot censure when the intention was noble," the wave rumbled. "Very well, you may dive within my waters to seek your gold. I shall withhold any grasping tendrils or menacing water-dwellers; I shall see you return safely to the surface. But be quick!" And with that last admonition, the spirit sank, the waters flattening again with a huge roar. The companions leaped back from the reaching waves, staring at the surging surface that was suddenly only a lake again.

Yocote went limp with a huge sigh of relief. "Thank heavens! Your pardon, my friends—I mistook my spell!"

"An easy mistake to make, but quite understandable," Illbane assured him. "Never seek to command the elements, for each has a spirit. Indeed, never seek to command where you can petition. Now—who will dive?"

"I shall," Culaehra and Lua said in one voice, then turned to stare at one another.

"*You*, little sister?" Kitishane stared, too.

"Women's bodies are better suited for diving," Lua said, "if there are no dangers to fight off, if it is only a matter of going down to fetch something, then coming up—and gnomes are far better divers than humans, if the waters are underground."

"I would not know how to swim where the only light is the water about me," Kitishane admitted reluctantly.

Culaehra scowled. "I do not like the sound of danger within it."

"There is no danger unless the chest lies deeper than I can swim," Lua assured him. "The water itself has promised us that."

"It is all true," Yocote said, then visibly plucked up his nerve and stepped to the edge of the water. He made passes with his hands, chanting.

"Yocote, no!" Lua cried, running toward him—but Illbane stopped her with a hand on her shoulder.

"He only asks the water how deeply the chest lies, and where. Culaehra, give her a coil of rope. Gnome-maid, tie an end through one of the chest's handles, then leave it where it lies and bring the other end to us. Let Culaehra's be the back that bends to haul the gold ashore."

Culaehra stepped to the pack, drew forth the coil, then handed it to her. "I lost it. It is certainly my place to draw it up."

Lua took the rope, nodding. "As you will, then."

Yocote finished chanting, and huge bubbles floated up, bursting off to their left, perhaps fifty feet out.

"The chest lies there," Yocote said, then counted bursting bubbles. "One . . . two . . . three . . . four . . . five . . . six! It lies six fathoms down."

"That is easily within my depth." Lua stripped off her furs, standing before them in her shift, but not standing long; she waded through the little waves till she was waist deep, then dove and swam.

"There!" Yocote called, and Lua kicked her heels high, then disappeared beneath the waves.

"You do not seem at all concerned," Kitishane said caustically.

"Concerned? I am." Yocote stared at the spot where Lua had disappeared, eyes fixed with an intensity that seemed to will her safe return. "But I cannot argue with her decision to go. Gnomes are good swimmers and good divers in underground water, but we have always known that the women can dive deeper and more safely than the men—so long as there are no huge fish to fight, or mermen, or buried snags to catch and hold."

"Can we trust the—" Kitishane bit her lip in time to keep from saying the words aloud. Surely they could trust the water spirit, when it had spared their lives—but voicing the question might have angered the elemental and moved it to revenge. She held to Yocote's shoulder, meaning comfort and not realizing that she was seeking reassurance until she felt the little man wince under her hand.

"Here, maiden." Culaehra offered his great paw. She took it gratefully. "Squeeze as hard as you please," he rumbled, and she did.

The water broke in a small fountain, and Lua jetted halfway out, gasping in a huge breath. She fell back into the water and struck off swimming toward them. Yocote cried out and waded into the water to catch her up in his arms in relief, then turned quickly away to limit himself to holding her arm and helping her through the little waves.

"You found it, then?" Illbane asked, and Lua nodded, gasping and holding up the end of the rope. Culaehra took it and began to draw.

CHAPTER 18

Culaehra hauled, and the pack erupted from the water. He pulled it ashore, water streaming off its leather sides. "Quickly! Is it damaged?" he cried, tearing the flap open.

"Peace, warrior," Yocote said. "Water cannot harm gold, neither salt nor fresh. If the chest is not broken, the metal is safe."

Culaehra's panic ebbed; he threw back the flap and opened the lid of the chest without wrenching it. Sure enough, the golden coins gleamed in the candlelight, unspilled and unspoiled. He sagged with relief. "I have not yet failed in my promise."

"You have not," Illbane agreed. "However, we must still bring the chest to the Wondersmith."

Culaehra sighed, closed the chest, latched it, pulled the leather up about it and buckled the flap, then stood, heaving the burden up to his back again. "Well, it will be a long climb, but I am pleased to have this load on my back nonetheless. Lead on, gnome-folk."

Yocote turned away, but Illbane stayed him with a touch of his staff. "Not that way—not upward."

The gnome turned back to him, frowning. "How, then?"

"Take us to the lake of molten rock."

Yocote and Lua both stared at him, rigid. Then Lua said, "How did you know of that lake, Illbane?"

"He knows many things," Yocote told her, "very many, and I am not surprised that he knows of that. But Illbane, that place is very dangerous!"

"It is indeed," Illbane returned, "but we will not come so close to it as that."

"We need not," Yocote said sourly. "The heat will bake us long before we see its glow, and if that is not enough, the bad air will choke us!"

"Not even so close as that, Yocote," Illbane said, smiling. "We shall find what we seek before danger rises."

"The noise is horrendous," Lua protested. "That horrible clanging will break our ears."

Culaehra frowned, puzzled. "How can rock be molten? And why would it make a clanging sound?"

"Rock, too, melts if the fire is hot enough," Yocote assured him, "even as iron comes running out of rocks when charcoal burns beneath it. As to the clanging, I have no idea what makes it."

"You shall discover it," Illbane told them. "Come then, Yocote— lead us past this lake, to hotter water."

"As you will," Yocote sighed, and turned to lead the way with an anxious Lua beside him. Culaehra glanced at Illbane, decided he didn't like the old man's smile, then bent his back under the load and followed his diminutive guides.

They threaded through subterranean passageways all that day and the next, sleeping around a campfire of torches that stayed burning but never shortened. Now and again the narrow corridor opened into caves—some large, some small—then closed about them again. Twice they paced long galleries, and Culaehra and Kitishane marveled at the paintings of animals that cavorted on the walls, seeming almost to dance in the torchlight.

"Who made these?" Kitishane asked, her voice hushed.

"Our ancestors tell us only that it was men who painted them, long ago," Yocote replied. "We do not know why they did so strange a thing."

"Men's deeds are frequently unexplainable," Kitishane said, and followed the gnomes, leaving Culaehra to scowl at her back.

Onward they went, through night divided only by the light of their torches. Culaehra did not realize how much warmer it had become until the first time he wiped his forehead. Then he stared at the sweat on his hand and felt fear coil through him. Was there truly a lake of molten rock? But there was no way to avoid it—and no way to know why Illbane wanted to go there. Of course, Culaehra could have asked, but he felt certain Illbane would only tell him to wait and see. Onward he strode, following the gnomes.

Toward the end of that day, they began to hear the clanging. It was distant and muffled, as if by layers of rock, but it was insistent as a heartbeat. It would sound several times, then lapse, then sound again, over and over for an hour or more at at time. Then it would stop for a while, but would unaccountably start up again.

Culaehra was tempted to say that they were nearing the heart of the mountain, a heart that was ill, but he glanced at his companions' faces and thought better of it.

They spent another night in the rocky tunnel, camping at a place where it broadened almost into a cave. They piled several torches together to boil water and for the comfort that light gave amidst all that darkness, but they certainly did not need it for warmth.

Mercifully, the clanging did not sound the whole night.

They woke, broke their fast, then marched onward, sweat streaming from every pore as the heat grew worse and worse. Culaehra had to remind himself that Illbane had said they would not actually come to the molten lake—but halfway through the morning the gnome stopped where the tunnel branched. "To our left lies the path around the Forge," he said, "but if you wish to see it, we must go right."

Kitishane frowned. "What is the 'Forge'?"

"The lake of liquid rock of which I have told you. The gnomes and dwarfs alike call it the 'Forge of Agrapax,' because there is an old legend that it once was the fire for the god's smithy—pure silliness, of course."

"How close would we have to come to see it?" Culaehra asked.

"Close enough to be very hot, not close enough to burn. It is a sight to overawe, they say." Yocote fairly quivered, his eyes gleaming.

Culaehra recognized the signs and smiled. "But you have never seen it, is that it?"

"Never," Yocote confirmed, "and I would most surely like to."

Culaehra turned to Illbane. "Is it important for a shaman?"

"Very important," the sage told him.

Kitishane smiled. "Then let us see."

Yocote laughed and leaped, knocking his heels together. "Then let us go!" He turned away and strode smartly up the right-hand tunnel. The companions followed, only Lua hanging back in misgiving.

The heat grew worse and worse as the tunnel climbed. Several times Culaehra touched the rock carefully, ready to snatch his hand away, but it never grew truly hot. Finally, they came out onto a broad lip of rock and found themselves in a huge cavern, lit by a ruddy glow.

"Carefully now." Yocote lay down on his belly and crawled forward till his face thrust over the edge. He gasped and froze, staring.

Curiosity triumphed. Culaehra shed his pack, lay down, and crawled forward; so did Kitishane and, after a few minutes, even Lua. Only Illbane stepped near the edge, leaning heavily on his staff.

The caldron seethed below them, glowing red. It was the full width of the cavern, a roiling expanse of thick, viscous liquid. Here and there it mounded into huge bubbles, which swelled and burst. Culaehra stared, spellbound, and might have stayed so for an hour or more if it hadn't been for the blast of heat that struck his face on an updraft. He pulled back quickly, and so did the rest. They stared at one another, shivering in spite of the temperature. "If ever there was a home for demons," Culaehra finally said, "that is it!"

"Hotter than any furnace." Yocote's habitual self-possession seemed shaken. "No wonder they call it Agrapax's Forge!"

As if it had heard him, the whole cavern suddenly reverberated with a clang that seemed to engulf them all. It went on for several minutes, three clangs, a pause, then four or five, a pause, then some more. At last it stopped, the echoes fading away, and the companions stared at each other, pale and shaken. "It couldn't really be . . ." Kitishane stammered.

"Could it?" Yocote asked.

"Not in here, no." Illbane beckoned. "Come."

He led them down from the lip of rock, back into the sloping tunnel, and they gasped with relief as the heat abated. Culaehra was amazed—only minutes ago he had been thinking how hot this tunnel was, and now it seemed cool!

Illbane stopped at a branching of the way. "Through here."

Yocote stopped, staring. The tunnel they had climbed slanted downward to the left; this one led off to the right, level but turning. "This was not here when we came by! I never saw it!"

"Never saw it, though it was here," Illbane agreed. "We would not see it now, if Agrapax the smith had not become curious about us."

"But generations of gnomes have passed this way—I can see their signs! Dwarfs, too! How could a door to Agrapax's smithy be here, and they not know it?"

"Because dwarfs and gnomes are natural things underground, and part and parcel of the stone and ore that Agrapax knows and loves so well," Illbane explained. "But human beings belowground are very much out of place; we have aroused wonder in the Wondersmith. I doubt not that he wishes to see who has come so near his domain, and knows that the natural curiosity of our species will draw us in."

"He judges me wrong, then!" Culaehra said. "Murrain take you, Illbane, for you have taught me fear!"

"I only reminded you of it; you had learned it in your childhood," the sage said absently, and led them into the branch. The clanging began again, seeming to sound all about them.

Suddenly, the tunnel opened out, leading them to a huge archway. The clanging was louder now, much louder, and the cavern beyond was lit with a sullen glow, like that of the molten rock, but highlighted and shot through with the bright yellow and orange of flame, with flashes of something much brighter. The companions froze, for through that archway they saw two mighty legs wide apart, each as thick as an old oak, hairy and scarred with burns here and there. The feet wore sandals that were bound with crossed leather straps, up as high as they could see.

Illbane stepped up to the edge of the archway, beckoning them forward. Slowly and with fear coiling within them, they came, and found themselves staring up, up, at a torso that seemed far too large for the legs, shoulders far too broad for the torso, and arms as thick as the legs, knotted with muscle and gleaming with sweat.

Above all was a huge head with a grizzled beard and bright eyes that reflected the fire. It was a homely face, smudged with soot and filled with the intensity of the fanatic.

He stood three times the height of a man, surrounded by neat stacks of metals and gems and other materials that receded into the gloom of that huge cavern. He worked before a forge that bubbled with molten rock. As they watched, he took tongs to hold a bar of metal just above that liquid fire, raising his other hand to pull on a beam that must surely have been the trunk of a century-old tree. When he did, flame roared up from the molten rock to surround the metal bar. The giant smith released the handle; the roaring and the flame ceased as he transferred the bar back to an anvil that stood taller than a man, as large as a rowboat, made of black metal that must surely have weighed a ton or more.

He worked in silence, his eyes glowing as he beat the bar into shape. Kitishane could have sworn he had not even noticed their entrance, that they were far beneath his notice—but finally he set the bar aside to cool and spoke in a voice that reverberated through the great cavern like the rumble of an earthquake. "What are you doing here, Ohaern?" He turned to glare down at Illbane. "Why must you come blundering into my smithy? Isn't it enough for you to spend your centuries bedding my wife?"

The companions stared at Illbane, thunderstruck.

But Illbane's face swelled with anger, and he spoke to the giant as though he were an interfering village gossip. "She was never your wife, Agrapax!"

"No, but she should have been, for there are precious few Ulin left, and we two are the mightiest of them. You stole her from me, mite!"

"I could not steal what you did not own! You never had any claim to her, nor should you have, for she could never have commanded your attention for long! Always, always, your mind would have drifted back to your forge, and off to your smithy you would go, to pursue your next project and leave her forlorn! No, never could you have been a true husband, for you were ever wed to your art!"

"The same old cant." The giant smith turned and spat into his forge. "The truth of it is that I am too ugly for any woman—except the one time when she wished to number the Wondersmith among her trophies. I am bandy-legged and lame, singed and squint-eyed, big-nosed and lumpen. Well, no matter—my metals love me, and I love my metals."

That last, Kitishane thought, was the only true claim. Well, no, the giant was homely, but certainly not ugly—and though his proportions were odd, those huge muscles exerted an attraction all their own. He was not the sort of man a woman would choose for a lover—but for a husband? Quite possibly, if he were not so bad-tempered.

For Culaehra, though, the effect was devastating. He was a man of action, a warrior who had always felt strangely superior to the smiths whose weapons he used—but here was a smith who could have crushed him absentmindedly, flattened him with one stroke of the huge hammer and gone back to shaping his iron, scarcely missing a beat! Here was a smith who had so little regard for anything but his art that he might just have done it, too, had Culaehra come there alone.

But he had not—and that made it worse. To feel himself dwarfed by a smith was bad enough, but to find that the teacher who had disciplined him and trained him, and whom he had dared defy, was the fabled Ohaern, made him feel a total fool for ever having had the temerity even to think of rebellion! A perverse desire rose in him to deny it, to tell himself that this oldster was only an ordinary mortal named after the great hero. But to hear Agrapax himself address the man as an equal, almost a familiar—though a disliked one—and to hear Ohaern respond in kind, daring to rebuke a god, made Culaehra's very soul seem to shrink within him. And, if he could have denied anything else, he certainly could not mistake the focus of their quarrel. Ohaern had been lover to an Ulin woman! His vagabond teacher Illbane had been, perhaps still *was*, her paramour!

Who could they be speaking of, but Rahani herself?

The mortal sage Illbane, whom he had tried so hard to regard as a contemptible old beggar, was consort to a goddess, to *the* goddess!

No. Not a goddess—an Ulin, Culaehra amended. Only an Ulin. After all, Illbane had said so—and what mortal man could know better than Ohaern?

"I should still like to strike you down for the blasphemy of loving an Ulin woman, Ohaern," the smith rumbled. He drew forth another bar of metal and inspected its surface.

"Strike, then." Ohaern smiled. "Strike, if you are willing to suffer Rahani's displeasure; strike, if you are willing to risk the certainty of never seeing or hearing her again."

The smith snarled and thrust the bar into the forge.

"Strike," Ohaern said, in a voice lower and, in some way, almost sympathetic. "Strike, if you dare risk the displeasure of Lomallin's ghost."

Agrapax stared at the dull glow of the metal. "Ghost or not, Lomallin is still mighty."

"Ghost or not," Ohaern replied, "you would still rather not risk losing the liking of one of the few Ulins who befriended you."

Agrapax shrugged impatiently. "Lomallin befriended everyone."

"Even me," Ohaern said.

Agrapax stood staring into the fire. At last he turned to give the sage a curt nod. "He did, so I shall speak to you with courtesy, for you are the friend of a friend. Tell me, then, Ohaern—why have you come here? Why have you sought me out?"

Ohaern nodded at the biggest of his companions. "This warrior is named Culaehra. He has taken upon himself the fulfillment of a promise made to you by another."

The Ulin turned his gaze directly upon Culaehra. "Taken another's risk and burden when you did not need to? What manner of fool are you, mortal?"

At that moment Culaehra felt very much a fool indeed. "A human fool, great Agrapax."

A gleam of approval showed in the smith's eye. "He has a civil tongue, at least, and perhaps the beginnings of wisdom. Whose promise is this you have taken up?"

"A—A king, some weeks' journey from here," Culaehra said. "His name is Oramore."

"Oramore . . . Oramore . . ." The smith looked away, frowning and rolling the name on his tongue. "The name has no meaning for me. Still, there are not so many humans who seek me out, that I should have forgotten him completely. What was his promise?"

"To give you the first fruits of his pastures and his fields, O Wondersmith."

"Why would he promise me that?"

"In repayment for invulnerable armor and magical weapons, and the wisdom to use them well, so that he might protect his people from barbarians and bandits."

"Ah! The breastplate, helm, and greaves of bright bronze, alloyed with traces of antimonium and adamant!" Agrapax nodded. "Yes, I remember it well. But he is somewhat late with his first fruits, is he not? That must have been several years ago."

"Twenty, at least," Culaehra said, his voice seeming very small.

"Twenty? Yes, that is not so much. But first fruits of grain and meat do not last so long as that, do they?"

"They do not." Culaehra's voice seemed still smaller to himself. "He sold them all for gold."

"For gold!" The Wondersmith's voice rang harshly. "Then he broke his promise? Do you tell me he broke a promise to an Ulin?"

"I do." Culaehra's heart raced with fear.

"The more fool he, then! Had he no notion of the consequences that fall on the head of a man who breaks faith with his god?"

Now Ohaern spoke. "An emissary from Bolenkar came to him, great Agrapax, and so bedazzled and befuddled him with spangling words and curling lies that he forgot to think of consequence."

"Bolenkar? What thing is that?"

"The eldest of Ulahane's half-human children."

"Ah, the Ulharl brat! Yes, I remember him now! Ever skulking about his father's halls, sulky and brooding. Has he come to power, then?"

Culaehra could only stare, amazed at the Ulin's lack of awareness.

"He has," Ohaern said. "He seeks to take up the mantle of his father and purge his hatred of Ulahane by surpassing him."

"Surpassing him!" Agrapax snapped upright, staring. "The audacity of the creature! He seeks to slay all the younger races, then?"

"That is his intent, I am sure," Ohaern said evenly.

All the companions felt their stomachs shrink and churn within them. They had never allowed themselves to feel the reality of the Ulharl's plan before.

"Why then, no wonder this human king was bamboozled! I should have given him tin ears, not bronze armor. And *you* have taken it upon yourself to right what the agent of Bolenkar sent wrong?" The huge eyes burned into Culaehra's again.

"I . . . I have," the warrior said, faltering.

"Great folly was that, to take on such a burden when you did not need to! Why did you do it?"

"Why . . . I . . . I could not say," Culaehra stammered.

"Could not say? Of course you could! You have lips and tongue, and lungs to drive the breath past them both! Speak, man! Why did you undertake to mend this broken promise?"

Culaehra could only stare up into those huge, bitter eyes and search his heart.

"Speak!" the Ulin commanded again.

"It . . . it was the right thing to do!" was all Culaehra could say.

"Right! How? Why?"

"Because . . . a promise must be kept." Words began to come. "Because, in breaking his promise to you, he broke faith also with his peasants, simple folk like those who bred me, like I myself! He ground them into the dirt they ploughed, to squeeze himself a few more pieces of gold! They lived in wretched hovels, while he built his castle high and adorned it with every luxury his wife could find! No, great Agrapax, that was wrong, pure wrong!" Culaehra realized he had finished with a shout, and stood stiffly, trembling, as he stared up at the Ulin defiantly.

But Agrapax nodded, slowly and with approval. "So because you could see yourself in his peasants, you made him keep his promise. Tell me, how did you manage that?"

"By . . . by combat, great Agrapax. Personal combat."

"Combat! How could you win against him, who was armored and armed with my sword and armor?"

"Ohaern took them away," Culaehra said simply.

"Took them away!" The Wondersmith turned on the sage. "How did you manage that, O Mortal Smith?"

"I knew your work when I saw it," Ohaern answered. "I touched it with my staff and bade it fall away from any unworthy of it."

The Ulin's homely face split in a grin. Then he laughed, a rich booming, though somewhat rusty. "Well done, well done, Ohaern! Then, if you had been wrong and the man right, the armor would have stayed to shield him! Yes, wisely done!" He turned back to Culaehra. "So you, a peasant, defeated a king, and made him swear to keep his promise! But why did you not make him bring me the first fruits himself?"

"I did not trust him," Culaehra said simply.

Agrapax nodded. "Wise, especially with an agent of Bolenkar's beside him."

"Oh, Ohaern banished that one."

"To the grave, I hope." The smith slapped his thighs. "Well, then! Bravely done! You have undertaken to bring me the first fruits the king yielded to you—but they rotted long ago! No, I forgot—you said he sold them for gold! Where is it, then?"

"Here, great Agrapax." Culaehra swung the pack down and unbuckled the straps, then pulled out the chest, unlocked it, and threw back the lid.

The smith's breath rasped in as he gazed at the rich gold within. "Lovely, lovely! True gold, pure gold! It is a wonder your back did not break, young human, for pure gold is heavy, very heavy! Yes, when you said you had taken up the king's burden, you meant it quite truly, did you not?" He beckoned. "Hold it up to me!"

Culaehra bent, set himself, then straightened with a convulsive heave, managing to lift the treasure as high as his breast, then shoved with all his might to lift it high above his head. The Wondersmith reached down and took it from him; his fingers grazed Culaehra's palms, and the man trembled from the Ulin's touch.

But Agrapax did not notice. He held the chest up near his face, lifting a few bars out between thumb and forefinger. "Beautiful, beautiful indeed! You may tell the king his promise has been kept, far better than if he had brought me grain or cattle! Yes, this will adorn my most precious work, it will be the illumination of my art!"

His glance caught Yocote's stare. "Yes, gnome, I could have found it myself, purified it myself, far more easily than making arms and armor for that unworthy king—but he amused me at the time, with his deep concern for his people, and the gold is beautiful whatever its source!"

He turned back to Culaehra. "You deserve reward for this service, mortal. What do you want in return?"

Culaehra could only stare.

"Come, come, no human does service without reason!" the smith said impatiently. "What would you ask?"

"Why . . . nothing, great Agrapax." Culaehra found his voice again. "I did it because it was right, because I could not abide seeing the peasants so wronged; I brought it here because I did not trust the king. I never thought of asking recompense."

Agrapax frowned, then swung to Ohaern. "Is this true? Yes, I see it is, because you are fairly swollen with pride and your face glows! You have made a man out of this lump of flesh, have you not? You have made him a noble man, far more worthy to be a king than the one he defeated, for this man at least has come to some understanding of rightness for its own sake!"

He turned back to Culaehra. "But such rightness deserves armor to defend it, arms to enforce it! You are a warrior, you must desire steel! Speak, human! What would you have the Wonder-smith make for you? Ask!"

Culaehra stared, so amazed that his mind went blank.

CHAPTER 19

"Come, your kind is even more avaricious than the dragons!" Agrapax boomed. "I have offered you reward, mortal! Do not fear to ask!"

"I . . . I cannot," Culaehra stammered.

Kitishane stepped up close to him, muttering fiercely, "This is your chance, Culaehra! Ask what you will, and none will be able to beat you!"

That was the pebble that started the landslide. That Kitishane, whom he had wronged and assaulted, who should be afraid of him even without arms and doubly afraid to see him accoutered with an unbeatable sword, should urge him to ask! Her goodness and forgiveness overwhelmed him, and the warrior fell to his knees, head hanging, borne down by the majesty of the Ulin and the hidden greatness of the old vagabond who had become his master, shamed by the unassuming nobility of the woman who was his companion.

"What is this?" the Ulin rumbled. "A hero, sunk in self-contempt? That must not be!"

Something bumped into Culaehra's head; the pain stirred anger.

His head snapped up, eyes glaring, and he saw the smith's hand stretching down, forefinger touching his head. He froze, staring up into the giant's eyes as light seemed to explode in his head, and with it a vast understanding—how all things were ultimately bound together into one single whole, how nothing existed without the Creator's attention, how that attention was within and without everything that existed, or it could not exist. He suddenly understood that the smith and his metal were really akin, that the hammer that struck was truly a part of the anvil, that enemies were really two outthrusts of the same life-force, but tried to deny their kinship, that Evil was the denial of human nature as extension of the life-force, and that the life-force was an aspect of the Creator itself. He comprehended with astounding clarity that he had nothing to fear from Agrapax, for the smith understood the secret of kinship and would never strike down any but those who tried to deny it.

Then he reached up to touch Kitishane's hand and heard her gasp, and knew that she, of a sudden, understood as he did that the bonding of man and woman, the continual struggle to join two souls, was only a very small manifestation of that ultimate Union of All in the Creator, an attempt to realize anew the bond that had been struck from their minds at birth. Love seemed trivial next to that desire for union, somehow—but that very desire seemed also to be the true meaning of Love, to be the sum and total of it, the greatest and most all-embracing force that human beings could know.

"Culaehra . . ." she murmured, shaken, and he turned a radiant face up to smile at her.

"I was right," he breathed, "all along—I was right to want to love you, even though the manner of it was the crudest sort of denial of that rightness. Oh, the assault was wrong, it was all denial, but beneath it lay a twisted and convoluted craving for rightness."

"Have you found it now, then?" she quavered, her hand taut in his.

"Oh, yes! Yes, I have—or have found where it is, and can now begin to seek it."

"What nonsense they talk, the young who are still enslaved to desire!" the smith said to the sage.

But Ohaern shook his head, eyes shining upon his pupils. "There is as much desire in your crafting and your art, Agrapax, and it is ultimately desire for the same thing."

The smith looked down at him for a minute, then gave a snort of derision. "We all know what *you* desire, Ohaern! And at your age, too—you doddering rake!" He turned away before the sage could answer and said to the warrior, "*Now* do you know what you want?"

"Oh, yes," Culaehra said, his gaze still on Kitishane, then turned back to the Wondersmith. "I know now—and have gained it. Thank you, O Agrapax. I cannot thank you enough."

The Ulin stared down at him, amazed, then turned to Ohaern in disgust. "Why, how is this? Have you transformed him so well that he has not an ounce of greed left in him?"

"No—but you have turned that greed toward its true end, Agrapax. I must thank you for that."

The giant stared down at the sage, affronted. "You brought him here deliberately, Ohaern! You used me to forge him!"

"What greater accomplishment for the Wondersmith?" Ohaern challenged. "And who more fit to have wrought it?"

"Yes . . . perhaps." The Ulin stared down at the kneeling man in speculation. "Still, he is now so fired for Right and so filled with zeal that he is apt to charge out to seek and smite Bolenkar, unarmored and unready. We cannot waste our work in that fashion, can we, Ohaern?"

"We cannot," the sage agreed, "but he shall have no need of your swords, Agrapax, for I shall forge his blade."

"Forge!" Agrapax looked up, suddenly alert. "The Star Stone, you mean? It shall be the death of you, Ohaern!"

"Of my body, at least." Ohaern nodded, accepting. "That is the price I must pay, and well worth it, if the Starsword slays Bolenkar."

"You must not risk yourself!" Culaehra cried, before he realized the words were out of him.

Ohaern fixed him with a gaze at once proud and sad, but Agrapax ignored them both and turned to his forge. "Well, if he will supply your sword, mortal man, than I shall furnish your armor and shield. Retire out of my forge, all of you! Oh, you may stay, Ohaern—you still have something to learn about smithing, and you shall need to quite soon. Away, small ones!" He pointed at a small archway. "In there! Dine, drink, rest! Refresh yourselves and renew your strength, for this doddering sage shall lead you a weary chase yet! Come back when I call, but for now, get you gone!"

Then he frowned down at the metal, and they all felt the sudden lifting of the pressure of the Ulin's attention and knew he had forgotten them as surely as if they had never come to his smithy in the first place.

Yocote stepped forward, beckoning, and Culaehra finally rose to follow him, scowling to hide a vast feeling of relief—and an equally vast sense of exaltation. He followed Yocote—but did not let go of Kitishane's hand.

The gnome led the way through the archway, which narrowed into a tunnel that turned through a double bend to open out again into a fairly roomy cave. Torchlight cast their shadows on the wall behind the gnome; glancing back, Culaehra saw that Lua had brought the flaming brands with them.

Yocote turned about, hands on hips, to glare up at Culaehra. "How now, wolf's head! I think you have become even more a shaman than I!"

Culaehra stared at him in astonishment, then frowned, seeking within himself, and discovered that he had an understanding of arms and of enemies that was virtually instinctive now. "Perhaps," he said slowly, "but only as regards warfare and feats of arms." He smiled down at the gnome with genuine affection. "Fear not, Yocote—I can never be a rival to you."

The gnome stared, then stood stiff and belligerent, taken off guard—but Lua slipped her hand into his, and he glanced sideways at her, then back at Culaehra, still glaring, but with something more of understanding and acceptance now.

For a time, Culaehra merely sat staring into the torch flames and relishing the quiet glow, the sense of complete well-being that filled him so thoroughly that he felt it must be radiating from him; and Kitishane's hand in his only made the wholeness more perfect. Finally, he lifted his head and looked into her eyes—wide, still amazed, a little frightened, but altogether delighted, so that he could tell she shared at least something of his joy.

Finally, though, he realized that the clanging had begun again, had been going on for some time, brief bursts of it punctuated by the roaring he had heard in Agrapax's smithy. He realized that the Wondersmith was at his work again. The clanging was the hammer on the iron; the roaring was the blast of air through the forge. Culaehra wondered what a supersmith used for a bellows.

Turning, he saw Yocote pacing the chamber, hands behind his back, muttering to himself. At the fire, Lua was cooking something in a pot—stewed jerky, by the smell of it.

"The smith will be done soon enough," Culaehra said. "Be at peace, little brother."

Yocote's head snapped around, staring at the warrior. "I have not given you leave to call me that!"

His anger and distress struck Culaehra like a body blow; he was amazed to discover that he could feel the little man's emotions. "Your pardon, Yocote. I stated only what I now see to be true—that all men of all races are brothers, and any enmity between us is denial brought about by deception."

"That the differences are only on the surface, and the things we have in common are far more important?" Yocote frowned. "Well, I can accept that. But what begins this illusion that we are enemies, then?"

"The agents of Bolenkar," Culaehra said simply, "and our own vices, our selfishness and greed and need for someone to look down upon. Heaven knows we give him enough to work with!"

Yocote's gaze strayed; he frowned. "There is some sense in that," he said, and sat on his heels by the fire, staring into the flames and musing.

Kitishane squeezed Culaehra's hand; he turned to smile at her, not sure what he had done right, but not about to argue with the consequences.

When the stew was ready, they shared a meal. Afterward, they talked in low voices awhile, halting to listen when the clanging rang out, for beneath it they could hear the voice of the smith chanting in a language they did not know. Yocote in particular stared at the entrance to the tunnel with longing, straining his ears and trying to make sense of it, but failing. Culaehra felt a twinge of sympathy for him—so much to learn so short a distance away, and to have it denied! But there was nothing any of them could do to change that; the Wondersmith had banished them while he worked his magic.

Finally, they slept. After all, there was little else they could do.

They woke at Illbane's call, a gentle urging: "Come, it is time to rise! The Wondersmith is done with his forging, and we must go up into the world again!"

Culaehra was on his feet in an instant, and Yocote was almost as quick, but Illbane made them take time enough to break their fasts before they went. Yocote wolfed his food, chomping at the bit, and Culaehra was in little better mood, but both of the women seemed faintly amused by their impatience. Finally, they packed their leavings, and Illbane led them out through the tunnel.

The smithy was quiet now, only a seething murmur coming from the forge. Agrapax himself was nowhere to be seen.

"He has gone deeper into the bowels of the earth, to mine more of the rare minerals he used in this forging," Illbane explained.

But Culaehra scarcely heard him, scarcely saw anything but the breastplate, helmet, gauntlets, hip plates, greaves, and sandals that lay against a slab of rock in the center of the smithy. He came over to them slowly, reached out to touch them with reverence and awe. "These are objects of beauty! How could I wear them in war, Ohaern?"

"Call me Illbane, as first I told you to," the sage told him, "for I will always be Illbane to you. As to the armor, no blow will dent or mar it; you may wear it secure in the knowledge that its beauty will remain undimmed." But his eyes were shining again. Kitishane saw, and understood: the old Culaehra would never have seen beauty in anything, not even a woman's face and form. He would have seen them as objects of desire, but not of beauty.

Still, the armor was indeed beautiful. It lay glowing in the light of the forge and the torches, golden with inlays of silver wreathing about and across it. "What are those figures, Illbane?" Yocote asked, his voice hushed. "I would almost think them to be flowers and leaves, if they had not so many straight edges."

"They are flora, even as you have said," Illbane replied, "but the plants are herbs and simples of great power. The straight edges are runes, marks that stand for words, and that only the wisest of shamans yet know."

"I must learn them, then!"

"You shall," Illbane promised, "and when you do, you shall read in that breastplate and shield spells of protection that shall amaze you by their power." Then, to Culaehra, "Come, put on the wondrous bronze! Agrapax is already impatient to begin his next work, and will be wroth to find us if we are still here upon his return."

"Put it on?" Culaehra looked up, astounded.

"Of course, put it on! Agrapax did not forge it only that folk might stare at it and exclaim upon its beauty! Put it on, Culaehra— he made it to ward you when you battle Bolenkar!"

"But . . . but . . . should I not at least carry it until battle looms?" Culaehra found himself strangely hesitant to wear such wondrous armor. "Surely it will be too heavy!"

"If it is, then I have failed in driving you to strengthen your body to its fullest! Besides, be assured—*this* armor will seem almost weightless upon him for whom it was forged! Put it on, Culaehra— it will keep you warm in the cold, and you will need that soon. It will cool you in the heat, too, and you will need that later. You will scarcely notice its weight, but it will lend you its strength."

Slowly, almost shyly, the warrior buckled on the enchanted plates of bronze. Kitishane stepped forward to help; the gnomes stepped up to fasten his greaves. Illbane himself set the helm grandly atop his head, its crest waving proudly as it fell down to guard his neck. Kitishane gasped at the sight. "Oh, Culaehra! You look as grand as a hero from the fabled tales of Dariad's war!"

"Dariad never wore such armor as this," Illbane assured her. "Come now, let us seek the surface again! A hero you look to be, Culaehra, and a hero you are within—but you cannot become one truly until you have faced and overcome your challenges, and they await you in the light of the sun!"

"Take me to them, then," Culaehra said, his voice quivering with impatience, and Illbane turned away to lead them back into the tunnel from which they had first come into the smithy.

Their way branched often, but seemed short enough to Culaehra and Kitishane, for they talked in soft voices as they climbed the ever-ascending ramp of the twisting tunnels. They spoke of their childhoods and their maturity within their home clans, of their enemies and their few allies, of the experiences they had shared and those they might have, if they had grown in the same village. They spoke of the war Bolenkar sought to loose upon the younger races, they spoke of the old tales of the Ulin, they spoke of everything and nothing, and were amazed that they could speak of so much and never tire of it. Lua gazed up at them with misty delight, and Yocote cast them occasional spiteful glances of envy. His one consolation was that they did not talk about themselves as a couple, but even that was undermined by the feeling that they did not need to.

The way was far shorter than that by which they had entered the underground realm, for they came into a small sunlit cave just as they were growing weary with a full day's exertion. They all squinted in pain, their eyes no longer accustomed to the brightness of daylight, and the gnomes quickly tied on their goggles again.

"Sit and dine," Illbane bade them, "and when your eyes are once more comfortable with the light that fills this cave, we will go out to see the sunshine itself."

"Well thought." Culaehra nodded, and sat by the torches as Lua set them in the center of the cave. "But I cannot waste time, Illbane. You have given me a mission now, and I must be off to the south to find and slay the monster Ulharl!"

Kitishane looked up at him in alarm and shivered, then realized that there was a chill in the air, and Culaehra was rubbing his hands not in expectation, but to warm them by the little fire.

"All in good time, eager hero," Illbane told him, amused. "You would be foolish indeed to run into battle before you are ready."

"But I must find Bolenkar before *he* is ready!"

"You can only do that by assembling strong forces to lead against him. Your companions will do well enough for a beginning, but they are not an army in themselves. Even they, though, grow chill in this northern climate."

Culaehra looked up, startled, and saw Kitishane and the gnomes shivering. "The armor *does* warm me! I should have realized, when my hands felt chilled! Forgive me, friends!" He started up. "I shall go kill a bear or two, and bring you some furs!"

"Nay, peace, my hero!" Kitishane stopped him with a hand, laughing. "Accustom your eyes to the brightness, and do not go hunting without your archers beside you! As to the furs, Lua and I have packed them away, when we shed them as the caverns became hot about us. Warm your hands while we dress!"

They left Culaehra to stir the stew while they pulled furs on over their tunics and leggings, then ate in hooded coats of fur. When they were done and their leavings cleaned, the companions all pulled on gloves, even Culaehra, who also needed boots, which Kitishane had thoughtfully supplied. Thus equipped, they stepped out to view what was left of the day.

They gasped with pain as they stepped out of the cave, squinting their eyes against the brightness, then slowly opening their lids—and gasped again with pleasure at the sight. They were still in the mountains, and the golden sunlight of late afternoon lent a glow to evergreens decked with whiteness. It was snow, and lay deep on the ground as well, and on the rocks all about them.

"Winter has come while we have been underground!" Kitishane cried. "Have we been below so long as that, Illbane?"

"Only a few days, as you know, Kitishane," the sage replied, "but winter has been growing about us as we have marched northward, and has come all the quicker up here in the mountains. It will only grow colder from this point onward, for when we come down from these hills, we will not come very far; the northern land to which we go is a high plateau, and we have yet some farther distance to go."

"To the north?" Culaehra bleated. "That is the wrong way, Illbane! I must go south now!"

"You must have a sword first, Culaehra, and I cannot forge it for you until I have found the Star Stone. Come, let us march!" He led the way off toward the north again. Culaehra stared after him, thunderstruck, then lowered his head and slogged off through the snow after the sage, muttering darkly. His companions followed, sharing glances of amusement.

They only marched for a few hours more that day; sunset came quickly, and they were happy to camp under a huge fir. Culaehra chafed at the delay, ready to march out into the night in his enchanted armor. "I must go south, Illbane!"

"In good time, Culaehra," the sage returned, and sipped from his spoon.

Good time certainly was not the next day; they set off toward the north again, and Illbane sent the hero in his enchanted armor ahead, to forge a path through the drifts for them all. Culaehra grumbled continually, but not at the cold. "I go the wrong way, Illbane! Bolenkar lies to the south!"

"So does sunshine and warmth, Culaehra. Can you not suffer the chill for a few weeks more?"

"A few weeks!" the hero bawled in distress, but Kitishane caught up with him and squeezed his hand. "Patience, big man. I am not eager to see you go to brave dangers, but even less eager to see you without a sword."

Culaehra looked up at her in surprise, then subsided into grumbling as he turned back to slogging ahead. But he glanced up at her again and could not help smiling before he set to his work.

That work became harder, for the wind blew more and more briskly. Then snow began to fall, but Culaehra felt it only on his arms; even his toes stayed warm in the bronze sandals the Wondersmith had fashioned for him. Kitishane slipped around to his back, letting him break the wind for her, and the gnomes followed close behind her. Illbane came last, striding through the drifts with his head high, long grizzled hair whipping in the wind, disdaining to show any sign of chill.

That night around the campfire, Culaehra seemed resigned to his fate; he laughed and chatted with the others, replying to Yocote's sour remarks with gibes of his own, then lay down by the fire, reminding Yocote to waken him for his watch—but when his companions breathed with the deepness of sleep and the gnome had fallen deeply into his trance, Culaehra rolled slowly to the side, farther and farther out of the gnome's line of sight, so slowly and gradually that he did not disturb the little shaman's contemplation of whatever arcane mystery occupied his meditations. When he was sure he was far enough out of sight, Culaehra climbed to his feet and moved quietly into the darkness beneath the evergreen trees. He picked his way away from the campsite with stealthy movements until the light of the fire had disappeared behind him. Then he increased his pace until he came out from beneath the pines onto a broad, windswept slope, stark beneath the starlight. There he drew a long breath, grinning at the feeling of freedom. He looked up to find the North Star, turned his back upon it and set off toward the south, walking quickly.

His path twisted between giant boulders. He set himself against the wind, thinking that he would welcome a brief respite among those rocks. He stepped in among them, relaxed as the wind's pressure let up, turned and turned again to follow the shallowest depth of snow, then braced himself as he saw the end of the outcrop ahead. He stepped out into the wind—and stopped dead in his tracks, staring at the black-robed, white-haired figure before him.

Illbane smiled, amused. "How rude of you, Culaehra, to leave your friends without a word of parting!"

"How . . . how did you come here, Illbane?" Culaehra stammered.

"Very quickly, I assure you."

"But *how*?" Then Culaehra realized how useless that question was with a shaman, and changed his tack. "How did you know I had gone? You were asleep!"

"Never so deeply asleep that I would not know where you were," Illbane assured him. "I shall be alert to your every movement from this night forth, Culaehra, no matter how deeply asleep I may be! Come now, let us go back to our friends, for it would be uncivil indeed to leave them alone in this wild land."

There wasn't the slightest trace of threat in his voice, but he set both hands upon his staff as he said it, and the gleam of anticipation in his eye was enough to remind Culaehra how poorly he had fared against his teacher in the past. For a moment, though, the feel of the magical armor on his body was almost enough to tempt him to resist, and the memory of the thousand drubbings that staff had given him sparked enough anger to drive him—but he remembered also how he had come to have that armor, and how Illbane had stood by him in danger, and realized that he could no longer summon even mild dislike for the old man. He sighed and capitulated. "As you will have it, Illbane. Back to the campfire, then."

The sage laughed, clapped him on the shoulder, and went with him back into the outcrop of boulders.

CHAPTER 20

T hat was not his last try, of course. With all the fervor of the penitent, Culaehra now burned to make amends for all his past wickedness, even at the peril of his life. He tried cajoling, nagging, and exhorting Illbane for hours on end as they marched.

"The deed must be done, Illbane! The younger races cannot wait! Every hour that we tarry, Bolenkar's agents are corrupting another gnome, another elf, another human! Every day of delay yields another battle, building to another war! We must go south!"

"We must go south when we have a chance to win," Illbane corrected. "Let it ride, Culaehra. If you strike before you are ready, Bolenkar will win, and there will be a thousand times more misery than arises while you wait for your sword!"

But Culaehra would not let it ride—he kept after Illbane until Yocote finally snapped at him to stop, for he was boring them all to the breaking point.

The next day, Culaehra started in on Illbane again, nagging and pleading until the sage finally rounded on him and said, "Go south without that sword and the final readiness it bestows, and you die yourself, with nothing accomplished and nothing to show for your life, Culaehra! Do you truly wish that?"

"I certainly do not!" Kitishane stepped up to him wide-eyed. "Don't you dare to make me a widow before you have even made me a wife!"

Culaehra turned to her in surprise.

Kitishane blushed and lowered her gaze. "Well, perhaps you had not planned to . . . but I had flattered myself that—"

"Of course I had! Or desired to, more than anything in my life. Though I had no certainty you would agree if I asked."

Her eyes lighted with merriment and delight; she tossed her head and invited, "Try."

"I dare not," Culaehra said through thick lips. "I dare not ask until all this turmoil is done. Then, if Bolenkar lies dead and I live, I may dare to ask."

Kitishane quivered with a sudden surge of desire that amazed her, and pressed close to his arm. "I cannot bear to think of you lying dead! But perhaps I spoke foolishly, about waiting to be a wife—"

"You do not," Illbane said sternly. "Wed him or bed him, and you weaken his stroke out of fear for your fate. You must remain a maiden, Kitishane, a maiden and an archer until this war is aborted or ended. Then you may begin your world, when it is new."

Kitishane lowered her gaze. "It will be hard, Illbane, hard to wait."

"Never let me say that there are no wonders in the world," Culaehra breathed, his gaze fast upon her, and he said nothing more about going south for the rest of that day.

That night, though, he tried to escape again.

Once more he waited until everyone slept; once more he crept out by inches; once more he climbed to his feet and ran silently through the night. This time, though, he stopped at a rocky outcrop, then walked backward very carefully, setting his feet in his own footsteps until he neared a tall pine. There he crouched, jumped high, caught a limb and pulled himself up. He climbed twenty feet, then settled himself next to the trunk with one arm around it, waiting for morning.

He had no chance to wait nearly so long, though. In less than half an hour a huge bear came ambling across the snow. Culaehra watched it with curiosity—what manner of bear would be abroad in winter? And what had wakened it from its long winter's sleep?

Hunger!

Suddenly, Culaehra's curiosity was anything but mild. He watched the bear with the first tendrils of fear snaking through his vitals as the beast meandered here, meandered there—and came to his tree!

The bear stood as if stretching itself, then looked up through the boughs. Its gaze met Culaehra's. He stared back in horrified fascination, then found himself whispering, "Go away, bear! Go away!"

It was a very contrary bear. It set its huge claws into the bark; it began to walk up the trunk.

The fear gripped Culaehra's belly now. He ached for the sword Illbane had promised him, but not having it, he slid his common sword from its sheath.

The bear reached the limbs and began to use them as a sort of ladder, pulling itself up on a branch, then catching its huge feet on the one below. Higher and higher it climbed, closer and closer. Culaehra glanced up; he might climb another five feet before the trunk became too thin to bear them both. He glanced at the next tree over, wondering if he could jump the intervening space without falling to his death. He decided that he could not and turned back, his eyes going cold as he set himself for the battle. If he must die, better to die fighting than running—and he might not die at all, if Agrapax's armor was as virtuous against bear's claws as against men's swords.

The bear climbed a little higher; its head was just below his foot, and Culaehra readied himself to kick when it gained one more branch. But the bear gazed up at him, its eyes neither hungry nor angry. Its muzzle opened but it did not snarl, only said, "Come down, Culaehra. There is no point in your spending the night in so uncomfortable a place when I will only find you in the morning."

The voice was Illbane's.

Culaehra sat, staring. Then he unfolded himself and began to climb down, cursing.

The bear listened with interest as it backed down the trunk, watching him. When Culaehra dropped into the snow again, the bear said, "Let us go back to the campfire; you must be chilled to the bone."

"No, Agrapax's armor keeps me warm, even as you said it would." Culaehra fell in beside the huge animal. "I am rather stiff, though."

"Not surprising, in this weather," the bear said judiciously. "You know, we both lose sleep this way, Culaehra."

"It would have been worth it, if I could have slipped away to the south."

The bear sighed. "You wished for a sword to fight this bear. How do you think you will fare against Bolenkar, if you cannot even fight a bear without a sword?"

"There are many swords," Culaehra muttered.

"Yes, and most would be of use against a bear—but only one can strike down Bolenkar."

Culaehra raised his head, frowning. "What would make this particular sword so powerful?"

"The Star Stone, the shard of Lomallin's spear that fell to earth during his battle with Ulahane. With the virtue of Lomallin's touch within it, it will prevail against the son of the Scarlet One."

"The power of the human-lover will be vested in a piece of his spear?" Culaehra frowned in skepticism.

But the bear nodded. "Virtue, not power—the unselfish, outgoing spirit that still resides within Lomallin's ghost. So rich was that aura that it spread to anything he touched. His staff would have great power indeed, if any could find it—the staff he carried when he took human guise. But the scrap of his spear has far more virtue in battle, for he used it to fight the Scarlet One, and it is might imbued with goodness directed against Evil."

Culaehra was silent, plodding on beside the bear, turning the matter over and over in his mind. He hated to delay a single day when he might be traveling south to the battle that would make amends for all his past deeds, and he knew the forging of a sword took many days, perhaps weeks! But what the bear said was true: there was no use going up against Bolenkar with ordinary human arms.

"Ah, warmth!" the bear said.

Culaehra looked up and saw the campfire ahead of them—with Illbane sitting beside it, gazing into the flames! The warrior stared, astounded, then whirled to ask the bear how this could be—but the great beast was gone as if it had never been. Culaehra stared foolishly at the space where it had stood, then looked down and, sure enough, saw huge prints in the snow, prints that turned and went back in the direction from which he and it had come, though they angled off a bit toward the west. The bear had moved quickly, though, for it was already lost in the night.

Scowling, Culaehra strode through the snow and sat himself down by the campfire, hissing, "How did you manage that, slave driver?"

Still Illbane sat, then slowly lifted his head, turning to Culaehra, and the warrior realized that he had come out of a trance. He smiled and said, "The bear is my totem, Culaehra, and the shape in which I visit the shaman world. This bear was quite willing to be host to my spirit; I roused its limbs from its winter's sleep, and have sent it back to its cave now. It will not even remember the waking." His tone turned to reproach. "But it was unkind of you to create a need for the poor beast to waken."

"It was unkind of you to make it chase me," Culaehra retorted, then remembered that he was talking so disrespectfully to the legendary hero Ohaern, the one who had lain so long in enchanted sleep, the one who had led the hosts against Ulahane himself!

But Culaehra could not really believe it in his heart of hearts; the old man looked no different, spoke no differently than he ever had. Illbane he had been, Illbane he would ever be—to him. He collected his wits and demanded, "Can you not let me begin my task?"

The sage sighed. "I have been at great pains to transform you from a brute to a man, Culaehra. I would not willingly see all my work erased with one stroke of Bolenkar's war club."

The thought rocked Culaehra; he sat unspeaking for a moment and was just managing to work up another retort when the sage smiled and said, "The hour grows late, and we must march long tomorrow. Sleep, now."

The next thing he knew, the sky was light with dawn, and Ill-bane was nudging him with a foot. "Waken, warrior. You have had as much rest as you are going to have, and it is your own folly if you did not have more."

Culaehra pushed himself upright with a halfhearted snarl and began his day—but when breakfast was done and he strode after the sage beside Kitishane, and Kitishane asked him, "Did you have a bad night?" all he could truthfully answer was, "Not bad, no. Odd, perhaps, but not really bad."

That did not mean he was about to give up, of course. That night, he rested a little while they dined, then told stories—but when the others went to bed, Culaehra tried a new strategy. He claimed the first watch for himself and sat by the fire, watching the night and feeding the flames until he was sure everyone slept, even Illbane—though truth to tell, he was beginning to wonder if the sage could ever truly be said to be asleep. Still, it was worth one more attempt.

He would not leave them without a sentry, of course, so he set a few pine cones at the edge of the fire, knowing they would catch in a little while and explode with loud noises some while after. Then he rose and strode straight off into the night—but stepped down onto the ice of the frozen brook that ran nearby.

It was slippery, so he had to walk with care—but it was level and clear, so he made better time than he would have if he had been plowing through drifts over rocky ground again. On he went, following the bends and turns of the stream as a sliver of moon rose to light him on his way, alert for Illbane to be standing there waiting around every curve.

So, of course, he was taken completely by surprise when the voice spoke at his shoulder. "Will you lose sleep again another night, Culaehra?"

The warrior jumped a foot off the ground and spun to the side even as he landed—but there was no one there. "Where are you, Illbane?" he cried.

"Still back at the camp," the voice said, still at his shoulder.

Culaehra spun back, but there was still nothing to be seen. "Can I never be rid of you?"

"Never," Illbane's voice said with a tone of absolute finality. "I will always be with you from this day forth, Culaehra—indeed, I have been with you for months. There will always be something of me alive inside you now, and I will always be able to find you through that."

Culaehra cursed.

"Come, will you make me rise from my bed to bring you back?" Illbane chided.

"No, I suppose not," Culaehra growled. He turned and set off back the way he had come. After a while he asked, "Illbane?"

"I am still with you," the voice replied.

"How did you manage to reform me?"

"By discipline," Illbane answered. "By teaching you to see the world as the weaker sees it. By showing you that you could not escape the consequences of your actions. By stripping away the vain view of yourself as more important than any other, and letting you see yourself as insignificant . . ."

Old anger stirred.

"Then by showing you all the worst aspects of yourself, embodied in the hunter who persuaded you to slay me, then betrayed you by stealing from you."

The anger smothered.

"Then by telling you that you could be a true man, an excellent man, and leading you into dangers where you could prove your good qualities. By surrounding you with good companions who, when you really needed them, could not help themselves from helping you. By leading you into winning their friendship, and thereby beginning to believe in your own virtue. But through all this, at every stage and most especially the last, with magic. Magic, and praise, which has a magic all its own, if it is genuine—but more than anything else, by magic."

Culaehra trudged along, letting all the words sink in. At last he asked, "No one can really be changed by anything else, then?"

"Oh, folk can be ground down by oppression," Illbane said. "People can be transformed by bitterness and hatred, saved by love and sweetness, even bamboozled and confused into thinking they have become someone else—but no man can deliberately change another. If the other wants to change, the teacher can show him the way to grow, can lead him into circumstances that will change him—but without magic, no man can change another. Not truly change, no."

"But you led me into wanting to change."

"And you had the courage, the strength, and determination to do it," Illbane confirmed. "You had the staunchness to face what you were and strive to overcome it. You were born with the stuff of which heroes are made, Culaehra, or I could have done nothing."

"But you did," Culaehra said, "by magic."

"Yes, but even magic cannot make a hero of a man who is a coward and a fool. The heroism had to be there within you first."

"I thought you told me that we are all fools in some way or another," Culaehra said.

"No," Illbane corrected. "I did not tell you that. Mind you, it is true—but I did not say it."

When he came back to the camp, his companions all lay as still as they had when he left. Silently, Culaehra lay down beside Kitishane again, then lay still, studying Kitishane's sleeping form—until she turned, her eyes open and accusing. "Will you leave me so soon, then?"

Culaehra stared at her, frozen. At last he said, "No. Never."

She did not seem entirely reassured, only gazed at him a while longer, frowning, then turned over and lay still once more. Culaehra lay staring at her unmoving back and knew he would not try to escape again.

They forged northward steadily after that, marching through the day with brief rests, then pitching camp in the lee of a boulder or beneath a pine or, when it offered, in a small cave. They ate stewed jerky and journeybread, with now and then a snow hare or ptarmigan that Kitishane brought down with her bow. Then, exhausted, they dropped into their blankets. That was the pattern of their days for a week and more, and every minute of it was an agony of impatience for Culaehra.

Then, one night, as they were about to lie down, a glimmering light appeared in the sky, appeared and spread until it took the form of twisting, furling curtains winding and unwinding across the sky. Green they were, shading into blue, with here and there a red one that was soon swallowed up by the twistings of the green.

"I have never seen anything so grand," Kitishane murmured in awe. "What are they, Illbane?"

"The aurora borealis," he replied, "the Northern Lights. They are a sign that we near the Star Stone."

"Do they spring from it, then?"

"No, they come from the unseen parts of the sun's rays striking near the northern center of the world—but the green and the red are drawn to the Star Stone and hover near it."

Culaehra frowned at his teacher, wondering at the tension in his voice.

The next day they found a cliff of ice blocking their path. "It is a glacier," Illbane told them, "a sheet of ice that flows out of the valleys in distant mountains and covers all the plain to this, its southern edge. Help me now in gathering as much deadwood as we can carry, for there shall be no more firewood on yonder floe."

They did as he asked, picking up sticks and logs until their backs bent under their loads. Then they followed Illbane onto the glacier.

He led them up a tortuous path, climbing on ice as gray and hard as rock, though nonetheless slippery for that. Once up on top, the going was easier, for fresh snow had fallen deeply upon the glacier, and if it had not been for Illbane's assurances, there might have been grass rather than ice beneath it, for all Culaehra could tell.

He still carried Illbane's pack of tools, though its weight seemed far less than it had at first. He bore it in the sage's wake, watching him with brooding eyes.

"What worries you?" Kitishane asked as she plodded through the snow beside him.

"Illbane," Culaehra replied. "He grows tense and curt. If I did not know he were the hero Ohaern, I would think that fear grew upon him."

Kitishane looked up at their leader and her voice was low. "Even heroes know fear, Culaehra."

"I am not a hero, Kitishane!"

"No," she said, very low, "not yet."

That night, the aurora danced above them again, and the horizon was lighted with a green glow.

In the morning, when the fire was smothered, Illbane bade them bring the partially burned logs with them.

"Why, Illbane?" Yocote asked. "Is it not enough that we carry dry wood, for there is none to gather on the glacier? Will it be so scarce that we must carry the burned ones, too?"

"Yes," Illbane answered. "I shall have need of the charcoal. Put them in a bag and bring them, Yocote, even though this is magic of a sort you will never need to know."

"If it is magic of any kind, I need to learn it!" The gnome collected the sticks and solid coals into a bag and slung it on his back.

Illbane spoke rarely that day, growing more and more somber as they went. He insisted they burn new wood that night, not using the coals they carried. The aurora was brighter, and the glow from the horizon reached higher into the sky.

It was higher the next night and the next, and Yocote's bag grew so heavy that Kitishane took it from him. The day after that, Culaehra took it from her, and that night the aurora seemed to dance directly overhead, while the green glow lit half the sky. Illbane sat in his trance till dawn, not sleeping at all, and the next day he did not say a word.

As the sun lowered, they crested a ridge, and the glow struck them so that they recoiled.

It lay below them, far below, cupped between outthrusts of the glacier that seemed to have melted away in its presence to mere fingers, ones that seemed to cup it in an embrace—a huge, irregular, pitted form that glowed like sunshine through leaves, like a vast emerald caught in a sun ray, but the glow came from within its own substance. Around it for five yards the snow was melted away and lichens covered the ground in a patchwork of bright colors.

"Look your fill, then retreat and look upon it no more," Illbane said grimly, "for that is the Star Stone."

"The Star Stone?" Culaehra stared wide-eyed. "If that is a shard, how thick was the spear!"

"They were giants then," Illbane told him, "and their ghosts were more gigantic still. They gathered stars from the sky and formed them into weapons to smite one another. They were vast beyond our imagining." He lapsed into silence, leaning on his staff and gazing down at the Star Stone, and his companions looked upon his face and wondered.

Finally Illbane roused himself and turned away. "Come, then! Pitch camp below this ridge, where its radiance shall not strike you directly. Tonight I shall rest; tomorrow I shall begin work."

As they went back down the hill, Culaehra said, "In any way I can help, Illbane, only call upon me!"

"I thank you for that, my pupil," Illbane said with a gracious nod. "I will ask you to bring a boulder three feet high, with Yocote's magic aiding your strength, and I will ask you all to bring half the firewood that is left. Then, though, you must wait at the camp and not come near me while I work."

"Do you know smithing, then?" Yocote asked, and bit his tongue in chagrin—but the question brought the ghost of a smile to Illbane's face.

"Yes, my pupil, I know something of smithing."

To be sure he did, Culaehra reflected. Before he had taken arms against Ulahane and the cities of the south, Ohaern had been a smith, and one of the first of the northern smiths to learn to forge iron—taught by the god Lomallin himself, if the tale was to be trusted.

So that night they piled firewood into a huge mound by the Star Stone, then came back to kindle a fire from some of the rest. Thus they sat around a campfire dwarfed by the glow that filled the sky, that obscured even the aurora, and they banished the eldritch chill upon their backs by telling tales as they ate, trying to coax another smile from Illbane. They almost succeeded in this: he gazed upon them proudly from time to time. But he did not smile again.

The next morning, Culaehra and Yocote cast about and found a boulder waist-high. Culaehra could never have moved it by himself, but Yocote cast a spell to set it rolling, and all Culaehra had to do was push now and again to keep it on the right course. When it crested the ridge and began to roll down toward the Star Stone, Yocote had to try to slow it, and Culaehra cried, "'Ware, Illbane! It comes!"

"Let it come." The smith already stood near the Star Stone, laying billets of firewood in a grid. "It cannot damage the Star Stone."

Yocote cast him a doubtful glance, but Illbane beckoned, and the gnome threw up his hands, letting the boulder go. It rolled by itself, faster and faster down the slope, and Illbane stood calmly watching it come. Finally Yocote cried a warning, but even as he did, the boulder began to slow, its turns slackening more and more until at last it came to a stop, well within the lichen patch that surrounded the Star Stone.

"Bring my anvil plate," Illbane called. "Set it upon the boulder."

Culaehra caught up the bag of tools and lugged it down to Illbane, then took out the anvil—a rectangle of iron a few inches thick and a few more wide, a little more than a foot long, pointed at one end—and set it on the flattest place he could find on the boulder. He did it almost by feel, his eyes drawn to the Star Stone, and bright though it was, its radiance did not seem to hurt his eyes. It seemed far smaller than it had from the hilltop, not even as large as the boulder they had brought, and this close he could see threads of scarlet twining through its green glow.

"Bring me the burned wood," Illbane directed. "Then get you gone, and wait till I come."

His face was grim, so Culaehra stifled the urge to argue and set off back up the slope, Yocote beside him, casting many anxious glances back at the sage.

When they brought the sack of charcoal, they saw that Illbane had dug three long trenches in the earth before the Star Stone, the ends square, the bottoms beveled. He thanked them and stacked the wood around the base of the Star Stone, then brought a live coal from the pottery box at his belt and set fire to the charcoal. As the flames sprang up he turned and lit the cairn of firewood he had built, too, then turned again and said, "Go now. My work is begun."

There was a look of peace in his eyes. Mute, his students turned away. As they reached the top of the ridge they heard him beginning to chant. Turning back, they saw the flames leaping up all about the Star Stone, growing red, then orange, then yellow, then even brighter than yellow. A roaring sprang up that reminded them of Agrapax's Forge, and the flames whipped in the gusts of air—but they could not see the source of those blasts. Shuddering, they crossed the top of the ridge and went back to the camp.

CHAPTER 21

They could not resist looking now and then, of course. In fact, they could not resist keeping an anxious watch on their friend and teacher, though they did it in turns, and none watched for more than a few minutes at a time. Even then the watcher raised his head only enough to see above the ridge and make sure Illbane was well, then ducked down again and hurried back to bear word to the companions.

They really had little need to look to know he was well—his chanting sounded day and night, carrying to them steadily, even over the top of the ridge. After the first few hours, though, Yocote could not bear to stay away; he found a sheltered cranny under a huge old pine and sat, wrapped in his furs and with a small fire before him, watching through his goggles as the sage-smith chanted and hammered and wrought magic in metal.

Yocote was of no use to his friends, though, for he never came down to tell them what occurred. Culaehra, Lua, and Kitishane took turns climbing up to the ridge top for a quick look, then coming back to report, and similarly each took his or her watch in the night. Lua took it upon herself to keep bringing Yocote wood and food. Culaehra protested. "Yocote is my friend, too, Lua! Let me tend him now and again!" And he took up an armload of sticks.

But Lua stopped him with a hand on his arm and a gentle if cryptic smile. "No, Culaehra. This is my privilege, and I will take it unkindly if you seek to steal it from me." Then she took the wood from his arm and set off up the slope, leaving him to stare after her speechless, wondering how this woman whom he had beaten and degraded had come to be able to stop him with a gesture.

Then he wondered all over again how she could have forgiven him enough to become his friend.

"Let her go, Culaehra." Kitishane slipped her arm through his with a smile that mirrored Lua's. "It is her portion."

"Her portion?" Culaehra frowned down at her. "How so?"

"Do you not see it?" Kitishane chided. "She has fallen in love with Yocote at last."

"In love?" Culaehra stared, and tried to ignore the surge of indignation that followed the thought. "Why? What has changed? It cannot be proof of his constancy—she had that before!"

"Oh, but he has changed in so many ways, Culaehra!" Kitishane beamed up at him. "Even as you have." She leaned a little closer, tilting her chin up, her eyes shining, and Culaehra would have been a fool indeed to miss seeing the chance of a kiss.

Deeply worried about Illbane, Culaehra told himself he was being foolish—if anyone could keep himself well, it was a shaman who had surpassed all others of his profession so thoroughly that he was now a sage. How could Fate strike down the consort of a goddess? Still he watched, and his brief glimpses became longer and longer, though Illbane showed no sign of weakening. His voice was still rich and strong as he chanted to the iron; stripped to the waist, his muscles rolled beneath his skin like those of a man far younger as he lofted the hammer and brought it down, then bounced it on the metal and raised it again.

The first day, he only tended the fires around the Star Stone and the fire in the cairn, singing to the flames throughout the day and all that night through.

"What does he do?" Kitishane asked when Culaehra came back from his twilight trip.

"Still sings, and brings blasts of wind to fan the flames," Culaehra reported. "Only the fire under the rock, though—the cairn he lets burn slowly of its own accord." He shook his head. "I cannot understand how his voice endures!"

The next morning Lua came back to report, "The cairn burns no longer; in fact, it no longer stands! He has taken the charcoal from it and added it to the fire all around the rock. A green glow has sprung up about it, a green glow threaded by strands of scarlet!"

They ran to see—and sure enough, the Star Stone glowed green, though here and there threads of red undulated in its haze.

Halfway through the afternoon Yocote came back in great excitement. "The Star Stone is melting! Drop by drop it trickles into the trenches he has cut beneath it!" Then he was gone, back up the hill to watch, and the others came scrambling after. It was true—the whole form of the Star Stone seemed to have softened, and droplets came from it into the trenches as Illbane sang, his voice deep and heavy.

When Kitishane went to look the next morning, she saw no Star Stone at all—only a heap of slag at the center of six trenches. Illbane had dug them all around, and each now glinted with white metal. She came back and told what she had seen, adding, "He is digging the cooled metal out of the earth now. It is formed into bars!"

Then began the clanging and the roaring. Looking down, Yocote saw that Illbane had brought bellows and had thrust their long iron snout into the fire. When he pumped, flames roared out of it to bathe in brightness the glowing metal bar he held within. He sang a verse while he pumped, then laid the bar on the anvil and struck it with the hammer, chanting a different song, one of driving urgency. As he did, the green glow spread from the metal again, still with one or two strands of scarlet.

One verse, and he laid the bar in flame again, singing the forge song as he pumped the bellows, then brought it back to the anvil.

Culaehra, too, saw this, and reported, "He takes it back and forth between anvil and flame, singing first the one song, then the other."

"What words does he chant?" Lua asked, but Culaehra could only shake his head. "It is a language I do not know. The shaman's tongue, belike—though I confess it does sound like the canticle Agrapax sang to his forge. And the metal—again and again he beats it. It shall be flat ere long, I doubt not."

That evening Kitishane reported, "He hammered the bar flat indeed, twice its length and breadth, then hammered another bar into it and folded them both with many blows. Now he beats them flat again."

In the morning Lua told them, "He has flattened four of the bars now, and beats them together, folding and flattening, then folding and flattening again."

"What of the other two bars?" Culaehra asked.

"He has set them aside—why, I cannot guess. The others, though, he has beaten into a single bar, though it seems little bigger than any one alone."

On the morning of the fourth day Yocote whistled shrilly, and the others came running up to his pine. "What moves?" Culaehra panted as he came up.

"Look!" Yocote pointed, his whole face taut, and somehow Culaehra knew his eyes were wide behind the mask. Turning, he saw Illbane beating out a long, straight length of green-glowing steel—surely it must be steel, to glitter so in the dim light of the overcast North! And what could it be but a sword? A long sword, a broadsword, a double-edged sword. As they watched, he laid it in the flames again, pressed the bellows and sang to the roaring, then laid the sword on the anvil once more and beat it with his hammer, bouncing on the steel in a rhythm like that of horses galloping. At last he heated it one more time, then thrust it deep into a bank of freshly fallen snow. It hissed; steam rose; the green glow sank into the white mound and was gone. Illbane drew forth the sword and laid it in the flame again, crying, "Culaehra, come forth!"

Culaehra stared, taken aback, then rose and ran down to the smith, hearing Kitishane's cry of alarm behind him. But his trust in Illbane was absolute now; he came panting up to the singing smith, crying, "What would you have of me, Illbane?"

"When I lay the sword on the anvil, grasp the tang!" Illbane snapped, then swung the sword over to the rock. He himself held it by the crosspiece, no longer with tongs. Culaehra laid hold of the tang where the handle would be bound and nearly cried out in pain. The tang was hot, very hot! How could the smith hold the sword even nearer to the glowing blade? But if Illbane could stand the pain, so could he! Culaehra grasped it hard while Illbane sang to it, not beating now, then shouted "Come!" and ran with it to the finger of glacial ice that strayed near. Culaehra ran with him, matching steps, and Illbane cried, "Thrust it in!" He let go of the sword. Culaehra thrust as he had been told, and the sword pierced the ice with a vast hissing. Boiling drops struck Culaehra; he gritted his teeth against the pain and kept up the pressure as the sword slid into its icy sheath and the smith stood by, singing. At last he stopped, sighed, and said, "Draw it out now, Culaehra. Your sword is forged."

Culaehra drew the sword forth, staring at the blade in wonder. It seemed to shimmer as the light glanced off it, a grain almost like that of wood running down its length. The edges glittered with the sharpness of obsidian flakes, though it was fresh from the forge and not yet whetted. The wind blew past, making it vibrate. It almost seemed to sing with a deep note that Culaehra could feel through his very bones, and it scarcely felt as if he held any weight in his hand at all. "It is beautiful," he whispered. "It is a marvel!"

"It will cleave any armor, be it iron or bronze," Illbane told him, exaltation in his voice. "It will cut through any other sword save those few that were forged by Agrapax himself, no matter the steel of which they are made—and because you held it while it was tempered, it will accept only your grasp or that of one of your blood; it will twist from any other's hands, so that no enemy can wield it against you."

At last Culaehra turned to stare at the smith. "How can I ever thank you for this, Illbane?"

"By bearing it in the mission I have given you," the sage answered. "Kneel, Culaehra!"

The warrior did not ask why; he only knelt before his teacher, bowing his head.

Illbane took the sword from him and laid the blade on his

shoulder, chanting a deep and weighty song, then laid it on his other shoulder, and finally across his breast, leaning down to fold the warrior's arms about it. "I name thee Corotrovir the Star-sword," he intoned, "to be wielded only when the cause is just. Do thou, O Prince of Swords, summon up in this man all virtues that lie within him, magnifying and expanding all until he is a Prince of Men!"

A glow sprang from the sword then, and Culaehra nearly cried out in alarm—but he held the blade tightly to his chest as that green glow shimmered all about him, then shrank in on itself and buried itself in his breast. He knelt staring down at the sword, feeling numb—then began to tremble as forces he had never guessed pounded through him, making his whole body vibrate with their shaking. Power itself seemed to rise into his head, making him dizzy; it seemed to rise like a heat haze between himself and the world. Then it subsided, sinking deep within him; he saw the world clearly again and saw himself more clearly still, saw his every fault and every virtue, knew himself as he truly was without boast or regret, and felt the iron resolve growing within him never to yield to his weaknesses or let his faults grow. He saw how to balance vice with virtue, to heal every breach, to become all that he could be . . .

But he saw, too, that he would have to temper those qualities in battle, even as the sword had been tempered in centuries-old ice.

Then he felt hands upon his arms and looked up to see Illbane raising him to his feet, taking the sword from him, and setting its tang in his hands. "You are a prince among men now, Culaehra," he said, "but you must still earn your crown and grow into king-ship." Then his eyes glittered and his voice sank low, almost feverish with exultation as he said, "Now go, and slay Bolenkar!"

Illbane bound wood to the tang, of course—not firewood sticks, but seasoned dark ebony that he brought from his smith's pack. He fastened it with rivets, fashioned a scabbard of the same dark wood, then whetted the blade and polished both wood and steel until they reflected the sky. He strapped it on Culaehra's back, bound up the anvil and his tools in his pack, and bound the two bars of Star Stone metal in a leather bag that he tied to a rope, to drag behind. Then he led the companions away from the ground where the Star Stone had stood. They looked back once from the crest of the ridge to see that the slag pile had already crumbled away into the ground, and that snow was already rising upon it, as the glacier began to reclaim its own.

Then off they went, through gently falling snow.

"I must carry your pack, Illbane!" Culaehra protested. "It is my place!"

"Not yet," the sage told him, "not yet. You bear a heavier load now, Culaehra."

"I scarcely feel the weight of the sword at all," Culaehra protested, though he knew quite well what Illbane meant—but the sage did not even deign to reply, only strode through the snow with a glow in his eyes. Culaehra would have thought him a man who had finished his work and rushed to his reward, if he had not known that the greatest task of all still lay before them. Nonetheless, the thought gave him a shiver.

The next day, however, Illbane seemed to lean more heavily on his staff, and after the first hour his pace slowed. Culaehra slowed with him, reining in his impatience and silencing questions from Yocote and Lua with a warning glance. Kitishane did not ask; she, too, had seen.

On the third day, though, Illbane's back began to bend under the weight of his pack of smith's tools. When they paused at midday, he set it down, and Culaehra snatched it up. Illbane glared at him, but Culaehra glared right back and said, "It is my place, Illbane, and my burden. It is time for me to bear it again."

Illbane tried to stare him down, but his glance wavered; he knew the younger man spoke truth.

They ate and rested, then forged into the wilderness again. A light snow fell about them as they strode across that featureless plain that was the top of the glacier, toward the mountains that rose still higher in the distance. Illbane walked with his back straight now, but his steps were still slower than they had been. Culaehra ventured a word. "We do not retrace our steps, Illbane."

"We do not," the sage agreed. "We must march eastward as

well as southward, Culaehra, for if we seek to find Bolenkar, we must go to his city in the Land Between the Rivers."

On they went into land none of them knew, but Illbane's steps slowed even more, and by evening his back had begun to bend again. When they sat around the fire, Culaehra saw with a shock that the sage's face had lost its color, taking on a shade of gray.

Yocote saw, too. "By your leave, Illbane," he said, taking the sage's wrist in his fingers.

Illbane frowned. "Do you think to heal me, Yocote?"

"You taught me that no shaman should seek to tend himself," the gnome said evenly. He frowned, pressed a hand against the sage's chest, then shook his head. "You are not well, Illbane. We must rest until you are healed."

"We must not lose a day!" Illbane snapped. "I will be restored tomorrow, Yocote! Leave me now!"

The gnome retreated with misgivings, and Lua murmured to him, "He did not tell you what to do if a patient would not accept healing."

"Oh, yes he did," Yocote replied, "but he is still too strong for me to knock him down and tie him up, and I would not put such a doom upon Culaehra."

True to his word, Illbane looked almost healthy the next morning as he strode briskly off into the snow. The clouds dispersed and sunlight waked all the snowfields to blinding intensity. Illbane bade them bind cloth over their eyes; so they did and, squinting behind their masks, strode ahead. By noon, though, the sage was wilting again, and by evening he was moving so slowly that his companions had to drag their feet as they followed.

Over dinner Culaehra decided to take the bull by the horns. "You must rest until you are well, Illbane. We will stay in this camp!"

"You will go on!" the sage snapped. "Even now Bolenkar brews war among the younger races! Leave me if you must, but march!"

Then the vomiting began.

Illbane turned pale and pulled himself up by his staff, hobbling quickly away behind a boulder. They heard him retch, then retch again. Yocote was on his feet, starting toward the sound, but Lua held him back. She detained him until the noise stopped, then let go, and the gnome bolted forward, but he met his teacher as Illbane came limping back. Yocote took his arm as he sat, concern wrinkling his face. "You cannot march farther, Illbane!"

"Even so," the sage admitted. "Go south without me, Yocote. I shall endure."

"You shall not stay by yourself!" Kitishane snapped, and Culaehra nodded. "We shall fare more strongly against Bolenkar with you than without you, Illbane. It is worth the wait while you mend."

The sage was silent a moment, then said, "I shall not heal."

They all stared, not daring to speak, frozen by his words.

Yocote finally asked, "What has brought this illness, Teacher?"

"The Star Stone itself," Illbane answered.

They stared. Illbane breathed heavily a few times, then explained. "The Star Stone is a force for good, yes, for it is imbued with the power of Lomallin—but it was struck from his spear by Ulahane, whose power poisoned the metal within it. Only traces of poison, it is true, but they would have been enough to sicken anyone who stood near it for any length of time."

"As you did." Lua's breath caught in her throat.

Illbane nodded. "I did not stand near it so long as that—but as I forged the metal, I beat the poisons out . . ."

"And they took root in you," Yocote whispered.

Heavily, Illbane nodded.

"You forged me a wondrous blade by taking its poisons into yourself," Culaehra cried, tears in his eyes. "You cleansed the steel at the cost of your own life!"

"And you knew you were doing it," Yocote accused.

Illbane's nod was slow and ponderous. "There is no curing this sickness. Go, go on without me, for there is no time to wait!"

"We cannot," Lua cried, and Kitishane agreed, thin-lipped. "We cannot leave you to die alone, Illbane."

They did not. They dug their camp in; Kitishane went out to hunt while the gnomes did what they could to ease Illbane's pain—but they could not stop the vomiting, nor patch old skin as it sloughed off, leaving new and tender skin behind. They could not make his scalp cease shedding, nor his cheeks. Perhaps it was a mercy that the end came while his beard and hair were only sparse, not gone completely.

They built a hut of ice blocks to shelter Illbane, then settled in for the death watch, their campsite sunk in gloom, partaking only sparsely of the game that Kitishane brought in and Lua cooked so well. Culaehra had to hold himself from speaking, for fear that he would snap or snarl at the others from the weight of grief within him that demanded release. He contented himself with holding Kitishane's hand and with trying to feel Yocote's grief as well as his own, for the little man's face was bleak and drawn whenever he came back from tending his teacher—which was not often.

On the fifth day he emerged from the brush hut to say, "He wishes to speak to us all. Come in."

Silently, they filed in and knelt beside the old man's pallet. His eyes were closed and dark, his breath rasped in his throat, and his skin was so pale that it seemed to have been claimed already by the snow. After a few minutes he opened his eyes, looked from one to another, tightened his jaw against a spasm of pain, then spoke with great effort. "Go south and east. Go through the mountains, go down to the plain. When you come to a great river, build or buy a boat and sail with the current until it joins another river, equally great. Sail with the current of that river, too, until it comes to an inland sea. There, take ship; cross that sea to its eastern shore, then march eastward still past seven great cities. The eighth will be Bolenkar's citadel."

"He will not let us merely march toward him," Kitishane stated.

"He will not," Illbane agreed. "He will send monsters against you, packs against you, armies against you. You must gather forces of your own as you march, and you will fight several battles before you see his city. There you will fight the greatest battle of all, and Culaehra shall at last hew through the ranks to Bolenkar himself." His hand caught Yocote's with strength that was surprising in a body so wasted. "Do not let him go alone, O Shaman! Stick as closely to him as his breastplate then!" Turning, he caught Kitishane's hand likewise. "Do you stay as closely to him as the shield upon his arm, O Maiden!"

Culaehra cried out in protest, but the sage's glance stilled him. "There will be no peace for either of you, Culaehra, nor any chance of marriage and children, if you do not win that battle—and believe me deeply, it will be far better for her to die beside you than to be captured if you are dead."

Culaehra felt something turn very cold within him.

"When I am dead—"

Lua cried out.

Illbane smiled fondly, a ghost of his former beam, and transferred his hand from Kitishane to her. "Do not think to deceive me, little maid, for I know I die, and I welcome it. But when life has left this corpse, find some seam, some wrinkle, in the great ice field, and lay me in it with my tools at one side and my staff at the other. Then heap snow in atop me and pack it firm, and leave the glacier to carry me where it will."

Lua sobbed, but Yocote said gravely, "Illbane, we will."

"The two remaining bars of Star Stone metal, drag behind as I have shown you, then bury them when you come to the mountains and leave them to lie for long centuries. Most of the poison I drained when I smelted them, but there is enough left that no man should touch them until another smith comes who can draw their poison as he forges."

At last the sage laid his hand on Culaehra's and said, "Of all that I have ever forged, my proudest work is you."

Culaehra stared, amazed, and the old man beamed back at him, as strongly, as truly, as ever. His hand tightened on Culaehra's, and the warrior had to blink hard against a stinging in his eyes.

Then the old hand loosened and went slack. The old eyes glazed, then dulled, and the sage's body loosened in a way that told them all his spirit had departed. Still they knelt in frozen silence, hoping against hope for some sign of returning life, but the body lay most obstinately still. At last Yocote leaned forward to test his pulse, first in his wrist, then in his throat, then held his hand over nose and mouth to feel for breath. He waited long, but grudgingly and finally reached up to close the sightless eyes.

· · ·

They buried the sage as he had asked, in ice and snow with his staff and smith's tools beside him. They packed the snow atop the little crevasse where they had lain him, stood to pause awhile in prayer, then reluctantly turned away and set their faces toward the south.

"You must lead us now, warrior," Yocote said, but Culaehra shook his head, his face dark, eyes downcast. "I am still too full of grief, O Shaman."

So it was Kitishane who took his hand and Kitishane who led them out of that lifeless land, south and east into the mountains, where evergreens grew and where, after days of travel, they found a land swept bare of snow, where grass sprang new.

CHAPTER 22

"Come, hero, you must eat a little, at least." Kitishane held the soup spoon up to Culaehra's lips. "How will you slay Bolenkar for Illbane if you die of starvation before you meet him?"

Culaehra looked up at her, frowning and blinking, trying to puzzle out the meaning of her words. The whole world seemed darkened, and had for days, ever since they had left Illbane's grave. Sounds came to him dimly, as if muffled in a snowbank—the snow that mounded high on Illbane's grave. After a few minutes, though, he managed to remember her words, then puzzle out their meaning. He nodded, took the bowl from her and sipped. She rewarded him with a bright smile, then seemed disappointed that he did not return it.

She was indeed disappointed. Sighing, she returned to the campfire and told Lua, "He cannot love me if my smile will not pull him out of this morass of self-pity in which he wallows."

Lua nodded agreement. "It seems he enjoys his sorrow more than your company."

But Yocote shook his head. "It is not self-pity, ladies, but only grief, though very deep."

Kitishane frowned. "We are no ladies, Yocote, but only ordinary women of our own kinds."

"No longer," Yocote contradicted. "You ceased to be ordinary when Illbane chose you for Culaehra's companions."

"Chose us?" Kitishane stared.

"Well, perhaps it was Rahani who chose you," Yocote conceded, "but did you really think it was accident that led you to Culaehra? I mistrust accidents of that sort, ladies. A shaman learns that coincidence only seems accidental. And yes, you are ladies, for your experiences have elevated you above the ordinary—or will."

Kitishane frowned. "I do not feel special—or elevated!"

"Then you are remarkable indeed," Yocote said sourly, "for everyone feels themselves to be special—or should. Anyone who does not has had her own picture of herself crushed or debased—or is somewhat less than honest about her feelings."

Lua frowned. "You are bitter tonight, my shaman."

"It is my way of showing grief," Yocote replied, "so I will ask your pardons right now if my remarks become so tart and sharp as to be offensive. I will strive most earnestly to prevent that, but strong feelings must show in some way."

"You are pardoned indeed," Kitishane said softly. "Believe me, I feel the grief, too."

"And I," Lua murmured.

"I am sure that you do," Yocote said, "but I also suspect that something within you is stifling the worst of the feeling, for it realizes that you cannot give way so long as Culaehra is so numb."

Kitishane gazed at him, then looked down at the fire. "Perhaps."

Yocote nodded. "When the darkness that surrounds him dissipates, it will be your turn to be prostrate with grief."

"I do not doubt you," Kitishane said slowly, "but I wonder if Illbane meant as much to me as he did to Culaehra."

"Well might you wonder, for Culaehra certainly did not know it until the old man died."

"There is some truth to that," Kitishane admitted, "but I am a woman, so I was protected against trying to be like Illbane, to some extent. Culaehra was not."

"A deep and proper insight," Yocote said. "He was your protector and your teacher, yes, but he taught you only to fight and to forgive. He taught me also how to be a man as well as to be a shaman; he taught me how to be my true self, but I began by trying to be him."

"So you know that now." Lua looked up at him keenly.

"Now, yes," Yocote agreed, "though I did not see it until he had begun to tell me that I was turning into something he had never been, and could never be, for he was not a gnome. Still, for all of us, he was only a teacher. He taught us skills, taught us to become ourselves, set us on the road to becoming all that we can be—but he did not need to redeem and transform us."

"As he did with Culaehra," Kitishane said softly.

Yocote nodded. "In these few months, he has become as much a father to Culaehra as the man who sired him."

"So it is not Illbane alone whom Culaehra mourns," said Kitishane, "but himself, too."

Yocote looked up, startled. Then he said slowly, "I think you are right, maiden. But how shall we prove to him that he is alive?"

"I thought I could do that by my mere presence," Kitishane said with a sardonic smile, "but it appears not—and I am reluctant to take stronger measures."

"Understandably; I can imagine how you would feel if they failed." Yocote nodded. "No, we must wake him and revive him before we seek to bring him to embrace life again."

"How shall we do that, though?"

Lua said, with complete certainty, "Revenge."

"Revenge?" Yocote protested. "How can he revenge himself upon the Star Stone when it no longer exists? For it was that which slew our Illbane!"

"No," said Lua. "It was Ulahane's malice within it that slew him—and those same traces of evil exist still, within Bolenkar's mind."

"And through Bolenkar, in everything and everyone he has corrupted," Yocote said, musing. "Yes, I think you are right, Lua. How could I have failed to see it?"

"So we must find some agent of Bolenkar's for him to fight," Kitishane inferred.

"Where shall we seek?" Lua wondered.

"Oh, I would not be concerned about that, sister. I do not think that will prove difficult at all."

They came down from the mountains into the foothills. There they camped for the night, then set off in the dawn. As they crested a rise they saw a column of smoke rising against the washed blue of the sky.

"If that is not a campfire close by," Yocote said, frowning, "it is a very large fire indeed."

"I mislike large fires," Kitishane said, her face dark. "It might be a woodlot burning—or it might be worse. Let us hurry to see." She caught Culaehra's hand and pulled him along behind. He followed, uncomprehending.

They came in sight of the village at noon—or what was left of it. It lay in a little valley, and every hut was reduced to charred timbers and ash. Lua moaned in distress, and Kitishane cried, "What has happened here?"

"I would say that was clear enough," Yocote said sourly. "Raiders have burned this village. I think you have found the agents of mayhem you sought, Kitishane."

"Down! We must see if any still live!" she cried, and tugged furiously at Culaehra's hand before she set off running down the slope. He looked up, startled, then kept pace with her, looking about him as if wondering where he was and how he had come to be there.

Kitishane skidded to a stop in what had been the village green, and was now only churned mud. "Is there any still alive? Look about you!"

They looked, but all they could see were corpses—dead bodies of men, some so young as to be scarcely more than boys, some gray at the temples.

"Did they kill all the males?" Lua gasped.

"Yes." Kitishane's face hardened. "But none of the women or children."

Lua looked up, eyes wide behind the mask. "Why not?"

"Imagine the worst, sister," Kitishane snapped. "What could have churned the center of this village so, Yocote?" She gestured toward the central ring.

"Hoofed animals of some sort." The little shaman pointed. "See the sharp edges? And here and there a whole mark?" He stepped closer. "No cleft prints. These were horses."

"Did they pen their plough animals here?" Lua wondered.

"Either that, or the raiders drove a herd through, to trample the villagers." Kitishane turned livid. "The cowards and poltroons! Peaceful villagers these, but they dared not fight them without a herd of horses before, and twice as many men as the folk who lived here coming after!"

Yocote still studied the mud. "The only footprints are those wearing buskins . . . No! Here are harder edges! And long trails . . . wheels? The invaders were fewer, or they rode in wagons!"

"Either way, they were experienced fighters, reivers who live by plundering peaceful folk!" Kitishane raved. "Oh, that I had them within reach of my bow! Cowards indeed, to war upon those who were not their equals in arms! Vile lechers, to steal a whole village of women! Despoilers and corrupters, to steal all the children! They are heartless, they are vile!"

"They are servants of Bolenkar," Yocote suggested.

Culaehra's head snapped up as if he had been slapped.

"Is this the kind of evil the son of the Scarlet One spreads?" Kitishane said. "No wonder Illbane made us swear to stop him! This is no wickedness of greed alone, but cruelty that delights in pain!" She swung on Culaehra. "You, warrior! O Bearer of Corotrovir! Will you let these reivers carry away the innocent? Will you let them despoil these folk unpunished? Will you not revenge?"

"Why, so I shall." That suddenly, Culaehra's mind returned. He loosened the great sword in the scabbard on his back and stepped forward to Kitishane. "It is even as you say—such evil must be stopped, and the innocent rescued before they are harmed any worse. Where have they gone?"

Kitishane stared at him in surprise, then ran to throw her arms about him. "Oh, I was so afraid you would never awaken!"

"It is as if I have stepped forward from a land of mists and darkness, where I wandered," Culaehra admitted. He embraced her, briefly but thoroughly, then stepped back and called out, "Ho! If any still live, come forth! Tell us who we fight, how great their strength is, and where they have gone!"

The village stood quiet all about them. Then a burning beam broke and fell.

"Come forth!" Culaehra cried again. "If we venture on this chase in blindness and ignorance, it is more than likely that the enemy will slay us, and your womenfolk and children will be lost for good!"

His voice rang through the blackened beams; then the village was still again.

"Well, we must go, but go carefully," Culaehra said in disgust, and was turning away when an old woman rose from behind a pile of char.

"There!" Kitishane pointed, and Culaehra turned back.

The woman was old and bent; her clothes were stout cloth, but rent here and there, and singed at the edges. She came toward them, trembling, her eyes rheumy and red-rimmed, quavering, "All my pretty ones! My little chicks! Can you wrench them back from the hawks?"

Culaehra stood stiff, feeling dread prickle his scalp; the woman was mad! Scarcely surprising after what she must have witnessed, but still enough to make him shy away.

Kitishane, though, stepped closer. "Save thee, grandmother! What hawks were these?"

"Vanyar," the woman cried. "They were Vanyar, hard men with long moustaches and beards, with sheepskins for clothing and wheeled carts to ride in! They came upon us out of a peaceful sky, shrieking and riding down the hillside behind their horses, brandishing their axes and calling upon Bolenkar to give them victory!" She collapsed sobbing into Kitishane's arms.

But an old man came around the corner of a wall that had not quite fallen in, nodding. "It is even as old Tagaer says. They were all of them men in the primes of their lives, and they rode their devil carts through our village, slashing with their horrible double-edged axes before our men could even bring up their staves and spades to ward themselves. The rest of the men came running in from the fields, their forks and scythes at the ready, but there were three of the reivers for every one of them, and they had horses! They rode around and about, they cut our men off from one another, they struck down their tools and split their heads with those evil axes! And all the while they kept up that screaming, that dreadful warbling shrieking, to drive us mad!"

"It is even so." Another oldster came hobbling up, swatting at her smoking hem. "They slew all the men, and there were fifty of them, a hundred of them, or more! Then they set fire to the houses and caught the women and children as they ran shrieking out. The older women they raped right there, in front of their children; the younger they plagued with ribald insults, telling them they would save them to warm their beds at nightfall! Then they bound them all, hand and foot, slung them over their horses' backs and rode away, laughing and singing their triumph and praising their vile god Bolenkar!" She shuddered as she told them.

"I tried to stop them," another old man said, coming up to them. He held up a broken staff. "They cut this through with one blow and felled me with a swat, then left me to lie, dead or alive."

"They cared not!" another woman said, and looking up, Culaehra discovered that there were a score of the ancients all about them. "We all of us tried to stop them, to drag back our daughters or one or two of our grandchildren at least, but they beat us all away and told us that the little ones would have the honor of being raised as slaves to the Vanyar! The girls would grow to whore for them, the boys to guard them as eunuchs!"

An old man shuddered. "The weeping and wailing of mothers and children was horrible, horrible! And we could not stop them, we could not!"

"But *you* can!" An ancient caught Culaehra by the arms. "You are young and strong, you have armor and a sword! You can stop them, young man! You must!"

"Be sure we shall!" Kitishane strung her bow. "We shall find them, we shall slay them all! What vile things are they to wreak such havoc, to reap living men, to make such grief and take delight in it! We shall teach them what pain they have wrought! We

shall see how they die, how they delight in captivity, what pleasure they take in their own pain!" She set off toward the plain, and
Lua ran beside her, drying her eyes.

"Be assured, we shall do all this and more," Culaehra told the ancients. His blood was singing in his veins again, and the prospect of
action delighted him; he was alive once more! "We shall bring your
daughters and your grandchildren back to you, if they still live!"

"They do—the Vanyar will not kill them until they have taken
their pleasure," an old woman said. "But find them ere nightfall,
young man, if you can!"

"Shorten our journey, then! Did anyone see which way they
rode?"

"Down toward the plain, where your shield-maiden goes," an old
man said. "Belike they will follow the river, for it has already cut
through the hills for them, and there is something of a trail along its
banks, though there were more deer who made it than people."

"Many thanks, old one!" Culaehra turned away. "Find a hearth
and keep a fire burning, to guide us back if we come by night!" He
set off, striding quickly to catch up with Kitishane, who was moving quickly enough herself. Yocote ran beside him; the warrior
said, "Your pardon for my long strides, Yocote, but I must catch
Kitishane before she goes too far."

"I think she has gone too far already." The gnome wasn't even
breathing hard. "What the devil is she thinking of, pitting us against
a band of fifty wagon riders with axes!"

" 'Chariots,' I think they call those carts," Culaehra said, musing. "Do you really think your magic is not equal to their axes,
shaman?"

"Be sure that it is!" Yocote snapped. "The question, though, is
whether or not they will slay you while I am spell-casting."

Culaehra reached back to touch Corotrovir's hilt, and grinned.
"Be sure they shall not."

When they caught up with Kitishane, Culaehra asked, "Do you
have any plan for what we shall do when we find these Vanyar?"

"Slay, stab, slash, and maim!" Kitishane snapped. "What else
need we know?"

Culaehra glanced at Yocote. The gnome shrugged, and Culaehra turned back to his avenging Fury. "We might wish to set some sort of a trap for them."

"Why not merely let them try to capture us?"

"Possible," Culaehra said judiciously, "but you might let your anger carry you away and drop your bow in favor of the satisfaction of plunging your knife into their bodies."

"An excellent idea! I know just where to plunge it!"

"Valiantly said," Culaehra approved, "but if you come that close to their axes, they might cleave you—and I would be heartbroken if you lost your head."

Kitishane snarled at that, but her snarl faltered. "Devise a strategy, then, if you are so keen for it."

"I shall set my brain to it." Culaehra glanced at Yocote, and the gnome nodded.

The four companions came to the crest of a hill and looked down into a long, twisting valley. "There!" Kitishane cried, pointing.

"Be still!" Yocote hissed.

"What, do you fear they will hear me at this distance?"

"The air is clear, and it is only a mile," the gnome grumped. "Are there more than fifty?"

Culaehra looked down at him, surprised that he asked, then noticed anew the goggles Yocote wore. He remembered that gnomes usually saw no farther than a dozen yards underground, and turned back to count.

The Vanyar were still singing their victory song—doubtless at the tops of their voices, since the sound came to the companions' ears over the distance, though very thinly. The tone was gloating, and Culaehra suspected the words spoke of blood and maiming. They rode their chariots in an oblong with the captives stumbling along in the center.

Culaehra nodded. "Fifty-four, yes. Two men to a chariot."

"Forget the chariots; they will," the gnome told him.

"Shall we charge upon them now?" Kitishane asked, eyes glowing.

"Not unless you wish us all to be slain," Yocote replied, "and yourself and Lua used as toys first."

Kitishane's head snapped up; she stared at him, appalled.

Culaehra frowned. "I am sure I can kill ten of them, Yocote."

"Yes, and I can take another dozen with my magic, and the ladies can bring down a dozen more with their bows, perhaps two—but that still leaves eight alive, and after they bring you down, they shall slay me, and I do not need to tell you that Kitishane and Lua cannot run as fast as a horse. If we wish to slay these murderers, we shall have to do it by cunning as well as strength."

"You do not say we must let them ride!" Kitishane cried.

"Only until darkness falls," Yocote told them.

Lua shuddered. "What will they do to the virgins then?"

"Little, I think," Yocote told her. "I hate to admit it, but there is a hierarchy of hungers in a man, and I think the Vanyar will wish to feed and drink before they play with their new toys—and being horsemen, they will picket and feed their mounts before they do anything else. Even if they turn upon the women before they dine, we will have time."

"Time for what?" Kitishane said, frowning darkly.

"I shall tell you as we walk, or they will ride too far for us to catch," Yocote told her. He pointed. "They follow the river, but it curves around these hills. If we stay with this ridge, we should hew to a straighter line, and move ahead of them before sunset."

Kitishane looked, gauged distances, and nodded. "Their horses go at a walk. We should outpace them, yes."

"We have already," the gnome pointed out. "Let us march atop this ridge."

"Not atop," Culaehra said, "or they will see us against the skyline. Let us walk a little below."

He found a game trail along the side of the ridge, one that was screened by brush but high on the hill. They followed the Vanyar, then began to pull ahead of them, and as Yocote had estimated, they were well ahead as the sun set. They watched as the Vanyar picketed their horses and began to curry them.

"If you do not do something quickly, shaman, I shall fall upon them myself!" Kitishane threatened.

"Even so." Yocote began to draw circles and lines in the dirt, muttering a rhyme. His body tensed; sweat stood out on his brow.

In the distance, something howled.

"What was that?" Kitishane looked up in alarm.

"Not a wolf." Culaehra reached back to touch Corotrovir. "The note stretched too long—but if it is a dog, it is a huge one."

Another howl sounded, still distant, but from a different direction.

The Vanyar heard it, too, but more to the point, so did their horses. They began to shift about, whickering with fear. The barbarians had to soothe their mounts.

Another howl sounded from still a third direction, then another and another.

Finally, Kitishane understood. "It is you who causes that noise, shaman!"

Yocote nodded. "When I journeyed to the shaman's world, other shamans offered me the loan of their totem-animals if I would lend mine in return—though I fail to see why they would have much use for a badger."

Culaehra looked up in surprise, then turned away quickly to hide a smile and stifle a laugh. Kitishane looked up in concern. "What makes you cough, warrior?"

"I swallowed wrongly," Culaehra wheezed, avoiding the black look Yocote cast at him. "What totems have you borrowed, shaman?"

"Huge and gaunt ones," Yocote told him. "They will keep the Vanyar from taking their ease, never fear. Now let us slip up nearer to them, so that we can slip up closely indeed after full darkness falls."

"That will be too late for the virgins!" Lua cried.

"Oh, no," Yocote assured her. "Whether or not that howling disturbs the Vanyar, it will frighten their horses sorely. They shall have no time for their captives—you shall see."

He was right; the only attention the Vanyar paid to the women was to set them to cooking an evening meal. After that, whenever one of the warriors approached a woman with purpose, a howl sounded out across the valley, and the horses neighed with fear and began to pull against their picket reins.

The timing was no surprise; the howls were coming very frequently now, and from many directions; they seemed to encircle the camp. Gradually, very gradually, they were coming closer.

In their hiding place on the hillside nearest the camp, Yocote nodded with satisfaction. "They have no shaman with them, or he would have seen through my spell ere now."

The biggest Vanyar stepped up by the cook-fire, leaned back and spread his hands to the sky. He began to chant, and though they could not understand his words, they caught the name "Bolenkar!" several times.

"What does he, Yocote?" Kitishane asked nervously.

"He prays," the gnome said, tensing, "but he is no shaman." He muttered a few words in the shaman's tongue, accompanying them with a gesture, then nodded. "It increases the force of malice a bit—Bolenkar must have given these barbarians amulets to evoke his force—but it will impede me not at all. It will give his warriors more heart, though."

"Then there will be the more for us to take from them." Kitishane's lips skinned back from her teeth. "When, Yocote?"

"When the horses flee."

"The horses flee?" She turned to stare at him. "When will they do that?"

"In a matter of minutes." The shaman drew in the dirt again. "Lua and Kitishane, crawl out to the sides and string your bows. Warrior, be ready to reap death!"

Culaehra drew Corotrovir and felt its strength begin to sing through his veins.

Yocote chanted, ending with a bark.

All around the campsite the howls rose, hot with greed, and began to move inward, coming faster and faster.

Then the howlers broke from the brush, glowing with their own light.

CHAPTER 23

They glowed with their own light and were at least as high as a man's waist, but they seemed far larger—lean and sleek hell-hounds with fiery eyes and steel teeth, long ears and jowls, legs like jointed stilts and huge feet studded with iron claws. They fell upon the horses, howling with greed and anger.

The horses screamed and reared, tossing their heads frantically till they broke their tethers. Vanyar came running, calling to their horses—until they saw what had frightened them. Then they stopped where they were, hauled out their axes and set themselves to fight.

A huge hound launched itself at a Vanyar. The man swung his axe once, twice, but the blade passed through the nightmare with no effect. He screamed in superstitious terror just before the huge jaws engulfed his whole head. He stumbled and fell.

"Now, farmer!" Yocote snapped. "Reap your crop!"

Culaehra ran forward swinging the great sword. It vibrated in the rush of air, seeming almost to sing. He came upon the Vanyar warrior who struggled to free his head from the hound's jaws, but wherever he moved, the beast moved with him. Culaehra called up the memory of the murdered boys in the village and struck. The Vanyar convulsed once and lay still. The hound leaped away, baying, and launched itself at another Vanyar.

Culaehra followed, slashing until his arms tired. All about him nightmare hounds were bringing down Vanyar, frightening them into stumbling, though the hounds had no substance. Culaehra slew and slew; it almost seemed as if Corotrovir had a life of its own and hungered for Vanyar blood.

Not all the Vanyar who fell still moved. Arrows jutted from throats and chests. Culaehra had help enough.

He needed it. The chieftain had somehow stayed alive; even more, he managed to clamber onto a horse's back. Now he shouted commands that included Bolenkar's name, and the nomads looked up, startled, staring at Culaehra. Then some ran to catch horses—but the nearest turned on Culaehra, teeth bared in a snarl, charging as he swung his axe.

Corotrovir lopped the axehead from its handle. The Vanyar howled in frustration and launched himself, hands reaching for Culaehra's neck. Corotrovir swung again, Culaehra stepped aside, and the barbarian hurtled on past, dead.

But other barbarians had reached their horses and clambered onto their backs with a crudeness that told how strange this was to them. Nonetheless, they shouted commands in their own tongue, and the horses sprang forward, galloping down on Culaehra from every side. Two or three men toppled, arrows in their chests, but their horses kept on. Nightmare hounds leaped past Culaehra on every side, howling in anger and hunger, and horses shied, throwing Vanyar from their backs, but three managed to fight their mounts down and keep them running—through the hounds, straight toward Culaehra!

Now it was steel against iron, sword against axe, and skill against skill. Culaehra sprang to the side, putting one horseman between himself and the others. He pivoted, swinging even as the Vanyar chopped downward. Corotrovir slit the man's leather coat and bit into his chest, throwing the axe stroke wide . . .

But not quite wide enough. The side of the blade struck Culaehra's head. Pain rocked him. He caught at the Vanyar, struggling to hold to consciousness, but the whole world slipped around him, slipped and slammed up to strike him. *I will* not *lose consciousness*, he ordered himself fiercely, and his vision cleared—to see Kitishane standing over him, a gnome to each side of her, and Vanyar lying dead before her with arrows transfixing them.

Culaehra scrambled to his feet, caught her in his arm for one brief, hard kiss, then turned to face the enemy, sword up in case one should rise—but the only men still alive were dying quickly.

"I cannot believe I have slain so many!" Lua cried, stricken—but she did not drop her bow.

Instantly, Yocote forgot his magic and turned to take her in his arms. She sobbed into his shoulder as the hellhounds faded from sight.

Culaehra looked up at a distant drumming and saw two riders galloping off down the riverbed. He cursed. "Whatever horde spawned this band will know what happened here!"

"Perhaps that is just as well," Kitishane said slowly.

"Why? They will seek revenge!"

"Yes, and the villagers will have to flee to the forest—but they have nothing left to return to as it is, save their grandparents. And word will run through the barbarian horde of a mighty warrior with an enchanted sword who leads a band of nightmare hounds to hunt Vanyar and spear them with arrows."

"Then they will hunt *us*! How is this good?"

"Because they will begin to fear," Kitishane said simply, "and because they called upon their god, but he did not save them."

Culaehra frowned after the fleeing barbarians, rolling the idea over in his mind.

As the night quieted, sobbing came to their ears—the sobbing of terrified women and the wailing of children.

Lua broke away from Yocote on the instant and went to the nearest mother, holding out her arms. "Do not fear! I am a gnome, not a goblin."

"But . . . but the hounds!" the woman stammered.

"They came at the command of our shaman." Lua gestured toward Yocote.

"Shaman?" The woman stared. "A gnome shaman?"

"Rare, I know," Yocote said, frowning, "but it is true—I summoned the hounds, and have banished them. My apologies for your fright, good woman, but our effort has succeeded—not a one of you has been worse hurt than when you were taken from your village."

"Why—that is true!" the woman said, wondering. "But you have captured us now! Where will you take us?"

"Back to your village." Kitishane came up behind the gnomes. "We have freed you, not captured you."

"This is her doing," Yocote declared. "Kitishane was so angered by the Vanyar's cruelty to your village that she led us to seek justice, and to free you. She brought us all to you."

"But the battle plan was yours!" Kitishane said quickly.

"I thank you, I thank you all!" Tears brimmed in the woman's eyes. "But who is the warrior who slew so many of our enemies?"

Culaehra finished wiping his blade, sheathed it, and came up behind Kitishane.

"His name is Culaehra," Kitishane said, "and if it had not been for him, we would all be dead—or worse. Tell the others—you are free! But we must go now, before the Vanyar send more warriors."

"Yes, yes! We shall go!" The woman rose and went to tell her neighbors, pressing her children close against her.

"Let us catch a few of those horses if we can," Culaehra told Kitishane. "The Vanyar seem to have left their chariots, and these folk will travel faster if the horses do their walking for them."

Kitishane nodded and went to try to make friends with the Vanyar's pets.

Yocote nodded, and began to gesture, muttering. The horses calmed; those who had strayed began to turn back toward the campsite.

Half an hour later the horses left the camp, going back where they had come during the day, with very inexpert, feminine hands on the reins. Kitishane and Lua rode another chariot with them. Culaehra and Yocote stayed only long enough for Corotrovir to chop apart the four chariots that had no horses; then they boarded one last car and drove after the women.

The old folk could scarcely believe their eyes when they saw their daughters and grandchildren coming back. Glad cries rose from both sides, and women rushed forward to embrace elders. The children ran in for their share of hugs and reassurances. Then all turned to see the carnage wrought about them anew, and tears flowed.

"It is time to bury the dead," Lua said, tears on her cheeks.

"Yes, but quickly." Kitishane frowned. "The Vanyar may not leave us an abundance of time."

Even digging graves, Culaehra did not doff his armor; as Kitishane had said, the Vanyar might be upon them sooner than they expected.

"Dig only a few inches," Yocote told him, "then leave the rest to me."

"Save your strength." Lua touched his arm. "You shall need it, and magic over rock and earth is such as all gnomes know."

Yocote's face darkened; he remembered that he had very little of such inborn magic.

"You are a mighty shaman," she assured him, "such as has never been among gnomekind. Let me do what any other gnome may."

The gratitude that flashed from his eyes was intense, but gone almost as soon as it was seen. The look on his face was vibrant, though.

Culaehra did not understand, but he knew better than to argue with magicians. He lifted a few inches of dirt in a line, six feet by three feet, again and again for the number of bodies that lay in the village street. Then Lua chanted, making an upward gesture with both hands, and dirt and stones began to pour out of the ground, mounding up high along the lines Culaehra had drawn. In half an hour the graves were ready, and Kitishane and Culaehra began the grim work of bearing bodies to their final beds, carrying first the one ancient who lay dead. Weeping, the women began to join in the work; sobbing, they buried markers in the ground carved with pictures that told who was buried in each grave. Then all the survivors stood about, their sobs filling the night.

Culaehra looked up, frowning. "Have you no priest?"

"He lies in that grave." An old woman pointed. "Aged though he was, he stood in the path of the Vanyar with his staff raised, praying to Ojun to stop them. Ojun did not hear. How well would he guard these dead?"

"Ojun?" Culaehra turned to Yocote. "Do you know of an Ojun?"

"He was an Ulin who was slain in their war," the shaman answered. "Illbane made me memorize all their names, and who had died, and how."

The old woman stared. "Do you say our god is dead?"

"Dead, but his spirit still may aid you," Kitishane told her. "Still, he was an Ulin, not a god. The only real God is the Creator."

Puzzled frowns surrounded her, and the old woman said, "You must explain this when we are safe. For now, though, cannot one of you say a prayer?"

"That is for the shaman." Culaehra stepped back, deferring to Yocote.

The gnome stared up at him, appalled—but Kitishane nodded agreement, and Lua stood watching him, huge eyes glowing. Yocote locked gazes with her, then nodded and stepped up before the circle of graves. He bowed his head a moment, summoning magic, then raised his hands and intoned, "May all who lie here ascend to a land of happiness and plenty. May they never want, never grow bored or restless, but remain for all of eternity in bliss. Lomallin, we pray you—lead these innocent victims to the Land of the Blessed, where they may bask in the glory of the Creator, their souls singing with the joy of His presence."

"May it be so," Lua replied.

"May it be so," the whole village chorused.

Yocote lowered his hands, but still stood gazing out over the field of dead. At last he said, "What is a lifetime, measured against eternity? And what matter the pains of life, if they are balanced by joys? Those who have sought to do good to one another in life, rejoice in the company of other good souls in death, and all rejoice in the presence of the Creator, from whom all goodness flows. May these dead, in their rapture in the Land of the Blessed, forget all pain and misery they have known on earth. Lomallin, guide them to their Creator in death, as you ever sought to do in their lives."

"May it be so," Lua said.

"May it be so," they all chorused.

Yocote turned away. "Come, let us give these dead the greatest gift that we may—which is your own continued life. Show us where you may be safe in this wilderness."

Slowly, the women turned away.

"Take the chariots," Kitishane urged.

The old woman shook her head. "Where we go, horses cannot follow." They led the way up a slope and in among trees.

"Go with them," Kitishane advised, and the gnomes turned to accompany the women. Culaehra and Kitishane stayed to drive all the chariots together, then cut the horses loose and drive them away before they kindled a blaze under the Vanyar cars. They followed the women with a bonfire at their backs, and brushed away all signs of footprints as they went.

The old men advised, but it was one of the mature women who emerged as leader of the village now. Her name was Alsa, but she turned frequently for advice to her mother, Temla, the old woman who had asked about Lomallin. Yocote told her what he knew; she asked for prayers to both Lomallin and the Creator, and for ceremonies to honor them. Again Yocote told her what he knew, but stressed to her that worship needed no set forms, only sincere words from the heart. He told her, too, that the Creator needed no sacrifice of goods or lives, but only of self-denial—refraining from cruelty or malice, and, more important, self-dedication to trying to help others and increase their happiness. Temla taught Alsa, and both of them taught the rest of the women.

While Yocote taught religion, Culaehra taught staff-play, showing the women how they might use scythes and spades and pitchforks as weapons. Kitishane and Lua taught them archery, for they all knew the Vanyar would come back.

Return they did, a thousand strong. Their chariots darkened the valley; the hoofbeats of their horses filled the hills with thunder.

"Get you down and hide you behind the largest ruin in the village," Yocote told Culaehra. "Kitishane, find archers to slay any who come near him! Culaehra, when their shaman comes forth to battle me, let him cast one spell, then step out and slay him. When he is dead, run back here, for the Vanyar will pursue. Run up that ravine, and archers will slay them from the evergreens on the slopes."

Culaehra did not stay to question. He went to hide.

The Vanyar slewed to a halt beside the heap of ash that had once been chariots, recognizing the iron hoops that had bound the wheels and the iron rods that had been axles. Their anger was great, and they set up a deal of shouting and swearing in their barbarous tongue. Finally, one of them stepped forth wearing a robe made of a wolf's skin, with the head perched atop his own. His eyes were darkened with soot; scarlet symbols adorned his cheeks. He drew a wand from his belt, faced the hillside nearest the village and chanted. Points of light began to glitter in the air, moving about, gathering into a swarm that was pointed at the hillside.

An owl swooped from the sky, an owl abroad in daylight, and struck into the center of that glittering swarm like a hawk seizing a mouse. The points turned, darted, pierced the bird—and it exploded, sending showers of darts everywhere. Several struck the Vanyar shaman, who cursed.

Now was the time. Culaehra leaped out, hoping that Yocote was readying his next spell, and ran at the Vanyar, sword swinging. The warriors saw and shouted, whipping their horses into a run. The shaman turned, stared, then began to gesture and chant.

Culaehra struck. The sword hummed as it bit, and the shaman screamed; then something exploded inside him and he fell dead.

Culaehra stared, not understanding. Then he heard the massed shout of fury, glanced up to see the Vanyar charging down at him, remembered the plan, turned, and ran.

The very earth exploded beneath the Vanyar's wheels. Gouts of dirt shot high into the air. Chariot after chariot overturned; others slammed into the gaping holes in the ground and jarred to a halt. Horses screamed, rearing to avoid the blasting dirt and kicking over the chariots behind them. But a hundred chariots swerved around the disaster and kept coming, converging on Culaehra as he darted into the mouth of the ravine.

The walls narrowed quickly. Chariot slammed into chariot; axles broke, oaken sides cracked. Cursing, fifty Vanyar climbed from the wreckage and set off after Culaehra, who darted far ahead, but the sun glittered off his bronzen armor, showing him clearly. The Vanyar followed, roaring anger.

Arrows sprang from the hillsides. Intent on their prey, the Vanyar failed to see them until points pierced their throats and shafts sprang from their chests. The survivors turned, roaring, to charge the hillside—and flights from the other slope took them in the back. At least a dozen living men turned to flee, but more shafts struck, and not one of them survived.

On the plain, the earth was still exploding around and under the Vanyar. Finally, a poor remnant of the host turned and ran, chariots rattling over the valley and out along the riverbank.

On the hillside Kitishane cried, "Enough!" and Yocote nodded, lowering his arms.

"Lomallin has borrowed power from the Creator to win us this day," he cried out to the villagers. "Let all see that Lomallin has greater power than Bolenkar!" Then he turned away—and tottered, nearly fell.

As he slept, villagers moved among the Vanyar, slaying those too badly injured to live and calling Culaehra to tend to those who might. He disarmed those who still bore axes and fought one or two who were not yet badly hurt. He took a few cuts on his arms where Agrapax's armor did not protect him, but disarmed them all, then set those who could still walk to carry litters bearing those too badly injured to bear their own weight. He sent them off along the riverbank with dire warnings of the fate that would befall any servant of Bolenkar's who came this way again. Then he turned to begin the long process of dragging the dead into the ravine. A few chariots were still intact, a few horses had not yet fled, so the task went more quickly than it might have.

When Yocote woke the next day, the ravine was filled with Vanyar dead. He looked down upon them and scowled. "We cannot have them lying unburied; it will bring disease." So again he chanted, and with a roar the sides of the ravine caved in, burying the slain under ten feet of earth. When the dust had settled, the astounded villagers found themselves staring down at sloping, raw hillsides with a broad, flat field between.

"Sow this field with gorse," Yocote bade them, "and let no one build or farm there for twenty years. Call it 'Culaehra's reaping.' "

But they did not—they called it "Yocote's Reach."

At last the companions assembled to resume their journey.

Temla came to thank them, with all the villagers behind her. "Be ready to run if the Vanyar come again," Kitishane advised her, "but I think they will not. Still, post sentries on the hilltops for two years before you think yourselves once more safe."

"Kitishane, we will," Temla promised, but Alsa came up with half a dozen grim-faced women behind her, each bearing a staff in her hand and a Vanyar axe at her waist. "These women have lost both husband and children," Alsa explained. "There is nothing for them here, no life to live. They wish to come with you and slay Vanyar."

Yocote and Culaehra were startled, but Lua only nodded slowly, understanding. Kitishane recovered from her surprise and frowned. "You understand that the journey will be hard, and that we will give you training in the use of arms that will be harder still."

"Anything! We will endure all gladly!" the tallest woman said. "Only give us Vanyar to kill!!" She was slender and hard-faced.

"Vira is . . . dedicated to the cause," Alsa said, her voice low.

Yocote stepped forward. "They will not always be Vanyar whom we fight. Bolenkar has many agents, of many different nations, even different races, for some among the elves and dwarfs and, aye, even the gnomes, have been suborned."

"We will fight any who have wrought this grief upon us!" Vira snapped. "Take us with you, we pray!"

Kitishane nodded slowly. "Illbane told us we must gather forces to throw against Bolenkar's armies. You shall be the first. Come."

They found two more chariots, and the women rode three to a car. Off they went down the river road. The companions turned to wave farewell to the villagers, who sang an outsong, waving—but Vira and her women did not look back even once.

They avoided the Vanyar horde by taking to the ridges, but found other hill tribes beset by the invaders. They fought and slew these Vanyar squadrons, shamanry against violence, sword against axes— and Vira and her women made sure there were no survivors to carry tales back to the main horde. In every village a few more farmers or herdsmen joined them, to learn fighting and take revenge for the deaths of loved ones—and though the tale of their prowess did not run back to the Vanyar horde, it ran through the hills, so that even in villages that had not been attacked, there were young men and women who asked to go with them. Their progress was slow, for they needed to pause daily for instruction in fighting, and for practice—but they trended steadily southward, and as the first hint of summer came, they found the great river, as Illbane had told them they would. They traded with the river-folk—Vanyar axes for small sailing boats, then more axes for lessons in their use.

They sailed southward with the current. Now and again river pirates would put out from shore, paddling fast to catch them, but a few waterspouts beneath their boats made most of them change their minds. A few righted their craft and came on with renewed determination; they turned and fled in horror when a monstrous creature with long and flailing arms emerged from the water. They could have paddled right through it, of course—but they did not know that.

Some of the village folk came out in peace and asked to join the company, for the tale of the hero and his companions who fought against the Vanyar and all the evils of the world was running before them. By the time they came to the river junction, they led a fleet.

The people who had built a city at the joining of the rivers sent their own fleet out to demand tribute of those who wished to pass. Kitishane explained the importance of their mission; Culaehra stood by, smiling brightly as he whetted his sword, and the men and women in the other boats gradually drifted to surround the tax ships, axes and scythes much in evidence. The tax collector decided the companions' mission was too important for interference and bade them go in peace. Yocote responded by offering to trade for food, and the collector settled down to haggle. By the time they drifted into the eastbound river, they had full cargoes of food—and a dozen recruits from the city.

They crossed the inland sea, but there they disembarked and began to march again. They had an army behind them, everyone laden with provisions—but when the grass became sparse and the living trees gave way to dead, many of them began to have second thoughts.

Then even sparse grass ended, the last blasted trunk fell behind, and they found themselves facing a land of baking heat, of naked rock and baked mud. The troop drew up in a line to stare in dismay. Culaehra turned with a frown. "Bolenkar's hold is far from here; it lies across this wasteland," he said. "I will blame no one who does not wish to risk his life in crossing this—but I do mean to go. If you wish to come with me, step forward. If you do not, remain, and have a camp ready to give us succor if we come back again." He paused, looking from one end of his little army to the other. At last he said, "Who comes?"

CHAPTER 24

Everyone stepped forward. Everyone came.

Culaehra stood staring at them in disbelief. Finally he said, "Do you know what you do? This is such a journey as may kill us all without ever sighting an enemy!"

"We know," Vira said. "Our lives have no purpose otherwise. At least let us die with a chance of finding our enemy."

Culaehra looked up and down the line, noticing all over again the scars, the hardness in the eyes. Vira and her villagers were not the only ones who had suffered from people who had listened to Bolenkar's notion of good living through others' pain. None had come who had any ties to keep them back. All had either had loved ones torn from them by bandits, like Vira, or were outcasts, like himself.

"They are faithful, warrior," Kitishane told him.

Culaehra nodded. "So be it, then. There was a pond half a mile back. Did you all fill your waterskins?"

Everyone nodded.

"We shall camp here and rest," Culaehra told them, "for I do not trust this heat. When the sun hides its face, we will march."

When the sun went down, night fell with a suddenness that surprised them. They struck camp, drowned their cook-fires, and strode out into the desert a hundred strong. Within the hour it was almost cool.

They marched all that night, then camped during the day. Yocote came up to Culaehra and said, "I sense no water, hidden or open. I have cast bones and read omens, but I see no hint of moisture during our next march."

Culaehra nodded and turned to Kitishane. "Tell them all not to drink unless you command it."

Kitishane stared. "Why me?"

"Because left to myself, I would drink too frequently or too sparingly, but never what is needed. You have the feel for it—you tally the water."

They marched again when night had fallen, and Kitishane called out three swallows each hour, then called when the hour was up. When the night was darkest, when the chill was almost uncomfortable, Vira let out a cry. The troop stopped; Culaehra turned to see. She was pointing off into the distance. Culaehra looked where she was pointing but could see nothing. He ran over to her. "What do you see?"

"Blobs of white approaching, and they seem to drift above the desert floor!"

"Ghosts! Ghosts!" Scarcely a whisper, it ran through the ranks.

"Form a circle, spears outward!" Culaehra barked. "Whatever it is, it shall find us thorny!"

They scurried to form up, taking heart merely from the action and the notion that they were ready. When everyone was in place, though, they all turned to stare into the darkness, waiting for some sight of the ghosts.

There they came, bobbing white shapes high off the sand, even as Vira had said! But as they came closer, Yocote cried, "They are not ghosts—they are men! But Heaven alone knows what manner of beasts they ride!"

"Have arrows nocked," Kitishane called, "but do not draw or loose unless I bid you do so. They may be friends." But she did not sound very hopeful.

The strangers were almost upon the little troop before the riders drew rein and the northerners could see the shape of their mounts. They were tall, long-necked, long-legged, gangly creatures whose backs rose in humps. The riders sat in saddles strapped atop those humps, swathed in loose robes that would have been white if they had not been so filled with sand. They wore cloth about their heads, held in place with circlets of rope. They were sunburned and bearded. In the center of the band the tall mounts wore small cur-tained huts instead of saddles. Swords glittered in the hands of the men; there were no women or children in sight.

The two bands stared at one another in mutual hostility, each line bristling with weapons—but each side also uncertain.

"They cannot be enemies," Kitishane finally said, "or they would have attacked."

Culaehra nodded, then stepped forward, transferring his sword to his left hand and holding up his right. "Peace!"

"Culaehra!" Kitishane gasped, then held her breath, for one of the riders nudged his beast forward, transferring his sword to his left hand and holding up his right in imitation. "Solam!"

"Could that be their word for peace?" Lua asked.

"Likely enough." Culaehra kept his eyes on the rider's face, try-ing to look friendly. "What do we do now, Kitishane?"

"We try to talk with them," Yocote answered. He stepped for-ward, holding up his right palm, and called out a string of syllables his companions did not recognize.

A man in the second rank of riders looked up in surprise, then moved his beast forward beside the leader's. He called out a ques-tion in a foreign language—foreign to his own people, too, judging from the looks of surprise they gave him.

But it was not terribly foreign to Yocote. There was gladness and relief in his voice as he called back to the second rider; his friends started as they heard him end with the name "Bolenkar." The rider seemed startled, too, and replied with considerable force and energy. The companions recognized the word "Bolenkar" again.

Yocote replied with a broad smile, then turned to his companions and said, "He is their shaman. They, too, are enemies of Bolenkar. He has given me a proverb of their people: 'The enemy of my enemy is my friend.' "

"Why then, we are most assuredly friends!" Culaehra said fervently. "What is our friend's name, and how is it they have come riding upon us?"

Yocote turned and spoke to the shaman. He replied at some length, and as he spoke, Yocote's face became darker and darker. When the man was done, Yocote returned a brief comment, then turned to his own people. "His name is Yusev, and he is shaman of the Tribe of Dariad. They came upon us because they sighted us in the distance, and it is their way to ride toward trouble, not to flee it."

Culaehra nodded vigorously. "A sound policy."

"Yes, so long as they do not make trouble where there was none." Kitishane frowned. "But what sent them riding across the desert in the darkness?"

Yocote turned to ask, and the dialogue between himself and the riders' shaman went more or less as follows, as he translated it for his friends:

Yocote: "How is it you ride in the darkness?"

Yusev: "Because in this merciless desert, it is too hot to ride in the day."

Yocote: "So I thought; it is what has sent us abroad by night. But why do you ride at all?"

Yusev: "To find pasture for our flocks. It is our way; we are nomads because the pasturage is scarce. When our animals have eaten all the grass in one place, we must go to another."

Yocote: "I am amazed that you can find grass at all in this wasteland."

Yusev: "We know where the grass grows and where water lies; this knowledge has been given from parent to child for many generations. Now, though, many water holes are drying up, and the palms about them die. The grass becomes brown and sere, then turns to powder and blows away. The desert is spreading, even as it did in the days of Dariad the Defender, and we who eke out a living at its edge must needs go farther and farther to find pastures."

Yocote: "A sad tale, and certainly reason enough to travel. You ride very quickly."

Yusev: "We ride to escape the soldiers of Gormaran."

Yocote: "Gormaran! Do they chase you, then?"

Yusev: "They hunt us. They have not yet found our trace, and we mean to see they do not."

Yocote: "What have you done, that they should hunt you?"

Yusev: "We exist. That is all the reason they need to hunt down all the Peoples of the Wind, all the nomads like us. Bolenkar has sent his armies out to build strongholds around each oasis, denying us water to sustain life and the pasturage that grows by water. Thus we are driven to the desert's rim, where the Gormarani can find us more easily. Those whom they catch, they slay. They mean to exterminate all those of us who wander freely over the desert."

Yocote: "I can see that; free people are threats to those who would rule everybody. Do they mean for none of your people to survive?"

Yusev: "Some, if you can call it survival—or if you can call them still the People of the Wind. Those who give up heart, those who weary of living in fear for the lives of their spouses and children, are welcome to go to the forts to live—if they swear allegiance to Gormaran and take up the worship of Bolenkar. Then the soldiers give them food and allow them water to grow grass, so that they may pasture their flocks. The women learn to grow food, like the farmers who surround the eastern cities; the men are taken into Bolenkar's army. Little Gormaranis are springing up all over the desert as the People No Longer of the Wind build houses of mud brick around the strongholds and study to become city dwellers."

Yocote: "Can they truly succeed in that?"

Yusev: "How do you succeed in a living death? For certainly, it is death for the People of the Wind to become rooted to one place. Oh, the body survives—but the spirit dies, until they come to truly believe that Bolenkar is a god."

When Yocote was finished translating all of this for his companions, Culaehra demanded, "Can they not beat off these soldiers? The legends say that the People of Dariad were fearsome fighters, and surely these are the descendants of those people!"

Yocote translated the question, albeit a bit more diplomatically, and Yusev replied, "The People of the Wind are still valiant fighters, and slay them each ten soldiers or more before they die—but die they do, and more soldiers come marching in to take the places of the slain. Bolenkar seems to have no end of soldiers. They march into our land over the bodies of our dead in an endless stream. They shall drown us by sheer numbers, no matter how badly they fight."

"Surely you do not believe that Bolenkar cannot be killed!" Culaehra cried in indignation.

"Of course not," Yusev replied to the translation, in equal indignation. "We know that only the Creator is God, and that the Ulin were people, very much like ourselves—more powerful people, surely, and longer-lived, with inborn magic and greater intelligence—but with passions and flaws of character very much like ours, though perhaps those were greater, too."

"And with virtues like ours, but perhaps also greater," Kitishane said through Yocote.

Yusev nodded. "Perhaps so. Surely Lomallin was great in courage, and great in his ability to sacrifice himself for others. Still, the Ulin were only super-humans, not gods—and an Ulin's half-human son is only a more durable kind of man. He can be slain; even an Ulin can be slain by another Ulin, so an Ulharl must be vulnerable even to humankind."

"Even so," Yocote said. "Culaehra slew one."

Yusev's gaze snapped up to the warrior in astonishment. "You? You slew an Ulharl?"

Culaehra shrugged at the translated words, uncomfortable with the praise. "We all did. Mine was the sword that dealt the death-blow, that is all."

"All? Only four people together, and you slew an *Ulharl*?"

The companions' army began muttering among themselves; they had not heard this before. But Vira and her fellow villagers kept silent, though their eyes glowed.

"Yocote countered the Ulharl's magic," Culaehra said. "Kitishane and Lua distracted him with arrows, and finished him completely by shooting him in the eye. And, too, a sage stood by us, to protect us."

"But he did not help in the slaying?"

"He did not need to, no."

"That is the sword that struck the death-blow?" Yusev stretched out his hands. "Let me touch it, I pray you!"

Culaehra did not understand, but he drew his sword and held it up by the blade. Yusev touched the hilt with awe—then stared with awe greater still. "This blade was forged by Ohaern, the companion of Dariad the Defender!"

Murmurs of awe and excitement swept both ranks. Warriors craned their necks to look more closely.

Culaehra would have said that Dariad was Ohaern's companion—but he could understand why legend would have made it otherwise to these people. He frowned, turning to Yocote. "How can he tell that?"

"He is a shaman," Yocote said simply.

"Amazing!" Yusev stroked the blade, staring at it in admiration. "Ohaern has been gone for five hundred years, and the sword he forged still looks new!"

"It *is* new," Yocote said.

Yusev whirled to stare at him, first in amazement, then in accusation. "You blaspheme!"

Culaehra hissed, "What are you doing? They will think us madmen or liars."

But Yocote seemed sure of his course. He said loudly, "I do not blaspheme. Ohaern woke from his centuries of sleep and found us. He bade us call him 'Illbane,' and trained us all without our knowing who he truly was."

"Ohaern woke! Ohaern woke!" The words ran through both ranks in hushed but excited tones.

"Where is he?" Yusev asked, eyes glowing.

"Dead, I fear." Kitishane turned somber. "He waited until we had come to love him—then he died on us."

Moans of disappointment sounded. Yusev turned to her in surprise, then smiled gently. "Do not be angry with him, maiden. I am sure he did not choose to die."

"But he did!" Kitishane was near tears. "He led us to the Star Stone, the fragment of Lomallin's spear that fell to earth during his battle with Ulahane, and bade us stay far away as he smelted its iron and forged it into the sword Corotrovir. But there was poison in the Star Stone, poison that came from Ulahane's weapon when it nicked the fragment from the spear, and Ohaern drew that poison out into his own body, so that the Starsword would not slay its bearer. But the poison wracked his body with pain and killed him."

Silence held that benighted plain. Yusev whispered, "He gave his life for you."

Culaehra bowed his head, taking the guilt upon himself.

"He gave his life for us all!" It was Lua who spoke, quivering with anger. "He told us that we four must slay Bolenkar, and he forged the sword Corotrovir to do it!"

"And forged Culaehra into a hero able to bear the sword," Yocote added.

Now it was Culaehra whom Yusev regarded with awe. "Truly? But yes, I see it must be true, for I feel it within the steel! You are the one whom Ohaern has chosen to slay the monster Ulharl! You are the one who shall strike down the soldiers of Gormaran! Kinsmen, rejoice! He who shall lead us to freedom has come!"

The People of the Wind shrilled triumph in loud, treble ululations. Culaehra stared about him, dazed.

Yusev turned to the nomad leader. "Send riders to all the other tribes that still wander free! Tell them the Chieftain of Chieftains has come, sent by Ohaern!" He turned back to Culaehra. "What would you have all the tribes do, O Chieftain?"

Culaehra stared, dumbfounded. Kitishane noticed and forgot her grief; she stepped up beside him with a smile. "Well asked, O Chieftain. You have found your army—what will you do with it?"

The camels—or so the odd-looking beasts were called—were picketed several hundred yards away under the care of the women and youths who had been riding in the curtained houses borne by the camels in the center of the party. The men lined the banks of a dry riverbed, waiting with the patience of stones. Culaehra knew they were there, for he had seen them take their positions. Then he had turned away to converse with Yocote, and when he turned back, the People of the Wind had disappeared.

"Do not fear, O Chieftain," Yusev had said. "We are here, as you have bade us be. We await the Gormarani, as you do."

Now Culaehra knelt with a large boulder before him, ready to hide at the first sign of the troops Yusev had promised him. There was no point in his keeping watch, really—Yusev's chieftain Chokir had sent out sentries of his own, and Culaehra was sure they would see more than he did, with far less chance of being seen themselves.

"It seems your plan will work well, Yocote," he said. "How did you think of it?"

The gnome shrugged. "You had to set them a task quickly, warrior, or they would have grown disappointed and left you—and if there are soldiers abroad, they are the sensible target."

"A force small enough for our few hundreds to defeat, but only a finger of the enemy hand," Kitishane said, nodding. "Well thought, Yocote." She turned as Lua came trotting up. "Are the women against us?"

"They are excited, but were fearful at the thought of losing husbands and sons," the gnome reported. "I showed them that they must risk that, or risk even more deaths if the soldiers catch the People of the Wind in their own time and at their leisure."

"Did no one say it would be better to go to one of Gormaran's strongholds and build houses?" Culaehra asked.

Lua shook her head. "In truth, I began to wonder about that, and finally risked telling them that was the only safe course."

"Lua!" Kitishane chided. "You could have lost us our army!"

"My curiosity gained the best of me," the gnome admitted. "But the women turned on me as one, scolding me and telling me of the misery the People endure at the strongholds. A few have escaped—yes, escaped! Once the soldiers have them, they are little better than slaves! At least as many men are executed for breaking the soldiers' rules as would be slain in battle, and their wives and daughters are used most shamefully. All the women agreed that clean death is better than a living one."

Kitishane shuddered. "I must agree. So that is why they were so willing for the men to ride! And why they were as quick to pledge loyalty as their husbands were."

"Sand!" The word swept toward them as if borne on the wind, passed from mouth to mouth from far away. Culaehra looked up, wondering at the excitement in the tone. If there was one thing that was not unusual in this place, it was sand.

Then he saw what they meant. A plume of sand rose into the morning air and seemed to be moving toward them.

They had ridden all night to this dried-up watercourse. The Darians had known exactly where each band of Gormarani had been, and the nearest marching column had only been a few hours distant. Culaehra suspected that if they had not ridden to find the column, it would have come to find them.

He strained his eyes, watching the bend in the watercourse between themselves and the plume of sand. Only a large body of creatures could be raising so much dust, and what creatures would travel in such numbers in this devastated country except men? A few minutes later he began to hear the beating of hooves and the rumble of chariot wheels.

A voice spoke near him, and Yusev translated for Yocote, who translated for his companions: "The fools! To bring horses into this country! They must carry their own weight in water!"

"Fools, perhaps, but deadly fools," Culaehra replied. "Let no man move until I give the word."

"Even so, Culaehra," Yusev replied, and translated, passing the message.

Culaehra glanced nervously at the bluff nearby, where Vira and her northern army stood waiting. They would have been furious to be left out of the fight, and Culaehra knew they needed a victory to lift their spirits as much as the Darians did—but the desert folk knew best how to fight in the desert. So Culaehra had positioned his little army in hiding, as reserves. He was only worried because he would have to call upon them at some time, or risk their resentment.

Of course, all their archers lay in hiding atop the bluff. Perhaps some Gormaranis would escape far enough to become targets. The problem might resolve itself.

Culaehra found it difficult to believe the city soldiers could be so stupid as to march along the bottom of a dry watercourse. "Do they not know that such a gully as this is ideal for an ambush?"

Yocote translated the question, and Yusev replied, "They think the sides to be natural breastworks, and they march sentries along the top, to warn them if enemies approach."

"Have they never thought those enemies might be hiding in the banks already?"

"How should they?" Yusev grinned. "They do not know that the People of the Wind can disappear even where there is only empty sand to be seen."

"I can well believe it," Culaehra muttered. He had seen them disappear into the very sand of the banks themselves, but still found it hard to credit that mere human beings could vanish so completely—and that without magic!

Closer came the plume of sand, and closer. Culaehra slipped behind his pillar, the Starsword in his hand. Surely it was only a vagrant gust of wind that made it begin to vibrate, almost to sing . . .

There they came, chariots two abreast, two men in each, one holding the reins, one with a spear in hand—though the driver had a spear slung across his back, too. On they came, as another pair rounded the bend . . . and another, and another . . .

Culaehra stared, amazed, as they came and kept coming. Past his position the chariots rumbled, and he was in the middle of the Darians! He began to think his northerners might be truly needed, after all.

Then the lead chariots were past the bluff, and still they came! No . . . there were no more! The last had come!

They had to spring their trap, or let the quarry escape. There were far more than Culaehra had planned on, but they had to begin somewhere. "Attack!" he snapped.

Yocote translated, Yusev passed the message—and ululating howls filled the air as the sides of the riverbed seemed to explode, hurling forth cloaked demons who fell upon the chariots.

The spearmen turned to defend, but the Darians took them by pairs, one to catch and break the spear, one to stab. Spears flew from the rear chariots, beyond the desert men, and a few struck Darians who screamed more with rage than pain and turned to slit another throat before they died. Horses neighed in terror and reared, bucking; chariots overturned. In minutes the riverbed was chaos. The lead chariots beyond the attackers tried to turn back, but there was not enough room.

Culaehra howled like a northern wolf. Other throats caught the sound and repeated it until it reached the ears of Vira's band. Arrows fell like hail from the top of the bluff, slaying the lead charioteers, halting the survivors in confusion as Vira and her folk ran out, spears flashing. They skidded and jumped down the sides of the riverbank and set to, thrusting and blocking.

Yocote was gesturing and chanting, as was Yusev nearby. If there was a shaman with the soldiers, his spells had no chance. Kitishane knelt beside them, panting with eagerness for the fray, but remembering her assigned position; she knelt with an arrow nocked, waiting for a Gormarani to climb the slope, trying to escape. Lua knelt beside her, smaller arrow at the ready, and just as lethal.

But one charioteer slew and slew, one who caught up a battle-axe when his spear was thrown, a battle-axe and shield, and beat off the Darians who came near him. Several already lay dead around him, but he could not move, for his chariot was blocked in by others overturned about him.

The wind blew, and Corotrovir whined for action. This task, Culaehra knew, was his own. He strode down the hill toward the big soldier.

CHAPTER 25

Culaehra picked his way through overturned chariots. The big
soldier saw him coming and drew back his lips in a sneer. His uniform was different from the others'—an officer, no doubt. He wore
a short robe over his leather armor, and his leather helmet was
surrounded with a fringe of small carvings—animals and monsters.
Culaehra stepped in, slashing. The soldier leaned aside just enough;
then his battle-axe blurred. Culaehra leaped back and swung at his
true target—the axle. Corotrovir bit through the oak as if it were
cheese, and the chariot lurched, throwing the big soldier to his
knees. Culaehra swung horizontally, his sword whining, but the
soldier raised his battle-axe in the nick of time, blocking the swing.
Corotrovir rang off the sharpened iron, bounding away—but a
wedge dropped from the edge of the axe.

The soldier stared. Then his brows drew down, and he began to
chant as he clambered from the overturned car.

Culaehra couldn't understand the words, but he comprehended
the blood lust in the man's voice. "Pull back the chariots! I have
no wish to fall and be unable to rise!"

Willing hands yanked the overturned chariots away, and in seconds there was clear ground for the two fighters. The soldier stepped into it. He struck his chest with a fist, roaring, "Ataxeles!"

Culaehra frowned, wondering what the word meant—until his enemy speared a huge finger at him, shouting something that sounded like a question—and the warrior understood. "Ataxeles" was the man's name!

Culaehra struck his own chest, opening his mouth to call out his own name—but at the last second Yocote shouted, "Do not!"

That made no sense to Culaehra, but he had learned to trust the little shaman. Instead he shouted, "Fight!" and slashed his sword at the enemy.

The big Vanyar jumped back, raising his war-axe. Then he advanced, chanting his battle song, and for the first time in his life Culaehra found himself looking up at another human being—nearly a foot. For a fleeting second he felt the same dread rise in him that he had felt when he faced the Ulharl—but he quelled it with a laugh; this man might have been huge, but he was still only a man.

His laugh enraged his enemy, though. The soldier shouted his verse and swung. Culaehra swept his sword up, deflecting the blow—but Corotrovir jarred back, nicking his shoulder; the man was unbelievably strong! And here came that bloody axe, sweeping backhanded. Culaehra leaped away from the clumsy blow, then leaped in, slashing. Corotrovir swept down toward the man's helmet, then jarred to a stop an inch from the soldier's head. The big man grinned through his long moustaches and chopped downward two-handed.

"He is a shaman!" Yocote howled. "Back, Culaehra!"

A soldier-shaman? Culaehra had never heard of such a thing! Then he realized that this was what Yocote was—now. He leaped back, sweeping Corotrovir up to parry. The axe turned, but not enough—it slammed into the ground, slicing off Culaehra's little toe.

"Pick it up!" Yocote cried.

Pain seared through Culaehra, generating anger. He shouted in rage and leaped in, swinging and slashing and parrying, too quickly for the clumsy axe to keep up. Corotrovir bounced off the Vanyar helmet again, bit into the leather of the breastplate but no farther, then swept downward toward the man's knees—

The enemy soldier shouted a last line. Light seared Culaehra's eyes; he shouted and thrust blindly, felt a tug on one side of the sword. But the light coalesced into flame that died into a cloud of foul-smelling smoke. Coughing and gagging, Culaehra slashed through and through it, but Corotrovir met no resistance, and when the smoke cleared he saw why—the soldier-shaman had disappeared.

Culaehra cursed.

Yocote came running up. "Your pardon, Culaehra! I should have realized at once that the man was a shaman, but I did not expect to hear a soldier chanting a spell, so I thought it was his war song. It was minutes before I realized he was singing in the shaman's language."

"I should have realized it, too," Culaehra said, "and called upon you. Your pardon, Yocote—I fear I may have begun to take you for granted."

"Given, and gladly! Ho! Where is that toe?"

A Darian dropped Culaehra's toe into Yocote's cupped palm. He held it against the foot and Culaehra stifled a howl of pain—but Yocote was chanting.

Yusev was nodding. "Both ask each other's pardon—good. I, too, ask pardon—I was fighting instead of watching for sorcery."

Culaehra clenched his teeth against the pain, but managed to say, "Given and gladly again. *Two* of you, both warriors and shamans! I should certainly have realized the enemy might have some, too! *Aieeeeee!* What are you doing there, Yocote?"

"Putting your toe back on." The gnome stepped back. "Wiggle it."

Astounded, Culaehra stared down. Sure enough, his toe was back in its place. He willed it to move up and down, and was amazed that it responded, however sluggishly.

"It will take time to heal completely, of course." Yocote sounded a bit defensive.

"I had not known it could heal at all! How can I thank you, Yocote?"

"By your pardon, which you have already given." The gnome held his hand over Culaehra's other wound and began reciting.

He healed Culaehra, then wandered among the other wounded, healing where he could. Yusev did likewise. Lua picked out those who were near death and did what she could to soothe their passing, then to comfort the widows who wailed beside the corpses. Kitishane stared as if startled by the novelty of the idea, then went to imitate her. After a while the Darian women followed their example, those who had not lost husbands or sons.

Culaehra looked out over the field, wondering why there was no rejoicing. Only a half dozen of the nomads lay dead, after all; there should have been victory songs before they realized that some of their own folk lay lifeless. He solved the riddle when he saw a knot of the Darian warriors gathered to glare down the gully after the soldiers who had fled. Culaehra realized that they did not count it a victory, because some of the enemy had survived—and, worse, had fled back to their fortress. He could sympathize—the fugitives might well bring back an army of ten times their number.

On the other hand, if the whole garrison left the fortress, it should be easy pickings for the nomads . . . He nodded judiciously; it was a thought to keep in mind. In the meantime, though, he had a better plan.

He went over to the knot of warriors and beckoned. They looked up in surprise, then with misgiving, but they followed him. Lua and Kitishane had begun to seek out dying soldiers, but found few—the warriors had already prowled through the slain, finding the few who still had some life in them and finishing them with quick sword strokes.

Culaehra led the Darians to a cluster of enemy dead and began to unbuckle the armor of the biggest soldier he could find. The Darians watched him in disgust; Culaehra guessed that they had a taboo about robbing the dead. But when he began to buckle the Gormaran armor over his own, they exclaimed with sudden understanding and turned to take harness off the other dead.

Kitishane saw and came up, frowning. "What do you intend?"

"A little surprise for the soldiers," Culaehra explained.

Kitishane nodded slowly, liking the sound of the plan. "Only a few of you, though," she said. "The fugitives would notice if three score of their dead comrades had recovered and joined them."

Culaehra frowned. "There is that, yes. Well, we shall have to open the gates for the rest."

"Well thought." Kitishane turned away and began to unbuckle the armor from a dead soldier.

"You cannot go with us!" Culaehra caught her shoulder. Fear for her was plain on his face, but he only said, "The Gormarani did not have women among their warriors. I doubt they allow it."

"They shall not see a woman." Kitishane thumped the leather breastplate, smiling. "Armor has more purposes than those for which it was intended."

When the dead were buried, the Darians rode off down the dry riverbed, seeming no different from their usual selves—but under their robes, twelve of them wore Gormaran armor.

The routed soldiers were not hard to follow—they had left a trail as plain as a herd of camels. The Darians rode along the top of the gully. When Culaehra saw the soldiers in the distance, he held up a hand. His twelve picked Darians dismounted, laid each his robes over his saddle, skidded and slid down the sides of the gully and began to lope along after the soldiers. The rest of the warriors followed on their camels, slowly enough to be unseen, closely enough to keep the fugitives within earshot.

The Gormarani had tired and were plodding along, their hearts heavy, making quite a bit of noise as they went. It was easy to keep them barely out of sight until emerging from the riverbed, almost under the palisade of the fortress.

The palisade was made of sun-dried brick, not wood, but it was a high, strong wall nonetheless. Culaehra looked up at it and felt his heart sink. What chance had tribes of desert nomads against such a stronghold?

On the other hand, he knew what chance *this* tribe had. "Now, quickly!" He waved his men on. They understood the gesture if not the words and followed, grinning.

They were right behind the fleeing soldiers as they came to the gate. Startled shouts echoed down from the top of the wall, and the sentries at the huge portal stood aside, staring, as the weary, defeated troops streamed in. There were cries that Culaehra was sure meant, "What happened to *you?*" and the fugitives called back terse sentences that probably meant, "I will tell you later." They picked up their pace as they hurried through the gate to safety.

Culaehra, Kitishane, and their warriors came right behind them.

No one looked too closely at their faces—they were far too concerned with the calamity that had befallen their friends and were already bedeviling the others for the story. An officer pushed his way through, barking questions. Ataxeles the shaman-soldier began to answer him, every word angry.

Kitishane muttered under her breath, "Will Yusev remember when to charge?"

Ululations erupted outside the wall. The sentries turned to look, startled—and Kitishane cried "Now!" in the Darian language.

Yocote dropped from under Culaehra's cloak and began to chant. Ataxeles must have sensed his magic, because he whirled, eyes widening—but Yocote finished his spell, crying out the last syllable, and something unseen buffeted the enemy shaman; his head snapped back and his eyes rolled up. He slumped, unconscious.

None of the other soldiers noticed—they were all staring out at the charging nomad army.

The false soldiers struck.

A pair of Darians converged on each sentry; two more pairs converged on the porters behind the gate. Knives flashed, and the Gormarani slumped in silence. Quickly the nomads dragged the bodies out of sight behind the panels, then assumed the posts of the dead men, standing in readiness. When the officer called down from the wall, they stared up in blank incomprehension—as well they might, since his words meant nothing to them. The officer turned purple, shouting at them in anger. Still they stared up, not understanding. The officer bellowed, running down the stairway inside the wall.

At the bottom Culaehra leaped, Corotrovir swinging.

The captain fell, blood spreading. Soldiers shouted and leaped forward—but Kitishane loosed two arrows, and the sentries atop the wall fell, dead before they struck the paving below, while the other four Darians turned to meet the soldiers, knocking aside their spears and stabbing with nomad knives. The soldiers weren't prepared to have their own men fight back at them; they died astonished.

Then the camels burst through the gate.

Suddenly the nomads were everywhere, blades scything, spears stabbing. A dozen Darians sprang down to guard the gates. Culaehra shouted, and his false soldiers ran to follow him. Looking back, he saw there was one missing, and he hardened his heart— there would be time enough for grieving later.

Soldiers were running toward the gate from all over the compound, but Culaehra could see from which building the men with more ornate harnesses came. These would be the commanders. He sprinted toward that building, then swung Corotrovir at the first of them. The man howled with pain, staggering back and clutching his side. Four more commanders shouted in anger and converged on Culaehra, battle-axes flashing.

Blood sang in his veins even as Corotrovir sang in his hand. He blocked axe blows and slashed at men—but one axe struck through, slamming Agrapax's armor against his side. Pain exploded, but he ignored it and slashed at the man, who fell, a virtual fountain. Then another axe struck through the leather armor, slamming the magic breastplate in front so hard as to knock the breath from him. Pain wracked him, but Culaehra swung and slashed anyway, stiffening when another axe struck against the small of his back. Pain again, but he whirled and struck down the last man, then stood panting, looking about him in quick, darting glances, knowing that if it had not been for the Wondersmith's gift, he would have been dead on the paving stones that moment.

All about him nomads fought officers. Three more of his advance guard lay dead, but virtually all of the Gormarani had been made corpses, too. One or two still breathed—or groaned, trying feebly to move.

"Put them out of their misery," Culaehra told a Darian, and when the man frowned with lack of understanding, said briefly, "Kill them, " in the Darian language—the two armies had learned a few of each other's words already. The nomad nodded, with a grin that made even Culaehra shudder, and turned away to deliver the coup de grace to the two surviving officers.

To the others, Culaehra recited the words that Yocote had taught him: "Go among the soldiers, now, and slay their officers in any way you can. Have no more concern for honor than they would."

The Darians responded with hard smiles and turned away to do their work.

They were only just in time—the soldiers outnumbered the nomads three to one, and though the Darians were each slaying five times their number, they were being slain at an alarming rate. Culaehra stripped the harness from the most high-ranking officer he could find, exchanged it for his own, then caught the Darian who had slain the wounded and pushed the Gormaran uniform at him. The man understood; he changed harnesses quickly. "Tell them to surrender," Culaehra said in the Darian language as clearly as he could, and hoped the words he said were really the ones Yocote had taught him.

The nomads had not learned very much of the soldiers' words, but they had learned that. The man grinned again, nodded, and trotted off.

Culaehra plunged back into the crowd, looking for Vira and her women.

He collected a few more cuts on the way, on the upper arms and lower thighs, where the magical armor did not cover him. He dealt blow for blow, but could not take the time to choose his targets or aim his strokes, and so did not know if he had given anything more than superficial wounds. He found Vira and her warrior women by the gate, and Yusev with them. There was also a nomad whom Culaehra did not know and thought he had never seen, one whose robes were the deep yellow of saffron and whose eyes gleamed with zeal.

"Name Ronnar," Yusev said by way of introduction. Ronnar raised both hands, open and empty, in greeting.

"Me Culaehra." The warrior returned the gesture, then asked Yusev, in very broken Darian, "Him know what do?"

Yusev nodded. "Will talk soldiers."

Culaehra grinned and waved them on. "Up! Do!"

Up they went, with the saffron-robed nomad in their midst—or he who had been a nomad. Yocote had told them to find one of the People of the Wind who had settled by the fort and learned the Gormaran language, to translate for the Darians.

Culaehra's officer-clad Darian stood tall upon the wall and shouted a Gormaran word. Vira swerved, leading her charges toward him. Kitishane emerged from the crowd and blended into their group, holding a captured battle-axe ready to ward off blows—but none came, for the soldiers had all whipped about to stare at the "officer" who stood on the parapet, shouting to them to surrender. They were at a loss, then even more confused as the "officer" stepped down and disappeared among the crowd. Soldiers began to shout questions, but no answers came—until Kitishane and Vira led their group up to the parapet, and the saffron-robed nomad shouted to them in their own language. The soldiers whipped about then, seeking.

Culaehra knew what they were looking for—officers. One officer had inexplicably told them to surrender, then disappeared. They had shouted for other officers to explain, but none had answered—and one of their captured nomads, one of their own slaves, now stood above them telling them that all other officers were dead! They looked about them, searching, lost—for these were men who had been trained to obey, and nothing more; they were soldiers who had never been taught to think for themselves, had indeed been taught *not* to think, to leave that to their officers.

Now there were no officers.

The Gormarani, unable to think of any other course of action—or not daring to attempt one—began to throw down their axes and raise their hands in surrender.

The nomads shouted with victory. Kitishane spoke to the saffron-robed man, and he called down a translation: "Go to the long houses where you live! Sit on your pallets! Wait there till our commanders tell you what to do!"

Numbly, the soldiers turned to obey, trooping back to their barracks.

As soon as they were away from the gate, Culaehra ran to the spot where Ataxeles had fallen, Corotrovir ready to hold the shaman at bay when he regained consciousness. He found the stair to the parapet easily enough—but he did not find Ataxeles. He had come too late; his enemy had disappeared again.

· · ·

The interpreter learned more about Ataxeles simply by asking the soldiers. They were eager to speak of him, even boastful.

"He is a priest of Bolenkar," Ronnar said. "He is a mighty sorcerer, not a shaman only, and delights in the pain of his enemies."

Yocote's face darkened as he heard this. He gazed at the night outside the window of the chief officer's dwelling. Its former owner lay in a shallow grave beyond the cultivated land. The gnome turned back to Ronnar and asked, "Does he sacrifice living people to Bolenkar, making sure they die slowly and painfully?"

"He does." Ronnar frowned. "How did you know of this, shaman?"

"Because I know what a necromancer is, and this Ataxeles is one of them." Yocote's face worked as if he were about to spit. "His sacrifices do not work, of course—Bolenkar has power of his own, but cannot give more than a small fraction of it, since he is not an Ulin. Besides, he is not about to make any of his minions more powerful than he must. But I suspect Ataxeles glories in the illusion that sacrifices increase his power—or, if he has learned that they do not, enjoys others' pain so much that he is eager to slay even more."

"He is truly evil, then," Kitishane said, frowning.

"He most certainly is," Yocote said grimly. He turned back to Ronnar. "Are all the priests of Bolenkar so bad, or is he remarkable?"

"He is foremost among their priests," Ronnar answered. "The soldiers call Bolenkar the Scarlet One—"

"Ulahane's title." Culaehra remembered Illbane using the term.

"—so they call Ataxeles the Scarlet Priest," Ronnar finished.

"But what was he doing here, at a minor outpost in the desert?" Culaehra asked.

"Seeking victims for sacrifice," Yocote answered, and Ronnar nodded, explaining.

Yusev's face darkened; he translated for Yocote, whose face froze, his voice tightening with anger. "The expedition we ambushed was not sent to squash rebellion—it was sent to search for victims for Bolenkar's altar. If it found rebels to capture, all well and good—but if it found only peaceable herders, they would have been quite satis-factory in themselves."

Yusev said a string of syllables, very softly, but with great vehe-mence.

"What does he say?" Kitishane demanded.

"Nothing that I would care to translate," Yocote replied.

CHAPTER 26

Ronnar's robes were saffron because the soldiers had forced the settled nomads to dye their clothing, so that the Gormarani would know wild Darians from tame. The settlement people were all for burning their garments and making new ones, but Kitishane bade them not to—it could suit their purposes for Gormaran soldiers to think they talked to captives when they really spoke to free people.

Without exception, the settlement people wished to be free again. The soldiers had turned cruel once their nomads were more or less captive—arrogant and swaggering, beating any who disagreed with them, killing any who refused to live by Gormaran law, and taking any woman who struck their fancy. The former nomads were all glad to become nomads again. They packed up their belongings, mounted the soldiers' horses, and rode off into the desert, leaving the Gormarani without mounts and no food other than that which lay in their storehouses or grew ripening in the fields.

"Let them learn how to become desert dwellers," Kitishane advised, and the nomads answered with a cheer—but as they rode away, Kitishane looked back and saw a few of the soldiers walking down the rows of growing plants. She pointed them out to Culaehra and said, "I think those men were farmers once."

Culaehra nodded. "They will be again. Frankly, Kitishane, many of them did not look at all unhappy at being left without officers."

"And without the need to go back to Gormaran." Kitishane nodded. "We may have done good where we meant to cause pain, Culaehra. Is that bad?"

The warrior grinned. "I think not, beloved."

She looked up at him in surprise, then answered the look in his eyes with a shy smile.

So they rode back into the desert with their numbers tripled, for two separate tribes had settled around the stronghold. Vira seemed somehow impressed with Yusev; she rode by him, though warily, and began to teach him her words. In return, he taught her his. In a matter of days all the northerners were exchanging words with the People of the Wind and were well on their way to working out a pidgin dialect encompassing both languages. The settlement Darians, moreover, were teaching their limited Gormaran to any who wished to learn it. Foremost among their students were Yusev and Yocote, of course, but Culaehra and Kitishane were close behind, and Lua, surprisingly, seemed to soak up both languages without even trying. Certainly she learned at a faster rate, so quickly that she was chattering with the Darian women in a matter of days. It was almost as if she felt so strongly about giving reassurance and establishing ties, she wasn't about to let a little thing like language stand in her way.

The Darian women had been quite astonished by the gnomes at first—being desert dwellers, they had scarcely heard of the underground people, let alone seen them—but they quickly recovered from their surprise and wariness and were soon including Lua in their conversational circle as if she were an old friend they had not seen for a long while. Kitishane eyed her diminutive friend with envy, for the Darian women were much more circumspect with her. She was, after all, one of the war leaders, and seemed to them to have more in common with the men than with themselves.

Well, if her hunger for feminine companionship became too intense, she thought, she could always ask Lua to bring her into the gossip.

It was odd to think of a human turning to a gnome for help, but Kitishane was growing accustomed to it.

They fought with two other strongholds, overcoming the Gormarani by much the same tactics—wherever Ataxeles had fled, it did not seem to be in the desert. They marched away with more Darians augmenting their force, and by the time they came out of the desert into fertile, cultivated land, their little army numbered more than a thousand. The peasants in the fields looked up, saw their approach, and ran.

They bore word to their headmen, Kitishane knew, and the headmen would no doubt send word to the soldiers. How long would it be before they faced a pitched battle?

But before they did, they ran across a raiding party of Vanyar.

The barbarians took one look at the mounted force that outnumbered theirs ten to one and ran, their chariots sending dust high. The Darians howled with delight and gave chase. Kitishane let them run half a mile before she passed word for them to go more slowly. "We shall have no difficulty following these charioteers, after all, and they may be leading us into an ambush."

The thought was sobering, and the People of the Wind slowed to travel with wariness. At Kitishane's suggestion, Culaehra sent scouts ahead. Then the two of them conferred with Yocote.

"We must learn if these Vanyar recognize us," the gnome said. "The ones we fought were far to the north, after all. They might well be a different tribe and may not even have heard of our victory."

"A point." Culaehra nodded. "What warrior willingly tells of his defeats?"

"Perhaps we can parley," Kitishane said, though without much hope. "We may even be able to pass them without bloodshed."

"Anything is possible." But Yocote didn't seem terribly optimistic, either.

So, they cautiously followed the raiding party back to the main host of their tribe. As they came in sight, a huge mob of chariots came rumbling out to bar their way, horses galloping, riders shouting—but there were no more of them than in the allies' force, so they did not attack, but only took up position in a long line, barring the way.

"Who speaks their language?" Culaehra called.

No one replied.

"Can we not even talk to one another?" he cried in exasperation. "Yocote! Call for a shaman!"

"I shall try, but I do not hope for much in a band of warriors." Nonetheless, the gnome climbed upon a camel's back and called out to the Vanyar.

All eyes turned to stare at him, for the Vanyar did not recognize a gnome, especially wearing goggles and in bright sunshine—but one young man started violently before calling out to the war chief. The leader replied, his tone hard, and the young man turned his chariot, speeding away around the end of the line.

"He goes back to their main camp," Yocote called down.

"He seems to have recognized the shaman's tongue." Culaehra frowned, not all that certain he liked the development.

"Perhaps he is one who began shaman's training but chose to be a warrior instead," Kitishane said, guessing. "I think he has gone to fetch a real shaman."

"Certainly there seems to be no sign of their attacking until he comes back," Yocote called down. "Let us wait, but with watchful eyes."

Culaehra agreed, calling out to the rest of his chiefs. They rested their spears on their knees, waiting—but ready to fight at a moment's notice. Still, the Vanyar did not advance, only worked to calm restless horses and equally restless young men.

Then the messenger came speeding back, raising his own private dust cloud, with a gray-haired woman in his chariot. He swerved the chariot to a halt between the two lines of warriors, and the woman climbed down. She stepped toward Yocote with authority in every step, then stopped, raised both arms and called out to him.

Yusev translated for the companions. "She says her name is Masana and that she is all this tribe has for a shaman now that old Dwelig has died. She asks to know who Yocote is and why he has brought his tribe here."

Yocote replied at some length. Again Yusev translated, only a few syllables behind the gnome. "He says that we are a federation of many tribes, come to attack Gormaran for revenge."

"But we do not seek vengeance!" Kitishane protested.

"We do not," Culaehra said, "but it is a reason the Vanyar can understand. Yocote tells them that if they will let us pass, we will not harm them, for it is Gormaran we quarrel with, not them—but if they do not let us pass, we must fight."

A rumble went up from the Vanyar ranks. They shook spears and war-axes, and their noise built toward a roar.

Kitishane seized Culaehra's arm with sudden inspiration. "Warrior! Challenge their chief to single combat!"

Culaehra stared at her in surprise, then realized the sense of what she said—the fight would certainly forestall a battle, and might prevent it. He had no doubt that he would win. He stepped forward, calling out, "Yocote, translate for me! Tell them I am Culaehra, war chief of this band! Tell them that I challenge their chieftain to single combat, here between our battle lines!"

"Culaehra! Do you know what you do?" Lua cried in fright.

"Be easy, sister," Kitishane called out. "He knows well, and it was my idea."

"Well . . . I know you would not truly risk him willingly," Lua said, but she seemed still doubtful.

Yocote called out the message, and the Vanyar quieted to hear Masana's translation. She shouted it out, and the Vanyar roared indeed, but in delight. When they quieted, the war chief shouted two syllables. Masana turned back to Yocote, calling out one word. "He says 'yes,' " Yocote translated.

"Well enough, then." Culaehra stepped out between the lines, drawing his sword.

"Yocote! Confer!" Kitishane called.

The gnome frowned, but grudgingly gave up his high seat and dodged between camel legs, coming to her.

The Vanyar chief stepped down from his chariot and out between the battle lines, opposite Culaehra. He was an inch or two taller than the warrior, and even more muscular. Suddenly, Culaehra wondered if this was such a good idea after all. Still, the chieftain was at least ten years older than he, probably twenty, for there were streaks of gray in his beard.

Behind him, Kitishane conversed quickly with Yocote. The little man nodded, then sat down on the ground, closing his eyes in order to settle into a shaman's trance. Meanwhile, Yusev stepped up beside him, guarding. Seeing this, Masana frowned blackly. She turned to the young man who had driven her, beckoned, and went back through the Vanyar lines, in order to settle into her own trance.

As Culaehra strode off, Kitishane called, "Do not kill him, Culaehra, but make the fight last a long time."

Her faith in him was touching, he thought sardonically as he advanced to meet the Vanyar chieftain, who was looking harder and more grim with every second. The man thumped his chest with a fist and called out, "Singorot!"

His name, at a guess. Culaehra mimicked the gesture, calling back, "Culaehra!"

The Vanyar chief grinned and reached back behind his shoulder. He drew not a battle-axe, but a huge curved sword. His grin widened; he stepped forward, leveling the blade.

Relief shot through Culaehra's veins. A battle-axe might have given him trouble, but a sword he was more than sure he could deal with—especially since an axeman like Singorot would probably wield the blade as if it were double-bitted instead of double-edged, and from the dullness of the metal, it was probably simple forged iron, perhaps not even steel at all. Corotrovir would probably go through it as if it were cheese—which created a different problem for Culaehra. How would he keep the fight going? He would have to be careful indeed not to chop through that blade!

But also careful to stay alive. Singorot leaped forward, huge blade swinging down like a crescent moon with a honed edge. Culaehra leaped back and parried, turning the sword's path downward. Singorot chopped into the dirt and roared with anger and frustration. Before he could yank the blade free, Culaehra leaped in to nick his upper arm—not enough to lame him, only to show blood. The watching warriors saw, and a cheer erupted from the allies, echoed by a shout of anger from the Vanyar. Weapons waved and rattled—but no one struck.

Singorot yanked his blade free with a snarl and advanced on Culaehra, sword sweeping from side to side and up and down in huge diagonal slashes. Culaehra gave ground again and again, waiting for his opening, knowing he must let Singorot strike him to save face—but also knowing he dared not risk a blow of that cleaver on any place vulnerable. Finally, he decided he must have faith in Agrapax's armor, and swung his own sword up as he slowed his retreat. Singorot shouted with triumph and swung. The sword cracked against Culaehra's breastplate. He staggered, feeling as if butted by a bull. For a moment the scene swam about him and he had to struggle for breath—but he came back to himself in time to see Singorot's huge cleaver swinging down at his ankles. He leaped, the blade passing beneath him, and swung at Singorot's helmet even as he was in the air. The blow did not have a great deal of force behind it, since he could not brace himself, but it was enough to gouge the metal and send Singorot staggering. Knowing he had to make it look realistic, Culaehra stalked him, looking wary, but really waiting for the man to recover so he could go on with the charade. Fortunately, Singorot did not seem to realize it was a sham—and Culaehra knew he did not dare let the man know.

Singorot pulled himself upright with a snarl and strode forward, holding his sword in both fists straight in front of him. Then he began to swing it from side to side, as if man and blade were a serpent trying to judge the best target for a strike.

Culaehra held Corotrovir rib-high, angling up, ready to parry. He was beginning to tire of this shamming, and wished that he could really fight, but had seen enough of Singorot's style to know that if he did, the Vanyar would not last a minute. Of course, without magical armor and an enchanted blade, they would have been evenly matched, Culaehra reflected, and without Illbane's teaching, he would have been meat for the vultures.

But he did have Agrapax's armor and Ohaern's sword and, more important, Illbane's training. He leaped to meet Singorot's swing and whirled Corotrovir in a circle, twisting the Vanyar's sword against the natural turning of human arms, then leaped back at the last instant, a moment before forcing the blade from Singorot's hands. The big Vanyar stood frozen, staring at his adversary, and with a sinking heart Culaehra knew that Singorot had realized he was being toyed with. There was fear in that glance, but more—there was a dread of being shamed in front of his troops.

Oho! Culaehra thought, suddenly seeing a way out of his dilemma—but how to manage when he could not speak the Vanyar tongue? He met Singorot's next onslaught with parry after parry, yielding ground, then suddenly reversed, stepping in and whirling Corotrovir to bind the Vanyar's blade. For a moment the swords froze on high, and Singorot stared down in disbelief at the smaller man.

Culaehra winked.

Singorot stared, confounded. Then his face darkened; he leaped back with a roar, and leaped in again, huge sword slashing down.

Yocote crossed a blasted heath to the huge trunk that rose from its center, and this heath itself was the Center of the World. He paused a moment, looking up at the huge tree that towered above him, disappearing into the clouds that overcast the day. When he had come here before, the sun had shone and the Tree had disappeared into the blueness of the sky itself. This day, though, was ominous; he hoped it was not a day of omen.

He set foot on a root, lifted hands to find holds in the rough bark, and began to climb the World Tree into the shaman's land.

Yocote had climbed the Tree only once before, and had known then that Illbane watched his entranced body and would be by him in an instant at the slightest sign of trouble—but it was Yusev who watched over him now, and he knew no more of the shaman's world than Yocote did.

He climbed up through a layer of clouds and saw the misty, magical land of shamans all about him. Carefully, he climbed down off the Tree, unwilling to trust his weight to ground that was cloud underneath—but it held him as well as real dirt, only giving slightly beneath his step. The gnome held out his arms, looked down at his body and saw it was covered with fur. He gave his tail a shake and felt it move, saw his stubby limbs and knew he was a badger.

Then the leaves of the World Tree shivered and shook, and badger-Yocote leaped back, watching warily, to see in what form the Vanyar shaman came.

It was not an animal that emerged from the opening in the ground, though—it was a bird that soared up, a wide-winged bird with angry eyes and cruel beak: a hawk. Yocote stared, amazed—he had not heard of a bird-totem before. Of course, now that he thought of it, there must be some—there were far too many tribes and clans of humans, elves, gnomes, and dwarfs for the number of fur-bearing animals.

The hawk settled to the ground, folding its wings, dwarfing Yocote; he had to fight himself to keep from shrinking in fear. The beak opened and spoke human words, shaman's words. "So, then. Now we fight, you and I?"

"If we must," Yocote replied through the badger's mouth. "But you seem to me to be a good person, and I would rather fight only enemies."

"We must be enemies, you and I," the hawk said sadly, "for the Vanyar must have all the land we can."

"Why?" Yocote asked, but the hawk had already leaped into the air. Its wings clapped open and it cried, "Defend!" Then it stooped on the badger, its talons reaching for his throat.

Even as a badger, Yocote remembered Illbane's training. He reared back, balancing on short, stumpy legs, and swatted the talons aside with one paw, then bit the leg from which they sprang. He did not bite hard—he still did not wish to hurt a good person. His reward was a buffet with the hawk's wing; then the leg yanked itself out of his mouth, ripping itself on his teeth. The hawk squalled with pain, and its blood tasted acrid in Yocote's mouth. It spiraled high, and as it flew it called, "Bolenkar, hear your worshiper! Come now to aid, and give me victory!" Then it began to sing a song of blood and death and maiming.

A red aura sprang up all around the hawk. It swelled in size; its talons glinted with sharpness.

What else could Yocote do but call upon his own protector? "Lomallin, if you hear me, lend your strength to aid! I battle in the shaman's world with one I would befriend, but she fights with the remnants of Ulahane's power, left within the soul of his misbegotten son Bolenkar! Come, I plead! Lend me the strength of your goodwill to oppose the malice of your old enemy!"

The world seemed to turn light green about him, and he knew Lomallin's aura surrounded his badger-form.

The hawk screeched in surprise and fright—but the scarlet aura about it deepened almost to black. Crazed with blood lust, it folded its wings and struck.

Yocote knew better than to use the same tactic twice—and sure enough, the hawk veered at the last second and struck from the side. But Yocote was already falling away from it, and the claws only pushed him, making him fall harder. He felt warm wetness spreading over his side and knew the talons had scored through his fur—but he kicked with his hind paws, striking with claws of his own.

Black badger's claws met tan talons—and light exploded all about them, sound blasting their eardrums.

CHAPTER 27

Yocote held on to consciousness, though he was frozen stiff by the energy coursing through and around him. The light about him seemed to darken, leaving the whole day indistinct and murky. Then suddenly light shone again—green light, rich green, the green of forest leaves. It showed him the hawk lying senseless on its back, claws up in the air.

Strength returned, and Yocote leaped to his feet in alarm. He surely had not wanted the Vanyar shaman dead! But the green light gathered about him and coursed away, burying itself in the hawk's body, then springing forth to form an aura all about it. After a minute the light sank back, pulling itself within the hawk's feathers, then was gone, and the even, pearly light of the always overcast shaman's world remained.

Yocote froze, knowing he must not try to help any further.

The hawk tipped over and rolled to her side. Slowly, then, her wings opened; she pushed herself to stand on her talons, shaking her head as if dazed. Her gaze alighted on Yocote, and she stared at him, wings shuddering then closing—but even as those wings closed about her, the hawk began to change, its form fluxing and growing until a young and comely woman stood before him, wearing Vanyar leggings gartered under a brown dress bright with embroidery in geometrical designs that Yocote recognized as mystic symbols, though not the ones he knew.

Yocote understood. He stood up on his hind legs again, willing himself to return to his proper shape. The world blurred about him for a few minutes, then steadied again, and he glanced down, seeing again his gnome's hands and arms, body, legs, and feet. He looked up at the young woman, then gave a little bow. "I salute you."

"And I you." The Vanyar shaman returned the bow, then swept a gesture that included all of herself. "This is how I appeared when I was young—and how I still see myself inside."

"Must we still fight?"

"No," the Vanyar shaman said. "I have seen for myself which force is greater—Bolenkar's or Lomallin's. Your god is a channel for the life-force from its Source to us—and that life-force has vanquished the death-force of Bolenkar."

"Of Ulahane, rather," Yocote said, "and he is dead."

Masana stared. "Can gods die?"

"He was not truly a god, only a man of the Ulin—an elder race," Yocote said. "He hated all the younger races and sought to slay us all. Has Bolenkar not told you of him?"

"We have never seen Bolenkar," Masana said. "How often do humans see a god? No, we have seen those who carry his word—but none of them have ever spoken of this Ulahane, nor any of the elder race."

"Ulahane raped a human woman," Yocote told her. "Bolenkar is the bastard son of that crime. His father made many other slaves that way; they are called Ulharls. No, Bolenkar would not tell you that he is less than his father, for he seeks to become greater. He *can* not, so he is doomed to perpetual anger."

"What could kill a god?"

"Another Ulin," Yocote said. "Ulahane slew Lomallin—then Lomallin's ghost slew Ulahane. Both ghosts mounted to the heavens and fought with stars for weapons, and Lomallin's ghost slew Ulahane's. All that is left of Ulahane's spirit is the residue that resides in the Ulharls, and the hatred and lust and greed that they imbue in humankind and the other younger races."

"So the green god lives, and the scarlet god is dead?" Masana asked.

"Even so." Yocote sighed and gave up trying to convince her that the Ulin were not gods.

"Then assuredly we worship the wrong god! I shall do all I can to turn my tribe to the worship of your Lomallin! What sacrifice does he wish?"

"Your arrogance, your cruelty, your greed and hatred," Yocote told her, "all the emotions that might cause you to fight with other people of any race. These Lomallin wishes you to give up, to try to exterminate in yourselves as if they were victims on his altar. He wishes you to live, not die; he wishes happiness and joy, not misery and pain."

Masana stared, eyes round in wonder. "He would have us give up conquest?"

"It would be a sacrifice indeed," Yocote said with a straight face. "Why do you Vanyar love to conquer so?"

"It is not a love only, but a need. We have never seen the lands from which our kind sprang; we have been riding and fighting in conquest for three generations now. Our grandfathers began it when they fled from the centaurs who rode down from the north and conquered our ancestral country."

"The Vanyar were chased from their own lands?" Yocote asked, surprised. "What manner of people were these who pushed them out?"

"Half man, half horse; they have horses' bodies, but are men from the waist up," Masana said. "They wear long moustaches and cut their black hair short. They shoot with short bows made of horn and wood, and are as numerous as the grass on the plain."

Well, that last was how the western folk thought of the Vanyar. Was there a people so vast in numbers that even the Vanyar thought them uncountable? Yocote shuddered at the thought. "They are hard, these centaurs?"

"Very hard; they show no trace of pain, and delight in slaughter and in rapine—or so said our grandmothers; we ourselves have never seen them." Masana shuddered, too. "Pray to all gods that we never shall!"

"So your grandfathers needed to conquer new lands in which to live." Yocote frowned. "But why do you continue to do so?"

"Because the centaurs might come again," Masana said, "and because by the time our mothers were born, we Vanyar had filled the lands our grandfathers had conquered. If we were to live, we must needs do so by conquering more."

"You must bear many babes. Do your women bring them forth three and four at a time?"

"Litters like those of dogs?" Masana scoffed, but her eyes brightened with anger. "No. We only know it is a woman's duty to bear as many children as she can."

Yocote was astounded. "What blasphemy is this? Women die from too much child-bearing—their bodies wear out!"

Masana shrugged. "There are always more women to take their places—or so say Bolenkar's priests. They tell us a woman must always be willing, no matter whether she wishes it or not." Her tone was becoming bitter. "If she is not willing, so much the worse for her! I wonder if those priests would say this if they had themselves been raped—but rape is all to the better, they say; Bolenkar would rather have rape than have the woman knowing pleasure. Thereupon he tells us another reason to conquer—to capture unwilling women and beget children upon them by force. If a man wants slaves, says Bolenkar, he should get them himself—get their mother by conquest, then get them upon her!"

"So your men have many slaves." Yocote shuddered. "Are the children reared as slaves, or as Vanyar?"

"The boys are Vanyar. The women are slaves." The sardonic set of her mouth told him that even the full-blooded Vanyar women were slaves, but she dared not say it.

"But children require food, clothing, warmth, and shelter," Yocote replied. "How is a Vanyar warrior to gain them?"

"By conquest," Masana replied.

"And if he fails?"

"Then they die."

Yocote shuddered. "It is otherwise among the western peoples, even among us gnomes! Among humans a man may not wed until he has built himself a house, cleared land to farm, and proved his ability to provide by raising crops and bringing home meat from the hunt for a year or two—and must prove also, of course, that he can slay a bear who threatens them, or even a bandit."

"And how many children does he sire *before* he weds?"

"Some do," Yocote admitted, "but they must bring home food for the babes nonetheless, even should they marry another—and they are viewed with contempt for years after."

Masana nodded slowly. "That is better for the women, yes—but once they are wed, how many children do they bear?"

"As many as the Creator gives them," Yocote replied. "Some have none, some have fifteen—but most have only four or five."

"Four or five in a woman's whole lifetime?" Masana said in disbelief. "How comes this?"

"I am still a bachelor," Yocote said sheepishly, "so I do not truly know—but our shamans say that a man must not lie with a woman, even his wife, unless she wishes it." He could not help a sly smile. "Of course, I am told that many men are quite skilled at bringing their wives to wish it."

"A wondrous law!" Masana cried. "Is this what Lomallin teaches his people?"

"Lomallin's ghost, and the still-living Ulin woman Rahani," Yocote told her.

"But if what you say is so, a man who has four or five wives would father only twenty or twenty-five children!"

"Twenty-five?" Yocote stared. "Where would he find food for so many? No, most of our folk wed only one wife—or only one at a time, at least; there are some couples that divorce and find new partners."

"Only one wife?" Masana said with surprise. "How could he be content?"

"Ah." Yocote smiled. "Therein are our *women* skilled. You might as well ask how a woman can be content with the same husband for a whole lifetime, and I must admit that some cannot, even as some men cannot—but most of our men seem skilled at keeping their wives content with their lot, and with their men."

"Rahani must teach them both wondrous things," Masana muttered.

"We are told that this is better for the children," Yocote added. "They are secure in their parents' love, and in having the attention of one man and one woman, whom they know to be their mother and father."

"It is true, it is very true! For a child to have to struggle for the father's attention, against the children of the favorite wife, is as cruel as the mother struggling for some small part of her husband's regard! In fact, many have no more attention than he gives his cattle, and less than he gives his horse!"

"Even so," Yocote agreed. "Thus we limit the number of marriages, and folk wed later—and thus are there fewer children born to our folk. That is sad in itself, perhaps, but happier in that there is more assurance that none of the children will starve. But we boast that more of our women are happy than among the city-folk of the south, and that more men are happy, too."

"I think that I like your notion of happiness," Masana said. "But what happens when a father dies in war?"

"Then all the other folk of the tribe band together to see to it that his wife and babes do not starve, or go too badly in want," Yocote told her. "Still, wars are rare among us, and generally nothing more than a hundred men or so in one single battle." His face darkened. "At least, so it was until Bolenkar's emissaries came among us."

"I shall be his emissary no longer," Masana said, with sudden and total conviction. "I shall match my spells against those of his priests, and if I die, I die—but if I live, I shall free the Vanyar from his tyranny!"

Yocote stared, amazed at the transformation he had wrought.

Masana saw, and smiled. "Do not be so surprised, little shaman—you have told me things I never knew, given me knowledge that Bolenkar and his priests have withheld from us! Of course I have embraced a teaching that could so bless me, and all my kind! It is not you who have persuaded me, but truth itself—and the truth shall free us all! Come, let us go back to the world of men and women, and I shall sing the Vanyar this song of freedom! Away!"

With that, her form seemed to melt, to vibrate, and to harden again into the shape of the hawk. She climbed aloft in a crackling of wing beats and shot off toward the World Tree, then began to slip and slide through the air in a spiral about it, descending.

Yocote hurried to follow her, changing back to the form of the badger as he did.

Singorot stood panting, and Culaehra could visibly see the man summon the last of his energy. He swung his huge broadsword with a convulsive heave, and Culaehra ducked under its path with ease. The Vanyar tried to change the direction of the slash at the last moment, and Culaehra, with a flash of inspiration, rose just enough for the blade to catch Corotrovir and slam it back against his helmet—and he could have sworn the sword snarled at him for it. He fell to the side, rolled up to his feet, shaking his head as if to clear it, and heard the murmur of satisfaction from the Vanyar with the groan of his own people—but in truth, the stroke held very little force compared to Singorot's first blow. The man had tired, and badly. So had Culaehra, of course, but with a lighter sword and lighter armor, he was nowhere nearly so weary as Singorot.

He was sick to death of this pantomime, though. He wished heartily that Yocote would waken so he could end it.

Then he heard a thrum of exclamations from the Vanyar. With a quick glance he saw the Vanyar shaman returning, her warriors supporting her as she came. She was still alive! Anxiety for Yocote thrilled through him, and he almost turned to glance at the little shaman, but saw Singorot swinging his sword back and up in a great circle. He was mightily tempted to kick the fellow in the belly and be done with it, but knew he had to let Singorot save the esteem of his own men, or he would have a blood-feud with full hatred on his hands. Again a lucky thought rose, and he rolled up his shoulder, tucked down his head, and charged the Vanyar, for all the world as if they held no swords.

Singorot saw him coming, of course, but could not bring the great sword around in time to stop him. They met with a crash, and the Vanyar went sprawling. So did Culaehra, but it was the Vanyar's people who shouted in anger.

Culaehra was first to roll back up to his feet. Singorot floundered, finally managing to roll to hands and knees, looking about, dazed, for his sword. Everyone could see that Culaehra had time and more to cut off his head . . .

But by that time no one was looking, for the Vanyar shaman was calling out, and all her people were turning to look. Culaehra risked a quick glance at Yocote and saw the little man unfolding and rising, blinking, bemused. Culaehra turned back to Singorot; the big man was on his feet again, his sword raised to guard, but taking many quick glances at his shaman. A moment later he was watching his shaman but taking many quick glances at Culaehra. With vast relief, Culaehra stuck Corotrovir into the ground before him and folded his arms. Singorot stared, first with surprise, then with quick calculation. The message was clear—Culaehra could seize the sword again in a second, but was not now brandishing it. What could it mean, but truce? The big Vanyar slowly lowered his own sword, then jabbed it into the ground before him and let go. His relief was hard to miss.

Culaehra gave him a little bow; Singorot returned it. Then, very deliberately, Culaehra turned to watch the Vanyar shaman, as if he could understand her words. Surprised, Singorot stared, then turned to the shaman eagerly.

Whatever she had said, it provoked a storm of controversy. Singorot caught up his sword, sheathing it as he ran to join the knot of people around the shaman. They were arguing furiously, arms waving, some voices angry, others high in delight.

Culaehra caught up Corotrovir and sheathed it as he sidled back to Yocote. "Welcome back, shaman. You do not know how glad I am to see that you live."

"I can guess," Yocote said sourly. "Be ready to defend Masana, warrior. She may need it more than any of us, in moments."

"Masana? The Vanyar shaman?"

"The same."

"You have been busy in your trances, have you not?"

"We have established that Lomallin is mightier than Bolenkar if the two must confront one another, yes—and I told her our notions about marriage and family life. She seemed to prefer them to the Vanyar code."

"As well she might," Lua said with a shudder.

Culaehra glanced down with a frown. "What do you know about Vanyar ways?"

"I have spoken with Vira and her women. They heard great boasting and bragging from their captors—how they would rape them all again and again, begetting children upon them time after time. Then as soon as the children were born, they would resume raping, until they got them with child again." Lua shuddered. "I am not surprised that a female shaman would prefer the way of Lomallin and Rahani."

"Nor am I," Kitishane said.

"Then she is preaching the worship of Lomallin to her people?"

"Teaching them to turn away from Bolenkar, at least—and his priests will not take it lightly." Yocote stiffened. "There they come!"

There were three of them, clad in tunics and leggings, but with black cloaks whipping from their shoulders, hats made of ravens on their heads, and twisted staves in their hands, each carved to resemble a huge viper. The foremost, gray-bearded, shouted a question at Masana. She drew herself up, giving him a frosty look—so frosty that Yocote could see her fear—and answered in a sharp but measured tone.

The oldest priest went berserk. He screamed at her, yelled at her, shook the snake's head of his staff in her face. She recoiled perhaps an inch, then glared up into his face and spoke sternly. The man turned pale, then spun about, raising his arms and waving his staff aloft as he shouted to the people. A murmuring sprang up, anger mingling with incredulousness, but with wonder underscoring all. One warrior shouted a question. Another cried out in tones of agreement and asked another question.

The eldest priest turned purple and thundered his rage at them. Those nearest him shrank back, but glared defiance; those farther back began to shout questions, then statements. The priest turned pale, then whirled to bellow at Culaehra and Yocote. Lua translated. "He tells us that we are blasphemers to say that Bolenkar's way can be wrong. He says we must die for that sin."

So saying, the priest threw down his staff. The two younger

priests threw theirs down beside his. The wood seemed to ripple; its twists began to move. The staves came alive, and three gigantic vipers came crawling toward the companions, mouths yawning wide to show huge fangs. Droplets glistened at their points. The high priest shouted, and Lua said, "He says their bite is instant death."

Yocote stepped away, lightly and on his toes, shouting at the priests in the shaman's tongue. They only grinned with delight and watched. Yusev shouted at them in his turn, but heard only gloating laughter in answer. "They would not have laughed at an insult like that if they had understood it. These priests do not speak the shaman's language."

"Then they are not shamans, but only charlatans," Yocote replied, "messengers who bear Bolenkar's message of hatred and war. Come, Yusev, you slay one snake and I'll slay another!"

"No!" Lua stepped forward, eyes bright. "This is my work. Leave them to me."

"No, little sister!" Kitishane cried.

But Yocote replied, "Let her fare. She is filled with gnome-magic, and vipers are creatures of the earth. She may slay them more quickly, and more certainly, than we." But he watched wide-eyed, every muscle stiff, jaw clenched, and sweat stood out on his brow.

Reluctantly, Kitishane held still—but she kept an arrow nocked on her bow.

Lua began to dance, singing in low tones that seemed to caress. The snakes slowed, then lifted their heads. They began to weave back and forth, following her movements to time their strikes.

The high priest shouted encouragement to his pet. The snake seemed not to hear him, though, for slowly, ever so slowly, its fangs folded as its mouth closed. So did those of its mates.

Lua's dance became more sinuous, her voice building heat. Yocote began to move to her rhythm very slightly, the sweat rolling down his face, and the look in his eyes was hunger and yearning. The snakes began to show something of the same appetite themselves, two of them turning to gaze at the third.

Suddenly, Kitishane understood. Two of the snakes were male, the other female! And Lua's voice was becoming heavy with desire. Kitishane blinked; surely she must be wrong, she thought.

Surely there was not really a faint green haze surrounding the little woman!

But the snakes seemed to lose interest in her as they gained interest in one another. The males undulated toward the female.

The high priest shouted, nearly screeching.

Suddenly, the two males seemed to see each other. Mouths yawned, emitting long hisses. They poised to spring—

Lua sang more loudly, and the aura about her deepened, becoming more blue than green, then blue indeed.

The snakes' eyes glazed; their fangs folded again, their mouths closed. They appeared to forget one another and turned back to the female.

The female had begun to writhe, undulating slowly in time to Lua's music. Her curving grew, and the males slid up next to her, one to either side, matching her undulations and her rhythms.

The priest screamed in rage; his assistants joined him. They came striding down to their erstwhile staves, raising their hands and chanting. The companions could understand only the repeated name, "Bolenkar!"

A red aura sprang up about the three snakes. They stilled, then turned cold eyes on Lua.

Yocote grasped his dagger and braced himself. Kitishane raised her bow.

But Lua's chant deepened; they heard her call, "Rahani!" Other than that, her sounds seemed hardly words at all, but she called again, "Rahani!"

The blue aura seemed to stream from her, from her and out to envelope the snakes. Sparks shot as it touched the red aura; then the two mingled, deepened, becoming a purple that lightened to lavender.

The snakes began to twine about one another.

The high priest howled and drew a long and curving knife. He swung it high . . .

Kitishane shouted.

The priests looked up—and saw an arrow pointed at their chief. Beside the archer stood Culaehra, panting, but lifting his sword, the sword that had fought Singorot to a draw.

344

The curving knife froze, poised.

Lua's voice thickened with passion. The snakes wrapped about one another so tightly that they seemed to be only one writhing, interlocked mass.

Face dark with anger, the high priest bellowed a chant. His assistants joined in.

The three snakes turned back into wood.

Lua stopped dancing and glared accusation at the priest. He snarled in return and leaped at her, the curved knife sweeping down.

CHAPTER 28

Yocote shouted, leaping forward; Kitishane loosed her arrow; but Lua was faster than them all, streaking forward to catch up the huge triple staff, which must surely have weighed twice as much as she herself, and the green aura glowed about her again as she whirled to strike the high priest on the side of the head with the huge, knobbed, triple head.

The man dropped like a stone as Kitishane's arrow caught one of the younger priests in the hip. The other stood, staring in shock, as Lua dropped the staff, beholding the dead priest. She stood trembling, eyes unreadable behind her goggles, then fell to her knees, face in her hands, sobbing.

Yocote was at her side in an instant, folding her in his arms.

Kitishane stepped up behind the two, glaring defiance at the whole Vanyar horde, another arrow nocked and ready.

The two remaining priests fell to their knees, the one groaning and the other crying out, but both with the same words. Masana turned to the companions, smiling, and spoke.

"She says they will turn away from Bolenkar," Yusev translated. "He is weaker than Lomallin and Rahani. She says they call Lomallin to protect them."

Culaehra nodded. "Thank you, Yusev." He stepped forward, sheathing his sword and holding up his hand, palm open, toward Singorot. After a moment the Vanyar chieftain pressed his own palm against Culaehra's.

Fortunately, the Darians had some spare knives of excellent workmanship that made ideal goodwill gifts for the Vanyar. The barbarians, not to be outdone, pressed several battle-axes on the nomads. They parted with declarations of goodwill.

"We will carry word of these events to all the Vanyar," Masana told them. It was no promise, but only a statement of fact. "We shall turn the Vanyar from their mission of death to the worship of life." She smiled. "I thank you for all of this."

"We thank you, for your courage and persistence," Kitishane returned. "May we meet again, as allies."

"May we meet again," Masana echoed, and turned away to mount a wagon that carried women and household goods. She turned back to raise a hand in farewell, and so did most of the dozen other women in the wagon.

Culaehra noted that. As they rode away he asked Kitishane, "You and Lua have been busy talking among the women, have you not?"

"It was not so hard," Kitishane said breezily. "Lua taught me the words to say, and they answered one another's questions."

Yusev lowered his hand from a farewell wave, then turned to Culaehra with a knot of nomad warriors behind him. In the patois they had developed, he accused, "We saw, Culaehra! We saw you aim your blade at his hip, not his head! We know the sharpness of your blade, we know that it could have shorn his sword at the hilt!"

"We have seen you move with twice, three times the speed you showed him!" a warrior claimed.

"Aye," another said, "and strike with two and three times that force, too!"

"Speak truly, Culaehra," Yusev said. "You could have slain that Vanyar in a matter of minutes, could you not?"

"Yes, but do not let it be noised abroad." Culaehra kept his voice low, as if Singorot were ten feet away. "None knows this except yourselves—and Singorot, of course."

"You mean that his tribesmen know it not? Of course, but why did you do it?"

"If I had killed him, we would have had a blood-feud on our hands, and they never would have turned away from Bolenkar. Have I not won a greater victory this way?"

"Yes, I see," Yusev admitted, though Culaehra could tell the words had a bad taste in his mouth. "What lasting good will it do, though? Will not Bolenkar simply have this whole tribe slain for treachery?"

But Yocote stepped up, shaking his head. "Be sure they are not such great fools as to send an emissary to Bolenkar to tell him they abjure his worship."

"But he will know when he does not hear them pray! He will know when he feels that a priest of his is dead!"

"Bolenkar is not a god, to know such things without being told," Yocote said severely. "I do not doubt that a few of these Vanyar will stay loyal to him, or that they will send one of their number to another high priest, who will send report to Bolenkar—but by that time the new ideas I have told Masana will have passed from mouth to mouth, not through this tribe alone, but through many other Vanyar tribes."

"I see." Yusev's eyes widened. "Once the truth has spread so far as that, Bolenkar will never be able to stop it, no matter how many he slays!"

"And if he does slay many in trying to stanch it," Kitishane said, "the Vanyar will know him for the tyrant he is."

"Yes, yes! But not all the Vanyar will accept this news and turn from Bolenkar."

"True," Yocote said, "and that will cause fighting within the ranks, Vanyar against Vanyar."

"Which will weaken them further, and make them less able to fight! Most excellent, Yocote!"

"At the very least, none of our folk have been slain or even wounded," Culaehra explained, "and our strength is still full, to meet whatever foe we next encounter."

Yusev turned to Culaehra again. "But you did not think of all that when you drew out the fight and refrained from slaying that slogger, did you?"

"No," Culaehra admitted, "though I suspect that Kitishane did."

"Kitishane! You withheld your hand only because she told you to?"

Culaehra looked into their eyes and saw that their opinion of him wavered in the balance, for how could they respect a chieftain who only took orders from another? "Who among you will not heed the words of your shaman?" he asked.

Their heads snapped up; furtive glances sought out Yusev, who frowned and returned the glances.

"Is Kitishane a shaman, then?" one warrior asked.

"No, but she has a kind of magic all her own," Culaehra told them. "I have never known her to give bad counsel. I did as she advised, not only because I trusted her, but also because I sought to avoid as much bloodshed as possible."

"You, the hero, thought of avoiding bloodshed?" a warrior demanded. So did the others.

"Oh, yes," Culaehra said softly. "Be assured, if I call upon you to risk your lives in battle, it will be because I see no other way."

Onward they marched, eastward still. They encountered other tribes; some they fought; with others they were able to parley or bargain. Yocote conferred with their shamans, and from almost every tribe they gained at least a dozen recruits. Where they were able to succor those who were threatened by other tribes of Vanyar, they gained whole clans, who traveled with them as much for protection as to aid in battle.

They bypassed the cities of the Land Between the Rivers where they could, and fought the armies of those who sought to stop them. There were no shamans here to listen to word of Lomallin and Rahani; they had been slain by Bolenkar's priests, and only the raven-masked ones counseled their people. Culaehra fought three more duels, but with no hope of winning new friends. When they had chased the city-folk back behind their walls, though, many of the farm-folk who dwelled around the city came to join them.

These Yocote and Yusev interrogated sharply, wary of spies—but as Kitishane pointed out, it mattered little; surely Bolenkar was aware of their coming.

They passed beyond the eastern river, where the land rose to a high plateau. Now they began to meet monsters, giant misbegotten mixtures of animal and reptile, of insect and even plant. They dealt with them easily, for they never traveled in numbers—but they lost a few warriors.

They replaced them, though, from the villagers who toiled under the lash of Bolenkar's soldiers. Those troops were never great in numbers; the allies defeated them easily, and villagers thronged to swell their ranks—in gratitude and, frequently, in search of revenge. Many shamans joined them, closely coordinated by Yocote with Lua by his side; oddly, the shamans seemed to feel there was no loss of face in hearkening to gnomes, since everyone knew they were too weak to be able to rule. The two developed amazing persuasive abilities. Together, the shamans called game small and large to their armies every night—game that had to travel for days to come to them. Others planted grain each evening, chanting spells; in the morning it was ready to harvest. Thus they traveled through the land without despoiling it and came to the eastern mountains without arousing the enmity of the people who dwelled in the plateau.

So by the time they began to climb the winding trails up into the foothills of the eastern mountains, their army was nearly ten thousand strong. Soldiers appeared to roll boulders down upon them, but the massed shamans caused the huge rocks to swerve around the army or, in many cases, to roll back upon those who sought to push them. Bolenkar's priests appeared, chanting spells to bring down the hillside in an avalanche—but Lua set her hands against the earth and, with her gnome's magic, bade it remain still. Thus they climbed higher and higher, chopping their way through skirmish parties and monsters, always wary at every turn of the path, until they finally came out at the top of the ridge. There, they looked down upon a valley with a hill rising from it, and upon that hill, Bolenkar's citadel, Vildordis. But they also discovered the reason Bolenkar's army had not fought them in force before, for monsters roamed the hillsides, and the valley floor was filled with campfires and tents.

"Bolenkar has summoned all the Vanyar here to stop us!" Yocote cried, staring down in horror.

"All the Vanyar, yes," Kitishane returned. "Perhaps Masana is among them."

Yocote looked up, startled at the thought. Then he began to smile.

Yusev called out something in his own language, and a young woman hurried up next to him. He asked a question; she frowned, staring down at the horde in the valley below, then answered. Yusev smiled and reported, "She says she sees knots of people sitting around campfires, each listening to someone who gestures often. She also sees other knots of men who argue fiercely."

"No knots of women arguing with each other?"

"None."

"I am not surprised." Kitishane turned to Lua. "Would any woman choose Bolenkar's way over Lomallin's, sister?"

"Not freely, no," Lua replied.

"Masana has been as good as her word," Yocote said, grinning. "She has converted many of her tribe, and they have gone among the other Vanyar to preach."

"How many will fight for Bolenkar?" Culaehra asked.

"All, if his monsters and his soldiers stand ready to slay any who turn back." Yocote stepped up atop a rock. "Let us see if we can forestall that." He spread his hands and began to chant. Yusev looked up in surprise, then grinned and spread his hands, too, chanting in unison with Yocote.

"See two men argue angry," the Darian woman said, her accent so strong it was barely understandable. "See one hit other. Other hit back. Them fight."

She went on to report the events. Here and there throughout the horde fighting broke out. The men around the fighters took sides, then began to join the fight. The fighting grew and grew, spreading out like ripples in a pond.

Yocote lowered his arms and jumped down off the boulder. "Let it work, like yeast in beer." His eyes gleamed with satisfaction.

But Kitishane frowned. "Bolenkar cannot ignore this."

"He never could," Yocote replied. "It has only escaped his notice till now."

"What will he do when his spies bear him word?"

The answer came quickly. The monsters on the hillsides turned, roaring, and started to descend. The gates of the citadel opened, and a hundred more came loping and flapping down—camelopards and manticores, harpies and chimeras, dire wolves and other monsters too bizarre to name. They descended on the Vanyar, roaring, and tore into the rear of the horde even as their kindred were running down the valley sides. Vanyar screamed as huge claws ripped them apart, roared in anger of their own just before serrated teeth tore them apart.

Then the whole horde jolted into realization—with help from Yocote's and Yusev's spells, of course. They stopped their fighting, staring in horror.

Then, with a vast shout, they turned on the monsters. Battle-axes waved, rose, and fell as a hundred humans fell upon each monster, and the shouting took form, becoming words: "Lomallin! Rahani! Lomallin! Rahani!"

Culaehra sucked in his breath. "I must give these Vanyar their due. They are brave."

The monsters began to retreat. A score of them lay dead.

The gates of the citadel opened again, and soldiers poured out.

Down the hill they came and struck into the churning mass of Vanyar, straight between two monsters and the men who fought them. Some stopped to attack the men from the back; the Vanyar turned with howls of rage and struck. Most of the soldiers, though, plowed on into the Vanyar horde as far as they could. They neared the center before they bogged down. There they spread out, slashing and hacking, leaving a sort of channel behind, walled by soldiers fighting Vanyar. More soldiers came running into that channel and joined in; the pool of fighting spread and spread again.

"The fools, to set themselves to be surrounded!" Culaehra cried.

"The better for us," Yusev told him. "We need only watch, and battle with whatever is left."

"Stand ready for that," Lua told him, and caught Yocote's hand. "Come, shaman! If that castle stands on a hill, surely there must be a way to it through the earth!"

Yocote frowned, then knelt and set his hands to the ground, beginning to chant. Lua knelt by him, singing a song of her own. The only familiar word was a name: Graxingorok.

"Behind you!" Kitishane gasped.

"What moves?" Yocote asked, then went back to chanting.

"A stone! It rolls . . . There is a cave! Something moves within that cave! It is a stone, but it walks!"

Yocote whipped about.

The "stone" stood twice his height, almost to Culaehra's belt, but its arms were long and thickly banded with muscle, as was all its body. Its skin was gray and rough, as if it were stone indeed, but its beard and hair were almost black. "Who calls by the name of my kinsman?" it asked in a voice like the rattle of falling pebbles. "Who calls by Earth?"

"Yocote of the gnome-folk, O Dwarf," the little shaman replied.

"Are you he who aided Graxingorok?"

"I am," Yocote answered. "We all are."

"Then ask. We owe. I am Tegringax."

"I am Yocote; these are Lua, Kitishane, and Culaehra." Yocote indicated his companions with a sweep of his hand. "We seek your help in fighting those who hold that keep yonder." He pointed to Bolenkar's castle.

The dwarf frowned, not even bothering to look. "Is there any true chance you might slay them?"

"Step forward, Culaehra," Yocote commanded. "Touch his sword, O Tegringax."

Culaehra did as he was bade, frowning in puzzlement. The dwarf set his stony hand on Corotrovir. His eyes flew open in astonishment. "This sword was forged by Ohaern!"

"Forged by Ohaern, for the purpose of killing Bolenkar," Yocote agreed. "Touch his armor."

Tegringax reached up to the breastplate, then snatched his hand away, trembling. "By all the earth! This came from the hand of Agrapax himself, and is newly forged!"

"Even so," Yocote confirmed. "Do you doubt we stand a chance against the Scarlet One?"

Tegringax laughed, a sound like rust flaking under a whetstone. "You do indeed! Come, I shall lead you there! But only you four, mind you!"

Culaehra whirled. "Kitishane, stay to guide the battle!"

"Never!" Kitishane trembled with anxiety. "Stay, and never know what happened to you? If you think I will let you go away from me to great deeds or doom, you are mad!"

Culaehra stared down at her, not really amazed. A fond smile curved his lips, and he caught her up in his arms to kiss her, deeply and well. When she could lean back, stunned, he said, "We live or die together, then."

He spun to Yusev. "It is for you and your war chief to order the battle! Wait until they are done chewing each other up down there, then harry them as your people always have—do not let them march straight against you!"

Yusev's teeth shone in a grin. "Never fear. The People of the Wind know how the sandstorm strikes."

"Well enough, then!" Culaehra clapped him on the shoulder. "Stay and wreak havoc!" He whirled to the dwarf. "Lead us, then, Tegringax! Down into the bowels of the earth!"

The dwarf laughed again and, laughing, turned to lead them back into the cave.

Darkness closed about them, and Yocote said, "Tegringax, we have folk whose eyes do not see well in darkness. If you could—"

Light flared, seeming bright in the underground night, but not so much as to hurt their eyes. Culaehra saw that the light was a glowing ball that floated above Tegringax's head. He wondered what it could be and how the dwarf could bring it into existence so easily.

Lua and Yocote took off their goggles.

The way branched, two caves opening off of one. Tegringax chose the left without pause. Culaehra wondered how, then remembered that the dwarf had spent his life in passages such as this, probably in this very valley. Down they wound, the floor sloping beneath their feet. Kitishane stumbled, but Culaehra reached out to catch her arm before she could fall. A few minutes later he stumbled, and it was her hand on his arm that kept his balance. So, clinging to one another, they descended. They came to more branchings, but Tegringax never hesitated, always choosing one without even seeming to consider.

Finally the floor leveled off. They came out into a huge chamber, halfway up one of its walls. Some strange quality in the stone took the dwarf's tiny light and multiplied it, as if any gleam at all were enough to trigger the mineral into imitation. By that eerie, sourceless light they saw below them a sort of honeycomb, intersecting and meandering walls without a roof.

"It is a maze!" Culaehra cried.

"And we must cross it," Yocote moaned.

Lua only stared down with wide, frightened eyes.

"Be sure to stay close behind me," Tegringax told them. "I shall have no trouble crossing through there, but if you are separated from me, you shall be lost, to wander till you die."

"We shall stay close indeed," Culaehra promised.

They started down a series of long sloping ramps, Tegringax leading, Yocote and Lua close behind.

"Do you go ahead, little sister," Kitishane told Lua. "I shall come last."

Lua flashed her a grateful smile. "Concerned that I might be lost? Not likely underground, big sister—but I thank you!" She went ahead.

Kitishane followed. She was indeed concerned, for if the others went too fast, the gnomes might be left behind. Coming last, she could call out if they lagged.

Thus they went into the maze, and Tegringax did not slacken the pace at all, for he knew exactly where to turn. He threaded his way through at a constant, plodding rate—but his legs were short, and he did not seem to feel any urgency, so the gnomes kept up easily.

Onward they went until it became almost boring, for the walls all looked alike, light gray and smooth, though far from polished. The sourceless light was confusing, and Culaehra was glad indeed for Tegringax's glowing ball. The eeriness of the chamber dampened his spirits, and seemed to do so for the others as well, for conversation lagged, then stopped, and they followed Tegringax in silence.

Finally they saw that the tunnel far ahead opened out, and Culaehra said, "At last! Are we come to the end of this maze, Tegringax?"

"We are," the dwarf replied.

"Praises be! I shall be glad to see sunlight again, even if it shines on Bolenkar!"

"I, too," Yocote grunted.

"And I," Lua agreed. "Will not you, big sister?"

There was no answer.

Culaehra stopped on the instant and swung back to look. Kitishane was not to be seen.

"Kitishane!" Lua cried. "Where have you gone?"

There was no answer.

"She is lost in the maze," Culaehra groaned. "Call loudly, all of you, then listen sharply! Tegringax, your pardon, but we must go back to fetch her. *Kitishane!*"

"*Kitishane!*" they all three cried together.

Then they listened, straining their ears.

Kitishane had been following, but lagged behind, to give Lua room—and to see if the gnome slowed even slightly, so that Kitishane might call out to Tegringax to go more slowly. Thus not even Lua noticed when the huge hand reached out from behind to slap over Kitishane's mouth and yank her back against a leather breastplate. A deep, harsh voice muttered something in the shaman's tongue, and all the world went gray and misty about her.

She stood frozen a moment in shock, then began to struggle violently, and in silence, for a minute or two. Then she heard laughter, huge guffaws bellowing in her ears, and the hold on her face and arm loosened. She thrust herself away, feeling her face burning, the laughter still echoing about her as she yanked her sword free—and saw Ataxeles standing there, lifting his battle-axe from the loop at his belt, grinning as his laughter calmed.

Only Ataxeles, nothing more—they stood in a realm of mist,

gray clouds swirling all about them, scattering light that told of a sun somewhere, but never here. She risked a quick downward glance and saw that the ground was hard, with a straggling of grass blades, brown and sere. She glared back at Ataxeles, heart thumping in her breast, and knew he could see her fear.

His laughter stopped abruptly and his eyes narrowed to slits. His voice was a hiss as he said, "You do not deceive me, slut!"

Anger flared, instant and harsh. "I am a maiden!"

"You are a slut in your heart! All women are, save one! You do not deceive me about that, either!"

"Either?" Kitishane eyed him warily.

"Aye! You hide behind the warrior, but I know you for what you are—Bolenkar's true foe!"

Kitishane could only stare.

Ataxeles laughed again, but this time his laughter was harsh and little more than breath. "Oh, you pretend well, pretend to be amazed—but I know that without you to unite the plans of the shaman-gnome with the sensing of the enemy's heart of the slut-gnome, and harness both to the warrior's fighting, he would be able to do little or nothing! He would flail about with his sword but never strike, or worse, hit only allies; he would wreak havoc, but do as much for Bolenkar as against him!"

With a sinking heart Kitishane realized that what he said was true. She had never dared think that Culaehra could need her that badly.

"I shall win the battle he brings against our scarlet god," Ataxeles said, his eyes glinting. "I shall win it here and now, by slaying you!"

The battle-axe swung high.

CHAPTER 29

K itishane whipped her sword up with a sinking heart, knowing a common blade was little use against an axe like that, knowing her only chance lay in always turning its stroke, never meeting it head-on.

Knowing, too, that if she died, the allies died, every one of them, and with them, hope for peace and harmony in the world, she summoned up every last ounce of resolve. She would win, she must win! She summoned, too, a vision of Culaehra lying battered and bleeding. Fright and anger flowed, and with them absolute determination.

She danced to the left, meeting the axe with a slanting blade, pushing, deflecting it just enough so the stroke hissed past her shoulder. Before Ataxeles could recover, she thrust at his throat just above the breastplate. She felt it strike bone and cursed inside, riposting quickly to guard—but blood sprang and Ataxeles roared with pain and anger. He charged her, axe slashing. Kitishane nearly wilted from fear—nearly; but she wilted to the side, leaving one foot behind, and Ataxeles tripped, stumbled, and went crashing to the ground. He whirled about, pushing himself up with a bellow, up enough to hurl the axe. It flew too fast; she tried to sidestep but it caught her in the belly and the side, whirling her around and knocking her down. She could not breathe; everything seemed to darken about her. Dimly, she heard Ataxeles' triumphant laughter, heard him coming nearer. Holding the sword, she frantically fought to move, to keep moving, remembering what Illbane had taught them about night fighting, about sensing where your enemy was even if you could not really see him.

She thrust upward.

Ataxeles howled with rage and anger, a howl that moved away. Kitishane scrambled to her feet, turning to face the howl, holding her sword up in both hands.

Then her body shuddered as her lungs filled with air again. Her vision cleared and she saw Ataxeles moving around her sideways, still facing her but shuffling his feet to the side, his face dark with anger and pain, blood welling from his thigh. "What unnatural sort of woman are you?" he bellowed. "Women do not fight, and when they do, they cannot fight so well or so long!"

"I am a woman trained to fight by Ohaern," Kitishane snapped.

Ataxeles went rigid, eyes wide at the name—and Kitishane leaped forward, slashing left to right, then right to left. Her first stroke bit into the haft of Ataxeles' battle-axe; he shouted with anger and fear and yanked it free. Her second slashed the laces that held his hip plates to his breastplate; blood welled from his side. He roared with rage and charged her again, axe swinging. She ducked under it, but his fist came up, filling her vision, smashing pain through her head, and the world went dark again. She felt herself flying through the air, felt herself land, hard ground shocking the air out of her as pain wracked her body and his shout of triumph filled her head. Desperately, she tried to roll up to her knees, clinging to her sword at any cost, struggling to bring it up, knowing it would be too little and too late, and her heart cried out *Culaehra!* but he was not there.

Then some strange reassurance swept through her, lending her strength; it was almost as if Illbane stood beside her again, almost as if she heard his voice shouting *Lua! Yocote!* but that had to be her voice, not his. Even so, she struggled to rise; if that horrible axe was going to kill her, she would meet it on her feet!

.   .   .

"We must go back!" Culaehra insisted. "She must be beside us in battle! We have come so far together—we must not be separated now!"

"She must be beside us," Lua agreed. "Do not ask me why, Yocote, but I will have no heart without my human sister!"

"But do you not see! That is exactly what the enemy intends!" Yocote cried. "That is their surest way to win the battle! If they can keep us wandering down here searching for one another, Bolenkar's soldiers can chop up our allies piecemeal! Without you to lead them, Culaehra, they will fall apart! Instead of one army a thousand strong, you will have six armies, none of more than a hundred, none knowing or caring what the others do! Bolenkar will triumph and will chew up all the younger races!"

"The younger races can go hang, if I do not have Kitishane!" Culaehra snapped.

"Only by slaying Bolenkar can you save Kitishane!" the gnome cried. "Do you not see? He has stolen her away; she is his hostage against you! If you do not slay him, you will lose her!"

"If I do not have her, I cannot slay him!" Culaehra returned. "Trust me, Yocote! I do not know a great deal, but I know this!"

"I, too." Lua stared at Yocote, huge-eyed. "I feel it all through me, Yocote. If Bolenkar's minions have taken her, we must find her, or all is lost!"

Yocote cursed and turned to Tegringax. "Can you, at least, not see sense?"

"I see the trail ahead and the trail behind," Tegringax returned. "Tell me down which you wish to go, and I shall take you."

Yocote frowned. "You can take us back the way we came, with no fear of becoming lost?"

"No fear at all," Tegringax assured him.

The gnome threw up his hands. "All right, then! Let us seek her! It will be quicker than standing here arguing with you two. Tegringax, lead on!"

Chuckling like gravel rolling down a rocky slope, Tegringax led them back into the maze.

Three turns and Culaehra was lost. He could not have said whether this was the way they had come or not, so much sameness was there in all the rocky walls. But Tegringax plodded on ahead, and Culaehra, trusting, followed.

Abruptly, Yocote stopped, eyes huge, arms outspread to halt them all. "It is here! Here she disappeared! I feel it!"

Lua crouched down, palms against the rock, and stared unseeing. "I, too! But not alone. Another, a male—"

"Ataxeles!" Yocote made the name an obscenity. "And if it is that soldier-shaman who has taken her, I know to where they have gone! Culaehra, hold fast to me! Lua, hold! Tegringax, stay you here and await us!" He added as an afterthought, "I prithee."

"Have no fear, I shall stay," Tegringax answered, amused. "And have no fear that Bolenkar's minions may find me, for I can melt into rock if I must."

"Well and good, so long as it is a rock near here! Hold fast, my companions! We go!" Yocote began to chant in the shaman's tongue, gesturing as well as he could with the arms they held. He stopped in mid-sentence, eyes huge.

"What is it?" Lua asked.

"Illbane! He calls us!" Yocote frowned, eyes on some distant scene. "And . . . Kitishane . . ." He threw back his head and chanted.

Culaehra felt anger building. If Illbane was taking them away from Kitishane when she most needed them—

Then the ground slipped from beneath his feet. Instantly, another surface pressed up against them. They were surrounded by mist, but it cleared quickly ahead of them, and he saw Kitishane on her knees with Ataxeles raising a sword over her. He shouted and sprang, but Yocote was already gesturing and chanting, and Lua had her hands pressed to the ground, singing. The surface beneath Ataxeles suddenly turned into a mire. Ataxeles sank to his knees and shouted, flailing for balance.

Kitishane saw her chance, pushed herself to her feet, stepped forward and swung. A thin red line appeared across Ataxeles' throat. He cried out in fear, but it was only a gargle. Dropping his sword to pinch the edges of the cut together, he frantically mouthed another spell. The flow of blood slackened . . .

Lua hurled a stone.

It struck Ataxeles square in the forehead. He lurched, his eyes rolled up, and he fell backward into the mire.

Kitishane's sword hissed by two feet above him. She froze, staring down in disbelief.

Then Culaehra was beside her, sword high, ready for the slightest movement, and she turned to throw herself into his arms, stiff for a moment, then loosening with sobs that wracked her whole body. Bemused, Culaehra folded his arms about her. He glanced down at the body beside him, then sheathed his sword and held her with both arms, murmuring soft words and caressing her back gently.

Yocote watched them for a moment, his eyes sardonic, but a smile touched his lips. Before it could grow, he turned to Lua. "Well aimed, maiden—but where did you find a stone? There are none here—there is barely ground!"

"I have been gathering pretty pebbles all through our journey, shaman," she informed him. "I had a notion I might need a weapon—and if I did not, they had beauty enough to treasure."

"Beauty." Culaehra frowned, turning. "Let us see what manner of . . . Ho!"

Yocote and Kitishane both snapped their heads up at the alarm in his words—and saw the ground hardening where there had been mud, and no trace of Ataxeles.

"The earth has swallowed his body," Lua breathed.

But Yocote shook his head. "There is no earth in the shaman's world, but only a hardening of the mist."

"Then the mists have taken him, and the mists can have him!" Culaehra said. He turned back to Kitishane. "Though I will own I would have preferred to have him alive, that I might be revenged upon him for attacking you."

She smiled up through her tears, then raised one hand to dash them away as she took his great paw with the other—but she said only, "Come. There is a world to save."

Culaehra stood looking at her for a moment, then smiled. "Well, if it has you in it, it is worth saving. Lead on, maiden—I shall follow."

Her smile broadened, but she still held his hand as she turned to Yocote. "Come then, shaman! Lead us back to the maze!"

"Join hands and hold my arms." Yocote tried to hide his misgivings, but he had a bad feeling about the loss of Ataxeles' body. Still, he put it from his mind and began to recite the spell.

The world swam about them again, and when it firmed once more, gray stone surrounded them instead of gray mist. Yocote dropped their hands, looking about anxiously. "Tegringax!"

"Here." Tegringax stepped forth from one of the walls; he had blended with it so perfectly that they had not seen him until he moved.

"Lead us up to Bolenkar!" Yocote implored.

"Gladly." Tegringax looked them up and down, then turned away and started walking. Over his shoulder he called back, "I had not thought to see you again."

"His faith in me is overwhelming," Yocote growled.

"But it is a delight to prove that faith is merited," Lua replied.

He looked at her in surprise and saw her eyes glowing into his. His heart turned within him and he fought the urge to take her into his arms. The thought of the coming battle saved him. "We must go fight," he said, and turned away.

Lua sighed and wondered when she would have done enough penance.

Tegringax led them up, up, to a circle of darker stone at the top of a spiral tunnel. "Farther than this I dare not go," he said. He placed the glowing ball in Lua's palm, saying, "Take hold, ye of Earth," then raised a hand in farewell. "Good fortune in your battle!" He stepped back against gray stone, blended into it, and disappeared.

"Many thanks, Tegringax," Culaehra called, but softly. Turning, he set his hands against the portal and pushed, then pushed again.

"What trouble?" Yocote asked.

"It will not move," the warrior answered. He felt over the surface. "I feel no hinges."

"Let me." Lua pushed up beside him, set one hand against the rock and began to sing to it. Culaehra fingered his sword hilt, wondering how well Corotrovir would bite stone.

Incredibly, the portal began to move.

It swung aside on pivots they could not see, swung with less grating than Tegringax's laugh. Culaehra set a finger across his lips, then moved through the doorway, drawing his sword.

They came out into a dungeon, a long and narrow hallway hewn from rock and lighted by a lone torch in a sconce. Silently, Culaehra prowled the length of the corridor. His companions followed.

At the corner, he flattened himself against the wall, then motioned to Yocote to look. The gnome edged up, darting his head out for a quick peek. He looked up at Culaehra and said, "None moves, warrior."

"I thank you, shaman." Culaehra led the way again. This time, halfway down the corridor, they found a stairway. Up they went, Kitishane to the rear, but with Lua keeping one hand on her friend's shin to make sure she did not disappear again.

As they neared the top, they heard a sound like a distant storm. Then a voice as deep as a quarry and as harsh as a rasp thundered, "How dare they retreat! Do you value your neck, fool, that you come to tell me my own soldiers are overborne?"

"My lord, I must say what I see!" a human voice cried.

"Then go back and see it again! Go back and rally them and throw them against this human rabble! My magic shall strengthen you! Go! All of you, go and triumph, even if you die in the attempt—for if you retreat, I shall slay you far more painfully than the enemy! *Begone!*"

Culaehra looked back and locked glances with Kitishane. As clearly as words, they both thought, *Bolenkar!*

Culaehra beckoned Yocote back, then stole out of the opening.

He saw a great hall, thirty feet high and twice that across, hung with tapestries and battle trophies, floored with rich carpets, and dominated by a huge gilded chair, a throne half the height of the room. Before it paced a figure only a few feet shorter than the chair, twelve feet at least, wearing a sword as long as Culaehra was tall and a dagger as long as Corotrovir. He was bare-faced and ugly, a face as craggy as a mountainside, with narrow eyes too small for so huge a face, eyes drawn down in a perpetual scowl. He was burly and knobbed with muscle, bandy-legged and splay-footed, clad only in a gilded breastplate and kilt, with golden greaves, sandals, and gauntlets—but instead of a helmet, he wore a crown. He paced the carpets, mouthing obscenities.

It could be no one but Bolenkar. Badly as he had wanted to find this being, Culaehra's heart quailed within him at the sight. How could he defeat one so mighty?

Then Corotrovir began to glow with a green light and, even here where there was no wind, to vibrate in Culaehra's hand. He heard no sound, but there must have been one too low to hear, for the giant whirled and saw him, then drew his blade. "So you have stolen into my stronghold like the vermin you are, pawns of Lomallin!" He eyed the green glow and sneered. "Do you think that puny stick could hurt *me*?"

Culaehra felt power flowing from the sword into his very being, pushing the fear back, holding it at bay. "Yes—for this is the sword Corotrovir, forged by Ohaern from the Star Stone!"

For an instant Bolenkar's face went slack with fear. Courage surged, and Culaehra sprang forward with a wordless shout. He swung at Bolenkar's knee. The giant roared with anger, yanking the leg high, then stamping down at Culaehra. Dancing aside, Culaehra swung at the back of the giant's knee. Corotrovir bit, and Bolenkar shouted with pain and fear as his knee buckled under him. He swatted at Culaehra with his sword, but the blow was so clumsy that Culaehra dodged it with ease, then leaped inside the swing to thrust at the joint between breastplate and kilt.

A huge fist came out of nowhere and slammed into his whole torso. Culaehra shot up into the air, frantically holding onto Corotrovir. Bolenkar's shout of satisfaction filled his ears, then the floor slammed against Culaehra's back, driving the air out of him. The room started to darken, but he knew that losing consciousness was death. Clinging to the light with the strength of fear, he struggled to rise, waiting for the sword stroke that would sever his neck, or the huge foot that would flatten his ribs . . .

It did not come. As the darkness dissipated, just before that first huge, shuddering gasp of returning breath, Culaehra heard the rumbling voice droning syllables in a foreign tongue.

The shaman's tongue! Or an even older magical language, older than humankind! Culaehra tried to force himself to his feet, but his body would not obey his will. Then a huge invisible hand seemed to grip him; force pressed in from every side, imprisoning his lungs; he could not breathe. He opened his mouth to gasp in air, but his mouth would not open. Fear clawed its way up to his gorge, turning into panic.

A high-pitched voice finally penetrated his ears, and he realized it had been there for some time, floating above Bolenkar's sub-basso, chanting incomprehensible syllables—Yocote's voice! The pressure began to ease, then slackened abruptly. Culaehra's jaw dropped, the waiting gasp flooding his lungs, and his body rolled up to its feet.

Bolenkar roared with anger and turned to pound Yocote flat against the stones—but the gnome hopped to the side, and the great fist came down on flat stone, down with too much force; Bolenkar cried out in surprise and pain. The mere attempt was enough to madden Culaehra, though; he clamped his teeth against a yell and charged, Corotrovir swinging.

The sword sang as it bit through the bronzen cuirass and into the Ulharl's side. Culaehra yanked it free as Bolenkar turned, howling, his huge sword slashing at Culaehra's midriff. The warrior dropped to one knee, swinging Corotrovir up to parry; Bolenkar's blade glanced off and swung on by.

But Culaehra froze for an instant, staring in horror at Corotrovir. Where the sword had twice bitten through Bolenkar's flesh, his blood had eaten away the steel! It was far deeper than a nick, almost half the width of the blade.

No time to ponder—Bolenkar, still roaring, was swinging again. Culaehra leaped back, but the Ulharl leaned forward even as he swung, and Culaehra raised Corotrovir to deflect the six-foot blade. Sword met sword, exploding in a burst of light. The force of the blow sent Culaehra reeling; he stumbled and fell, but scuttled back, dazzled, unable to see, and hoping the vast roaring that filled the chamber meant that Bolenkar, too, was blinded . . .

Then the light faded and he saw the Ulharl hiking himself forward on knee and foot, raising the huge sword in two hands. Culaehra swept Corotrovir up to guard—and saw that the blade was broken in half, broken where the Ulharl's blood had eaten away the steel! He held up the remnant in both hands, knowing it could not be enough. He struggled to regain his footing, knowing he could not stand in time, knowing that huge downsweeping blade would slice him in half like a pear under a kitchen knife—

The giant froze in mid-swing. Culaehra stared, unbelieving, then saw his companions frozen in mid-movement, too—but saw also the tall, translucent figure, bearded and robed, staff in hand, and the vast green form that towered behind it, indistinct and wavering, not even clearly male or female, but seeming human, greater than human . . .

Take this, too, the ghost of Ohaern said in his mind. *I forged it when I forged your sword, forged it first, to test the metal. Take and strike!*

Then he faded, the great green form behind him faded, and Culaehra, raising his left hand, found a spear in it, a spear with a green-glowing head. Bolenkar was striking, his vindictive roar shaking the hall. Culaehra dropped the half sword, raised the spear with both hands, threw himself to his feet and charged.

Down swept Bolenkar, bowing forward with the force of his blow, and up shot the spear. The two came together with another explosion, greater this time, for red sparks and green mingled to darken Culaehra's vision, darken the whole room. Then a huge weight slammed down on top of him, crushing him beneath hard metal. He struggled frantically, letting go of the spear, pushing and shoving, but whatever had fallen on him was far too heavy . . .

Then it moved, at least one side of it, and Culaehra rolled toward light and life, tears in his eyes. He rolled out and up, and nearly fell—but Kitishane was there beside him, holding him up. He stared down, unbelieving, at the huge corpse before him, and there could be no doubt it was dead, with that spear shaft rising from its back, exactly where the heart would have been. Yes, he had slain Bolenkar, Culaehra realized, dazed—but the Ulharl had helped in his own death, for the vicious momentum of his final swing had thrown him onto the spear, and his own weight had driven it home.

It was a spear that was rapidly diminishing, though, as the Ulharl's blood ate it away. The head was corroded almost to a scrap, and even as Culaehra watched, the shaft broke and fell against the giant's bronze-armored back. Wood and metal both rotted, hissing, vanishing into air, and the smoke of their passing rose to fill the chamber with a foul, acrid stench.

"We have won," Culaehra whispered, unbelieving. "We have slain Bolenkar!"

"*You* have slain him, you mean." Yocote was beside him, insisting on honesty. "Well done, O Hero!"

"Well done, bravest of the brave!" Lua cried, tears filling her eyes—but she seized Yocote's hand and would not let go.

"Yes, brave indeed, and worthy of any reward." Kitishane gazed up at him with awe.

Awe he did not want, not from her. "I would be dead this minute if Ohaern had not given me the spear."

"Ohaern?" Yocote frowned. "But when did he . . . " Then he realized the answer to the question and his eyes went wide.

"His ghost." Culaehra nodded. "And a greater ghost behind him."

"Lomallin," Yocote whispered.

"Why not?" Kitishane asked, her face glowing up at his. "You did his work, after all."

Culaehra looked down and saw with relief that the awe was gone from her eyes—but he saw something else there, glowing, making her whole face vibrant and beautiful. He froze, entranced, but those luscious lips moved and said, "We have not finished that work, have we, my hero?"

Her words brought him back to the world like a slap. Suddenly he became aware that the roar of battle still rose from the windows. "No, we have not! We must stop this warring before all are dead!"

"How?" Yocote spread his hands. "We cannot carry so vast a form, and even my magic cannot raise him long enough to bear him forth from this stronghold!"

"No—but there is not a man of his who will not recognize *this*!" Bending, Culaehra scooped up the huge sword—or the hilt, anyway; the weight of the full blade nearly buckled his knees. Shifting down the blade, he straightened with a grunt, balancing it on his shoulder. "Quickly, lead me to the wall! I cannot bear it long!"

Yocote muttered, gesturing with quick movements, and the sword lightened amazingly. "That much, I can help bear." He ran ahead toward an archway. "I feel fresh air moving! Come, hero!"

"Do not call me that!" Culaehra protested as he followed.

"You shall have to grow accustomed to it," Kitishane said, smiling up beside him.

It was Lua who glanced back, then whipped off her cloak and ran to gather the broken pieces of the sword, being careful not to touch the metal with her hands. Then she settled her goggles back over her eyes and rushed to follow her companions.

CHAPTER 30

Up they went, out onto the roof of the stronghold. Below them in the valley, armies contended, and the carnage was great. Most of the monsters had been slain or had fled, but those left fought alongside the soldiers, chewing up the allies as badly as the allies slew and maimed them.

"We cannot stop them if they do not look up to see us!" Kitishane cried, nearly in despair. "How shall we do *that*?"

"Call out," Yocote said simply. "Call long." Then he began to gesture, chanting.

Culaehra looked at him as if he were insane, but Lua reached up to touch his hand and said, "Do as he asks."

Culaehra frowned down, but held the great sword aloft above his head and filled his lungs. Then he called out "Ooooooooooh!" as loudly and as long as he could.

Yocote spread his hands, turned the palms up and lifted them slowly.

Incredibly, the very stones of the fortress began to vibrate, echoing Culaehra's call. The sound rolled out over the battlefields and struck the hillsides, rousing echoes that poured back over the warring soldiers. In less than a minute the whole valley was filled with Culaehra's cry.

Here and there a soldier or a warrior glanced up, then leaped away from his opponent and stared. Sometimes the opponent followed his glance, then whirled to gaze, eyes wide; sometimes the opponent started after, but followed the pointing arm. In only a few minutes all the fighters had stilled to stare at the big warrior holding the sword that was as long as he was tall—and the soldiers, recognizing it, cried out in despair, for they knew that Bolenkar would never have loosed his hold on that sword, that the only way Culaehra could have come to lay hold of it was if the Ulharl was dead.

"Tell them to surrender," Kitishane muttered.

"Surrender!" Culaehra cried, his voice booming out over the valley. "Throw down your weapons and plead for mercy—for be sure, you cannot win if your god is dead!"

A moan began somewhere among the soldiers, then soared up the scale as it gathered force, echoing and reechoing from thousands of throats into a keening wail of despair. By hundreds, then by thousands, the Vanyar threw down their arms and fell to their knees.

Here and there, though, an officer raged, laying about him with his sword. "Fools! Do you think Bolenkar's soul will not come hotfoot after those who desert him? Take up your spears! Fight! Slay! Murder!"

The Vanyar near them scrambled back to escape their wrath, but the officers followed close, screaming and slashing. Here and there a soldier fell, streaming blood. His fellows shouted in outrage, but dared not strike, so intimidated were they. But they stepped aside as a corps of Vanyar warriors barged in with angry shouts. A dozen warriors piled on top of each officer. Axes rose and fell.

"Bind the arms of each soldier!" Culaehra cried. "Herd them together, and mount guard over them!"

Among the Vanyar host, angry shouts arose. "Betrayal!" "You told us Bolenkar was strongest!" "You have brought us to defeat!" As one, they turned upon Bolenkar's priests. Those who could not reach them turned back to clasp the arms of those who had fought for Lomallin, crying, "We shall follow the Green Way now!"

They only began it. With the priests dead, all the Vanyar embraced one another with shouts of joy.

But the allies, grinning, followed the Darians' lead, waving their swords aloft and chanting, "Culaehra! Culaehra! Culaehra!"

Atop the fortress, Culaehra beheld the sudden truce, and lowered the great sword. Grinning, he threw up his arms in rejoicing. The allies saw, and shouted their joy in return.

Then Culaehra turned away, his face suddenly haggard. "I cannot accept such acclaim! I did not slay the Ulharl by myself!"

"But you must accept the praise," Kitishane said sternly.

"Yes!" Lua agreed.

"Who would cheer a gnome?" Yocote pointed out.

"But they must acclaim someone," Lua said, "for thus are they all united again."

"Only in this fashion can Lomallin and Rahani triumph," Kitishane said. "You must represent us, Culaehra—you must accept the glory for us all!"

His face was haunted. "Must I truly?"

"You must—and besides," Kitishane said, "I think that I shall find a way to share it." Culaehra gazed down into her glowing face, then realized the import of what she had said. Slowly, beginning to smile again, he lowered his head to claim her lips with his own.

He kissed her there before the horde. They shouted approval, and when he lifted his head, he gazed down at her for a moment, smiling now, and asked her, "Have I at last proved myself worthy of a wife?"

She gave him a shy, sly look and said, "You have."

His voice went husky and breathy as he asked, "Then will you marry me?"

"I will," she said, and he caught her up in his arms to kiss her once again. Below, the crowd whooped for joy.

Lua watched them with tears in her eyes, and her hand stole into Yocote's. She looked up at him shyly and said, "You, too, have proved yourself worthy."

"Oh, I know that," he said with a sardonic smile. "But I will not have a wife if she is not in love with me—and with me above all others that she might find."

"Why, *I* am in love with you," Lua said softly, "and in just such a fashion."

Yocote frowned at her, but her face glowed with so much love and desire that he could doubt her no longer. He, too, took his mate in his arms, and kissed her as only gnomes can.

The crowd bellowed joy again, and the two gnomes looked up in surprise, then blushed. "See what you have done now, woman!" Yocote said. "You have made me forget where I was and who looked upon us."

"I may take pride in that much, then," she rejoined, and he flashed her a smile before he turned her, and turned with her, to accept the crowd's acclamation.

"Ohaern," Rahani said lazily, "come back to bed."

"A moment only, beloved." Ohaern gazed down through the rift in the clouds, running a hand over his arm and chest to reassure himself that his skin was no longer wrinkled, that his muscles were as massive as ever.

Rahani pouted. "You have been absent from me for most of a year! What if each month was only a day to me? You have left me clamoring with desire! I cannot be assuaged in only a few encounters! Come back to bed!"

"I shall, most surely." Ohaern gazed down at the world, smiling. "But I must see the ending of what I have begun."

"Wherefore?" she asked. "You know what must be happening—the alliance of nomads and northerners have asked Culaehra to rule them all, the whole of the western world! You know he has been forced to accept, in order to forestall fighting and feuds! And most surely you know that he has married Kitishane, as Yocote has married Lua!"

"They are being wedded together, both couples in one ceremony," Ohaern told her.

"Even now, at this moment?" Rahani rolled up to her knees, then rose and came up behind him, gazing down over his shoulder.

They saw Yusev standing before the two couples, chanting and pantomiming the tying of a knot; they saw Culaehra kiss Kitishane as if he would never stop, and Yocote kiss Lua with more restraint but as much intensity. "I shall bless their union," she breathed in his ear. "They shall have each two girls and two boys, and none shall die till they are old."

"I thank you, my love. Forgive my abstraction, but I have put something of my heart into those four, even as a smith must always do with work he comes to love." But Ohaern felt her breasts against his back and could not prevent the desire that rose within him. He turned, bearing her back to the bed, and it was an even question as to which of them bore the other down.

Finally, Ohaern lifted his head and said, almost in apology, "You understand that it is not Culaehra whom I count as the hero I forged."

"Of course not," she replied. "It is all four of them together. But come and kiss me, Ohaern, or my lips will grow rough with waiting."

And what man could wish such misfortune on a goddess?

About the Author

CHRISTOPHER STASHEFF spent his early years in Mount Vernon, New York, and the rest of his formative years in Ann Arbor, Michigan. He has always had difficulty distinguishing fantasy from reality and has tried to compromise by teaching in college. When teaching proved too real, he gave it up in favor of writing full-time.

He tends to prescript his life, but can't understand why other people never get their lines right.

═══ DEL REY® ONLINE! ═══

THE DEL REY INTERNET NEWSLETTER (DRIN)

The DRIN is a monthly electronic publication posted on the Internet, GEnie, CompuServe, BIX, various BBSs, and the Panix gopher. It features:

- hype-free descriptions of new books
- a list of our upcoming books
- special announcements
- a signing/reading/convention-attendance schedule for Del Rey authors
- in-depth essays by sf professionals (authors, artists, designers, salespeople, and others)
- a question-and-answer section
- behind-the-scenes looks at sf publishing
- and much more!

INTERNET INFORMATION SOURCE

Del Rey information is now available on a gopher server—gopher.panix.com—including:

- the current and all back issues of the Del Rey Internet Newsletter
- a description of the DRIN and content summaries of all issues
- sample chapters of current and upcoming books—readable and downloadable for free
- submission requirements
- mail-order information
- new DRINs, sample chapters, and other items are added regularly.

ONLINE EDITORIAL PRESENCE

Many of the Del Rey editors are online—on the Internet, GEnie, CompuServe, America Online, and Delphi. There is a Del Rey topic on GEnie and a Del Rey Folder on America Online.

WHY?

We at Del Rey realize that the networks are the medium of the future. That's where you'll find us promoting our books, socializing with others in the sf field, and—most important—making contact and sharing information with sf readers.

FOR MORE INFORMATION

The official e-mail address for Del Rey Books is

delrey@randomhouse.com